HIGHLAND SEDUCTION

"Poor lad. Ye cannae conceive of a lass telling ye nay, is that it?"

The bite she had intended to put behind her words was very weak. It was hard to be cold and sarcastic when his nearness was making her short of breath. The way he was kissing her face, brushing his lips over hers, and nibbling at her ears was making her entirely too warm. She wanted to kiss him back, wanted to run her hands through his hair and all over his lean body, and she wanted to rub against him like some hungry wanton.

"It hasnae happened before," he drawled, and almost laughed at her look of outrage. "Ye want to say aye, lass," he said, and kissed her. "Say aye," he murmured against her throat.

"Why do ye press me so?"

"Because I ache for ye. Ye are a passionate woman, Kirstie."

"Weel, ye cannae have this one."

For a brief moment, she tried to resist his kiss, but with a sigh, gave in and wrapped her arms around his neck . . .

Books by Hannah Howell

Published by Zebra Books

HANNAH HOWELL

HIGHLAND ANGEL

ZEBRA BOOKS
KENSINGTON PUBLISHING CORP.
http://www.kensingtonbooks.com

ZEBRA BOOKS are published by

Kensington Publishing Corp.
119 West 40th Street
New York, NY 10018

All Kensington titles, imprints, and distributed lines are
available at special quantity discounts for bulk purchases
for sales promotion, premiums, fund-raising, educational,
or institutional use.

Special book excerpts or customized printings can also
be created to fit specific needs. For details, write or phone
the office of the Kensington Special Sales Manager. Attn.:
Special Sales Department. Kensington Publishing Corp.,
119 West 40th Street, New York, NY 10018. Phone: 1-800-
221-2647.

Zebra and the Z logo Reg. U.S. Pat. & TM Off.

ISBN-13: 978-1-4201-3292-2
ISBN-10: 1-4201-3292-X

First Printing: May 2003

20 19 18 17 16 15 14 13 12 11 10

Printed in the United States of America

CHAPTER ONE

"Are ye Sir Payton Murray?"

The fact that the voice coming from behind him was female stilled Payton's initial fear that he had been caught by the husband he was planning to cuckold. Then it occurred to him that anyone catching him lurking beneath Lady Fraser's bedchamber window could cause him trouble. Well, he mused as he tamped down the desire he had begun to feel at the thought of spending a few hours in the fulsome Lady Fraser's arms, he had developed a skill for talking himself out of trouble. It was time to use it.

As he turned to face this possible nemesis, he opened his mouth to begin his explanations, only to leave it open, gaping at the vision before him. The woman was very small and very wet. Her hair hung in long, dripping ropes over her equally wet gown. He suspected it was not just the moonlight which made her delicate, heart-shaped face look so pale. The dark gown clung to an almost too-slender body, but the hint of womanly curves was there. He wondered if she knew that she had more mud than slipper on her small feet. And, if he was not mistaken, that was marsh grass sticking out of one sleeve.

"Weel? Are ye Sir Payton Murray? The bonny Sir Payton?"

"Aye," he replied, then wondered if that had been wise.

"The gallant, brave Sir Payton?"

"Aye, I—" he began, wishing she would leave off the accolades, as they always made him uncomfortable.

"The bane-of-all-husbands Sir Payton? The lightning-quick and lethal-with-a-sword Sir Payton? The Sir Payton the ladies sigh o'er and the minstrels warble about?"

There was the distinct bite of mockery behind her words. "What do ye want?"

"So, ye are Sir Payton?"

"Aye, the bonny Sir Payton."

"Actually, I dinnae care if ye are as ugly as a toad's arse. I want the honorable, gallant, lethal-with-a-sword, and willing-to-leap-to-the-aid-of-those-in-need Sir Payton."

"The minstrels exaggerate," he snapped, then felt guilty as he saw her slender shoulders slump a little.

"I see. Ye did notice I was a wee bit damp, didnae ye?" she asked as she wrung out a handful of her skirts.

"Aye, I did notice that." He bit back the urge to smile.

"Didnae ye wonder why? 'Tis nay raining."

"I concede that I am a wee bit curious. Why are ye wet?"

"My husband tried to drown me. The idiot forgot that I can swim."

Although Payton was shocked, he forced himself to be wary. He had suffered from far too many women trying all sorts of tricks to get close to him, to entrap him in situations that could force him to the altar. Yet, Payton thought as he looked her over again, no one had ever tried dipping themselves in a murky river before. Nor, he mused as he recalled her words, had such a bucket of sarcasm been poured over him before. If she was trying to lure him into a trap, she was using some very peculiar bait.

"Why did your husband try to drown you?" Payton asked.

"Payton, my sweet courtier, is that you?" called Lady Fraser softly as she peered out her window.

Inwardly cursing, Payton looked up to see Lady Fraser's sweet face looking down at him, her long, fair hair spilling over the edge of the window. He glanced toward the other woman, only to find her gone. She had left as quietly as she had arrived.

"Aye, 'tis me, my dove," he replied, wondering why he felt so disappointed that the girl had left.

"Come to me, my bonny knight. The warmth of my chamber eagerly awaits ye."

"And a sweet temptation that is, my beauty."

Even as Payton stepped toward a cleverly arranged set of kegs, he heard a soft, gagging sound. He looked around, expecting to see that sadly bedraggled girl, but saw nothing. Uneasy, he turned back to the kegs, musing that Lady Fraser was clearly no novice to the intrigues of cuckoldry. There was before him a cleverly disguised stairway consisting of the kegs and several thick boards artfully nailed to the wall of the house.

"Are ye planning to just leave me here?"

That husky whisper startled him so much he stumbled a little as he again looked around for the girl. "I have an appointment," he whispered, hoping her reply would help him locate her.

A heavy sigh escaped the ivy on the wall to his left. Looking closely, he was finally able to make out her shape tucked neatly, and very still, within the shadows and foliage by the wall of the house. It was unsettling how well she used the shadows and how quickly and silently she had done so. Payton did not really want to contemplate the reasons a woman would learn such a trick.

"Go, then," she said in that same soft whisper. "I will wait here. Enjoy your conquest. I hope I dinnae catch the ague."

"I doubt ye will."

"Of course," she continued as if he had not spoken, "my deep, wracking coughs will no doubt disguise your cries of illicit passion and thus keep ye safe from discovery. I am ever ready to be helpful. If her husband should return, shall I just hurl my weak, shuddering self upon him to allow ye time to escape?"

"I am beginning to see why your husband should wish to drown ye," Payton muttered.

"Oh, nay, ye could ne'er guess that."

"Payton, my beau chevalier, are ye coming?" called Lady Fraser.

"I worked hard for this." Payton looked up at the window and knew he would not be climbing through it tonight.

"Oh, I doubt that, although she does like to play coy," said the girl. "Go on. I will just huddle here, though I doubt ye will be much help to me when ye crawl out of there later. 'Tis said she is insatiable, fair wrings a mon dry."

Payton had not heard that. Although he had not thought he was the first to coax Lady Fraser into breaking her vows, he had not realized she had become so well known for doing so. *Insatiable* sounded intriguing, he mused, then sighed. Payton hoped Lady Fraser would not be too offended when he forced himself to leave without partaking of her favors.

"Are ye talking to someone, my brave heart?" asked Lady Fraser, leaning out of the window a little to look around.

"Just my page, my sweet," Payton replied. "I fear I must leave."

"Leave?" Lady Fraser's voice held a distinct shrillness. "Tell the boy to say he could nay find ye."

"I fear the lad is an abysmal liar. The truth would

soon be told to all and ye wouldnae wish your husband to learn where the lad found me, would ye?''

"Nay. I dinnae suppose ye will return later, will ye?''

"It fair breaks my heart, my little dove, but nay. This problem could take hours, e'en days, to solve.''

"I see. Weel, mayhap I will allow ye to make amends. Mayhap. Later.''

Payton winced as she slammed the shutters closed on her window; then he turned to the shadowed figure near the wall. "Let us go and get ye dry and warm. 'Twould please me if ye wouldst stay to the shadows until we are weel beyond her sight.''

It was not easy, but Payton fought down the unease he felt as he walked away from Lady Fraser, knowing the girl was with him, yet unable to see or hear her. There was a part of him that began to ponder on ghosts and other creatures that could hide in the night, but he wrestled it into silence. The girl was simply very adept at hiding, he assured himself.

Once on the narrow street which led to the house his family owned, he stopped and looked for her, picking a spot where the light from a house would aid him in seeing her. "Ye can come out now.''

The first thing he noticed was that she was pale and shivering with the cold. Payton quickly took his cloak off and felt a twinge of relief as he wrapped it around her. She was real. He could touch her. Placing his arm around her slender shoulders, he hurried her along toward his house, deciding that he could get a good look at her once he got her warm. He noticed with a twitch of amusement that she had to hold his cloak up to keep from tripping over it, for she barely reached his armpit.

Payton ignored the astonishment on the scarred face of his man, Strong Ian, when he entered his home. The condition of the woman he had brought was intriguing enough, but Payton suspected the man was more star-tled by the fact that Payton had brought her into the house at all. None of his women were allowed across his threshold, in any of his homes. It was an old rule, one he clung to faithfully. When asked about it by family or friends, he glibly excused it by claiming he did not want to soil his own nest. Payton strongly suspected there was more truth to that than he cared to acknowledge.

"But, I need to talk to ye," protested the girl when Payton ordered Strong Ian and his wife, Wee Alice, to see to a fire, a hot bath, and dry clothes for his guest.

"When ye are clean and warm, ye can meet with me in the great hall," Payton assured her. "What is your name?"

"Kirstie, but my brothers call me Shadow."

Thinking of how silently she moved and how easily she could hide herself, Payton was not surprised. He nudged her toward Wee Alice then went to find himself some ale and food. Payton felt a surge of curiosity, both about her tale and how she would look when clean and dry. He hoped it would be worth what he had given up, for Lady Fraser would have allowed him to end a rather lengthy period of celibacy.

Kirstie winced as Wee Alice worked to unsnarl her still-damp hair. Clean, mostly dry, and well warmed by the hot bath and fire, she did feel better. It was easier to ignore the bruises and scrapes caused by the fight to stay alive, many of them soothed by the hot bath and a pleasant-smelling salve applied by a softly tsking Wee Alice. She did wonder where the clean, dry gown had come from, but sternly suppressed her curiosity. Kirstie even felt relatively calm about the approaching confrontation with Sir Payton.

"There, lass," murmured Wee Alice, the shadow of a smile lightening the dour expression on her round face. "Ye are ready to speak with Sir Payton now. I will just make sure that there is plenty of food set out."

The underlying implication that Kirstie was in sore

need of fattening up was clear and Kirstie inwardly sighed as she followed Wee Alice to the great hall. She knew she was now more thin than slender, for her husband was very fond of seclusion and long, enforced fasts as a means of discipline. It just stung the few scraps of vanity Kirstie had clung to, to have her sad condition openly recognized. Since she was now facing a fight for her very life, she doubted that would change much. Regular, filling meals might not only be rare, but could not take precedence over her own life or the lives of the innocents she sought to protect.

Even as Kirstie braced herself to face Sir Payton, Wee Alice gently but firmly shepherded her into the great hall and straight toward Sir Payton. He stood up, bowed slightly, and she was quickly seated at his side. Wee Alice set a large amount of food in front of her, then left. Kirstie felt almost dazed by how quickly she had gone from readying herself for this important confrontation to the confrontation itself.

She took a sip of ale and cautiously studied Sir Payton. Talk about the man was plentiful, but, although she had caught a glimpse or two of the man, she had never actually gotten a good, hard look at him. Following him through the shadowy streets to his tryst had not allowed her to study him, either. Now, looking him over as he sprawled so gracefully in a huge chair of carved oak, she could see why so many women sighed over him.

He was all grace and elegance, from his slender, long-fingered hands to his expensive boots. His dress was that of a courtier, an English or French gentleman, yet with none of the excesses too often seen. His jerkin was not too short, the toes of his boots not too pointed, and the colors of deep green and black nicely muted. And those clothes covered a form that made a maid's heart flutter, Kirstie thought, oddly annoyed by that realization. He was not particularly tall, but his figure held the lean, graceful strength of a finely bred animal. Or a predator, she mused, recalling his licentious reputation.

Facially, he was beautiful yet unquestionably manly, all
clean, perfect lines and temptation. Especially in the
hint of fullness in his mouth, she decided, fighting not
to stare at those lips. His eyes, an intriguing golden
brown enlivened with shards of emerald green, were
made to catch and hold a woman's gaze. Set beneath
gently curved brown brows and thickly lashed, they were
clearly a well-honed tool of seduction. His thick, reddish-
gold hair, neatly tied back, looked so soft that her fingers
actually twitched with the urge to touch it. Kirstie rue-
fully admitted to herself that his fabled licentiousness
could well be more a matter of taking what was freely
offered than of heartless seduction.

"So, m'lady," Payton said, "ye may now tell me why
ye felt compelled to seek me out."

Payton waited as she finished the bread she had just
filled her mouth with. Her looks made him think her
name Shadow did not come only from her uncanny
ability to become one. Thick, glossy raven hair, still
damp from her bath, was held in a fat, loose braid that
hung down to her slender hips. Her eyes were a grey
that seemed to lighten or darken with every glance.
They were beautiful eyes, vaguely slanted yet wide, mys-
terious in their changing hues, rimmed with long, thick
black lashes and set beneath dark brows that perfectly
followed their slight upward tilt. Nothing appeared to
mar her lustrous, milk-white skin. The features gracing
her slightly heart-shaped face were almost ethereal,
from the hint of an upward tilt at the tip of her pretty
nose to the vague point of her chin. *Innocent* and *elfin*
described her looks, until one glanced at the full sensuality of her lips . . .

Forcing his gaze away from a mouth that begged to
be kissed, he subtly studied the rest of her. Her neck
was a graceful length, slender enough to make him
wonder how it could support such a wealth of hair without snapping. She was almost too thin, but the curve
of her small breasts and her tiny waist were tempting

enough. Although she displayed excellent manners, he could almost sense the long-endured hunger she sought to appease. Payton doubted she would ever be well-rounded, but he suspected she should be more lithe than thin.

He wanted her now and he wanted her badly. Payton suspected his friends would be surprised by his lust for such a tiny, delicate female. In the past, he had always reached for women with fuller curves. He doubted he could explain what made him ache to pull her into his arms, but he could not deny that the feeling was there.

"Ye say your husband tried to drown ye?" he pressed, hoping conversation would cool his blood.

"Aye. I was wed to Sir Roderick MacIye when I was but fifteen, near five years ago. I did try to change my father's mind about his choice, for though Sir Roderick is pleasant to look upon, he made me uneasy. But, when I couldnae offer any sound reason for why I didnae wish to marry the mon, my father wouldnae heed me. I finally ceased to fight, kenning that my family sore needed the money Sir Roderick gave them. Poor harvests and other miseries had left us in sore danger of starving come the winter. So, convincing myself 'twas what my clan needed, I donned the cloak of noble martyrdom and wed the fool."

"But the union didnae fair weel?"

"Nay. It ne'er had a chance." Kirstie helped herself to some of the meat pie, still too hungry to care much that her audience was somewhat impatiently waiting for more information.

"Because of ye or him? Or, are ye barren?"

After taking a deep drink of ale, she replied, "Because of him and there was ne'er any chance of children." She sighed and shook her head. "Having bairns of my own was the one hope I had of enduring that marriage if naught else could be made of it. The mon wasnae honest with me or my kin. He kenned there was verra little chance he could or would give me bairns. 'Tis all part of why he wishes to kill me."

"Because he is impotent? I cannae see that a mon would kill anyone to keep that secret, shaming though it is."

"Oh, Roderick isnae impotent. Nay with everyone, leastwise. I thought 'twas just me." She grimaced and began to cut up an apple. "I am a scrawny thing and was e'en more so at fifteen. Young as I was, I decided he must have just wanted the lands I had inherited from my mother. It was a while ere I gained enough knowledge to ken that what I looked like should nay matter. That was when I began to look more closely at what was happening around me. It shames me to think I held myself blind and ignorant for almost three years, sulking o'er my sad lot like some spoiled bairn."

"Ye were verra young," Payton said, but she just shrugged off his attempt to console her. "Why didnae ye return to your family, seek an annulment?"

"And tell all the world my husband couldnae abide the bedding of me? Foolish it was, but pride gagged me. After almost three years, howbeit, I was thinking on it, for my husband is young and healthy. I began to see that I could be condemned to this empty marriage until I was too old to have bairns, tied for near all my life to a mon who seemed interested only in punishing me for every tiny real or imagined slight. Ere I acted upon that thought, I discovered the truth."

He watched as she finished off the apple and reached for another piece of bread. "And the truth is? He likes men?"

"Nay. Children."

Payton sat up straight, a chill running through his body. He did not want to hear this. It stirred sad, ugly memories. He had been a pretty child, a pretty young man as well. Although he had escaped any true abuse, he had been made painfully aware of the dark side of people at too young an age. A part of him wanted Kirstie to leave and not draw him into this particular mess, but a far larger part of him was prepared to battle such evil to the death.

"Wee boys?" he asked.

"And wee lasses," she replied. "Mostly the laddies, though. E'en now, I am oft mistaken for a child, and I have few womanly curves. I now believe that he thought he could mate with me, breed a child or two. Once I kenned the truth, I spent hours in the chapel thanking God that Roderick couldnae bed me, for he would surely have visited his sickness upon my bairns." Kirstie sensed how taut Payton had become and was suddenly, sadly, aware that such a beautiful man had probably been a beautiful child or pretty youth. "In truth, if he had favored men, I could have accepted that. The church and some laws condemn it, but, if 'tis two grown men, I feel 'tis none of my business. I was willing to try to come to some agreement with Roderick, keep his secret but also gain my freedom so that I might seek out a true marriage."

"Are ye certain 'tis children he uses? *Verra* certain?"

"Aye, verra certain." Kirstie took a bracing drink. "I began to understand the whispers swirling about him and was determined to seek out the truth. I had thought the silence, e'en the sadness, of the children about the keep was due to the brutality so carelessly meted out. Then I truly noticed how Roderick keeps the wee ones e'er close, that near all the children are pretty, and, sometimes, a child is about for a wee while, then gone. I soon recognized that all those touches, caresses, he gave the wee ones were nay paternal. I began to try and catch him when he thought no one was looking. I found a way to spy upon him in his solar and his bedchamber." She quickly had another long drink. "I dinnae think I can say what I saw. It haunts my dreams. I dinnae ken where I found the sanity to hold fast, to nay just rush in and kill the bastard, but I did. That might have failed and I would have been quickly silenced. E'en one child would nay have been aided then.''

"Ye did right. Ye could nay be sure ye could kill him and get ye and the child away to safety. Have ye proof of his evil?''

"I have my word and the word of a few children. Some of his people ken all; most of them just guess. They are all firmly under his boot heel, however, too afeared for their lives to act. There are two within his home who give me some aid, but only some, and only when the child's life is threatened. I tried to gain support amongst the common folk, for he steals or buys their bairns, but I have ne'er had the freedom to do much at all. The few who cared about the fate of the children could help verra little. I have tried to spread dark rumors about him so that fewer people would send him their lads for training. That seems to work, but it only causes him to turn more to the children of the poor upon his own lands or from the towns where the king's court is held. The children of the poor suffer the most. Not only does Roderick have no fear of retribution for how he treats them, but, once in his hands, they are forgotten and so he uses them to feed his other sickness.''

"How much sicker could he be?''

"He gains joy, pleasure, from inflicting pain and death. Now and then he is, weel, seized by an urge to kill.''

Payton drank down his ale and quickly refilled his tankard. It was not hard to believe that Sir Roderick found pleasure with young boys, for he had learned of such things long ago. What Kirstie told him, however, stretched the boundaries of any sane man's belief. It seemed impossible for a man to continuously abuse and murder children yet never be discovered.

"Ye doubt my tale,'' Kirstie said after watching his changing expressions for a moment.

'' 'Tis difficult,'' Payton confessed. "I ken all too weel that some are unusually stirred by the beauty of a child.

The child's own sense of undeserved shame would help keep Sir Roderick's dark secret. But, for so long? And so completely that he can e'en murder these innocents? And to believe that none of his people would try to speak out or help the bairns?" He sighed and shook his head. "Ye ask me to believe the unbelievable with no proof."

"Why should I tell such lies?"

"To be rid of an unwanted husband?"

"Then come with me. Mayhap ye need to hear more than my voice."

Payton nodded and within moments they were slipping through the back streets of the town. Yet again he had to marvel at her ability to move so swiftly, silently, and secretively. He had to work hard to keep up with her and had the lowering feeling that she was not using all her skill in deference to his lack.

They finally stopped at a wretched little house well hidden in the foul warrens the poor were forced to live in. Kirstie abruptly disappeared and Payton was reaching for his sword when he felt a tug upon his ankle. He looked down to find her peering up at him from a hole in the crumbling foundation of the house. Cautiously, he followed her, although it was a tight squeeze. Once inside, she covered the hole with a board, then lit a torch revealing a damp, long-unused storage area. The light also revealed the wary faces of five children.

"All is weel, my sweetlings," Kirstie said as she pulled a small sack from beneath the cloak Payton had lent her. "I have some food."

Payton suspected Kirstie had cleared the table while he had gone to find cloaks for both of them and weapons for himself. Despite the rough platform made to keep the children off the floor, the blankets and other small comforts, it was a sad, unhealthy place. The fact that Kirstie so clearly cared for the children and they obviously made no attempt to leave this dismal place added the weight of truth to her dark tale.

He studied the children—four boys and one girl. All were beautiful in the way only a child can be. Despite their interest in the food Kirstie gave them, however, they watched him. The fear and wariness upon their faces struck him to the core. He took a step closer to them and the largest of the boys immediately shifted so that he was between Payton and the other children, his expression turning nearly feral. The little girl began to cry silently.

"Nay, my loved ones," soothed Kirstie. "He is nay the enemy."

"He is a mon," said the oldest boy.

"He is Sir Payton Murray and no danger to ye, Callum. I swear it. He found it hard to believe all I told him. I brought him here so that ye may help him see the truth and then he will help us."

"He is willing to kill that monster?" asked the little girl. "He will kill the bad mon who hurt me so that I can go outside again? Can he get my brother back?"

"Ah, nay, Moira. Your brother is with the angels."

"Aye, that bastard cut—" hissed Callum.

"Little Robbie is with the angels," Kirstie said, interrupting the boy quietly but firmly.

Callum looked at Payton. "Ye want me to tell ye all that swine did?"

There was such anger and hate in the boy that Payton was surprised he did not shake apart from the force of it. "Nay. 'Tis said I was a verra bonny child."

"Then ye ken what I would say."

"Aye, though, through God's mercy, I was saved."

"Are ye going to save us, sir?" asked Moira.

"Are ye going to kill the bastard?" demanded Callum.

"Callum," said Kirstie, "Sir Roderick is a mon of power and wealth. I have told ye, we cannae just kill him, nay matter how much he deserves it. Proof of his evil is needed and it takes time and skill to gather such proof."

Callum kept his gaze fixed upon Payton. "Weel, sir?"

Payton held Callum's gaze, almost feeling the torment and pain the boy suffered. "Aye, I will kill him."

"Sir Payton," Kirstie protested softly.

"It may take days," Payton continued, ignoring her, "weeks, e'en months, but I will dig out every foul secret the mon has. I will rob him of his allies, of places to hide. I will expose his evil to the world. I will break him, corner him, haunt his every step."

"And then?" asked Callum.

"I will kill him. As of this moment Sir Roderick MacIye is a walking dead mon."

CHAPTER TWO

Little Alan trembled in her arms as Kirstie led them all through the dark, rank streets back to Payton's home, Payton and the other four children following at her heels. She wished she could do more than hold him close and rub his thin back, but silence was necessary. Kirstie also wished she could have discussed the moving of the children with Payton first, but a dark hidey-hole with five frightened children listening was no place to discuss such things. She tried to calm her unease by telling herself they could always find another hiding place if needed.

Kirstie realized they must have reached an area Payton recognized, for he quietly took the lead. She was surprised at how readily Moira had accepted him, even letting him carry her. The boys stayed close to her, however, revealing their lack of trust in any man. Callum watched Payton as if ready to tear Moira out of his arms at the slightest hint of any wrong. When Payton led them in through the rear of his house, startling Wee Alice and Strong Ian at their meal, Callum stayed taut and glowering near the door. Kirstie knew the boy would require gentle, patient handling.

"Sir?" Wee Alice asked even as she rose from the rough kitchen table to set kettles of water over the fire.

"These children need a safe place to hide," Payton told her. "This bonny lass is Moira, the lad snarling near the door is Callum, m'lady holds Alan, David stands to her right, and William to her left. Baths, clean clothes, food, and beds. In that order."

"Aye," agreed Strong Ian as he stood up and looked pained when all the children backed away. "I will find the clothes, then ready the beds. All in one room?"

"Aye," all the children replied.

"Fair enough," he murmured, and left.

"I suspect Callum will be wanting a private place to bathe himself." Payton looked at the tense child who curtly nodded, then looked at the others. "The rest of ye can be private with him or have one of us lend ye a hand."

After a lot of discussion, it was decided the children would bathe in the kitchen with the women to help them and with a very large sword close at hand. Once Strong Ian brought the clean clothes, Payton led the man to the great hall and poured them each an ale. Slowly, fighting to control his anger, Payton told the man everything from the moment Kirstie had approached him.

"Ye believe it all?" said Ian after a long, weighted silence.

"I believed a mon would visit his lust upon a child." replied Payton. "But, as the tale grew more vile, my belief wavered. Nay more. I could see the black truth in their eyes."

"And so ye will kill this mon."

" 'Tis my plan. Sadly, I cannae just go and slowly, verra painfully, end his miserable life as I would like to."

"Could cause a wee problem or two."

"Or two. Proof is needed, more proof than the word of a dissatisfied wife and five poor bairns."

"Servants? His men?"

"Too afraid, too much a part of his crimes, or of his own ilk, mayhap. One can only count on aid from some of them once they are sure he will fall, once he is too weak to be a threat to them."

Strong Ian rubbed a finger over the jagged scar on his left cheek. "Going to get help from your family?"

Payton sighed and sprawled in his chair. "Nay yet. I need to ken just how many pitfalls there will be in the pursuit of this swine. A few MacIyes are verra weel placed and can wield some impressive power. They are also connected by blood or marriage to other verra powerful people. We Murrays and our allies are nay without power ourselves, but I cannae see the gain in mustering it until there is proof to wield as a weapon. He has already made one error."

"Nay making sure that lass was dead."

"True," Payton agreed and briefly smiled, "but I was thinking on the fact that he has inflicted his sickness upon lads of good family. Since there has been no outcry, and he still lives, one must assume shame or fear keeps the poor lads silent. We need to try and find one or more whose sense of justice or need for revenge can o'ercome those feelings. There may need to be some lies told, some deceptions used, as fear of having others discover the truth may still tie the tongues of the better-born victims."

"Mayhap the truth can be used to stir their kinsmen to act, yet the world and its mother can be led to believe they act because they discovered what evil he visits upon the poor."

"Ah, thus allowing them to hide a need for revenge behind a banner of righteousness and moral outrage. Good thought. Ah, weel come, m'lady," Payton greeted Kirstie as she cautiously entered the hall and he stood to assist her in sitting at the table. "The bairns are abed?'' he asked as they all sat down, Strong Ian seating himself across from Kirstie.

"Aye. Since they had only recently eaten what I had brought them, their meal was a quick one,'' she replied. "The baths also made them sleepy. Aye, and so did being warm again. Wee Alice took food and drink up to their room, thinking one or two of them may wake in the night feeling a pang of hunger. She insisted on making herself a pallet near the door, which seemed to comfort the children. And Callum sleeps near the window with a large knife close at hand.'' She helped herself to some bread and cheese as Payton served her some wine.

"How old is Callum?''

"Eleven. He was to be killed, for he was swiftly outgrowing Roderick's interest. Aye, and he was rapidly gaining the guile and size to make his anger a true danger. For once, I caught word of the plans for the boy ere they could be carried out and helped him to hide. I think that is when Roderick began to become suspicious of me. Helping and hiding Moira sealed my fate.''

"How long have ye been doing this?''

"Two years, more or less.''

"And ye have only been able to save five bairns?'' He saw her wince and quickly added, "I dinnae condemn. If ye had saved but one, 'twould be a worthy thing. I but try to grasp some idea of how difficult it may be to end this.''

"Verra difficult. In a wee bit over two years I have saved but ten children. Two were taken back by their families, for they truly cared for them and had thought they were giving their bairns a chance at a better life. I helped them get away to my father's lands. My brother Eudard helped slip them into the village with little notice taken. Our lands have sheltered others and our people ken the need to act as if the new ones in their midst are nay so new.''

"Ah, so your family aids ye?"

"Only Eudard. He agreed that, for now, 'tis wise to keep the others ignorant." She smiled faintly. "They are, weel, emotional, and if told, would approach this trouble bellowing and with swords swinging. My family, my clan, would be swiftly decimated if they turned the ire of Roderick's kinsmen upon themselves. Eudard and my Aunt Grizel helped hide away the other three children. They were to come for a visit and take away these children, but Eudard broke his leg. When I realized Roderick was now certain I kenned too much, I sent young Michael Campbell to Eudard to tell him to stay away and that I would get word to him when I could. I also told Michael to find some way to stay with my kin, or to hide somewhere. He was close to me and often my messenger, so he, too, will be in danger, suspected of kenning far too much."

"But, he is of good family," Payton said. "Would Roderick risk the lad's kinsmen asking too many questions?"

"Lads die all the time," Kirstie replied in a sad voice. "Howbeit, kenning that his life is threatened may be enough to make Michael finally turn to his family. I have spent many long months trying to convince him to speak out, but fear of Roderick's retribution, doubts that he would e'er be heeded, and e'en fear that his own family will turn from him, see him as soiled or the like, stills his tongue. I believe I have nearly banished the lad's sense of shame, his sad belief that somehow 'tis his own fault. Eudard will continue to try and persuade him to speak out. 'Tis wrong, but Michael's word will carry more weight than Callum's or the others'."

Payton nodded and took a long drink of wine. He needed to look away from her, to regain some control, and ease his fascination with the ever-changing shades of her smoky grey eyes. Watching her far-too-tempting mouth was not helping him hold fast to his concentration, either.

"Can any of these children seek shelter with their kin?" he finally asked.

"Nay," Kirstie replied. "Alan, David, and William are orphans. Roderick is considered a kind and generous benefactor by those who take on the care of such waifs. He treats such places as his own private stable. If any of those who give him such abandoned bairns ken his evil, the weighty purse he sets in their hands silences all doubt. Moira and her brother Robbie were sold by their mother. The mon she lived with was of Roderick's ilk and she believed she was saving them. I sought her out, but she had died, beaten to death by her lover when he realized what she had done. Callum is a child of the gutter, a near-feral child. If he had any kin, they deserted him so long ago he has no clear recollection of them."

"Did Callum see wee Robbie die?"

"Nay. He kens nay more than I—that some children are, weel, hurt, then gone, and we ken where some of the bodies may be buried. Wee Robbie tried to keep Roderick from Moira. He was sorely abused for that. I found him in a tiny, dark room, still alive, but had to leave him for a short while to prepare a way out. When I returned, the lad was gone."

"Could he have escaped?" asked Strong Ian.

"Mayhap," Kirstie replied, then shook her head. "I dare not hope nor give Moira such hope. He was a wee, underfed lad of but seven years and sorely injured. The only way out was through the tunnel I used to reach him, yet I cannae see how he would have kenned it was there. And, it has been near to a fortnight since he disappeared." She tried and failed to smother a yawn.

"Ye are nearly asleep on your feet," Payton said quietly. "Go to bed. Get some rest."

"But, shouldnae we make plans?"

"We will. In the morning."

Kirstie nodded and stood up. "Aye, I dinnae think I

could recall much anyway. Where am I to sleep? With
the children?"

"Nay. The room across from them. I suspect Wee
Alice has set out a night shift for ye."

"Where do ye get all these clothes? I can understand
the women's, though, remembering the fair Lady Fraser, I am surprised ye have any small enough to fit me
so weel. But why so many clothes for the bairns?"

Payton almost smiled at the cross note in her voice
when she spoke of the women's clothes. "My family uses
this house, too. All the clothes are ones they have left
behind, either apurpose or have simply forgotten. I was
beginning to think I should give them to the poor, but
'tis glad I am I hesitated."

"Oh." It had been a somewhat rude question, but
Kirstie decided she was simply too weary to be embarrassed. "Just one last word. I suspect ye dinnae really
need to be told, but ye must tread warily around the
children. 'Twill be a while ere they feel they can trust
any mon, I think. Especially Callum."

"Aye," agreed Strong Ian. "That one is like a cornered animal and now he has a knife."

"Oh, dear," Kirstie murmured. "Sorry. I just thought
he would rest easier."

"He will. 'Twas a good thing to give him. Mayhap he
will let me show him how to use it."

"Do ye think that is wise?"

"Aye. I cannae think of any lad who more needs to
ken that he can protect himself."

Kirstie was still considering that when she crawled
into bed a short while later. She murmured in delight
as she snuggled into the bed beneath the warm blankets
and smoothed her hand over the fine linen night shift
she had been given. The fact that the children were
enjoying similar comforts pleased her immensely.

As she relaxed and let sleep creep over her, she
thought of what Strong Ian had said one last time. He
was right. There was little chance that a child of Callum's

age could defeat a full-grown man and suspected Callum
had the wit to know it. And, yet, learning to fight would
give him the hope of escape. It could make him feel
less helpless. That could only be for the good. Finally
giving in to her exhaustion, Kirstie briefly wished there
was some way she, too, could lose that chilling sense of
being powerless.

"'Tis a sad business," Strong Ian said the moment
Kirstie left.

"Aye, and with no easy or swift route to justice," said
Payton. "There are many ways I could simply kill him,
but there are just as many ways my part in his death
could be discovered. Without proving his crimes, his
evil, that could plunge my family into a bitter feud. I
cannae risk that. Such an act could also seriously endanger Lady Kirstie."

"A brave lass."

"She is and 'tis clear she cares for the children. She
is verra gentle and loving toward them."

"Which means she has a softness for the bairns, for all
children. To discover such evil must trouble her deeply."

Payton nodded, then frowned slightly. "It does. Do
ye think she needs watching, might need to be re-
strained from acting on her own?"

Strong Ian shrugged. " 'Tis possible. 'Twill be a while
ere we can make it too dangerous for Sir Roderick to
continue his evil ways. The lass appears to be acting
wisely, using her wits o'er her heart. Yet, something
could happen to make emotion o'erule good sense."

"A difficulty I understand completely," murmured
Payton. "She must be watched carefully, then. If naught
else, she is safe now, for her husband thinks she is
dead. She cannae be allowed to succumb to emotion,
act rashly, and mayhap lose that shield."

"It could certainly prove useful at some time, useful
in bringing the bastard to justice."

"True, but that usefulness must be verra clear, the results vital to the cause. She is his wife. The moment Sir Roderick kens that she is alive, he can take her back and no one could stop him. 'Twould be verra easy to make others believe she is naught but an unhappy wife and then anything she says will be ignored. Sadly, the fact that she sought me out will only make it worse. 'Twould be verra easy for Sir Roderick to act the wounded mon, one shamed by an unfaithful wife, or some such tale."

"Ah, of course," Strong Ian rubbed his hand over his forehead and then yawned. "It has been a long night. Just tell me what your first move will be and then I will seek my bed." He frowned. "Without my lass. I ken the bairns need her, but I hope that wanes soon."

Payton smiled faintly. "Sorry. 'Tis my hope it willnae take too long for the children to feel safer here, as safe as they can feel whilst that bastard still lives. And, my first move is to carefully start to blacken the mon's name, as Kirstie tried to do. A whisper here, a warning there. Aye, I will immediately seek the proof I need to bring him down, but through rumor and the spread of a suspicion, I can turn other eyes his way. I can start depriving him of victims and make him begin to feel the weight of that suspicion, and, mayhap, e'en condemnation."

Strong Ian nodded as he stood up. "And e'en your enemies ken that your word is good. If ye whisper a warning, 'twill be heeded. 'Twill be a good start."

As soon as Ian was gone, Payton sighed and slumped in his chair. He had told the truth about needing to keep an eye on Kirstie, to be certain that she did not lose the battle of logic over emotion. It was a battle he would be fighting himself every day until Sir Roderick was dead. Payton did not think he had ever faced such a challenge. It would be a fierce struggle not to immediately denounce the man, loudly and clearly; an even fiercer struggle not to give in to the keen urge to just cut him down. Payton hoped the need to keep Kirstie from letting her emotions rule would give him the strength to control his own.

It was also going to be hard not to involve his family. This was a crusade they would be avid to join. Payton knew he would be spending many long days soothing tempers and bruised feelings when his family discovered he had excluded them. But, exclude them he would until he either had no choice or there was no longer the risk of bringing the wrath of the powerful MacIye clan down upon them all. His family might be bigger and hold more power than Kirstie's, but he had the same fear of retribution. MacIye's kinsmen might not be able to decimate his clan and its allies, but they could bloody them far more than Payton cared to think about.

Payton tensed when the door to the hall eased open, then relaxed when Moira shyly entered. She was an enchanting little child with her thick, dark curls and her big, dark eyes. He smiled at her as she hurried across the floor and climbed up onto the chair to his right, her clean night shift billowing around her. Payton nudged the plate of bread and cheese closer to her. When she smiled at him, his heart nearly broke. She still wished to trust. Sir Roderick had not succeeded in stealing that from the child.

"Ye should be abed, lass," he said as he poured her a goblet full of clear, cool water.

"I was a wee bit hungry," she replied.

"Mistress Alice took food up to your bedchamber."

"She was sleeping." She took a sip of water, then asked softly, "Where is Kirstie?"

"She is sleeping, too. I gave her the bedchamber right across the hall from ye."

Payton was not surprised to see Callum abruptly enter the hall and stride over to Moira's side. He looked a child in the nightshirt he wore, his thin calves visible below the hem. The hot look of anger and suspicion in his green eyes and the knife he held stole away all hint of boyish innocence, however.

"Ye didnae have to bring your knife, Callum," Moira said. "They already have one to cut the bread."

"I wasnae looking to cut bread, lass," Callum snapped. "Ye shouldnae be down here with this mon."

"He isnae a bad mon."

"Wheesht, how would ye ken that?"

Moira looked at Payton for a moment, then looked back at Callum and shrugged. "His eyes. They dinnae look like my mither's mon's or Sir Rod'rick's." She looked back at Payton. "My mither is with the angels, like my brother. The angels willnae take me, will they?"

"Nay, lass," Payton replied. "I willnae let that happen. And," he nodded toward Callum who had been unable to resist the food and was gnawing on a thick slice of bread, "ye have a fine protector in Callum."

"Aye." Moira smiled at Callum. "And he has a big knife now."

"That he does," agreed Payton. "Mayhap he would like to learn how to use it," he said, fixing his gaze upon the boy.

"I ken how to use it weel enough," snapped Callum.

"Ah, then ye dinnae need any training from Strong Ian." Payton took a drink to hide his smile over the interest Callum was unable to hide.

"Weel, there may be a trick or two the mon could show me."

"There may be."

"I will do some thinking on it."

"Verra wise."

"I have the wee ones to protect and all, ye ken."

"That ye do, lad, and to be alert to do that important job weel, ye need rest." Payton stood up and, keeping his gaze fixed upon a wary Callum, helped Moira out of her seat. "I mean to seek my bed myself." He was surprised at how touched he was when Moira slipped her tiny hand into his. "Ere ye slip back to your beds, I will show ye where the Lady Kirstie sleeps."

Payton could almost feel Callum's watchful gaze as the

boy followed him and Moira up the stairs to their bedchamber. The fact that Kirstie had given him her approval
was obviously enough to stir a tiny spark of trust in Callum.
It would require a lot of patience, but Payton was determined to keep that spark alive and make it grow. He knew
one way was to accept the boy's self-appointed role as
protector of the wee ones. The fact that Callum had a
cause, an obvious need to be an important member of
this band of small survivors, could well help the child
recover from all he had suffered. There would always be
scars, but Payton was certain that strength and a restored
pride in himself would help the boy more than anything
else. Callum was a survivor, a fighter, and that was a charac-
teristic Payton knew how to work with.

He paused before Kirstie's bedchamber and eased
the door open so the two children could see that their
lady was still near them, still safe. She was sprawled on
her stomach on the bed, her slender body barely shap-
ing the thick blankets covering her. Her face was turned
toward them, one small fist resting near her mouth.
Payton thought she looked like a child and wondered
what there was about her that had made Sir Roderick
unable to truly see her as one. At the tender age of
fifteen she must have looked even more like a child,
yet, despite his hopes, the man had apparently been
unable to convince himself she was one when it was
time to bed her. The few of Sir Roderick's ilk Payton
had been unfortunate enough to deal with, had all had
wives and children, obviously able to act as a man despite
the demons lurking within them. Perhaps, he mused,
Sir Roderick's demon had conquered him. Inwardly
shaking his head over that puzzle, Payton silently shut
the door and escorted the children to their own room.

"Are ye going to fight Sir Roderick on the morrow?"
Callum asked in a near whisper, pausing in the doorway
beside Payton as Moira tiptoed to her small bed.

"I will begin the battle, aye," replied Payton in an

equally soft voice. " 'Twill be a long one, I am thinking. It must be a slow, cautious assault."

"Why?"

"Because we are the only ones who are willing to speak out against him. 'Tis nay enough. His family is a powerful one."

"We would be killed."

Pleased the boy had the wit to understand the difficulties, Payton nodded. "And my kinsmen and your lady's could find themselves in danger, e'en in the midst of a feud. Aye, Sir Roderick must die, but we want to be sure no innocents fall with him. We want him to die alone, his name nay more than a foul curse."

Callum nodded. "And that will take time."

"Aye, lad, especially since ye, the bairns, and your lady must all be kept weel hidden. The mon will taste the cold steel of justice, but ye must be patient."

"I will be. And, I will grow and get strong," he looked at the knife he held, "and I will learn how to fight." He looked at Payton. "And, when that bastard is dead, I will still grow and get stronger and become a mon of skill and cunning."

"Of that I have nay doubt."

"And then I will be able to protect the wee ones from all such men. Then I will be able to hunt down such evil and end it. On that I swear." He gave a sharp nod and strode to his bed.

Payton made his way to his own bed, thinking of what Callum had said. In his heart, the boy had already taken the oath to protect children. In his heart, Payton also took an oath. He and his clan would give the boy all he needed to fulfill that oath. By the time Callum reached manhood, he would have all the skill, learning, and weaponry he needed to be the guardian of innocence he wished to be. Payton knew that it would be a legacy to the world he could take pride in.

CHAPTER THREE

"Where are the bairns?" Payton asked Strong Ian as he met the man outside of the empty room where the children had slept.

"Been up and about for an hour or more," replied Ian.

"Jesu, I must have been weary to sleep through the rising of five children."

"Nay. 'Tis sad how quiet they were. Like wee ghosties." Ian shook his head as he started down the narrow stairs. "My Alice would have slept through it, too, except wee Moira woke her. The poor lass couldnae get her clothes on proper."

"Moira seems right ready to trust us," said Payton as he followed Ian.

"My Alice thinks the other wee ones will be quick to accept us, too. The lass was loved by her mother, it seems, so she kens an adult can have a kindness in him. The wee lads were probably not with that bastard long enough to have all their faith and innocence destroyed. Ah, but Callum lost much of his ere he was e'en cursed by Sir Roderick's attentions. As a street waif he would

have had a dismal life, nay much better than a stray
cat's.''

Payton sighed and nodded. "He survived. He is a
strong lad. He wants to be a champion of innocence.''

"He would probably be a good one if one can teach
him nay to just cut the throats of such scum.''

"Aye, that could be a problem," Payton agreed, and
laughed softly. "That dismal beginning could actually
serve him weel now. He was hardened, wise to evil and
brutality, ere MacIye got his filthy hands on him. As ye
say, there was probably no sweetness or innocence in
Callum to be destroyed." Payton frowned. "There is
something strangely familiar about the boy.'' He
shrugged. "No matter. Ridding the world of MacIye is
all that must concern us for now.''

"Are ye going to send word to your kin?''

"Nay, not yet. If I must ask them to assist me against
a clan as powerful as Sir Roderick's, I want to be sure
I have at least enough proof to avert the chances of a
feud. Or, that the danger to Kirstie and the children
grows too great, more than we can deal with on our
own.''

"Agreed," said Strong Ian as they entered the great
hall. "For now, we can deal with the bastard.''

Payton nodded and started toward his chair. After
serving the children, Kirstie was just helping herself to
some food as he sat down next to her. Callum watched
him closely, even as he continued to eat, but the other
children greeted him shyly before turning all their attention to their food. It was becoming increasingly clear
to Payton that the younger children had been saved
before they were too badly abused. They were wary and
easily frightened, but held none of Callum's intense
distrust or rage.

"Did ye pass a good night, m'lady?" Payton asked as
he helped himself to some bread and fruit.

"Oh, aye," replied Kirstie. "It has been too long since
I enjoyed such a warm, soft bed. And to have had a hot

bath and a meal ere I sought my bed as weel? Ah, there is heaven.''

"But, ye were wedded to a laird," Wee Alice muttered as she served Payton a large bowl of honey-sweetened oatmeal and moved to serve the children more of the same.

"And she was always irritating him," Callum said as Wee Alice sat down next to Moira.

"I wasnae," Kirstie began to protest.

"Oh, aye. Ye were. 'Tis what the mon said the last time he shut ye in the cage for near to a sennight. He said that ye irritated him like a bad rash."

"The cage?" Payton asked.

"My husband feels wives need stern chastisement," Kirstie replied. One glance told her Sir Payton would press for a more precise answer and she sighed. "He had a metal cage hung from one of the walls at Thanescarr, his keep about a half-day's ride south of here. Occasionally, he put me in it so I could ponder the error of my ways. A week was the longest I e'er had to rest there. Ye cannae be so verra surprised that my husband can be cruel."

"Nay, yet one can still be shocked by what form that cruelty can take. Ye ne'er told your kinsmen?"

"Nay. I am my husband's chattel, am I not? They could do little. And, they would be so angered they would strike out at him, so burdening them with the truth would only cost them dearly. I would gain little respite from my woes, but my family, my clan, would suffer most grievously. As I told ye, they could too easily be utterly destroyed."

"Yet, ye seek my help. Do ye nay think I might suffer for it?"

"Ye have the favor of those who rule. Ye have kinsmen and allies far greater than my family could e'er hope for. Ye also have a reputation for fighting on the side of the helpless. There are many reasons I could give for choosing ye, but all lead to the same conclusion. Ye will take up this cause and fight weel, with the power and allies needed to ensure it doesnae cost ye your life. My kinsmen dinnae. There is also the fact that no one kens that we have e'er met.''

Payton sat back in his chair and studied her for a moment. ''Ye have been planning all of this for a while?''

''Months,'' she replied. ''I might have waited e'en longer to seek ye out if I could have gotten these children away and if my husband hadnae decided I was too great a threat to him to live.'' She nudged her empty plate to the side, clasped her hands upon the table, and looked at him. ''So, do ye have a plan?''

''For now, ye and the children hide here. Ye shall remain dead or run off. 'Tis best if your husband feels he succeeded in ridding himself of ye. I shall go to the court. If there are already whispers about Sir Roderick, ones ye planted or others, I shall add to them. If there are none, I shall spread my own.''

''That is all?'' she asked, even though she knew he could not simply declare Sir Roderick evil and cut him down, that one had to move cautiously.

''For now. As I told young Callum, this could take weeks, months, e'en years. Sir Roderick must be brought low first and that could take time. We must hope he has few close friends and allies, and those he may have will step aside once the rumors and whispers begin to spread. My plan can change at any time, depending upon how many will heed the whispers that will soon swirl about the court, but the heart of it will remain the same. I will see him cut away from all support—then I will see him dead.''

'' 'Tis a good plan, the only one which may succeed. 'Tis just that I seem to have no part in it at all.''

''Ye cannae. 'Tis truly for the best if your husband continues to believe ye are dead. The moment he discovers ye still live, matters will grow more complicated, more deadly. Then we shall have to divide our time and strength between keeping ye alive and destroying him.

The children, too, must be kept weel out of sight. He must ken ye are the reason they slipped his grasp—thus they, too, could be seen as a threat. If they are seen to be with me, then I lose all chance to slip about, slowly weakening him. He will suspect we work together, that ye may have told me too many of his secrets, and again, I will need to turn to defending myself and the children. Callum most certainly must be verra careful to remain unseen. Sir Roderick has already marked the lad for death. Callum may be young and untrained, but Sir Roderick already sees him as a threat."

"I can take care of myself," Callum snapped. "I am no bairn to be coddled."

Payton looked at the boy, knowing he had to be careful not to sting the youth's pride. "I dinnae doubt that ye can care for yourself. 'Tis a wise mon who kens his own strengths and those of his enemy, however. Your enemy is a trained knight with other trained warriors at his command. All of whom are bigger and stronger than ye are. Ye are undoubtedly verra good at running and hiding, slipping about to see and hear what ye shouldnae without getting caught. 'Tis still an unequal battle ye would fight. Your heart and mind are equal to many a knight's, but your body is still that of a boy—easily grabbed, easily held, and verra easily broken."

Callum glared down at his too-thin body. "I just need to eat more."

" 'Twill help. So will allowing Strong Ian to teach ye how to use that knife ye now carry. Mayhap e'en a few other things a mon needs to ken to stay alive, to win his battles. And, think on this, my brave lad. If ye are found, ye could endanger Lady Kirstie and e'en the other children."

"I would ne'er betray them."

"Nay, I ken ye wouldnae. The simple fact that ye are still lurking about would probably be enough to start that swine to thinking, however. Why, when ye ken he wants ye dead, are ye still so close at hand? 'Tis the verra

first question he will ask himself. And, he willnae need
ye to give him answers. They will be far too easy to guess.
Help the others to stay safe and hidden, lad. Work to
grow strong and skilled. Your turn to fight will come
and 'tis a wise mon who prepares for it.''

It was another half hour before Kirstie found herself
alone with Payton. Strong Ian had taken Callum off to
begin training him and the other children had gone
with Wee Alice. Kirstie looked at Payton, silently praying
that the way his fair face could make her heart clench
would soon pass. She needed a warrior, not a lover. She
was in need of a champion for the children, not
romance or infatuation.

"What ye said to Callum," she began.

Payton held up a hand to stop her words. "The lad
has his pride. He needs to have it. He also needs to ken
that there is no shame in accepting that a thin lad is
nay match for a grown, battle-trained knight. Callum's
belligerence may hide it, but we both ken a lot of his
anger is born of shame. If the lad can come to see that
there was naught he could do, that he was nay at fault
for what was done to him, some of that shame might
fade. As Ian teaches him the ways of battle, he will come
to see that he was no match for his enemy. He will come
to see that the shame is all Sir Roderick's, that only a
dishonorable mon would use his greater strength and
power to abuse those he swore to protect.''

"Thank ye all the same for speaking to him nay as a
mon to a child, but as a mon to a mon. He is the most
wounded of them all and I think the hurting began ere
Roderick got his filthy fingers on the lad." She sighed
and shook her head. "I dinnae think all the scars upon
his poor, wee heart will e'er be healed.''

"Nay, probably not." He smiled faintly when she
winced. "He can still be a strong, good mon, Kirstie.
He has the strength, in heart and mind, and his plans
for his future are to grow strong, learn to fight, and

protect the bairns. The fact that he speaks of protecting, nay killing, should give ye some hope.''

"I suspect he means to protect by killing.''

"Aye, but he is still young. Restraint and clear judgment can yet be taught.'' He stood up, took her hand in his, and, ignoring her shock, kissed her fingers. "Now, I am off to the king's court to whisper in a few weel chosen ears and find out all I can.''

"And I am to creep off into a wee hidey-hole, aye?''

"Aye. And, it would be verra wise if ye crept into it and stayed there until I say ye can come out.''

Payton almost smiled as the soft-bellied laird he had been talking to hurried off to find his young son. The man was not particularly keen-witted, yet had understood Payton's subtle hints about Sir Roderick MacIye with an impressive speed. There had to be some past knowledge or crime for such a man to grasp the meaning of Payton's words so quickly, to look so stricken, and to race off through the crowded great hall to find his child as if a blade was already pressing against the boy's throat. It was quite possible that Sir Roderick had already shown an unhealthy interest in the boy.

"Greetings, my bonny knight,'' purred a familiar voice in his ear, followed by a few teasing licks of a warm tongue.

When Payton turned to face Lady Fraser, he was surprised to feel not even the smallest flicker of interest. He knew he was lusting after Kirstie, but he had lusted after more than one woman at a time in the past. He had also been without a woman for longer than he had ever been since he was a very young man. Yet, the welcoming look in the lady's eyes, and the press of her fulsome body against his side, did not move him at all. Payton was both intrigued and alarmed. Was he weary of the games one played with women like Lady Fraser or had he, for the first time in his life, become physically bound to only one woman? And, if he had, what could he do about it and how long would it last?

"My husband has been summoned to his father's bedside," she said as she stroked his arm. "He will be gone for days. And nights. Many long, lonely nights."

"Ah, my sweet dove, how ye do tempt this poor, weak mon," he murmured as he took her hand from his arm and kissed her fingers. "I weep to think of the treasure I must turn away from."

"Turn away from?" She snatched her hand away and glared at him. "Ye refuse me?"

"My fair one, I must, though it stabs me to the heart. The king's men rarely ask anything of me," he began.

"Ha! The old king and now the heir's regents keep ye at their beck and call." She frowned in the direction Payton's previous companion had fled. "And what could that silly fool have to do with the regents' business?"

"Now, my bonny pigeon, ye ken that a mon cannae talk about such things. But, I will say that that mon and I only spoke about his young son. He seeks to foster the lad, to begin his training and all. The mon sought my opinion on a few men." Payton suddenly realized there was one other thing Lady Fraser was well known for. She was an avid collector and disperser of gossip. "He was curious about Sir Lesley MacNicol and Sir Roderick MacIye. I fear I wasnae verra helpful. I dinnae ken Mac- Iye weel, though I have heard a whisper or two about the mon."

"He is odd," Lady Fraser murmured, glancing around the crowded room as if searching for the man. "He is frequently at the king's court, yet, e'en if hard- pressed, I doubt anyone could tell ye the name of e'en one woman he has favored with his attentions. I have seen him indulge in some flirtation, but it was light, fleeting."

"I heard he was married."

"And holds true to his vows?" Lady Fraser laughed,

but there was a bitter taint to her amusement. "Oh, I have heard that your family does, but if that is true, 'tis a verra rare thing indeed. And, if Sir Roderick was so verra enamored of his wife that he remained faithful to her, why is he here but a day after she drowned?"

"Drowned?"

"Aye, 'tis what he is telling all who will listen, although he doesnae seem to be doing so in order to gain the sympathy and comfort of some woman. 'Tisnae as if anyone needs to ken the news, either, for she wasnae one who was weel kenned or loved."

"Mayhap he but seeks aid in searching for her body."

"He hasnae asked for any. From what I have heard of the tale, he may have already found her body and buried her. It seems they were frolicking by the river and she insisted on cooling her feet in the waters. She went too far in and was caught by the current. There was nay saving her." She frowned. "That does sound as if she was swept away, yet I am verra certain he doesnae search for her. He certainly isnae indulging in any show of mourning." She nodded toward a handsome, sturdy man flanked by two large, very dark men. "There he is and he doesnae act like a mon who has just buried his wife. E'en ones ye ken had a wretched union at least observe some form of mourning. Most of them," she muttered, briefly scowling toward a rotund, greying man who had buried his third wife only a week ago.

"Some men simply dinnae see the need to pretend," Payton murmured. "Nay e'en to please the gossips."

Payton studied Sir Roderick, fighting the urge to walk over to the man and end his life—as slowly and as painfully as possible. It surprised Payton only a little that he could feel so viciously bloodthirsty. Sir Roderick was a man worthy of such intense anger and hate. It also surprised Payton that the man was not marred in some way, his evil staining him for all too see. There should be something to warn others about him.

Once he controlled his fury, Payton was able to more

closely observe the man he intended to destroy. There
was nothing unique or impressive about Sir Roderick.
The two men with him looked to be more of a threat.
Payton knew he would never trust Roderick or any of
his men to fight fairly, that Roderick much preferred a
stealthy knife thrust to the back to rid himself of a threat.
He also noticed that Roderick could not stop himself
from watching the pages who wandered through the
crowd. Unless his perversion had become too strong to
control or conceal over the years, it was astounding that
his sickness had remained a secret for so long. The way
the man watched the boys was chilling, for Payton began
to suspect that Roderick was on the hunt again.

"Ye are interested in Sir Roderick for some reason?"
asked Lady Fraser. "Ye watch him most carefully."

"I but search for some hint of grief, e'en a bit of
irritation o'er the fact that he must now find another
wife," Payton replied. "She must have been a sore curse
to the mon."

"Mayhaps. I saw her but a few times. Small, dark, nay
much more than a child. She appeared nay more than
a wee, timid shadow chained to his side. Spoke to few
and, when she did, Sir Roderick or one of his men was
quick to separate her from her companion or stand
close by until all conversation was strangled. Now that
I think on the child, I must wonder if her death was
truly an accident. She may have let the river have her
on purpose."

"Ah, aye, possible. And sad."

"Oh, curse it a hundredfold. Fraser's sister."

Before Payton could say a word, Lady Fraser was gone.
A moment later he saw a stout, grey-haired woman
marching in the direction Lady Fraser had fled. The
woman did not pause, but scowled at him as she passed,
and Payton nearly laughed. Clearly, at least one of Fraser's family was attempting to keep the man's wife from
behaving badly. There was a chance Fraser himself had
asked the woman to stay with his wife. That could prove

helpful. Since he had pursued Lady Fraser, he could not think of a kind or even reasonable explanation for why he was no longer interested. If Lady Fraser was now saddled with a dragon of a chaperone, he would rarely be pressed for excuses to refuse her sensual invitations. He did not really wish to insult Lady Fraser. If nothing else, his sudden obsession with a small, smoky-eyed woman could prove fleeting, and he might regain an interest in what Lady Fraser so eagerly offered.

Returning his attention to Sir Roderick, Payton tensed and had to fight hard to quell the urge to race over to the man, sword drawn. Sir Roderick had his hand on the shoulder of a small page. It was obvious the boy did not wish to be held there, and the way Sir Roderick studied the child made Payton's insides churn. He knew he could not openly drag away any boy who got near the man, not yet, but this time he could act. This boy was a kinsman, a MacMillan. As he walked toward Sir Roderick, Payton carefully and tightly tethered all his fury and disgust.

After nodding a greeting to Sir Roderick, Payton clasped the boy on the shoulder and gently tugged him away from the man. The way young Uven shuddered once and relaxed made Payton wonder if the boy had sensed the threat in Sir Roderick. Uven was, after all, Lady Maldie's grandson and Payton knew she had many a gift, as did others in his clan. Payton much preferred that possibility to the one that had Uven knowing about the evil in Sir Roderick because he had already been subjected to it. The mere thought of that had him wrapping his arm around the boy's thin shoulders and holding him closely, protectively, by his side.

"Are your parents here, Uven?" he asked the boy as he slowly walked him away from Sir Roderick. " 'Tis far too long since I saw Cousin Morna and old Iain."

"They are still at Dunncraig," replied the boy. "Cousin James will soon take his place as laird there, but Papa will be his mon still. Cousin James has given us a fine, wee piece of land and a good stone house."

"An honor indeed and one weel earned. Who are ye serving then?"

"Sir Bryan MacMillan, one of my fither's highborn cousins." He cast a brief, nervous glance back at Sir Roderick. "I am glad ye came to fetch me. I cannae like that mon." Uven trembled slightly and edged closer to Payton.

"Has he done something to make ye uneasy?"

"Nay, not truly. 'Tis just that he feels bad, ye ken? He seeks me out, and when he touches me, I feel ill. Mama told me to ne'er ignore such feelings, as many Murrays are gifted. So, I try to stay far away from that mon."

"Good. Continue to do so. And, tell Sir Bryan what ye just told me. He kens the Murrays weel. He will heed your words and help ye stay away from Sir Roderick MacIye."

When the boy looked up at Payton and smiled, Payton nearly stumbled. It was Callum. True, Callum had yet to smile, but he had the same eyes, the same features, the same hair. Uven was only eight, but the baby softness was already leaving his features, revealing the fine bone structure Payton saw in Callum's face. No wonder he kept thinking something about Callum was familiar. The boy was a MacMillan to the bone; he had to be. The only trouble would come in trying to gather enough facts to prove it.

"Is something wrong, Cousin Payton?" Uven asked.

"Nay, laddie. I was but suddenly taken by how much ye look like the MacMillans."

"Aye, Mama says I am a MacMillan to the verra marrow. She says she could think I took naught from her or the Murrays save that I have these feelings about people." He frowned. "They are a wee bit frightening. Mama says she will see that I visit with my aunt Elspeth and cousins Avery and Gilly more so that they might help me learn about this gift.''

Payton agreed and told him a few tales about the women until he found Sir Bryan. As he handed the boy into Sir Bryan's care, he studied the man. Callum was yet again brought to mind, there to glimpse in the older man's coloring and features.

He left the MacMillans without mentioning the boy. Not only was it safer for now if no one else knew where Callum was, but he needed proof of what he now believed. Payton knew he would not speak of it to anyone except Strong Ian, who could help him look for the proof he wanted. Someone, somewhere had to know who the boy's mother had been and when and how he had been tossed out to survive on his own. One look at Callum would be proof enough for many, and there was always a MacMillan or two at court, but Payton wanted more. He wanted enough to make Callum believe it, enough so that the boy would be certain just what clan he belonged to. Payton was certain that giving the boy a clan, a name, would help Callum far more than many another thing ever could. Once he had a name, became part of a small but proud and honored clan, Payton knew Callum would gain the pride and strength needed to overcome much of the pain he had suffered.

CHAPTER FOUR

Kirstie could not believe how easily she had slipped away from Payton's house. She conceded that, after a week of being so well behaved that none of her family would recognize her, the watch on her had eased considerably. It was nice to think she had been clever, however. There was the chance that the others felt she would not wish to foolishly put herself within reach of a man who wished her dead, but she banished the thought. Thinking of herself as clever and stealthy, even daring, felt a great deal better.

Tugging idly at her simple, black woolen doublet, Kirstie began to meander through the narrow streets and alleys of the town. She did not look rich enough to attract danger or intimidate anyone, but just prosperous enough to be able to afford a coin or two for a service. Since she had been slowly, painstakingly accumulating money for years, she felt she had enough to start loosening a few tongues. Surely if Roderick could use money to commit his atrocities and buy silence, she could use money to stop him. She had never had the freedom to wander amongst the people of the town, to speak to anyone, anywhere, for as long as she wanted. Now, at last, she had the chance to gather testimony against Roderick, to tell people about him, and to cut off his supply of innocents.

It took Kirstie five long hours to fully comprehend that she might well be wasting her time and money. Her head ached from banging it hard against indifference and disbelief. Her heart felt shattered from the constant shock and pain of confronting a deeply rooted apathy. She had thought fear silenced the people at first, and for some it might, but far too many simply were not interested. Or struggled not to be because they had too much else to worry about.

The mon gives the lads a chance at a better life. I willnae hear him spoken ill of.

I have eleven bairns of me own. I havenae time or strength to worry about others.

'Tis past time someone took those thieving rats off the streets. They are a pestilence.

Those words and far too many similar ones were branded on her mind. They were the words of the ignorant and the heartless. Worse was the silence of the fearful. To break it required a larger, more fearful threat than Sir Roderick presented, and even if she could think of one, Kirstie doubted anyone would listen and believe it. She could, if she tried very hard, find a few thin excuses for the heartlessness of the men, but not for that of the mothers. Even if they were too hardened and wearied by life, surely they should at least fear for their own bairns? Were they so blind they thought only the unwanted were in danger?

As she approached the back of Payton's house, she tried to raise her spirits by reminding herself that there were still hundreds of people to speak to. There might still be someone out there willing to speak up, someone who realized that only by understanding and confronting the evil in their midst could it be defeated. She would just have to work harder. She had been a naive fool to think it would be easy.

Wee Alice gaped at her as she entered the kitchen and Kirstie inwardly cursed. Sneaking in was not as easy as sneaking out, especially when lost in her own unhappy thoughts. Wee Alice was concerned about the children, however, and as Kirstie shut the door behind her, she smiled at the woman. She just might be able to gain herself an ally within the household.

"What have ye been doing?" Wee Alice asked, her tone heavy with suspicion.

"Trying to find someone in this wretched town willing to speak out against my husband," replied Kirstie.

"And ye needed to dress as a lad?"

"People will talk to a lad more easily than a lady, and I am supposed to be dead, aye?"

Wee Alice sat down at the table, cupped her round chin in her hand, and frowned at Kirstie. " 'Tis dangerous."

"Oh, aye. 'Twas also dangerous living with Sir Roderick. Someone in this cursed town *has* to ken something. A mon cannae keep taking children without someone seeing or hearing something."

"But they are nay willing to say anything, are they?"

"Nay." Kirstie sighed and sat down on one of the benches flanking the table. "I was a fool to think it would be easy. E'en so, the disbelief and utter lack of interest I met at every turn was a shock. Roderick kens what he is about. He kens people willnae believe or willnae care. Nay when it is the verra poor and the abandoned who suffer. I had suspected it, but only that some would feel that way. I fear 'tis everyone."

"A hard, bitter truth. Most have their own lives and kin to fear for and watch o'er. They havenae time or strength to fret o'er anyone else. So, there is no need for ye to do this again." There was the hint of a question in Wee Alice's voice.

" 'Tis a verra big town, Wee Alice. Somewhere out

there, there has to be at least one brave soul. And, as Sir Payton does amongst the wealthy and powerful, so I shall do amongst the poor and helpless. Aye, they may nay help me or openly accuse Sir Roderick, but I do feel sure they heed what I say. My warnings settle in some part of their hearts and minds. Whispers of evil can spread about the town as swiftly as they do about the king's court.''

"Och, aye. Verra swiftly.''

" 'Twill be slow, but, little by little, I will end Roderick's ability to take whate'er child he fancies from this town. His hunting ground will soon grow sparse of game. True, some may ne'er believe in the dark whispers, but whene'er Roderick seeks a child, those whispers will be there, making people hesitate, breeding suspicion. It will have to be enough. And, if Sir Payton vanquishes Roderick ere what I do can serve much good, it matters not. There may still be enough said and heeded for at least a few people to understand that one must be verra careful ere one entrusts a child to anyone—rich or poor.''

Wee Alice nodded. "Aye, 'tis possible. I can see the sense of what ye are doing, lass, but the laird willnae be liking it.''

"Nay, he willnae.''

Kirstie winced and slowly looked at the man standing in the doorway to the kitchen. She found it a little annoying that he could still look so breath-stealingly beautiful when he was acting the arrogant male. He had his arms crossed over his fine, broad chest, his long, well-shaped legs were braced apart, and there was a hard, angry look on his handsome face. She began to think Payton could not look bad no matter how hard he tried.

"Did all go weel at court this day?" she asked in as pleasant a voice as she could muster.

Payton slowly shook his head. She had been risking her life, disobeying him, and she acted as if nothing was wrong. She did it well, too. He walked over to her, grabbed her by the hand, and dragged her out of her seat.

"We need to have a wee talk," he said as he started out of the kitchen, pulling her along with him.

It struck Kirstie as almost amusing that the touch of his hand on hers could make her feel all soft and warm inside. The man was angry. He was dragging her off to some place where he could lecture her until her ears burned. She should be preparing her arguments, not thinking about how nice it was to touch him.

"What are ye doing to Kirstie?"

Forcing her gaze away from Payton's attractive back-side, Kirstie looked at Callum even as Payton stopped to face the belligerent boy. "He is going to lecture me," she replied.

"He is angry," Callum said, but eased his aggressive stance a little when he saw no fear in Kirstie.

"And ye think I might knock her about a wee bit, do ye?" Payton asked.

" 'Tis what angry men do," Callum replied.

"Nay this one."

It was clear by the look on the boy's face that he was not sure he believed that. "Mayhap I best come, too."

" 'Tis kind of ye to worry o'er me, Callum," Kirstie said, "but I think I wouldst rather suffer a scold without an audience. He willnae strike me," she added softly.

"Ye sound verra sure of that."

"I am."

After another moment, Callum stepped aside. Payton gave the boy a small bow, then dragged Kirstie off to the small room where he did his accounts. The confrontation with Callum had not only served to ease the boy's concerns, but to take some of the sharp edge off his own anger. Although, he mused as he gently but firmly pushed Kirstie down into a large, ornately carved chair, his anger did not seem to worry or frighten her.

In truth, the extent of the anger he had felt when

he had realized what she had done surprised him. It surprised him even more to realize a lot of it was born of fear for her. As he had approached the kitchen and overheard her conversation with Wee Alice, he had felt that fear and anger twist together within him. Even if Roderick did not catch her, wandering the streets alone was dangerous. His mind had become crowded with all manner of dire fates she could have suffered and he would not have been able to protect her, would not have even known where she was. Such thoughts had chilled him to the bone.

As he poured them each a goblet of wine, he covertly studied her. Her diguise was good, might even have fooled him if he had not known it was she. She had surprisingly long legs for such a small woman and her attire displayed their every slim, shapely curve to perfection. Payton did not like the thought of her revealing that beauty to so many, even if those who saw her legs thought her a lad. Since he had never before cared who else caught a glimpse of the charms of any lady he desired or bedded, he found that feeling astonishing as well. Obviously, avoiding Kirstie as much as possible was not curing him of his obsession.

When she took a drink of wine and idly licked a stray drop from her full lips, he felt his belly clench with want. He, who had thought himself well versed in sensuality of all forms, had lately discovered that watching a woman eat could stir a man, fill his poor beleaguered mind with all manner of licentious images. Even sharing the meal with five children, Wee Alice, and Strong Ian had not helped cool his blood. Dining at court last evening had helped except that he had missed everyone. Even worse, he had discovered that watching other women eat did not stir him in any way. It was only Kirstie who affected him so. Now, it appeared, he could not even watch her quench her thirst without feeling like a buck in rutting season.

Payton reached for his anger. The mere thought of

her wandering the dangerous streets alone thinking a lad's clothing would protect her was enough to clear the lust from his brain and replace it with clean, clear anger. "Mayhap ye can explain what game ye play?" he asked as he sprawled in the chair facing her.

"Ye mean ye didnae o'erhear it all?" she asked.

The look of pure male irritation that passed over his fair face almost made her smile. She had used the moments of tense silence to prepare herself for an argument, and to stop herself from staring at inappropriate parts of his lean body like some wanton. Kirstie had to make him understand that she had to help, had to do something to bring her husband to the justice he had eluded for so long. This was her fight, too. All other righteous and honorable reasons aside, her very life depended upon beating Roderick.

"Do ye have no idea of the danger ye put yourself in, wandering the streets alone?"

"Roderick thinks I am dead and he would ne'er recognize me like this."

"Mayhap not, but he isnae the only danger lurking out there, ye foolish wench."

"Foolish wench?" she muttered and took a deep drink of wine to quell the urge to toss her goblet at his head.

"A wee, pretty lad is nay any safer out there alone than a wee lass. And ye have dressed fine enough for some thief to think ye might have something worth stealing. And, where did ye get those clothes?"

"From one of the chests upstairs. I had thought of going about as a poor, ragged boy, but I couldnae find any rags."

"A poor, ragged lad? Ye mean such as the ones Sir Roderick steals from the street?"

She winced inwardly. It had not really occurred to her that she was probably no safer from Roderick as a beardless lad than if she had gone out as herself. That

Payton could find that flaw in her plan was heartily annoying.

"I think I look too old to interest him."

Payton cursed and got up to pace the room, which made Kirstie want to echo his curse. It was impossible not to watch him as he moved. Every step he took was embued with a grace born of strength. She was struggling not to look at inappropriate parts of his body again. As he ranted about all the threats lurking upon the streets of town, she found herself watching the flex of muscle in his calf and thigh. His court dress was richly made, the tunic short enough to give her a far too tantalizing glimpse of his taut backside. Kirstie thought it a little odd that she could stop herself from staring at his groin with relative ease, but had to work very hard indeed to stop watching his legs and backside. Perhaps, she mused, it was because she did not think he would catch her at it, as he was usually facing away from her at the time. Of course, it could also be because it was such a pleasure to watch him move. Then, abruptly, he turned to face her, and Kirstie quickly looked up.

"Ye are paying me no heed at all, are ye?" he said, his tone a strange mixture of irritation and amusement.

"Aye, I am," she lied and ignored his soft snort of disbelief. "I have to do something. I cannae just sit about and pray ye and Strong Ian can solve all my troubles. Nor can ye do it all by yourselves."

He crouched down in front of her so they were eye to eye. "Ye are the one Roderick wants dead."

"I ken it, but I am most careful. Dinnae forget, I ken all who aid him and serve him. I ken who to avoid."

"Ye wouldnae have to avoid anyone if ye would just stay in this house," he snapped as he stood up, walked to the fireplace, and leaned against the thick stone mantel.

Kirstie set her goblet down and moved to stand near him. "I ken how to be careful, to be wary and watch my back. Since I ken from where in the town so many of the children come, I ken where to search for witnesses, allies. I also ken what names to mention, what tales to tell to stir suspicion.''

''Which isnae working, is it?'' He turned to face her more fully.

''Nay as weel as I had hoped. But, your work at court goes slowly as weel, aye?''

''Aye.'' He took off her cap, almost smiling when her hair immediately started to slip free of the odd lump she had pinned it up into. ''Word spreads slowly but surely, however. Yet, there are so many other troubles at court that worrying about a mon with a liking for lads isnae something many have time for. There is a struggle for power o'er our wee king amongst the Board of Regents. The Boyds rapidly gain more and more power. There are whispers that Lord Boyd and his brother Sir Alexander may try to grasp full control o'er young James.''

Kirstie sighed and shook her head. ''So the only lad most wish to hear about or fret o'er is our young king.''

''And whether England may try to take advantage of all the squabbling and fighting for power.''

''Do ye think there will be war?''

''I pray it willnae come to that, but when the rule of a country is at stake, war oft results.'' Unable to resist, he took her hair down, combing his fingers through the silken mass to loosen the tangles. ''But, we have our own battle to fight and cannae fret o'er those who try to steal power from a too-youthful king who hasnae the strength to hold fast to it.''

''What are ye doing?'' she asked, knowing she should move out of his reach, yet liking the feel of his fingers in her hair too much to stop him.

''Fixing your hair. Ye willnae wander the town alone.''

''Oh? I willnae? I believe I requested that ye be my champion, my ally, nay my father.''

''As your champion and ally, 'tis my responsibility to see to your safety.'' He grasped her by her slender shoulders. " 'Tis nay safe for ye to wander these streets all alone."

"Then I will take someone with me."

"Curse it, ye barely escaped one attempt upon your life. Why do ye now court another?"

"Sir Roderick believes he succeeded in killing me, so he willnae be looking for me. Nor will any of his people. I need to do this. I cannae go to court and help ye. I cannae go to any of the few people I ken for I am supposed to be dead. I have been fighting to save the children too long to just stop now. There was danger in it before, wasnae there? And, that bastard tried to kill me. I cannae let that lie, cannae just sit by and pray he doesnae find me so that he can try it again. As ye make it impossible for him to get his filthy hands on the children of the highborn, he will turn more and more to the poor, to the ones in the town. I mean to sorely hinder him in that."

Payton could understand her need and agreed with her reasoning. Someone spreading the word about town and searching for allies and witnesses would be helpful. Strong Ian tried in what time he had to spare, but he was more apt to elicit fear than confidences. Logically, he knew her plan was a good one. Emotionally, he wanted to lock her in a room and surround it with burly guards until Roderick was dead and buried. That was not something he intended to confess, however, and he struggled to think of some compromise.

"I can take Callum with me," she said, fighting not to be too strongly stirred by the way he was stroking her arms.

"Roderick and his men would easily recognize the boy." He stared at her full mouth as she spoke, feeling nearly desperate to taste it.

"Nay when I am done with him. Two lads are in less danger than one and ye ken that I am verra good at creeping about unseen and hiding. Callum is nearly as good as I am. I swear that, at the first hint that my disguise is nay working or that I have roused my husband's interest, I will come back here and nay leave again until Roderick is dead.''

Kirstie could not fully suppress a shiver of delight when he gently held her face between his elegant hands. The shards of green in his golden eyes seemed to sparkle and gleam, fascinating her. She did not really want to find him so alluring; far too many women did. The very last thing she needed was to become just one more in an undoubtedly impressive line of women he had seduced. And yet, she mused with an inner sigh, to be seduced by such a man would certainly be a memory any woman would cherish.

"At the verra first hint of danger?" he asked, not sure why he was giving into her.

"E'en the suspicion of a hint." The way he was lightly caressing her face with his fingers was making her almost uncomfortably warm.

"And ye willnae go out alone."

"Nay." She almost squeaked the word when he touched his lips to her forehead.

"And ne'er at night." He kissed the outside corner of each of her eyes.

"Nay, ne'er at night."

Kirstie could hear herself speaking, but was not exactly sure what she was saying. Her mind and her body seemed to be melting into a heated pool at his elegantly shod feet. She hoped she was not promising anything she would regret later. With each soft kiss upon her face, she cared less and less about talking. In fact, she was increasingly desirous of seeing how fast she could tear those elegant clothes off his too-tempting form and get him down on the floor. Since she was not entirely sure what she would do with him after that, she thought it a passingly strange urge. When he brushed his lips over hers, she felt her whole body tremble and clutched at the front of his tunic.

"And ye will let me ken where in town ye mean to

be," he said softly, his mouth so close his lips brushed against hers as he spoke.

"Oh, aye."

Payton tangled his fingers in her soft, thick hair, cradling the back of her head with one hand. He curled his other arm around her tiny waist and tugged her body closer to his. It had been a long time since he had had to use such subtlety, to coax or steal a kiss, but he was pleased to see that he still had some skill at it. Kirstie was intoxicatingly responsive. He knew he ought to feel guilty for taking advantage of that, but he did not. If it took a sly maneuver or two to get a kiss, he would not hesitate. He felt as if he had ached to taste her full lips for most of his life.

A heartbeat after Payton pressed his lips against her, Kirstie wrapped her arms around his neck and held on tight. When he ran his tongue along the seam of her lips, she readily parted them. Roderick had kissed her a few times on their wedding night and, when he had stuck his tongue in her mouth, she had nearly gagged. Payton's kiss was beyond words, each stroke of his tongue making her feel hot and desperately needy. So many strong feelings were tearing through her, she was surprised she did not swoon. As he moved his hands over her body, she felt the urge to throw off her clothes so she could feel them against her skin.

When he placed a hand against her backside, holding his groin firm against her, Kirstie heard herself moan softly. She realized she ached to rub herself against him in a blindly wanton fashion, and she was so shocked she was able to finally grasp a few shards of control. There were a hundred reasons why she should not take what Payton offered. The fact that she could not think of a single one at the moment showed her just how much danger she was in. She quickly pulled free of his hold, staring at him as she struggled to calm her breathing. She was pleased to see that he was breathing as hard as she was.

"That must ne'er happen again," she said, wishing she did not sound quite so unconvinced and breathless.

"Ye want me." He reached for her.

Kirstie started backing up toward the door. "I want a lot of things, but that doesnae mean I can or should have them."

"Ye could have this." Payton wondered what had happened to his renowned skill with words, then decided that, when every bone and sinew in his body cried out to possess her, it was no wonder his lust-crazed mind could not conjure up any practiced words of seduction.

"Nay. I willnae just be one of the multitude," she said, grasping the latch on the door.

"Ye wouldnae be."

"And, I think 'tis wise to cling to my virginity. After all, if all else fails, I could still seek an annulment."

She fled before he could argue that. She could not possibly believe there was any chance of an annulment. Roderick wanted her dead, had already tried to kill her once. Since Kirstie was not dim-witted, Payton suspected that statement had been no more than some hasty attempt to make him leave her alone.

He poured himself some wine and emptied his goblet in one long drink. It did little to cool the fever in his blood. No woman had ever stirred him as Kirstie did. He wondered if some part of him had suspected that was how it would be, hence his obsession with her. Up until this moment, he had been struggling to be a perfect gentleman, to refrain from trying to seduce her. That searing kiss had ended that noble plan. For once, he rather hoped rumor did not exaggerate his seductive skills, for he was going to use every one he had on Kirstie. He would not, could not, rest until she was in his bed.

CHAPTER FIVE

"He wants to get under your skirts."

Kirstie nearly stumbled, then steadied herself with a hand on the rough stone wall of the building they stood near. She stared at the scowling Callum. He was well disguised, with a large cap hiding his bright hair and shadowing his green eyes, but it was still easy to see his anger. She wondered how long he had held it in. They had been wandering the town for eight days, then exchanging information with Payton and Ian in the evening, and not once had Callum revealed that he knew Payton was trying to seduce her.

And the man was doing a very good job of it, too, she mused as she calmed herself. Constantly touching her in small yet sensuous ways. Stealing kisses and speaking words that heated her blood. Kirstie grimaced when she realized she should have been prepared for this. Callum was too quick-witted, too worldly wise, not to have seen what was going on.

"What he wants and what he will get are nay the same thing," she said and started walking again.

" 'Tis said he could seduce a stone."

"Exaggeration. The mon is beautiful, holds all a woman favors, and he kens the art of seduction. Whether he kens it better than another mon or nay, I certainly couldnae tell ye. What I *can* tell ye is that I am a married woman and I believe in the vows I spoke."

"With Roderick?"

"True, he is nay what I want and he deserves to roast in hell's hottest fires, but the fact that my husband is a perverted, murdering swine doesnae change the fact that I said vows afore God. Payton is obviously far too accustomed to women who ignore such vows. Too long at court, I suspect."

Callum walked by her side and, after a moment of staring at his new soft boots, he said, "He hasnae bedded ye. Roderick hasnae, I mean. So, ye have no marriage."

"I havenae ended it."

"He did when he left ye unbedded for five years. There is naught holding ye in that marriage save the need to get some church mon to agree that ye have no marriage and sign a wee paper or two. I think ye ken that and Sir Payton does as weel. So, why are ye resisting him?"

"He is nay my husband."

Callum made a rude noise and shook his head. "That matters naught. I ken ye want the mon."

There was a sulky tone to his voice and Kirstie wondered if, like many boys do, Callum was suffering a first infatuation—with her. If so, she had to be very careful what she said. If he had feelings for her, they could not be openly acknowledged, but they could also not be callously ignored. She would have to tread warily.

"Sir Payton has kenned many, many women. E'en if one believes only half of what is said about him, 'tis still a longer line than I am inclined to join."

A brief, very male grin lightened Callum's face. "He is a rogue. Yet, I dinnae think he sees ye that way." He shrugged. "I dinnae ken. I ken about men and women and what they do, but I have ne'er seen the game ye two play. Where I grew up, if a mon wanted a lass, he took her, then paid her for the pleasure or smacked her to stop her wailing or wedded with her. Ye two kiss and hint and blush and argue. 'Tis a muddle.''

It was hard to maintain her calm. Kirstie was filled with horror over the life he briefly referred to and laughter over the way he described the strange courtship she and Payton indulged in. She was knotted up inside with the desire Payton so easily stirred in her and her head often ached from the numerous arguments she had with herself over right and wrong. If Payton's growing ill temper was any indication, he was also suffering, which pleased her. Such upheaval had to be confusing, however, even to a boy like Callum.

"There are rules, Callum. Rules that say a married woman should be faithful to her husband. Rules that say a maid should give her innocence only to her lawfully wedded husband. I will confess that Sir Payton makes me want to turn my back on all those rules, but then I would be nay better than all the adulteresses, courtesans, and licentious widows he has taken to his bed in the past.''

"Ah.'' Callum nodded. "Pride.''

Kirstie shrugged. "I suppose.''

"Which do ye think will win? Pride or the lusting?''

"I have no idea,'' she admitted softly.

"Would being with him make ye happy?''

She hesitated, then sighed. "Aye, I think it would.''

"Then ye should do as ye wish. Ye deserve to be happy.''

"Mayhaps. Yet, with a mon like Payton, that happiness could be verra fleeting, followed by a heart's pain.'' She slipped into the shadows of the wall surrounding the foundling home, Callum swiftly joining her.

"Weel, I will say one last thing on the matter,'' Callum said in a near whisper. "If ye decide ye want to reach for a wee bit of joy and pleasure, I will nay mind. S'truth,

I will kill any fool who dares to cry ye wrong or shameful.''

"Thank ye, Callum." Ignoring the way he hunched his thin shoulders, she kissed his cheek. "That will weigh most heavily in whate'er decision I make." She studied the large, thatch-roofed home that Roderick so often used to feed his dark hungers. " 'Tis verra quiet. I wonder if the bastard will come here today. Payton says more and more people are quietly keeping their lads from his reach. Roderick will be hunting new victims soon and this has always proven to be fertile ground.''

Callum watched as a too-thin, ragged boy stumbled toward the well with two heavy buckets. "I think I ken who that lad is.''

She quickly grasped his shoulder when he made to move toward the boy. "I think your disguise is good, but I daren't risk ye being seen by these people. They are Roderick's lackeys.''

"They willnae see, Kirstie. Trust me.''

He gave her no chance to reply, slipping free of her grasp and moving toward the well where the boy struggled to fill the buckets. Kirstie began to relax when she realized even she was having a difficult time keeping him in sight. Then he was gone, but the way the lad at the well suddenly tensed and chanced a peek around, told her Callum was there. She tried not to get her hopes up as she waited; yet, if Callum could gain them an ally within the foundling home, they could more easily help the children there. They might even be able to end Roderick's ability to help himself to the boys housed there.

It seemed like hours before Callum rejoined her, tense hours filled with the fear that he would be caught. Kirstie was compelled to grasp his hand when he reached her side and hold it tightly for a moment to reassure herself that he was safe. It pleased her when Callum made no attempt to free himself of her touch.

"That lad is Simon, a weaver's son," Callum told her.

"He only just arrived here. His father died and there was no one else to care for him." Callum frowned. "I think he will be safe from that bastard, for he isnae a pretty lad. He has a big nose and his skin is spotty."

"Ah, so he is a wee bit older than ye, is he?"

"Aye, twelve. He told me Sir Roderick hasnae been round for weeks. Said the mon what deals with Roderick has been acting nervous and afraid lately. O'erheard the mon and his bitch of a wife muttering about rumor and suspicion and needing to be verra careful for a wee while."

"Ah, good. The rumors are starting to work their magic."

Callum nodded. "Simon says the wife isnae happy about it, is whining about the money lost if they dinnae keep Sir Roderick happy."

"Jesu, 'tis times such as this that I wish I was a verra big, hairy mon so I could stomp in there and pound those wretched people into the mud." She ignored Callum's soft laugh, even though the sound of it made her heart soar. "Can the lad be of any help to us?"

"Aye, he says he will do what he can. Told him we would come round each day we could at this time, for 'tis when he fetches the water for the evening gruel. He will nod his head as he works if he has something he needs to tell us. I didnae tell him where we were to be found, for I am nay sure he could stand firm if pressed for the truth."

" 'Tis probably for the best," she said as they began to creep away from the wall, slipping into the deep shadows of an alley a few houses away before they eased their stealthy progress a little. "We will follow your plan for now."

"He is a good lad, Simon is. He will do all he can to help. Ye see, he kens what Roderick is. His father told him. Nay too long afore he died."

"How did his father die?"

"Stabbed in an alehouse. The mon went there every

Saturday evening for a drink and a tumble with one of
the maids. He had just returned from taking a few bolts
of fine cloth to Sir Roderick and had a full purse. Told
his son to nay get near the mon, went for his drink and
tumble, and died." Callum frowned. "The mon saw
something, didnae he."

It was not a question, but Kirstie still replied, "I believe
so. He was silenced. Roderick is verra good at silencing
people, either wih a heavy purse or a knife in the back.
Roderick must have kenned that the weaver was nay
one to be silenced by coin. I think we should tell Strong
Ian about it. He may be able to get some people to
tell him about how the weaver died, mayhap e'en get
enough information to lay the blame at Roderick's
door."

For a while they walked in silence, winding their way
through the narrow, sheltered alleys of the town. It was
time to return to Payton's home, but they were always
careful not to be seen coming or going. It was as they
made their way carefully through a refuse-strewn alley
that Kirstie heard an odd sound. She grasped Callum
by the arm, halting him beside her, and then listened
carefully.

"Did ye hear that?" she asked Callum a moment later,
speaking as softly as she could yet still be understood.

"Sounds like someone is crying," Callum whispered
back, even as he searched the alley all around them.

Kirstie bit back a protest when he moved toward a
bundle of filthy rags near one damp, moss-covered wall.
She carefully followed him as he bent down and, knife
held at the ready, began to peel away the rags. Huddled
beneath the filth was a small boy. Kirstie knelt down
and, murmuring comforting words, gently turned the
child's face toward hers. As the dim shaft of light coming
down into the alley from between the rooflines of the
buildings hit the child's face, Kirstie inhaled so quickly,
she nearly choked. Filth, streaked and smudged by tears,

and vibrant bruises marred the little face, but she still recognized it.

"Robbie?" she asked, not daring to believe that the little boy could have survived for so long, injured and on his own.

"M'lady Kirstie?" the boy mumbled.

" 'Tis Robbie, isnae it?"

"Aye, m'lady. Moira?"

"She is weel," she replied as she took off her cloak and, as gently as she could, wrapped his bone-thin body in it. "We will take ye to her."

"She is safe?"

"Aye. I got her away from that mon. Ye should have waited for me, lad. I came back."

"I needed to find Moira."

He gasped when she picked him up in her arms, then swooned. Kirstie tried not to think about how many injuries might be hidden from view. Callum quickly took the lead as they headed to Payton's house.

"Jesu, lass," cried Wee Alice as Kirstie and Callum entered the kitchens, "what have ye found?"

"Moira's brother," she replied. "I dinnae ken how he survived or how he got to where we found him, but right now he needs cleaning and his wounds seen to."

The next hour passed in a taut silence as they cleaned the child, tending all his bruises, and wrapping his ribs when Wee Alice decided that, although not broken, there was a need for binding them. Each bruise she put ointment on, each glance at the tiny, battered body of young Robbie, fed Kirstie's anger. There was no excuse for anyone doing such hurt to a child.

Moira edged up to the side of the bed even as Robbie opened his eyes. "Moira?" the boy called.

"Here I am, Robbie," Moira said, taking his hand in hers. "I thought the angels had taken ye away."

"Nay. Not yet."

"And they willnae," Kirstie said firmly as she helped

the boy to drink some of the thin gruel Wee Alice had hastily made and brought to the room.

"Do the bruises hurt?" Moira asked.

"Nay, not so bad. The old ones are near healed. 'Tis the ones I got a few days ago that sore pain me."

"What happened a few days ago?" asked Kirstie.

"I nearly got taken back to that bastard," the boy said in a surprisingly hard voice. "His men grabbed me and thumped me some, then threw me on a horse. I threw myself back off and went back into the town to hide."

"Such a brave, resourceful lad."

"I had to find Moira." Despite the swelling around his mouth, he managed a little smile for his sister. "I have to take care of her. Promised Mither."

"And I am sure her heart is fair bursting with pride as she looks down on ye, her braw son," said Wee Alice as she sat down on the edge of the bed and gently coaxed Robbie into drinking a potion that would ease his pain and help him sleep.

"What has happened?"

Kirstie looked at Payton, who stood in the doorway, a frowning Ian behind him. "It seems the angels didnae take Moira's brother, after all."

Payton cursed softly and strode to the bed. The little boy lying there fighting to keep his eyes open was sorely injured. Despite the bruises and bandages, however, he could see the resemblance to little Moira. Robbie had the same dark hair, although not as curly, and the same dark eyes. Payton found it difficult to believe that such a battered child, a boy of only seven, could have survived on his own for several weeks. Then he recalled that Callum had survived for years.

"I will care for Moira, sir," the boy said, his voice slurred as Alice's potion began to do its work.

"Aye, I am sure ye will," Payton said, deeply moved by how the small boy thought only of his smaller sister despite the travails he had obviously suffered through.

"Let the women help ye first, however. Ye need to be healed and strong so ye can care weel for your sister."

The boy's eyes closed. "I am feeling tired."

"He is just sleeping," Moira said as she climbed onto the bed next to her brother, but her voice shook with fear.

Payton stroked her thick curls. "He is truly just sleeping, lass. Wee Alice gave him some medicine so he can rest without pain."

"Thank ye, Wee Alice," Moira said as she lay down next to Robbie. "I will stay with him, I think."

"Aye, ye do that, lass. That will make him feel better." Payton took Kirstie by the hand and tugged her out of the room.

As Kirstie allowed him to lead her into his ledger room where he had stolen far too many kisses, she fought to control the rage writhing inside of her. Payton would have questions and she would need a clear head to answer them. Later, she would consider what needed to be done about this latest atrocity committed by Roderick. She took the goblet of wine Payton served her and drank it all down, then began to answer his questions.

Payton began to feel uneasy as Kirstie told him everything she and Callum had discovered. She looked and sounded a little odd, as if she was a too-tightly-drawn lute string. He told himself it was just shock, probably grief as well. No one with any heart could look at Robbie and not feel both.

"I will set Ian on the trail of the weaver's death immediately," said Payton. "He will sniff out the truth. It could give us a hefty club to wield against Roderick."

"But is probably nay enough to hang him, aye?"

"Aye. If he didnae wield the knife himself, if it was made to look like nay more than a tavern brawl, then the ones who actually committed the crime will be the only ones who will pay for it. That is, if anyone recalls who they were. And, Roderick's lackeys may curse and blame Sir Roderick all the way to the gallows, but they willnae be heeded. Sir Roderick may still fear that truth, however, e'en fear that his men may yet betray him.''

"If Roderick fears that, then those men are already dead and beyond answering any questions.''

They discussed the use they might make of young Simon, but Kirstie was soon unable to concentrate. Knowing she was rapidly losing control over the turmoil inside of her, she excused herself. She did not wish to succumb to hysterics in front of Payton. It would be too easy to tell him far more than she wanted him to know.

Once in her bedchamber, she downed yet another goblet of wine. It helped a little, easing the strength of the emotions trying to tear her apart. One clear thought emerged from all the others as she sipped at yet another drink of wine. This had to end. Payton's plan was a good one, but it worked too slowly. As they nibbled away at the power which kept Roderick sheltered from all punishment, children continued to suffer.

Kirstie sat on her bed and waited. Soon the house would grow quiet as everyone sought out their beds. Then she would go and do what she should have done years ago—kill Roderick.

Just thinking of it brought her a strange sense of calm. Even the knowledge that she would undoubtedly lose her own life did not trouble her. All she had to do was think of how poor little Robbie looked, and she knew any sacrifice was worth it to put an end to such horror.

"What does your wife think of the lad's condition?'' Payton asked Ian the moment the man joined him in his office.

"The lad should be fine if he doesnae take a fever,'' Ian replied as he sighed and sat down in the chair facing Payton. "He needs feeding, is near starved and thus weak.'' He shook his head. *"Weak* is, mayhap, a poor choice of word. No weak lad could have survived all that one did.''

"He had a verra strong need to find and protect his sister."

"Aye. So, did the lass have any news?"

"Quite a lot, yet mayhap not quite enough." Payton told Ian everything Kirstie had told him.

"I will seek out the truth about the weaver's death. It does carry the stink of murder. But there may be nay proving it, nay against that bastard Roderick, leastwise."

"So I thought."

"The lass probably didnae take that news verra weel."

Payton frowned and felt his unease return. "Weel enough. I think she was too shocked and upset o'er the boy to e'en think much o'er all the rest."

Ian frowned as well. "That doesnae sound like the lass I have come to ken. She should have been enraged."

"That feeling may take a wee while to work its way through all else she was feeling."

"Did she say she wouldnae go after the mon?"

"Aye." Payton thought over all he and Kirstie had said and then cursed. "Nay, not exactly." He shook his head, trying to dispel a growing sense of alarm. "The lass has seen this all before, and worse. She has kept her wits about her and planned weel. I cannae think she would do anything foolish now."

"Mayhap not. She is, indeed, a clever lass."

"But? I hear a *but* in your voice, my friend. Why, after so many years of being careful, would she act in a foolish way now?"

"Because everyone reaches that point where they can take no more."

"And she loves the children," Payton said, even as he stood up and headed for the door.

Ian followed him. "Loves them so much that she cares for the ones most others ignore or kick aside. E'en risks her verra life to keep them from harm."

"And, so, may finally decide 'tis a fine time to sacrifice herself?"

Payton walked into Kirstie's bedchamber and halted.

He did not want to believe what he saw, or, rather, what he did not see. Kirstie was not curled up in her bed. Her bed was empty, still neatly made, and her night shift was still draped over the covers, waiting for her to don it.

With a silent Ian dogging his steps, Payton checked the other bedchambers. He even looked into his, hoping she might have sought him out for some comforting. By the time he moved to look into all the other rooms in the house, he knew it was a waste of time. He finally accepted the truth as he entered the kitchen and found it empty as well.

"She isnae here, Payton," Ian said, his voice unusually gentle.

"She has gone after him." Payton finally gave voice to the fear rapidly knotting his insides.

There would be no trail to follow. Knowing Kirstie's skills, Payton suspected he could walk right past her and never know she was in reach. She was marching off to her death and, loathe Roderick though he did, Payton did not feel the man's death was worth Kirstie's life.

He cursed and dragged his hands through his hair. "Too many choices," he muttered, "and I have only one chance to catch her. If I choose wrong, go off to the wrong place in search of her, I shall lose all chance of saving her. Jesu, where would she go to first?"

"She went to the king's court."

Payton turned to see Callum in the doorway. The boy was dressed, had his knife stuck in his belt, and had a very determined look upon his small face. It was obvious that the boy was intending to go and rescue Kirstie.

"Are ye sure?" he demanded.

"Aye," Callum replied. "When we were slipping about the town, we heard that Sir Roderick would be at the king's court. He is supposed to return her dower lands to her family since she is supposed to have died childless, but that bastard hopes to get someone important to say he doesnae have to do that. She didnae tell ye about that?''

''Nay, she didnae.''

''I suspicion she forgot soon as we found poor Robbie.''

''Possibly.''

''Are we going after her?''

''Ye will stay here,'' Payton ordered the boy.

''But . . .''

''Ye cannae go up to the castle. Ye could easily be seen and recognized. I would feel a need to watch out for ye and that could cause me to fail to get to Kirstie before it is too late to save her.''

After a brief hesitation, the boy nodded his reluctant acceptance of the command. As Payton strode by the boy, he patted him on the shoulder. ''I will get her back.''

''Safe from Roderick?''

''Aye, safe from him. But, after this madness, she may nay be so verra safe from me.''

CHAPTER SIX

The candles and torches lighting the great hall of the king's court provided Kirstie with ample shadows to move in. She was surprised at how easily she had slipped into the royal keep. With all the current turmoil and struggle for power, she had expected a larger, more vigilant guard. Even when she had had no place to hide, had been forced to move in the open, no one had paid any attention to her. A boy was of no interest, no importance.

As she watched the crowd flirting and gossiping all around her, playing their games of seduction and power, she noticed the many boys and youths, the squires and pages, hurrying through the crowd or waiting for a summons. They, too, were ignored for the most part. It was sad. A child, especially one who survived those first treacherous years, was a gift from God. Yet, although she caught the occasional glimpse of kindness, most of these boys were ignored or treated as little better than slaves. It was no wonder they grew up into hard men eager to take up a sword at the slightest provocation. Where was the protection, the gentle guidance?

The way so few people seemed to notice where the boys were or what they were doing was appalling. No wonder Roderick seemed able to act with impunity. Kirstie had the chilling suspicion that Roderick saw this as yet another hunting ground, that he did not have to actually take the boy to Thanescarr to commit his crime.

Although it had been poverty that had kept her brothers from being fostered out, Kirstie was now glad of that lack. They were big, loud, annoying most of the time, and somewhat quick to anger, but they had many good qualities as well. She knew them all very well and they knew her, for they had not been parted until she had married. She had to wonder how much family feeling remained when a boy was sent away at such a young age. Kirstie knew boys had to be trained, had to learn how to survive in war and deal in courtly ways, but there had to be another way. Her brothers knew how to fight well and, although their manners could be appalling, they had been taught courtly ways, but they had never left home. If she was ever blessed with children, she would not send her sons away. Especially not when she now knew that predators like Roderick lurked in waiting for them.

Then she saw him and all the rage that had been briefly dimmed rushed back with such force she was made dizzy. Pressing herself against the wall to steady herself and remain hidden, she watched her husband. The man had his hand on a young boy's shoulder and she recognized the look on Roderick's square face. It was hunger.

Her knife was in her hand before she even thought about it, a blind need to protect the child directing her movement. Then, suddenly, another man appeared and, within but a minute, the boy was taken away. There was a brief look of fury upon Roderick's face, but the expression of a calm, pleasant courtier quickly returned. Looking around, Kirstie realized that none of the boys was near Roderick. She watched as one small page made a clear detour around the man as he went from one end of the hall to the other.

Payton's words were being heeded, she realized. Obviously, not enough to have Roderick cast out for the vile beast he was, but enough to make people wary about allowing him near the boys. Even better, word had gotten to the boys themselves. The boys who did not have caring, alert protectors now had the other boys. There would be no more easy hunting here for Roderick.

So, what was she to do now, she asked herself as she put her knife away. The proof that their campaign against Roderick was working had eased the blind grip of rage. Now she began to see the dangerous flaws in her plan to end the man's life here and now. There were too many people around. An attempt upon Roderick's life might actually gain him some sympathy, weakening all Payton's hard work. If she failed or was captured, her identity would quickly be discovered. That would start a whole round of questions, questions and answers that could lead Roderick or his family to Payton, to the children.

And, now that the hot fury which had brought her here was easing, she was not sure she could do it. Roderick was a foul stain upon the earth, but could she truly just walk up and stab him in the heart? She had the sinking feeling that, now that her wits had returned, such a cold-blooded execution would be beyond her. Which meant she could be caught, could find herself back in Roderick's hands, and she would die for nothing.

Trembling a little from the realization of what she had almost done, she began to work her way stealthily out of the hall. She struggled to ignore the voice of her lingering fury, which called her a coward and urged her to carry out her mad plan. A battle raged inside of her. One part of her wanted to do what she had come here for and put an end to the monster that was her husband, while the other part urged her to go home, to allow Payton's safer, wiser plan to work. Each time rage spoke, she hesitated; then good sense prevailed again and she would move ever closer to the doors. If this madness did not cease, it would take her days to leave the hall, she thought sourly.

As she paused in a shadowed corner, Kirstie surveyed the crowd again. A small page walked in front of her and she glanced at him, then froze. How did Callum get here and where did he find those rich clothes? She started to reach out, only to have an all-too-familiar elegant hand reach out from behind her and grab her by the wrist.

"Mayhap we should look about a little for the lass as we go?" suggested Ian as he and Payton rode to the castle.

"Dinnae bother. Ye willnae see her," Payton replied. "That lass truly can make herself naught but a shadow."

"She is *that* good?" he asked in astonishment as they rode into the courtyard.

After dismounting and ordering the man who came to take their horses to hold them right there, Payton fell into step beside Ian. "Aye, she is that good. Silent, swift, and able to blend into even the smallest of shadows."

As they entered the crowded great hall, Ian frowned as he looked around. "If she can do that, how do ye expect to find her in here?"

"Nay easily, but," he nodded toward Roderick, "there stands her prey, so she will be here somewhere. Ye watch him, keeping a close eye out for the lass. She will have to show herself, however briefly, in order to strike. I will search the shadows."

Leaving Ian to thwart an attack Payton prayed would not come, he immediately moved to the far edges of the hall, into the shadows where he knew Kirstie would hide. As he moved along the wall, Payton realized several advantages to slipping around in the shadows. He was not interrupted or delayed by women interested in flirtation or men eager to talk of the embattled regents or the ever-shifting alliances with the English, whether one should side with the House of York or the House of Lancaster. Payton felt the wisest thing to do was to leave both houses to fight over the English crown unaided by the Scots and, if they did not completely kill each other off, deal with the winner. At the moment, he was even less interested than ever in which English fool won the crown. All he wanted was to get Kirstie safely out of the castle and back to his house, where he intended to berate her for her foolishness until her pretty little ears rang.

Even as he idly noted his young cousin Uven walking away from him, thankfully oblivious to his presence, Payton saw a slight movement in the shadows the boy walked past. Despite his astonishment over how completely Kirstie could disappear into such thin protection, Payton hurried to her side and slipped behind her as she stepped away from the wall. He grabbed her by the wrist and yanked her hand back before she could touch the boy.

" 'Tis Callum," she whispered as Payton tugged her back into the shadows and began to pull her along toward the doors.

"Nay, 'tis my cousin Uven MacMillan," Payton said, breaching his cover long enough to signal Ian to go back to the horses.

"But he looked just like Callum."

"Aye, I ken it. I will explain it later when I am done telling ye what a complete idiot ye are."

Obviously, Payton lost his reputed skill with soft, seductive words when he was angry, Kirstie mused. She started to protest his somewhat rough treatment as he yanked her out into the bailey and tossed her up onto his horse, then decided it might be wiser to just be quiet for now. Payton looked so furious she doubted telling him that she had begun to change her mind would be enough to calm him. She sat stiffly in front of him as they rode away from the castle and wondered just how bad a scolding she would soon have to endure.

Once back at his home, Payton dragged her into his ledger room and pushed her toward a chair. Exhausted from the emotional battles she had been through in the last few hours, Kirstie sank down into the seat. She was a little startled when Payton served her a goblet of wine. Even though he thrust it at her without a word and walked away, she almost smiled. Even when furious, the man could not completely forget his manners.

She watched him as he paced and had to bite back another smile. Despite knowing that, at any moment, he was going to start lecturing her, she enjoyed watching him move. Kirstie wondered if emotional exhaustion had made her light-headed.

"Ye were going to kill him," Payton said abruptly as he turned to face her.

"Aye," she replied honestly. "I was going to plunge my dagger into his black heart." She took a drink of wine. "For a wee while, I thought of slicing his belly open so that he would die slowly and in agony. Then I thought about cutting off his manhood so he couldnae work his evil anymore." She took another drink of wine. "Then I—" Her eyes widened when Payton snatched her goblet out of her hand, scowled at the wine it still held, then scowled at her. "I am nay drunk," she murmured as she took her drink back.

"Ye would have been the one who was killed."

"Quite possibly. It didnae matter. I wanted that monster sent straight to hell."

"And those two brutes who stand by him at all times would just watch ye do it, aye?"

Kirstie decided she would prefer to dance on nails barefoot than admit she had completely forgotten Roderick's guards. They were blindly loyal to Roderick and as strong as they were stupid. One glimpse of a knife in her hand and they would have snapped her neck or taken her head from her shoulders with a huge sword, their favored methods of meting out death.

"I was planning to be quick," she said and inwardly grimaced when he gave her a look of furious exasperation.

"Ye didnae think at all," he snapped. "Ye didnae have a plan, either. Nay, ye just trotted off, knife in hand, prepared to do murder or die in the attempt. Or did ye think everyone would just step back when ye attacked Roderick and say, have at him, dearie."

She slammed her goblet down on a small table next to her and stood up, the smouldering anger still within her now aimed at Payton. The fact that he took a hasty step backward when she moved so quickly pleased her immensely. She did not need him to tell her she had acted hastily, but he could show some sympathy, some understanding of what had driven her to act so unwisely.

"They should," she said, her gritted teeth making her words terse and sharp. "Everyone there should be eager to pick up sword or dagger and cut that foul mon into a hundred bloody pieces. Nay, I didnae think or plan. All I did think of as I looked at poor wee Robbie was that Roderick had lived far too long. It had to stop. He had to be stopped. Roderick is a sick beast, a vile monster, and I wanted that monster dead. Dead and buried and with every child he has hurt able to spit upon his grave and curse his black soul."

She turned away from him and walked over to the fireplace to stare blindly into the flames. Kirstie realized she wanted to weep and inwardly cursed herself for such a weakness. Although a good, hearty cry might make her feel less twisted-up by conflicting emotions, it would solve nothing. She tensed a little when Payton stepped up close behind her and wrapped his arms around her.

"The wee lads wouldnae spit on that bastard's grave," he said against her ear. "They would piss on it."

Kirstie could not believe such crude words would

make her want to laugh. She recognized both the humor and the truth of them, however. It would certainly be what her brothers would do, even the gentle, refined Eudard.

"Why did that boy look so much like Callum?" she asked, hoping conversation would help her remain cool to his light embrace, to the soft kisses he placed against her ear and neck.

"Because I believe Callum may be a kinsmon of his," Payton replied.

Kirstie broke free of his hold and moved to the side, away from the heat of the fire and him, before facing him. "Are ye sure?"

"As sure as I can be, but, until I get a mother's name and, mayhap, a bit more information, I will say naught to the boy. The MacMillans will take one look at Callum and ken he is one of theirs, but Callum needs more if he is to believe and accept it." Payton moved to stand in front of her, then edged forward until she was backed up against the wall. "Then he will have a name, a clan to belong to. And, if I can actually find a close kinsmon, 'twill be e'en better."

"Would they want him?"

"Aye." He saw a brief flicker of doubt in her expression. "They are my Uncle Eric's clan. Trust me to ken how they will act. They will welcome the lad into the fold without hesitation or condemnation. A blood tie is verra important to them."

"Oh, that would be wonderful. To give Callum a name, a heritage, e'en a clan, would do so much good for him." She frowned a little when Payton placed his hands on either side of her head and drew so close that their bodies would rub together if either of them took a deep breath. "Move away. I grow weary of this game of seduction ye play."

When she tried to move away, he pressed his body against hers, pinning her against the wall. Payton gently gripped her chin in his hand and turned her face up to his. "So do I," he said and brushed a kiss over her mouth. "I grow weary of ye fighting what flares between us. I tire of waiting for your aye."

"Poor lad. Ye cannae conceive of a lass telling ye nay, is that it?"

The bite she had intended to put behind her words was very weak. It was hard to be cold and sarcastic when his nearness was making her short of breath. The way he was kissing her face, brushing his lips over hers, and nibbling at her ears was making her entirely too warm. His groin was pressed close to hers and the feel of the hard ridge of his manhood was making her knees weak. She wanted to kiss him back, wanted to run her hands through his hair and all over his lean body, and she wanted to rub against him like some hungry wanton. What he could make her feel was frightening and thrilling at the same time.

"It hasnae happened before," he drawled and almost laughed at her look of outrage. "Ye want to say aye, lass," he said and kissed her. "Say aye," he murmured against her throat.

"I cannae." She trembled at the feel of his warm lips against the rapid pulse in her throat. "I am a wedded woman."

"Ye are an unbedded widow."

Payton kept her distracted with kisses as he unlaced her tunic, then slid his hand inside it to cup her breast. It fit his hand perfectly. The way she gasped softly and arched slightly made him ache for more.

"Why do ye press me so?"

"Because I ache for ye. Ye are a passionate woman, Kirstie, and I want to revel in that."

"Go revel in one of your other women," she gasped when he brushed a kiss over the soft swell of her breast.

"Dinnae want another one." He moved against her as he brushed his thumb over the hard tip of her breast.

"Weel, ye cannae have this one."

For a brief moment she tried to resist his kiss, but,

with a sigh, gave in and wrapped her arms around his neck. This kiss was different from the others. It was more of a demand, a possessive urgency, than a seduction. She felt dazed yet vibrantly alive when he ended it. When he moved against her, his body acting out the possession he demanded of her, she could not fully stifle a moan. She clutched at his tunic and met his gaze.

"Aye, I can," he said. "I will. Your nay was merely troublesome ere ye tried to martyr yourself. Now 'tis nearly a sin. Ye tried to steal away something I crave ere I could e'en have a taste."

"Whether or not I would survive to warm your bed wasnae something I gave much thought to." It was difficult to sound firm, even derisive, when one's voice was husky with desire, she decided. It was no wonder the man ignored her words.

"Ye want this as much as I do, my wee Shadow," he murmured. "Ye tremble with need."

" 'Tis fright." His chuckle warmed her throat and the rhythmic press of his erection made her feel agitated, needy.

"Ah, lass, ye want this. Right now ye are thinking on how it would be if we were skin to skin."

"Nay!" She wondered how he knew what thoughts were in her head.

"I ache to see your beauty unclothed, to taste your fine skin. I want to bury myself deep inside your heat," he said softly as he pressed his cheek against hers. "Slow and deep." He grasped her backside in his hands, holding her close as he spoke. "At first. Aye, then fast, fast and fierce. Ye can feel how it would be, can ye not, lass? Aye, ye can. Your body can, too. I can feel your woman's heat against me. Ah, lass, let me in. Let me show ye paradise."

He moved back a little even as he devoured her mouth, his tongue imitating all he said their bodies would do. For a moment, she thought he was about to put a stop to this attempt at seducing her, but then she felt his fingers slide inside her hose. If not for the strong arm he had wrapped around her, Kirstie knew she would have collapsed when he stroked her between her legs. Although a part of her, the one panting and clutching at Payton, wanted to shove him down onto the floor and ravish him, another part of her, a sensible, calmer part, was alarmed by the ferocity of the feelings his intimate caress roused in her.

"Ye are so hot, so hot and wet, Kirstie," he said, his voice deep and seductive.

When she realized she was moving against his hand, the part of her which was frightened and shocked won out over the wanton side of her. With a soft curse, she pulled free of him. Kirstie started toward the door on legs that felt alarmingly unsteady and hastily fixed her disordered clothing. When she reached the door and grasped the latch, she looked back at him. The taut, hungry look upon his beautiful face almost drew her back into his arms.

"Ye, sir, are a pestilence," she snapped and fled, nearly running into Ian on her way out.

"That woman is determined to cripple me," said Payton as he quickly poured himself a tankard of wine, praying a few hearty drinks would drown the need twisting up his insides. He looked back at Ian, saw the man open his mouth, and quickly said, "I am in no mood for your teasing. One remark about how I may be losing my charm with my advancing age and I willnae be responsible for what I do next." He gulped down the wine and refilled his tankard.

"Mayhap the lass doesnae want ye," said Ian.

"She does. Mayhap e'en as much as I want her."

"She is a maiden and a woman who believes in vows given, I think, nay matter who they were given to."

"I ken it."

"Then why dinnae ye leave her be?" Ian asked as he sat down.

"I cannae," Payton snapped, then sighed and

dragged his fingers through his hair. "I think I have been hard for her since I first saw her in the light. I swear, I just hear her footsteps and my rod is on alert, trying to sniff her out. I wake up in the night, asweat and aching, and have to fight to stop myself from going to her room, getting into that bed with her, and ignoring her nay until it becomes a verra loud aye."

"Ah, nay, that wouldnae be good. She is nay one of your women."

"I ken it."

Ian stretched his legs out, stared at his boots for a moment, then looked back at Payton. "So, if ye do get her into your bed, what will ye do afterward?"

"Have her again." He ignored Ian's brief look of disgust and sat down. "I dinnae ken. Mayhap after I have rutted myself blind with her for a fortnight or two, I can once again start thinking like the sharp-witted fellow I always thought I was." He smiled faintly when Ian laughed. "I think I will see if it, weel, fades, if it is all just some brief madness. The moment 'tis kenned that she has stayed here with me, 'twill be thought that we were lovers, so I cannae save her from that by leaving her be. And, since she has been wed for five years, no one will e'er think I seduced a maiden. So, unfair or e'en unkind it may be, but I will make no decision on a future until I ken exactly what ails me."

"That may be for the best, mayhap e'en the kindest way." Ian fetched himself a drink of wine. "Do ye think she really would have killed that bastard today?" he asked as he sat down again.

"Nay," replied Payton. "She was already changing her mind, moving toward the door. She saw Uven. Thought it was Callum."

"Did ye tell her why the lads look like twins?"

"As little as I ken, aye. She willnae say anything. Have ye discovered anything?"

"His mither's name was Joan. She was the swineherd's youngest daughter. The mon still lives. I plan on speaking to him soon. Need to ready myself as I may have to control the urge to pound him into the muck. Ye see, he tossed the poor lass out soon as he kenned she was carrying.'' He nodded when Payton cursed. ''Most think he kenned exactly who Callum was.''

''The bastard! How could any mon turn his back on his own blood like that?''

'' 'Tis certainly a branch of the family tree Callum doesnae need to be told about.''

''Nay, he doesnae. There is a chance he already kens it, but I willnae put it to the test. Let me ken when ye have found out more,'' Payton said as he stood up. ''I will see if Sir Bryan kens a Joan, the swineherd's daughter, when I am at the castle on the morrow. It has been a long day and, if the past fortnight is any indication, I forsee a verra long night. Good sleep,'' he added on a sigh as he left Ian and went to seek out his still painfully empty bed.

Kirstie tightly gripped her covers as she heard Payton's footsteps hesitate briefly outside of her bedchamber door, then continue on to his own room. That she could recognize the sound of his footsteps irritated her. She did not want to be that aware of him. She could not be sure if she clutched her bedcovers to hold herself back from going to him or in anticipation of his entering her room, and that annoyed her as well.

The man truly was a pestilence. He left her so hot and agitated her night shift and the bedcovers felt oppressive. Her nipples were hard and they ached. She hardly dared breathe, for it caused the soft linen of her shift to move against her and she kept being reminded of his touch. Worse, she could still feel his hand between her legs, still wanted it there. Every word he had said seemed locked into her mind, refusing to be banished.

She closed her eyes and forced herself to think of every good, sound reason why she had to hold firm to her chastity, had to resist the temptation of the man. With each kiss, each caress, that grew more difficult. Kirstie was infuriated by her own weakness.

Behind her eyelids she could still see him, still see the desire on his beautiful face. In her mind she could hear his rich, deep voice promising to show her paradise. She cursed. It was going to be a very, very long night.

CHAPTER SEVEN

Callum and Moira looked up as Kirstie entered the room where the children slept. They sat cross-legged on the bed where a rapidly improving Robbie sat propped up by several fat pillows. She smiled at the children as she set down a tray of honey-sweetened oatcakes and cool cider she had brought for them.

"Wheesht, lad," she said to Robbie, "if ye can look this good after only four days, ye will soon be out of that bed."

"I wanted to get out of bed today, but Wee Alice told me I couldnae," said Robbie.

The hint of sulkiness in his voice delighted Kirstie. She considered it a sure sign that he was healing. He sounded exactly like any other little boy stuck in a sick bed.

" 'Tis best to heed what Wee Alice says, lad. Now, eat what she has sent ye. Ye need to put some fat on those bones. David, Alan, and William assure me that these are the best oatcakes they have e'er tasted."

"They are in the kitchens with Wee Alice again, are-nae they?" Callum said between bites of an oatcake.

"Aye. They like her," replied Kirstie.

"I think they like her a lot. Her and Strong Ian."

"Weel, they are verra good people."

"Oh, aye. Strong Ian isnae teaching them how to fight, though. They are still too wee for that."

"Aye. 'Twill be a few years yet ere they can be taught the monly art of fighting."

Kirstie almost smiled when Callum replied with a solemn nod. He was jealous of his position as Ian's student. Every morning he and Ian went down into the surprisingly spacious cellars of the house to practice fighting. As she had watched Callum grow less wary, less angry at the whole world, she had lost her uneasiness about that training. She had a suspicion that there had been a few man-to-man talks as well, talks undoubtedly aimed at taking away his guilt and shame. Kirstie sensed a blossoming pride in Callum and it thrilled her.

She stayed and talked with the children until they had finished the cider and oatcakes. Callum assured her that he was able to help Robbie if the boy needed anything so Kirstie took the tray back to the kitchen. She peered out the window and saw the three other little boys helping Alice in the garden.

"My Alice is verra fond of the lads."

A little squeak of alarm escaped Kirstie for she had not heard Ian approach. She turned to look at him. He was a very big man, dark, none too handsome, and scarred, yet she had quickly seen the kindness in the man. At the moment, however, he looked uneasy, almost nervous.

"I believe the lads are verra fond of her as weel," Kirstie said.

"Aye." Ian ran his fingers over the large, jagged scar on his cheek, then sighed. "Did ye have any plans for the children? When 'tis safe, I mean."

"Oh, weel, no firm ones. I was going to send them all to my brother Eudard, as I did the others."

He nodded. "I remember ye saying that."

"Of course, it then grew too dangerous to do so. None of these children has family so I rather think I shall keep them. Mayhap when we are all safe and with my kinsmen, I will find families who want them or e'en apprentice them to someone." She shrugged. "There is no hurry to decide."

"Nay, nay." He looked out the window at his wife and the boys. "I wed Alice near fifteen years ago. She was but fourteen and I was seventeen. She was soon carrying, but lost the bairn. Lost two more in the two years that followed. The midwife said something was damaged when she lost the last one. 'Twas for the best, I think, for she grieved so and was near death each time. The midwife must have been right in saying Alice was now barren for there has ne'er been another."

"How verra sad," she murmured, her heart aching for the couple.

Kirstie also felt uneasy for she knew what the man was struggling to ask her and, for a moment, she battled a selfish urge to hold fast to the children. She had not had such a feeling with the others, but suspected that was because she had sent them away so quickly. These children had been in her care far longer, had nudged their way into her heart. It took only one quick glance out the window to banish the feeling, however. She could see the bond between the three little boys and Alice. The boys had found their home and she would be the worst sort of wretch to deny it to them. When Ian finally looked at her again, she smiled encouragingly at him.

"Weel, if ye have no plans for the wee lads out there, mayhap ye would let them stay with me and Alice. Now, I havenae said a word to my Alice or the lads," he hurried to say. "Being as the bairns were in your care and all, couldnae be sure what ye intended or felt. Didnae want to give my Alice false hope, ye ken. Now, I ken I am nay a rich mon."

"Ian," she said, interrupting his nervous recitation

of his qualifications or lack thereof, "they were three ragged orphans or abandoned children. Nay sure which. I suspicion ye can give them far more than the foundling home did and a better future, too." His sigh of relief was so heavy, Kirstie was a little surprised she stood firm before it. "Ye just want those three, aye?"

"Oh, we would take them all and I mean to tell the others that. Dinnae want any bruised feelings." He looked out at his wife and the three little boys again. " 'Tis just that those three, weel, my Alice and them seem to be, weel . . ."

"Bonded," she said. "I can see it. It works that way sometimes."

"Aye. The others are nay the same. Moira and Robbie have each other right now. It may change. And, if they want to be with me and my Alice, weel, we will be glad to have them. My Alice will love them hard, she will. Callum is set for better things, I am thinking."

"Ye have found out more about his parentage?"

"Some, and Payton is speaking to Sir Bryan MacMillan. 'Tis nay him, but once Payton told him the lad looked so much like young Uven they could be twins, Sir Bryan kenned they were talking of a MacMillan. They breed true, ye see, and there are few who look like them."

"But, there are none of the mother's kin left?"

"None worth mentioning. Truth is, they would do the lad more harm than good. They kenned the lad was alone and wanted naught to do with him. 'Tis best he has naught to do with them."

"Quite right." She shook her head. "I dinnae think I will e'er understand such things."

"Nay. I got the lad's grandfather and uncle to tell me all they kenned, then thanked them as they deserved and left."

There was a look upon Ian's harsh face that told her he had meted out a little retribution on Callum's behalf.

" 'Tis their loss. Do ye want me to speak to Robbie, Moira, and Callum?"

"If ye could. I think ye would be better at making them understand that we but wait for them to make a choice. And assure Callum that I will keep training him nay matter what."

"Ye have been good for him." She smiled when he blushed slightly. "I can see the pride growing in him."

"Aye, weel, I think I will tell my Alice that she can stop trying to nay love the wee lads too much." He started toward the door leading to the garden, then paused. "He doesnae think of ye as just one of his women, ye ken."

Kirstie felt a blush heat her cheeks, for there was no mistaking who he spoke of. "He is a rogue."

"Oh, aye. A pretty lad like that could be naught else. The lasses have been sighing o'er him ere his voice deepened." He shrugged. "A free mon will take what is offered, aye? 'Tis the way of men."

"I am nay offering."

"I ken it and there is the puzzle. The lad has ne'er set after a lass like this before."

"Probably ne'er had to," she grumbled, irritated by the mere thought of how easily women fell into Payton's bed.

"Nay," Ian said and briefly grinned at her. "So, if 'tis so verra easy for him to get some loving, why is he making himself half mad chasing after a wee lass who keeps saying nay?"

"Because I do say nay?"

He chuckled. "Could be. I dinnae ken and I willnae try to. My Alice looked at me and I looked at her and that was that. We kenned we were mates. I daren't e'en try to guess what is going on between ye and Payton. All I wish to say is, if ye fret o'er what me and Alice might think, ye can stop. Whether ye keep saying nay or say aye, it matters naught to us. Ye willnae shame yourself in our eyes if ye grab yourself a wee bit of pleasure. As my Alice says, after five years of hell, ye deserve some. Do as your heart bids, lass, and dinnae fret so over the rest."

"I think it might be wise if I try verra hard to nay let my heart lead me this time."

"Mayhap. I just wanted ye to ken that my Alice and I willnae care if ye do or ye dinnae."

"Thank ye. Now, go. Make your Alice happy."

The moment he left, she peeked out the window. It was easy to see by the way the little boys rushed to his side that it was not only Alice they loved. She watched Ian pull his wife aside, bend down, and speak to her. Alice's eyes widened, then she flung herself into her husband's arms. Kirstie saw the look on Ian's face, watched him pat his wife's back a little awkwardly, and suspected she was crying. Deciding to give them some privacy, she turned around, only to find Payton walking toward her. By the time she thought to move, he had her pinned against the table set beneath the window, his hands set down on either side of her, and he was looking out the window over her shoulder.

"What is going on out there?" he asked, nestling himself between her legs and inwardly smiling when her breath caught.

Hearing the squeals of three excited little boys, Kirstie replied, "Ian just told Alice and the lads that they are now a family." She leaned away from him as far as the table would allow when he looked at her.

"Ian finally worked up the courage to ask ye, did he?"

"Aye, although I dinnae ken why he needed courage to do so. I am nay so fearsome."

"He didnae want to hear a nay. I understand how he felt." He kissed her before she could respond. "Thank ye."

"For what?" she asked, struggling to regather her wits, scattered by the heat of his kiss.

"For giving Ian and Alice such a fine gift."

"The children did that. They chose. It really wasnae my decision to make."

"Aye, it was."

He placed his lips against the rapid pulse point on her slim throat. Payton put his hand on her tiny waist and slid it upward to cover her breast, feeling the hard tip of it against his palm despite the clothing sheltering it. At the same time he pressed his groin hard against her, moving in a faint mimicry of the act he craved. The soft noise she made was sweet music to his ears. Something between a gasp and a trembling sigh, it heralded her desire for him.

"Do ye ken what I want, lass?" he murmured and stroked the life-giving vein in her throat with his tongue.

"Ye have made it most clear what ye ask of me, but . . ."

"I want to push up these petticoats, spread these bonny white thighs, and bury myself deep within your warmth."

"Jesu," she whispered and realized she was nearly panting. She also realized he was slipping a hand beneath her skirts, but she could not seem to grasp the willpower to stop him. "Ye shouldnae say such things."

"What? Nay speak the truth? Nay tell ye how I lie awake at night all asweat with the wanting of ye? Nay tell ye how I dream of all the things I want to do to this lithe, silken body of yours?"

Payton wondered just when it was he had decided it might be fun to drive himself completely insane. He could tell by her quick breaths and darkened eyes that his words were stirring her. Unfortunately, he was also stirring his own desires to a dangerous height.

Not that that was so uncommon anymore. He had had to start wearing longer tunics to hide the inconvenient and all-too-frequent hardening that occurred each time he thought of her. Or caught the hint of her scent. Or heard her voice. Or caught sight of her. Aye, Payton mused, he was definitely teetering on the edge of madness.

If she did not say aye soon, he knew that he would lose all patience. She desired him, of that he had no doubt. Soon, Payton feared, he would go to her room and do just as he had told Ian he would—ignore her nay until it became the aye he so craved. That would be folly, for after the delight there would be regrets, guilt, and recriminations. He needed her to be willing in heart, body, and mind.

His hand brushed against her garter holding her stocking up. Payton was just savoring the feel of her soft, warm skin above that when he heard a door open and shut. A moment later, even as he was pulling his hand out from beneath her skirts, something hard rapped him on the head. Muttering a curse, he turned to glare at Wee Alice, who was holding an impressively large wooden spoon in her hand. She put her fists upon her well-rounded hips and glared right back at him.

"What did ye do that for?" he asked crossly as he carefully rubbed the sore spot upon his head.

"Ye shouldnae be tormenting the lass in the kitchen," snapped Wee Alice. "Anyone could catch ye at it. And, ye certainly shouldnae be thinking of doing *that* upon the table where I knead my bread."

"Weel, I was thinking of doing a little kneading myself," he murmured and hastily backed away when Wee Alice threateningly raised her spoon.

"Make yourself useful. Go and help Ian keep my lads busy for an hour or two. They are eager to tell the others their news and I wished Kirstie to have time to talk to them first."

"Ye think that will take an hour or two?"

"Nay, but I need to talk to Kirstie myself first." The moment Payton left, Alice looked at Kirstie. "Have ye got your wits back yet, lass?"

"Most of them," Kirstie replied, torn between amusement over the way Alice had routed Payton and embarrassment over being caught with a man's hand under her skirts. "The mon is verra stubborn."

"Och, aye," agreed Alice. "Always has been. He is hungry, too, lass. Ye have put him in a sad state. Past time some lass did, I am thinking." She suddenly clasped Kirstie's hand in hers. "But, I didnae come to speak on that. I want to thank ye,"

"Nay, there is nay need. The lads need a family and ye want to give it to them. They want it, too. 'Tis all that is important."

"We will treat them as our own and do right by them."

"I ken it."

Alice set her spoon down and nervously smoothed her apron. "I need to ken, weel, if the lads were, er, hurt. If your husband, weel, did them any true harm."

Kirstie doubted Alice's small round face could get any redder and she felt the sting of a blush upon her own cheeks. "Nay. There was some, weel, nay-so-innocent touching and harsh punishments meted out if the children objected in e'en the smallest way. Roderick didnae do much more than that to a boy until he was eight years of age. 'Twas as if he had made himself some rule all his own, but he held to it. He would get them young and 'twas as if he tried to train them to his ways. He would touch them, the touches slowly growing more intimate, and any rejection of his attention brought harsh punishment. It was all aimed at making the lads accept Roderick without protest when he decided they were the right age for him. It worked with some, but nay all of them."

"Rather like ye might train a dog," Alice muttered and shook her head.

"Roderick is verra good at finding a person's weakness, sniffing out what terrifies one the most. 'Twas nay hard with most of the children. Once he found it, he used it against ye again and again, until ye would do anything, just so he wouldnae put ye through your greatest torment again. He ne'er found Callum's. A few times it seemed as if he had, but Callum seemed able to overcome that fear or weakness and Roderick would have to try and find another. Breaking the poor boy to his will became an obsession with Roderick. 'Tis why I couldnae free Callum for so long. He was always being watched, if only because Roderick kenned Callum would ne'er stop trying to escape. The older Callum got, the more the urge to escape became the urge to strike back."

"I am surprised the mon didnae use ye to try to break the lad."

Kirstie sighed. "He did, shortly before I freed Callum. We had already guessed that he might and I had made Callum swear he would stand fast nay matter what was done. He did. Roderick tried to use me to break the boy three times, but each time Callum stood firm. Unfortunately, it made the need to free Callum more pressing. Roderick was enraged and he finally noticed how swiftly Callum was growing, that verra soon the boy would be able to look him in the eye. That was when Roderick decided it was time to be rid of Callum."

Alice shook her head again. "I hear all ye say and I believe ye, yet a part of me just cannae grasp it."

"I ken what ye mean and I lived it all. Ah, weel, your lads werenae badly done by. And, although I think Callum may forever carry the scars of some heart-deep wounds, I can see now that he can be healed in many ways."

"Aye, he is a verra strong lad in heart, mind, and body. And, he is yours."

"Och, weel, I would keep him, but it appears he may have family who will want to take him in."

"The MacMillans, aye. Once the name was said, I could see it clear. But, that willnae matter, nay e'en if he goes to live with them. He will e'er come back to ye and he will always be ready to stand by ye. Ye ken all that happened to him, lass, and ye still care for him, have from the start. Ye endured pain for his sake and ye freed him from it all at risk to your verra life. Nay, Callum is yours. Moira and Robbie have yet to choose, but I am thinking they may be yours as weel. Although, if Moira was given a choice right now, I am thinking she would want our Payton."

"Ha, just like every other female." She smiled faintly when Alice laughed. "One last thing ere I talk to the others—try to get the lads to tell ye what Roderick did. I think it would help if ye could discover what he did to punish them for he may have discovered their fears, may have e'en made them worse. It might save ye an unpleasant moment or two, save ye or Ian from stirring up the same terror or torment by accident."

"I will do that. They are young enough for the bad memories to fade, but nay if Ian and I stir them up all unknowing-like. Go on with ye, then. Talk to the others. I ken ye will say all the right things."

Kirstie was not so sure of that as she faced Callum, Moira, and Robbie a few moments later with a distinct feeling of trepidation. She finally just repeated most of what Ian had said to her. As she waited for some response to the news she had just given them, she studied their faces and could see no hint of hurt or insult.

"Weel, I am nay surprised," Callum said, and the two younger children nodded. "Those three boys were always wanting to be with Wee Alice. Thought it was just for the food, but changed my mind."

"Ye do ken that they will take all of ye as weel, if ye wish it," Kirstie said.

"Och, aye. I think we just want to set steady for a while, just liking being warm, with full bellies and soft beds. And being as safe as we have e'er been." Callum glanced at the two other children and they quickly murmured their full agreement.

When David, Alan, and William arrived, all three trying to talk at once, Kirstie felt the sting of tears in her eyes. Three of her waifs now had a bright future and would be cherished. She saw only a responding happiness in the other children and knew there would be no hurt feelings or jealousies to deal with. Kirstie did wonder, however, what Robbie, Moira, and Callum wanted for their futures. They seemed perfectly content with matters as they stood now, but once Roderick was dealt with, some decision would have to be made. If they thought she and they would simply continue on at Payton's house, in his life, she was going to have to disillusion them. Payton was her chosen champion, nothing more, and when he succeeded in slaying her dragon, he would be gone from her life.

That realization sat like a cold stone in her belly for the rest of the day. By the time she retired to her bedchamber for the night, she felt as if the chill of it had seeped into the very marrow of her bones and doubted the hot bath waiting for her would ease it. Kirstie finally admitted to herself that, as the children did, she had not allowed herself to look closely at how this would all end. She had settled herself into Payton's life, worked with him in planning Roderick's downfall, and not truly considered that their time together was limited.

She placed a hand over her heart as if she could shield it from the pain that was already settling itself deep inside. It was suddenly clear to her that, although she had been successful in her fight to keep Payton out of her bed, she had failed to keep him out of her heart. Such folly, she thought, and sighed. A man like Payton was so far above her touch it was laughable. She was still locked into a hopeless marriage and now she had gone and plunged herself into a hopeless love. The only thing she could do was try very hard not to let anyone know just how great a fool she was.

Nay, she mused, there was one other thing she could do. Kirstie went to the chests of women's clothing that had been brought to her room. In only a moment, she clutched what she had searched for. Kirstie held the night shift up and blushed. It was made of the finest, sheerest linen and trimmed with silk ribbons and lace. One of Payton's kinswomen obviously liked to entice her husband.

"And she probably has what is needed to entice a mon, unlike ye, ye skinny fool," she muttered.

Then, she shook her head and began to shed her clothes. One thing she was sure of was that Payton desired her. He had been rubbing the proof of that against her in the kitchen only a few hours ago. She could even see his desire in his fine eyes, hear it behind every seductive word he spoke. It made no sense to her when women like the well-rounded Lady Fraser sought him out, but there was no denying Payton's desire for her.

"So, I shall take it," she said firmly as she began to give herself a thorough bath. "If 'tis all the rogue has to offer, then I shall take it, glut myself on it."

She had been married for five years. No one would believe her a virgin, even when they found out the whole ugly truth about Roderick. There was no need to cling to her maidenhead for an annulment, either, for there never would be one. At the end of this battle either she or Roderick would be dead. Did she really want to die without ever having known the fullness of the passion she and Payton could share? The answer to that question was a swift and resounding nay. Her love was greedy. She wanted it all, but good sense told her she was reaching for the moon. So, she would take all she could, all Payton would give. At least, when it all ended, she would have some very lovely memories to help ease her heartache.

When she finally donned the night shift, her slightly damp hair tied back with a silk ribbon, Kirstie felt her courage waver as she looked at herself. For all the shift hung from shoulder to toe, it hid very little. Then she stiffened her backbone. She was about to do some hearty sinning. This was the perfect attire for it. That she was acting out of love took away some of her concern over all the rules she was about to break. Not completely, however, and Kirstie decided she had better get herself into Payton's arms and his bed before thoughts of sin sapped the last of her resolve.

CHAPTER EIGHT

Payton slouched in his chair and sipped at his wine. Nothing was going right. Roderick still walked free and healthy. His campaign of blackening the man's name was beginning to bear fruit, but the man had yet to be shunned completely. It was proving far more difficult than it ought to be to get people to heed his warnings and to try to find any witnesses willing to speak out. People either disbelieved it all, were appallingly disinterested, or were too afraid to step forward. Payton knew patience was a virtue in a campaign against such evil, but he was rapidly running out of it. Every time one of the children flinched or their big eyes held dark shadows instead of sweet innocence, he wanted Sir Roderick MacIye dead.

And, most lowering of all in his slightly drunken opinion, was that his attempts at seduction were also failing. A full fortnight had passed since he had decided he would have Kirstie in his bed and his bed was still cold and empty when he crawled into it at night. Kirstie was not cold to him, but she was certainly resisting him with a frustrating success. A part of him was pleased that she

was not proving to be an easy conquest. He had had far
too many of those. Another part of him, he mused as
he glanced down at his aching groin, was not pleased
at all. Payton idly wondered if a man could suffer any
damage from a near-perpetual erection. His vanity was
stung as well. Why was she not tumbling into his bed
with the ease so many others had?

The soft sound of his bedchamber door opening drew
him from his thoughts. He hoped Strong Ian was not
coming to taunt or lecture him again. The man was
finding far too much enjoyment in Payton's failure to
get Kirstie into his bed and, far too often, too sternly
disapproving of Payton's attempts to seduce the woman
as well.

When Kirstie slipped into the room, softly shutting
the door behind her, Payton nearly dropped his tankard. Never taking his gaze from her, he finished his
drink and awkwardly fumbled around until he was able
to set the empty tankard down on the table next to his
chair. He surreptitiously tugged his shirt down to hide
the painfully visible proof that he could not be in the
same room with her and not want her. Especially when
that room was a bedchamber and most especially when
she wore only a too-thin night rail.

"Is something wrong with the bairns?" he asked, not
surprised to hear how raspy his voice was. Payton was
astounded he could utter a single coherent word.

"Nay, they are all sleeping," she replied in a soft,
somewhat unsteady voice.

"Why are ye here, then?"

Kirstie took a deep breath to steady herself and was
pleased with the calm, strong tone of her voice as she
replied, "I want ye to make love to me."

A heavy silence met her words. She had imagined
many responses to her approach, but never one where
Payton just sat there silently staring at her, acting as if
he had been hit in the head. Or, she mused as she
looked at his tankard, as if he was one sip away from

becoming a useless lump of drunken unconciousness. She had not considered the possibility that he would be too drunk. Then she frowned. In the three weeks since she had met him she had not noticed that Payton was given to indulging in too much drink.

"Ye have been drinking?" she asked.

"I have been doing rather a lot of it in the past three weeks," he replied, wondering why he was still sitting in the chair and not rushing her into his bed.

"Ah, so ye are drunk." She wanted to weep with disappointment, for she was not sure she would be able to work up the courage to approach him a second time.

"I dinnae think so, although I begin to wonder. Repeat the reason ye are here."

"Must I?"

"Oh, aye, I believe so."

"I want ye to make love to me."

Slowly, Payton got up and walked over to her. Just hearing her say those words had him so heavy with need he was surprised he could walk at all. Yet, the end to the long days and nights of aching hunger had come so abruptly, so simply and directly, he could not fully believe it. He grasped her by her slender shoulders and pressed his lips to her forehead.

"Again," he whispered against her skin. "Tell me again."

"I want ye to make love to me," she whispered back, then blushed when he leaned back a little to stare at her. "I dinnae understand why ye keep asking me to say it. 'Tis what ye have been trying to coax from me for a fortnight, aye? Jesu, have ye changed your mind?"

"Nay. Och, nay, I havenae changed my mind. I have been fair to crippled with the wanting of ye since we met."

"Och, aye? I believe ye were about to climb into Lady Fraser's bed when we met."

"Weel, then since I first saw ye in the light, without all the mud and marsh grass."

She shivered faintly. The thought that this beautiful man wanted her was enough to send her desire soaring. Slowly, she curled her arms around his neck, hoping he would hurry and start doing what he was rumored to be so good at. Although she had finally convinced herself to just reach out and take what he offered, what she so desperately wanted, too much hesitation could easily prove fatal to her resolve. There were just as many reasons why she should *not* be in his arms as there were reasons why she should be, and she did not want her mind to start thinking about the former again. Too much thinking could easily turn her *aye* back into a *nay*.

"What about your annulment?" he asked as he began to stroke her thinly covered back.

"I realized that wasnae possible now." She began to unlace his soft linen shirt. "This battle can only end with Roderick's death, or mine. He cannae let me live. In this instance, 'twill truly be only death which will end the marriage. If naught else, I will have to let it be known I am alive if I am to get that annulment." She opened his shirt and thought it had to be a sin for a man to have such beautiful skin. "But, I suspect ye kenned that." She softly kissed his chest and felt him tremble, his arms tightening around her and pulling her closer. "I suspected the flaw in that plan from the moment I thought on it. Ye ne'er argued it, however."

He pulled her close, nestling her against his groin, and was enthralled by how perfectly she fit him. "I decided it was but a ploy to try and hold me at a distance so ye would heed no argument." He gritted his teeth as he fought to control his desire, to allow her to keep touching him. "Ye are nay longer concerned about committing adultery? Can ye now see that ye are nay his true wife and ne'er have been?"

"Payton, why are ye trying to recall me to all the reasons why I shouldnae be here?" she asked.

"Because I am an idiot?"

"Weel, I would ne'er be so unkind as to say so. Still . . ."

"Aye, still. One last question ere I strip ye of this wee scrap of linen ye wear. Are ye certain Sir Roderick ne'er consummated your marriage?"

"I may be innocent, but I am nay ignorant. Nay, he ne'er did."

"Why?"

"Doesnae that make two questions?"

"Why?"

Kirstie sighed and looked at the wall, feeling the sting of a deep blush upon her cheeks. "I told ye that, at fifteen, I looked like a child. I truly did. I was verra late coming into womanhood, though I threatened the few who kenned it into silence. It finally descended upon me on my wedding night. Roderick didnae give me a chance to warn him, so, I fear, he discovered it in a rather embarrassing way."

"Ye mean he—"

"Aye. I didnae ken it at the time, but he had obviously stiffened his backbone and gritted his teeth, prepared to do the deed as quickly as possible. He staggered into my bedchamber, muttering something about a husband's duty and inheritances. I had prepared myself to tell him what had happened, only he kept sticking his tongue in my mouth. Then he yanked up my shift. He was ill all over the bed linen, then ran out of the room. After that I began to look a wee bit more like a woman and less like a child. He tried a time or two after that night but could ne'er get verra far. At first I thought it all my fault, that I repulsed him."

"Foolish." He began to kiss her neck, breathing deep of the clean scent of her skin.

"Weel, after I had a wee problem with one or two of his men trying to tumble me, I decided it wasnae me. It was him. Then I began to notice that there were verra few women about the keep and fewer still who were even allowed near him. That was when I decided he must prefer men. That also explained why he was increasingly angry with me, his faint tolerance rapidly turning into a somewhat brutal contempt, even hatred.''

"Mayhap he thought a wife would cure him."

"Mayhap. Or he felt, if he could breed me, it would help him hide his true self from the world."

The way he was kissing her face, her throat, even her ears, had desire flowing through her veins at an increasingly heady speed. She did not want to talk anymore. She wanted them both naked, wanted to feel those gently caressing hands against her skin, and wanted to touch his skin. Kirstie had the feeling Payton sought to go slowly, gently, to soothe any virginal fears she might have, or even to ease her free of any lingering doubts. She was not sure how she could tell him she did not need, or even want, such consideration. He had been promising her paradise for a fortnight and it was time he delivered.

As she had told him, she was innocent, not ignorant. She might not know exactly how they were supposed to fit together, but she did know that the ache she felt was demanding that they do so. On her wedding night she had been prepared to endure it all for the sake of her family and for the begetting of children. Now, she craved it. It was what Payton had been trying to make her feel, yet now that he had, he was dawdling.

When he kissed her, she wrapped her arms around his neck and let herself be swept away by the heat his clever tongue induced within her. It took a moment after the kiss ended for her to realize he had removed her night shift. His hands clenched slightly upon her shoulders as he held her away from him and looked her over. Kirstie fought the urge to try and cover herself with her hands. There was no place for such timorous modesty in what they were about to share. When his gaze met hers again, she trembled beneath the force of the desire she could see there.

Payton struggled against the urge to toss her down

onto his bed and immediately bury himself within her. She was ivory perfection. Her breasts were small but perfect, the rose-colored nipples hard and inviting. Her waist was small, her belly taut, and her hips slender but well shaped. Her equally slender legs were long, perfectly formed, and strong, with a space between her silken thighs that invited a man to settle in. The sight of the neat triangle of black curls shielding her woman's flesh had him trembling like an untried youth. He started to remove his clothes, hoping that chore would aid him in regaining some scrap of control.

Kirstie clenched her hands into tight fists as he undressed far too slowly for her liking. When he shed his shirt she had to fight the urge to immediately touch him. He was all lean, taut muscle and smooth, golden skin. It was no wonder the man's beauty was nearly legendary. Then he removed his boots and hose and she found it difficult to breathe. His legs were long and muscular, the fine coat of reddish hair only enhancing the light golden tone of his skin. What rose up from a tidy thatch of auburn hair at his groin was what truly held her gaze. Roderick's manhood had never looked so imposing. Kirstie began to wonder if some of Payton's reputation as a great lover was born of the fact that he had a little more than most men. She did not really think something of that impressive size was going to fit inside of her. Perhaps, when people whispered that Sir Payton Murray could make a woman scream, they were not meaning with pleasure.

The look of consternation on Kirstie's face, and the hint of alarm in her eyes, did a lot to help Payton cool his heated blood and grasp some semblance of control. He pulled her into his arms, lifted her slightly, and carried her to his bed. He sprawled at her side, then kissed her. To his relief, her unease was not enough to steal away her passion, for she quickly responded as she always had. Kirstie was a passionate woman and he knew he could use that to ease her introduction into the heady delights they could share.

Kirstie clung to him as he kissed and caressed her. All the hunger and need he had stirred within her over the last weeks swamped her when he turned his seductive attentions to her breasts. A strange wildness possessed her as he kissed, licked, and suckled at her breasts. She barely flinched when he slid his hand between her thighs. His long fingers both eased and heightened the hot aching there. It was as if every soft, seductive word, every stolen kiss, every subtle caress, and each heat-filled dream over the last three weeks had never been forgotten or fully recovered from. She enjoyed his kisses, his gentle caresses, but it took only a few of them to leave her shaking with need. Payton muttered something about needing to be sure she was readied for him, and Kirstie suddenly knew that she was. Completely, blindly, ready. She had been getting readied since the moment she had set eyes on the man.

"Payton," she cried, nearly bowing up off the bed when he slid a finger inside of her.

"Ah, lass, ye are so verra ready for me," he said, even as he prepared to enter her. "It still may hurt a wee bit."

"I dinnae care," she nearly growled and wrapped her limbs around him.

He laughed, but she heard no mockery in it. Then, for one brief moment, pain cut through her somewhat frenzied need. Kirstie held herself very still, every one of her senses fixed upon the joining of their bodies.

"Lass, are ye all right?" Payton asked through gritted teeth as he fought the need to move.

She shifted her legs slightly, felt him slide deeper within her, and shuddered. "Oh, my. Aye, I am all right. S'truth, I am verra fine, indeed, though I think ye still have some work to do if I am to see that paradise ye have been promising me for days."

Payton grinned, then echoed her gasp of pleasure

when he began to move. "Ah, lass, ye are a wonder," he managed to say before he lost himself to passion.

Kirstie smiled and ran her foot down Payton's calf. Her body still felt all atingle, but the near swoon she had fallen into had passed. If this was what Payton could make a woman feel, it was surprising that there were no women camped outside his door.

She frowned as she toyed with a lock of his thick hair, enjoying the feel of his slowly steadying breath against her neck. It would be wise to cease thinking about all the women he had bedded. Such thoughts were painful and she did not want them to spoil whatever time she had with Payton. It would probably be impossible to stop all pangs of guilt for breaking so many rules, but she intended to do that as well. If the wanton way she had behaved just now was any indication, Payton was right in saying she was a passionate woman. Kirstie was determined to enjoy that to its fullest. Aye, she thought, it was time to grasp all the delight she could, for in a way, she was living under a death sentence.

Payton enjoyed Kirstie's idle caresses as he waited for his pulse and breathing to return to normal. He hoped he would then find the strength to move. It was as if he had poured all of his strength into her lithe little body. His release had been the most powerful, most shattering he had ever experienced. Payton suspected that ought to concern him, and it might do so later, but for now, he simply wondered if there was any chance he could make love to her again tonight.

He finally found enough strength to stroke her hip and felt her snuggle against him. Little Kirstie MacIye was probably the most passionate, most responsive woman he had ever known. Not only did she go wild in his arms, but she had done so her very first time. There was no deception in it, either. She was not pretending, not simply making all the required faces and sounds. The moment desire started to creep through Kirstie's veins, she let it rule her, gave it her whole heart, and reveled in it. She was deliciously exhausting. He wanted to compare it all to another woman, another bedding, but at that moment, he could not recall any.

When Payton moved out of her arms and got up, Kirstie felt a brief flicker of alarm. She had thought the silence between them was simply because they were both too wrung-out to talk. Now she began to wonder if she had done something wrong, been too wicked and wanton and disgusted him. Despite her embarrassment over such an intimacy, she was relieved when all he did was fetch a cloth and water to clean them both off. When he slid back into bed beside her, she fought the urge to cling to him.

"I should return to my own bedchamber," she said, her voice a little unsteady as he nibbled her ear, restirring a desire she would have thought was well fed.

"Nay." Payton wrapped his arm around her waist and held her close. "Ye will sleep with me now."

"But, then everyone will ken what we are doing."

Considering the amount of noise she had been making earlier, Payton found it amusing that she would whisper now or that she could think, for even a moment, that her presence in his bedchamber was a secret. He would not say anything about that, however. There was the chance she would be embarrassed into silence and he found the sounds of her delight rather intoxicating.

"Nay, ye will stay here."

"But—"

He gave her a brief, hard kiss. "They will ken we are lovers e'en if ye creep back to your own bed. They willnae fault ye for it, lass. After what ye have done for the bairns, ye would have to do far more than take a lover to lose their respect. And, ere ye say it, nay, they willnae see ye as just another one of my women." He circled her nipple with the tip of one finger, delighted by how quickly it hardened, inviting his kiss.

"The children—" she began, fighting to ignore his idle caress.

"Are too young to see any harm in this or e'en to understand. Weel, save for Callum. He willnae condemn ye, but he may nay be too happy with me." He began to cover her plump, round little breast with fleeting kisses. "I think the lad is in the throes of a first love and that can be a sore trial."

Kirstie had begun to suspect the same. "He told me I should do what will make me happy."

"So, ye already spoke to the lad, aye?"

"He spoke to me. 'Tis difficult at times to recall that he is but a boy of eleven."

"In years and stature, but nay in heart and mind. Callum hasnae been a boy, as we think of one, for many a year. His childhood was stolen by abuse and abandonment. I think some of what he feels for ye is born of the fact that ye are kind to him. 'Twill soon settle down to a feeling more akin to what one feels for a mother, sister, or aunt."

"That would be nice." She wondered how he could keep talking as she was rapidly losing all of her wits.

Kirstie threaded her fingers through his hair. She trailed her other hand down to his hip. His skin felt so good beneath her fingers. She wanted to cover his body with kisses, but was not sure a lady would do such a thing. She inwardly grimaced as a small voice in her head tartly informed her that a lady would not lie down with a man who was not her husband nor do so with such vigor and enjoyment. But, she had. She was in Payton's bed and, despite her unease, she intended to stay there for as long as she could. The very last thing she wished to do was something that would give him a disgust of her. Since he was freely touching her, however, it had to be permissible to touch him. Kirstie slid her hand inward from his hip and curled her fingers around his erection.

"Jesu," Payton muttered as he felt her touch him.

"Did that hurt?" She started to release him only to have him put her hand back.

"Nay. It felt too good for a moment." His eyes widened slightly when she solemnly nodded, as if what he had just said actually made sense to her. "Stroke me, my dark beauty." He shuddered and closed his eyes as she did as he commanded, revealing an exquisite skill. "I am nay sure I have the strength to enjoy too much of that."

"I ne'er thought it would feel so nice to be touched."

"Neither did I. Too nice." He gently removed her hand as he wondered what had happened to the control he had perfected over the years. "Are ye sore, lass?" he asked as he stroked her taut belly.

"Nay. Should I be?"

"Ye may be, come the morning." He teased her hardened nipples with his tongue, savoring her soft gasps of pleasure and the way she arched her back, silently asking for more.

"Then I will worry o'er it come the morning." She clutched at his broad shoulders as he drew the aching tip of her breast deep into his mouth. "I believe I am getting agitated again," she gasped out as he turned his attentions to her other breast. "Verra, verra agitated."

"Verra, verra?" He kissed her stomach as he slid his fingers into the hot, damp welcome between her lovely thighs. "Oh, aye. Ye are so beautifully responsive, my dark beauty. So hot and wild in your passion."

"I am sorry," she said, even as she frantically wondered how she could hold back the feelings his touch stirred within her.

"Nay, ne'er be sorry. 'Tis beautiful, wondrous, intoxicating."

He wanted to devour her, but it was too soon. Payton did not want to shock or frighten her, to do anything that might dim her passion. She was a treasure, but one that needed to be uncovered carefully, gently. He slowly joined their bodies, her soft moan music to his ears.

She shifted her body and took him in deeper, revealing a natural skill that left him breathless. With a little experience, Kirstie could prove lethal.

As he slowly thrust in and out of her tight heat, he found just enough control to watch her this time. The open, unfettered delight reflected upon her sweet face was the most sensual thing he had ever seen. She opened her eyes to meet his gaze and he felt a hot spear of lust stab him. Her eyes were dark and glowing, like storm clouds.

"This time I will be in control," he said, not sure who he was promising that to—Kirstie or himself.

"That is important, is it?" she asked, her voice so thick and husky she barely recognized it.

"Control helps ye make the pleasure last longer."

"Oh, that sounds verra fine indeed."

Then she thrust her fingers into his hair and pulled him down for a kiss. At the same time, she pressed her small heels against his backside, arched her hips, and drove him deep within her. As Payton felt the thin strands of his control snap, he decided it was a very good thing Kirstie was too innocent to understand her own power. If she ever began to understand it and use it well, he could easily become soft clay in her small hands.

CHAPTER NINE

"How is young Simon?" Kirstie asked the moment she and Callum were a safe distance away from the foundling home.

"Fine enough," replied Callum, leaning against the wall of one of the buildings siding the alley they hid in. "That foul woman has all the children working harder than e'er before. Since they daren't be seen to be giving lads to Roderick, she wants to make more coin off the bairns' sweat. The bitch."

Since Kirstie agreed heartily with those last two words, she decided it would be a little hypocritical for her to scold Callum for using them. When she had first heard of the home for orphaned or abandoned children, she had thought it such a wonderful thing. Most children not taken in by family were left to fend for themselves, tended to by the church, or used as slave labor by whoever could grab them and hold them. This house was run by the Darrochs, who survived on the work the children were trained to do and any money contributed by kind or guilty people.

Or so she had naively believed until she had started

to gather information on it. It was appallingly run, the children given barely enough to survive and then worked nearly to death to fill the Darrochs' coffers. The children were also sold and, if Roderick was an example of the sort of person the Darrochs allowed to buy a child, Kirstie dared not think of the fate of the others. She could not save them all, however, no matter how dearly she wished she could.

"As soon as we rid the world of Roderick, I think I shall turn my attention to the Darrochs," she murmured.

"Aye, they are wretched scum."

"But, Roderick is nay longer welcome there?"

"Aye and nay. They are afraid, afraid if they are seen to deal with the mon now that all the rumors are flying about, someone might come and look a wee bit too closely at how they care for the children."

"Then, mayhap, they will cut their own throats, although I dinnae want another child to suffer in order for that to happen."

"The mistress will be the one who falters. She is hungry for the coin given for a child. Simon says Roderick has come round once more, but Master Darroch wants the mon to wait, pleads patience."

Kirstie started on the way back to Payton's home. She was so tired, weary to her soul over the misery that seemed to be such an intricate part of the world. The rich did so little and the ones who would help, such as herself, simply did not have the power or coin to do much at all. She had pulled only ten children free of the mire, but even those few had strained what few resources she had. Kirstie dearly wished she could harden her heart, close her eyes to the need all round her, and be satisfied with the little she could do. She was startled out of her dark thoughts when Callum took her hand in his and gave it a slight squeeze.

"Ye do what ye can, m'lady," he said. "Wheesht, ye

are willing to risk your verra life for us. There are nay verra many who would.''

"That was what was making me so sad. There are so many children in need, and there shouldnae be. I was raised to believe 'tis the responsibility of an adult to care for the wee ones, for any child in need. The bairns are the future, needed to replace the old and infirm. There are so many ways for a child's life to be cut short, so the ones who are strong enough to survive and grow ought to be cherished. I just cannae understand why so few people understand that.''

"The poor have too many of their own and the rich care only for the ones of their own blood.''

"And, sometimes, ne'er e'en them.''

Callum nodded, a very adult, very solemn look upon his face. "When I am full grown I will care for as many as I can. Mayhap, if I work verra hard, I can have a big house and fill it with the orphans and the abandoned bairns.''

"Ah, ye are a good mon, Callum.'' She bit back a smile at the way he puffed out his thin chest.

Their moment of accord was abruptly shattered. Two men stumbled into the alley she and Callum walked through. They had obviously just left the alehouse, for they were a little unsteady on their feet. Despite their best efforts, she and Callum were unable to avoid the men. Callum was knocked down and, even as she moved to help him up, one of the men stumbled into her. She was shoved hard into the wall of the tavern.

Dazed, Kirstie stepped away from the wall and felt a tug on her hair. Horrified, she reached up to hold her cap on only to find it was already too late. She quickly grabbed her cap off the jagged piece of wood that had snared it and yanked it back on, but it was hopeless. Her hair had already begun to fall down around her shoulders, revealing her sex. The two men stared at her, recognition in their eyes. Roderick's guard dogs, she realized, and felt her blood chill.

"Run," she ordered Callum, her gaze fixed upon the two large, dark men who served Roderick so well.

"Weel, weel, if it isnae his lordship's wee bride," said Gib, his grin revealing badly rotted teeth.

"Oh, the laird will be weel pleased with this." Wattie scratched his belly and looked Kirstie over in a way that made her skin crawl. " 'Course, he willnae be too happy that the bitch is still alive."

"She willnae be for long."

Even as Gib reached for her, Kirstie brought her foot up, hard, right into his groin. At the same time, a stout stick was brought up between Wattie's thick legs from behind. Both men screamed and slowly sank to their knees. Kirstie started running as fast as she could, Callum keeping pace at her side.

"I thought I told ye to run," she said, even as they fled the alley, followed by bellows of rage and the sounds of pursuit.

"And leave ye to that scum?" Callum cast a brief glance behind him. "We didnae hit them hard enough or they have ballocks made of stone. This way," he said, turning sharply and yanking hard on her sleeve to pull her along.

Kirstie willingly gave the lead to Callum. The boy had grown up on these streets and alleys. He knew his way around far better than she did. She just hoped he knew it far better than Wattie and Gib did as well.

The pain in her side was excruciating by the time they paused to catch their breath. Leaning against a wall, Kirstie fought to regain her strength. They had run for longer than she cared to think about. Although she knew ladies were not supposed to indulge in such rigorous activity, she found it a little lowering that Callum had been able to keep up such a pace far better than she had. She had often been able to outrun her brothers.

"I can hear them," she whispered when she finally regained enough breath to speak.

"They arenae verra quiet when they are on the hunt, 'tis true." Callum listened intently for a moment. "They arenae that near. We can rest for a wee bit longer."

"They willnae give up easily, will they?" She took her cap off, hastily repinned her hair, and covered it.

"Nay, dinnae think so. If they could bring ye to their master, they would soon have verra fat purses. Aye, enough to keep them in ale and whores for years."

Very soon she was going to have to have a talk with Callum about his language, Kirstie thought. She then wondered why she would be concerned about such inconsequential matters when she was running for her life. Lack of air had obviously disordered her wits.

This was exactly what Payton had been concerned about. It was annoying to discover he had been right. It would be even more so when she had to tell him that he was. Tempting though it was not to tell Payton about this, Kirstie knew she would have to. Once those two oafs told Roderick she was still alive, her husband would start searching for her. She was not the only one hiding at Payton's home. Some plan of escape would need to be formed, or a secure hiding place would have to be found.

"They sound verra close now," she said.

"Aye," agreed Callum. "We could rest a wee bit longer, but best we move. We can go slower for a while."

"Thank God. I must be getting old."

"Ye probably used up all your strength thrashing about in Sir Payton's bed last night."

"Callum!" She was both shocked and deeply embarrassed.

"Wheesht, m'lady, did ye think it a secret?" He looked around when they reached a brief opening, then hurried her across it. "I dinnae ken why ye are so worrit that we all ken it."

"Because it is shameful."

Of course, it had not felt that way in the dark of night. Or even in the morning light when Payton had reached for her again, she mused. It was only when he was away from her side, when he was not beguiling her with his smiles, his kisses, and his touch, that she started thinking on all the rules she was breaking. She slowly lost all her resolve; her decision that her love for the man made it acceptable grew weaker and weaker. If she managed to elude Roderick's grasp yet again, she was going to have to take time to truly understand what she was doing and why she should still feel uneasy about it.

"Ye worry on such things too much, m'lady," Callum said, even as he silently urged her to move a little faster.

The pursuit carried on until the approach of nightfall. Kirstie was afraid she would soon be caught simply because she would collapse at Gib's or Wattie's big feet, too exhausted to care what happened to her. Every time they turned toward Payton's home, Gib or Wattie was lurking in their path. Kirstie could almost believe they knew where she was hiding and with whom, but knew that was an impossibility. She and Callum would immediately turn in another direction, not wishing to take even the smallest chance that the other children might be found.

When Callum suddenly stopped and tugged her downward, she realized they had come to the place where she had first hidden the children. She followed Callum into the hole, then collapsed, sitting on an old barrel set almost directly beneath the window. As Callum set the piece of wood back over the hole in such a way that cracks were left, she wondered where he found the strength. When he sat down on the floor near her feet, she could hear him panting softly and felt a slight trembling in his body when he slumped against her legs. He would not be able to go much farther, either. She prayed this hiding place was still safe.

"Why did ye leave those cracks?" she whispered when she finally regained enough breath to speak.

"So we can hear anyone coming," Callum replied,

his voice hoarse with exhaustion. "I want to ken if we have to run again."

"But, there isnae any other way out of here."

"Aye, there is. Two. Went looking for another way out the first time ye set me down here. I like to ken where all the bolt-holes are. Dinnae like to be cornered."

She briefly stroked his bright hair, silently acknowledging the hard lessons he had been forced to learn and offering an unspoken sympathy. On the other hand, she thought, those hard lessons had just proven very useful. Some of them would probably prove very useful in the future as well. Kirstie had the feeling Callum would be a force to be reckoned with when he became a man.

It was strange to depend upon a boy for rescue and leading them to safety. She was the one who was supposed to be keeping the children safe. Although she had thought she was skilled in running and hiding, Callum was extraordinary, and it was not just his superior knowledge of the town. Callum knew how to listen and what to listen for. He had an uncanny sense of what his enemy would do next. When she had first met the boy, he had not learned the full value of the shadows that were everywhere, but he had obviously vastly improved that skill as well. Kirstie had the depressing feeling that she was slowing him down, perhaps even putting him at risk.

"Callum, if they find this place, ye are to flee and nay worry about my keeping pace with ye," she said.

"Nay, I willnae leave ye behind," he said.

"Callum, 'tis important to me that ye get away. I dinnae want to be the cause of ye falling into Roderick's foul grasp again."

"And I dinnae want to go back to Sir Payton's and tell them all I couldnae keep ye safe. Now, hush."

She opened her mouth to remind him just who was the child here and who was the adult, but closed it

again. It would do no good to recall him to the fact
that she was *Lady* Kirstie and he was just Callum, either.
Such reminders of birth and position were not her way
anyhow. Nothing would change the boy's mind, for this
was a matter of manly pride. And, after living with eight
brothers, she knew that manly pride could be far more
important and easily stung in a youth than in a full-
grown man. Callum would not desert her. Kirstie struggled to make her exhausted mind work so that she could
give him a way to elude capture, yet still maintain his
manly pride.

"If we get cornered, Callum," she said after several
moments of hard thought, "and ye can see there is nay
way to stop those two fools from dragging me off to
Roderick, ye are to do your verra best to free yourself."

"But, I must—" he began.

"What ye must do under those circumstances is get
back to Sir Payton and tell him what has happened. We
told him where we would be today, but we are nay
there now, are we? The moment he realizes we havenae
returned in a timely manner, that we are late enough
to indicate something has happened, he will search for
us."

"I told him I would take care of ye."

"And he kens that ye will, but he will still come looking for us. He is a knight, our protector, and our chosen
champion. He cannae do anything else, nay being what
he is. He would do the same if Strong Ian went missing.
So, he will need to ken where to look. And, if Roderick
does get me, he will take me to Thanescarr and ye ken
all the ways in, out, and about that dark place."

After a few moments of heavy silence, she felt him
nod. "Then, if there is nay saving ye," he said, "I will
save myself and go get Sir Payton." He suddenly tensed.
"Nay more talking."

It was another full minute before Kirstie heard what
Callum had—someone approaching their hiding place.
The boy had very keen hearing. She tensed and felt

Callum slowly, silently, get to his feet when the footsteps halted just outside the opening they had used to get into the dark cellar.

"We have lost them, Wattie," Gib said, his rough voice heavy with exhaustion.

"Curse them—I thought I would get my hands on that little bitch at last," muttered Wattie.

"Oh, aye, and ye have always wanted to get your hands on her."

"Weel, Roderick wasnae making any use of her."

"Nay, but I dinnae think he will let ye ride her. She is his wife and old Roderick isnae too fond of sharing what he considers his."

Wattie grunted. "He was starting to think on it. If he can breed a child there is something he gets from his kinsmen. Land or coin, I am nay sure which. And, he could keep her dower lands then. Just before he tried to drown the bitch, he talked of letting us get a bairn on her."

"He wouldnae let any bastard of ours have anything he considers his, or to inherit. Blood proud, he is."

"I suspicion he would have taken care of the little bastard ere that happened. Still, he was going to let us ride her and I was looking forward to riding her hard. I like 'em new and unbroke, too. There is naught as sweet and tight as a virgin. And she is clean and high-born. A fine treat, that is."

"Mayhap I would want to be the one to have first blood, Wattie."

"We could toss the dice for it, Gib."

"Fair enough. He just wants her dead now."

"Might let us have her first if only because he would like to see that proud, interfering bitch humbled. And I would humble her right and good. Would like to have me a taste of all that fine white skin."

"Weel, ye have missed your chance, Wattie. We have lost her. Wonder which brat was running with her."

"Probably that little bastard Callum. Always has been

a slippery, vicious lad. Roderick should have broke his skinny, insolent neck years ago. We will look for them for another hour or two.''

"And then what? I think they found a bolt-hole and we will ne'er find it now it be getting dark.''

"Then we will bring out the dogs.''

"Roderick isnae going to be happy we lost her, Wattie,'' Gib said as both men started to walk away.

"Nay, but it doesnae matter. He will be more pleased to ken we found out she is still alive. Now he will ken who is to blame for all the trouble he has been having of late.''

Kirstie wrapped her arms around her stomach as she tensely listened to the men's footsteps fade away. "I think I am going to be ill,'' she whispered when it had been quiet for a few minutes.

"They are swine,'' Callum said as he moved to the board covering the hole and cautiously removed it. "Nay worth ye losing what might be in your belly.'' He glanced around. "A fine bolt-hole, but it willnae be safe anymore. The dogs will sniff it out. To them, 'twill fair stink of us.''

"So will Payton's home,'' she said as she moved to his side.

"So will near all this town after tonight. Go on, get out there. They are gone.''

"Ye dinnae think we ought to wait an hour or two? 'Tis how long they said they would keep looking.''

"Aye, and then fetch the dogs. The sooner we can get back to Sir Payton's house, the longer we are off these streets, then the more time there will be for others to walk o'er our path, mayhaps muddle our scent.''

"Ah, of course.'' She crawled out of the hole, brushing herself as he crawled out behind her. "Ye are frighteningly good at all this. I thought I had some skill, but ye make me look like the veriest novice.''

"Nay, ye are verra good. Ye are a weel bred lady, yet ye kept pace with me, didnae need much direction at all as we skipped all o'er this town, and ye ken weel how to hide, how to be silent. The only thing ye didnae ken was where to go, all the little twists and turns.''

''I think it may be wise for ye to remember all these skills e'en though ye are now training to fight,'' she said as they started out on yet another attempt to reach Payton's home.

Callum nodded. '' 'Tis what Strong Ian said, too. Told me to keep such skills honed sharp. Told me that sometimes, part of defeating your enemy is to live to fight him another day. Said that if ye are outnumbered, 'tis nay shameful to run and hide so ye can fight again when the odds are much better. A clever mon is Strong Ian.''

''Aye, 'twould seem so. Do ye think he and Payton will be clever enough to keep the dogs from finding us, or Roderick when his hounds point the way?''

''Och, aye. He will ken what to do. Dinnae ye fret o'er that.''

Easier said than done,'' she murmured and fell silent as she carefully followed Callum on a torturous route through the town.

''Alive?''

Roderick stared at the two men who had intruded upon him in his bedchamber, forcing him to curtail his planned enjoyment. He had been reduced to purchasing a well-trained boy from Mistress Murchison, a base whore well known to provide for any and all tastes. It would serve for now, he thought as the boy slipped away to wait for his summons in the adjoining bedchamber. The boy lacked the sweetness, the innocence Roderick craved, however. He had already been broken to bridle, already been trained. Roderick preferred ones trained by his own hand.

Inwardly shrugging, he fixed his attention upon Gib and Wattie. He was not sure he should believe the fools, yet if his wife was alive, a great deal was suddenly explained. Although not sure how she could have accomplished it, if Kirstie had survived, then she was the one blackening his name, the one responsible for his having to hire a whore because it was increasingly impossible to get anything else. She probably had an accomplice and Roderick decided that person would have to die as well. Why could people not just let him be, he thought with an inner sigh. Self-righteous frauds, the whole lot of them, and his skinny wife was the worst of the lot.

"Aye, m'lord," answered Gib. "She and a lad we think was that wretch Callum." He proceeded to tell Roderick how they had bumped into the pair and pursued them for hours.

Ignoring a great deal of what Gib said, for Roderick was sure the man exaggerated his skill and effort during the chase, Roderick asked, "And ye are verra sure it was my wife?"

"With them odd eyes and that black hair? Oh, aye, 'twas Lady Kirstie. Nay doubt. Nay sure who the lad was, though he was the right size to be Callum and ye had suspected she had helped him."

"I suspect she robbed me of a number of children. Slipping about the place like some ghostie, spying on me, and robbing me of my treasures. I should have rid myself of the bitch years ago."

He felt a surge of rage at the thought of his wife. She had consistently betrayed him. Even now, when he had thought himself free, she still betrayed him, for he was certain she was behind all the whispers and gossip dogging his heels. He should have strangled her on their wedding night when she had revealed her deceit. When he felt the gorge rise to sting the back of his throat, he forced that memory away.

"We thought to set the dogs on her trail," said Wattie.

"Ye cannae set those hounds loose to run free through the town," said Roderick.

"Just a few, on a lead, ye ken. We could pick out the best of the pack."

"Nay tonight." Roderick poured himself a goblet of fine wine, ignoring the covetous glances his men gave it.

"But the trail will still be fresh now," protested Gib. "Come the morrow there will be more people walking about, making it verra hard for the dogs to catch her scent."

"There have been people walking all over whatever trail they laid since the moment ye saw them," snapped Roderick, and then he downed his drink. "Leave it 'til the morning. The moment I start hunting my wife, I shall have to explain why I told everyone she was dead. I need time to plan an answer to that question. And, since we now ken she is hiding in the town, a clear trail isnae so vital, only expedient. We can still sniff her out, find where she has gone to ground."

Wattie shook his head. "I dinnae understand why she didnae drown." He tensed and took a step back toward the door when Roderick cursed and flung his goblet against the wall.

"Apparently the bitch could swim, couldnae she? Curse her, she doesnae e'en have the grace to die like a lady." He took several deep breaths, but his fury only faded a little, strong remnants of it continuing to ripple through him. "This time I will make sure she is dead. Whether I decide to let her die quickly or make her suffer for all the trouble she has caused, I will still make certain she is dead. I want that boy, too. And whoever has been fool enough to help her. Now, go. We will begin the hunt at dawn."

CHAPTER TEN

"Where have ye been?"

Kirstie stumbled into the house when Payton threw open the kitchen door. She staggered over to the bench by the table before looking at him, noting absently that Callum did the same. Payton looked as furious as he had when she had gone after Roderick, dagger in hand. She suspected he had never spent so much time being angry, especially at a woman. Kirstie wondered if that should trouble her or if she should consider it an achievement.

"Running away from Roderick's hounds," she replied in a weary voice and greedily drank the cool cider Alice served her and Callum. "Running, hiding, running some more, and hiding some more. I dinnae think I have the strength left to move."

Payton felt his heart clench, and was astonished at how deeply he feared for this woman's safety. The woman seemed to leap from crisis to crisis with astonishing speed. If this was how he was going to feel each time she courted danger, he would be a madman in just a few days. He was tempted to find a mirror to see if his hair was turning grey.

Before he could speak, Ian strode into the kitchen and looked at Callum and Kirstie, nodded, then looked at Callum. "Saw Roderick's faithful hounds searching the town. Followed them until they fetched their mounts and rode out of town. Couldnae get close enough to hear much," he looked at Kirstie, "but they saw ye, lass, didnae they?"

"Aye," she replied. " 'Twas a wretched accident. They staggered into the alley we were slipping down. Knocked us both aside and I lost my cap. Unfortunately, there was enough light where we stood for them to get a good look at me. We managed to break away, but it took a long time to lose them so that we could return here. Of course, we cannae stay." She wondered if she would have time for a nice, hot bath before she had to flee.

"I think a hot bath and some food are needed," Wee Alice said quickly when Payton growled and dragged his fingers through his hair. "That will revive ye, lass," she helped Kirstie to her feet, "and then ye can clearly tell Sir Payton what has happened. Ye, too, Callum. They will be needing ye alert, too, for they will be wanting a mon's view of it all."

After looking around the kitchen that now held only him and Ian, Payton hurried out into the hall and called after a rapidly departing Alice, "My ledger room. One hour. Nay more."

"I think I must needs set a torch to that cursed ledger room," Kirstie muttered and was able to smile when Wee Alice laughed.

Payton was extremely angry this time, Kirstie mused as she sipped her wine. He had barely even looked her way from the moment she and Callum had come to the ledger room. Once she had been seated and given a drink, he had turned all of his attention on Callum. If the man was going to ignore her, she thought crossly, he could have just allowed her to go to bed. If he was trying to make some point or give her some lesson, she was too tired to understand. All she wanted to do was get up, give him a sound kick in his too-attractive backside, and then go to bed and sleep for a few days.

She looked at Ian, who occasionally took his solemn gaze from Callum and Payton. The man would then glance between her and Payton and look highly amused. Kirstie was not sure what could possibly amuse the man about the irritating way Payton was treating her, but perhaps it was some manly humor beyond her understanding.

The more she thought on it, the longer Payton did not even glance her way, the more annoyed Kirstie grew. She finally decided enough was enough. She would soon have to start running for her life, and she needed some rest. When she stood up and started to walk past Payton, she realized he was not ignoring her as completely as he had pretended to be. She released a squeak more from surprise than pain when he grabbed hold of her braid and pulled her to his side, only to quickly release it to grasp her hand in an iron grip.

Just as she opened her mouth to berate the beautiful tyrant holding her captive, Callum said, "Those two pigs cannae wait to get their hands on our Kirstie. They are thinking Roderick will let them tup her ere he kills her."

"Callum," she murmured, half in admonishment over his language and half in an attempt to get him to be quiet, "Sir Payton doesnae need to hear all that." Kirstie was a little concerned over how tense Payton had become and just what it might mean. " 'Twas all just empty boasting."

"What else did they say?" Payton asked the boy in a calm but cold voice.

"Seems Roderick was thinking on letting his men tup her to start her breeding. He needs an heir. Gib and

Wattie were nay sure why, just that Roderick would get something for it. Said he was talking on that plan when Kirstie forced him to try and shut her mouth.'' Callum glanced at Kirstie, shrugged, then added, ''They are thinking they might still get her because Roderick might like shaming her ere he kills her.''

''If she even survived those two brutes taking turns with her.'' Payton took a deep breath and was able to speak somewhat pleasantly as he told Callum, ''Ye did yourself proud, lad. Get some rest now.''

''We need a new place to hide, I am thinking.''

''Only if the bastard comes here and he willnae be kicking in my doors, nay the first time. Ian is already preparing a wee hiding place. There are several in the cellars.''

''Willnae the dogs sniff us out?''

''There is a chance of that, but I am nay too concerned about it. There are a few things one can do to put dogs off the scent and we will keep what is needed close to hand. Go on, lad. Get yourself to bed.''

Even as Callum and Ian left, Kirstie started trying to wriggle her hand free of Payton's hold. It annoyed her when he ignored her with apparent ease and dragged her along as he started out of the room. When she realized he was headed to his bedchamber, she started to protest, then tightly pressed her lips together to quell the urge. She did not think the anger she could feel in the man was directed at her, but she was not inclined to do anything to stop his obvious attempts to control it. Kirstie knew how easily such anger could singe anyone foolish enough to nudge at it, innocent or not.

Her resolve to remain quiet and let Payton wrestle with his emotions grew difficult to cling to as the minutes wore on and he remained tensely silent. He undressed her without a word. He set her on the bed with barely a glance. He undressed himself in that same heavy silence. When he crawled into bed beside her, and sprawled on his back with his arms crossed beneath his head, she decided she had had enough. Clutching the covers to her breasts, she sat up to frown at him. It pleased Kirstie to see that her rising displeasure had finally caught his attention.

"Just why have ye brought me in here if ye dinnae mean to e'en speak to me?" she asked when he looked at her.

"Oh, I mean to do more than speak to ye," he drawled.

"Do ye now?" She flopped back down and turned her back to him. "I will try to stay awake until ye finish with your brooding."

"I wasnae really brooding."

"Nay?"

"Nay. I was fighting down the urge to go and kill someone. Three someones, in truth."

Kirstie turned onto her other side to look at him. "Roderick, Gib, and Wattie."

"Aye." He slid his arm around her and tugged her close against his side. "Ye hadnae intended to tell me about what Roderick's faithful hounds had said, had ye?" He trailed his fingers up and down her spine as he waited for her to reply.

"Nay," she confessed. "Roderick wants me dead. 'Tis all that really matters. What Gib and Wattie said was but one possible way Roderick might accomplish the deed. I didnae feel it was so verra important, especially when I suspected what they had said would irritate you."

Payton laughed softly, but the sound was tainted by his lingering anger. "Aye, it irritated me. It was nay just the talk of whether or nay they would each have a turn at ye ere they killed ye, or Roderick did."

"Nay?" She had found the thought of that possibility somewhat chilling.

"Nay. Sad to say, 'tis nay uncommon for rape to precede the murder of a lass, e'en in battle. E'en if 'tis nay thought of as some right of conquest," Payton's tone revealed his contempt for that attitude, "there are far too many men who dinnae heed a nay or e'en think a lass has no right to deny him. A poor lass can e'en find herself used to deliver a blow or an insult to another such as was done to my cousin Sorcha by enemies of my Uncle Eric.''

"How sad." She kissed his chest, intrigued when that gesture of sympathy caused him to tremble faintly. "So, ye were nay angered by such talk?" Kirstie idly circled his navel with her finger, fascinated by the way his belly clenched.

"I wouldnae say that. I was, however, nay surprised. Nay, 'twas talk of the fate ye barely escaped, that your foul bastard of a husband thought to give ye to those two pigs until they got ye with child." He took a deep, slow breath in an attempt to control the desire she was rapidly stirring with her idle touches. "He couldnae treat ye as a wife or a woman," and Payton was a little surprised at how much that pleased him, "but he would-nae set ye free, either. Did he truly think he could use ye so and ye would ne'er tell your kinsmen of such an insult?''

Kirstie lightly bit her lip and cast him an uneasy glance. "He may have had some right to think that." She grimaced at his look of astonishment. "I had nay sought their help o'er anything else. Since that atrocity didnae happen, I cannae say I would have gone to them. My fear for them was e'en greater than my fear of Roder-ick, or any revulsion or unhappiness. By all the laws of church and mon, I am Roderick's chattel. He can do with me as he chooses."

"Nay that."

"Nay? How could I be certain which thing he did would be the one to make the law side with me, his wife? Or, more important, make his family believe he should stand alone against my family's anger? The other MacIyes I met seemed good men, fair men, and treated me kindly. But, I was slow to see the evil in Roderick so how much could I trust in my own judgments? The cost of being wrong, of stirring my family to righteous outrage, could be their verra lives.'' She shrugged. '' 'Tisnae so easy to ken what to do when ye ken a wrong move could bring destruction and e'en death upon all ye care about.''

"I will make him pay,'' Payton vowed and pressed his lips to her forehead.

She was deeply moved by his words, by the emotion she could hear in his voice. Kirstie's first reaction was one of delight, her besotted mind seeing the words as an indication that he cared for her, that she was more than just another lover. Common sense quickly reared its head, scoffing at her romantic notions. Payton was, in all ways, a chivalrous knight. His vow was born of such ideals, of his outrage that any of his ilk would act so completely against all rules of chivalry.

It was a shame he did not follow the rules of courtly love so assiduously, loving only from afar, she thought and nearly smiled. That might have ensured he did not have such a lecherous history, but it would also mean he would not now be in this bed with her. Kirstie shifted against him, and smiled faintly against the warm, taut skin of his chest. They also would not be skin to skin, as they were now, and that would be a sad loss.

"Ah, that is sweet of ye,'' she murmured and kissed his chest.

"Sweet? Ye call a vow of vengeance sweet?'' he muttered.

Ignoring his complaint, she said, "Make the vow for the sake of the bairns. They need a champion more than I do.''

"I am nay so sure 'tis more. Kirstie, your family will soon have to be told something. That lad ye sent may weel tell them enough to make them demand the full truth. If that happens, if their suspicions are raised, and the lad, your brother Eudard, or your aunt are forced to tell them everything, will they come?''

Thinking of how intimidating her brothers could be,

including Eudard if he felt the need, Kirstie sat up, a growing fear for her family making her unable to remain still. She smoothed one hand over the soft velvet cover on Payton's bed as she tried to decide if she was right to be afraid. In truth, she had been surprised Eudard had kept all her secrets so well, although she had not told him everything. Eudard, being her twin, had often sensed there was more, but he had not pressed and the need to help the children had consumed them both. Her other brothers would also feel for the children, but would still press for the full truth if they suspected someone was hiding something.

"Kirstie?" Payton sat up and stroked her hair.

"They will come," she said quietly. "Eudard is my twin and I am certain he sensed I wasnae telling him everything, but, ere he could press too hard, we became caught up in the need to help the children. My other brothers certainly notice the new people upon our lands, but would, and have, accepted the tale of a need to be charitable. Eudard and I were always gathering strays. But, Michael?" She shook her head. "I told him of all the reasons I kept certain secrets from my family, but he may nay truly understand. And, if Roderick sent word that I had drowned, or if the rumor of it drifts to the ears of my family, my brothers will turn to Michael and start asking questions."

"Then we shall send word to your family that ye live, that they are to ignore all word to the contrary."

"Which will certainly stir up their curiosity."

"Ah. Ye have kept them ignorant and safe for five long years, Kirstie." He gently pushed her back onto the bed and settled himself by her side. "I am nay sure they will thank ye for that."

"Och, nay, they certainly willnae. Proud, pigheaded lot of fools. My father is just as bad."

"And will be riding at their head when they finally hie to your side?" He slid his hand up her ribs and over her breast, delighted at how the nipple hardened at the slightest touch of his fingers.

For a brief moment Kirstie forgot what they were talking about. The mere touch of his hand stirred her need for him. One brush of his fingers over her nipples and they ached for him. She was a complete wanton, she mused. It should have shocked her except that she knew only Payton stirred her this way. Kirstie also knew that, even though his manly beauty could take her breath away, it was not the reason she was so lost to passion when he held her. The man's beauty ran deep, right to the heart which was so moved by the plight of children, so outraged over how Roderick had treated her.

"Aye," she finally managed to say. "Fither will be there, especially since he will feel betrayed by Roderick. He thought he was making such a grand match for me despite my small dowry. The bride price offered was tempting as weel, and, kenning that, Fither will feel guilty for nay looking at the mon too closely."

Payton moved so that he was on top of her, nudging her legs apart with his, and settling himself between them. She felt perfect beneath him. He did not miss the lushness he had become accustomed to, but enjoyed her lithe, soft body wrapped around his.

Bedding her had not ended his obsession with her at all. It had merely altered it slightly. Now, instead of spending hours thinking about how it would feel to make love to her, he spent hours thinking about how good it felt to do so and just when he might do it again. As he cradled her firm little breasts in his hands and licked the silken skin between them, Payton mused that he might be a fool to let this one walk away.

"So, I had best be prepared for a visit from your kinsmen." He cursed himself for an idiot when she tensed.

The mere thought of her kinsmen finding out about her and Payton had Kirstie thinking about leaping from the bed, grabbing her clothes, and finding some dark hole to hide in. Unfortunately, there was no place to go. There was also still Roderick to worry about and the children to protect. Nor could she leave Payton alone to face her kinsmen, especially if her family discovered she had shared his bed. Payton did not seem overly concerned about a possible confrontation with her kinsmen, but that could be both arrogance and ignorance. He had never faced nine furious Kinlochs before.

"Ye can do naught, Kirstie," Payton said as he warmed her throat with kisses.

Kirstie gasped, then murmured her delight when he lowered his kisses to her breasts. "Oh, my. That feels so verra nice." She inwardly struggled for some control as she recalled what they had been talking about. "Mayhap I *should* send word to them."

"We shall thrash out the wording of a message on the morrow."

"I may have to run away on the morrow."

"Nay, ye will do nay more running."

"But, he will bring the dogs." She was not surprised to hear how shaky her voice was, for she was nearly panting. The way he was caressing her breasts with his lips, hands, and tongue was driving her nearly mad with desire.

"Ye chose me as your champion, aye?" Payton moved his kisses to her silken midriff and taut belly as he stroked her legs with his hands.

"Aye."

Kirstie was not sure if she was answering his question or inviting the more intimate touch of his tormenting hands. He was stroking her thighs, then her hips, his clever fingers brushing temptingly close to the part of her that now ached for him. She was shocked that she could crave something so scandalous, but she did. When he finally touched her woman's flesh, the sigh that escaped her was a mixture of relief and delight.

"Then let your champion do what ye chose him for.

I have sworn to protect ye and the children.'' He slid his finger into her tight heat, enjoying the feel of her and the way she immediately raised her slim hips to welcome his touch. "At least let me have one chance to do so ere ye run again." He placed his mouth where his fingers had just been.

"Oh, my God."

For a brief moment, Kirstie's whole body stiffened in shock. When she reached out to try to push him away, he grabbed her hands to hold them captive at her side. His broad shoulders thwarted her attempt to close her legs against such intimacy.

Then a searing heat began to blossom outward from where he stroked her with his tongue. Kirstie felt her body soften and open to him as passion raced through her veins. Payton released her hands, but this time, she made no move to stop him, but simply clutched at the bed linen as if to anchor herself. Even when he draped her trembling legs over his shoulders and slid his hands beneath her bottom, exposing her even more flagrantly to his sensuous intimacies, she made no protest, no attempt to pull away. She heard herself stutter out words of praise and delight and knew she was a willing prisoner for now.

Payton did his best to keep Kirstie teetering on the edge of release, delighted and enflamed by how completely she lost herself to this pleasure. He almost laughed when she rather forcefully demanded he cease his tormenting play and get himself inside of her—now!—but he was equally as desperate for the joining of their bodies. As he thrust into her, he took her nipple deep into his mouth and suckled hard. The way Kirstie shattered in his arms was enough to drag him into passion's oblivion right along with her.

She was going to kill him, Payton thought, as he lay sprawled on top of Kirstie, still trembling faintly from the strength of his release. One quick glance at the woman beneath him revealed her with her arms out-

flung and her eyes closed. For a moment, he thought
he had made her swoon; then she lifted one arm and,
somewhat gracelessly, flopped it across his back. He
smiled faintly. It would have been something to be
proud of if he had made her swoon with pleasure, but
the clear evidence that he had sapped her of all strength
was almost as pleasing. It was also only fair since she
had left him as weak as a day-old bairn.

As his wits grew sharper, Payton became acutely aware
of the fact that he was still inside of Kirstie. He had not
withdrawn, had not spent himself upon the sheets, and
he had not done so from the first. With every other
woman he had bedded, he had done so, even with his
first. His brothers and cousins had been impressed with
his control, had said he must have been born with it.
That control was not there with Kirstie. Each time he
had felt his release upon him, he had not pulled away
at all, not even tried to. No, he had thrust himself as
deep into her lithe body as he could go and stayed
there, filling her with his seed.

He murmured his appreciation when her body briefly
tightened around him and he felt himself begin to
harden inside of her. Such a fierce lusting would explain
his unusual carelessness, but Payton was not sure it was
that simple. A small voice in the back of his mind whispered that it was not carelessness, it was calculation.
The possibility that he was seeding her on purpose, was
trying to get her with child so she could not leave him,
did not alarm Payton. That, he decided, was probably
verification enough of his subtle guile, a guile he had
even failed to sense in himself until now.

There would be time to think about that later, Payton
decided, as he felt desire reviving him. He slid his hand
up her body and caressed her breast. Despite the way
her nipple hardened quickly in welcome, Payton sensed
a growing tension in Kirstie that had nothing to do with
passion. He looked at her, but she blushed, and would
not meet his gaze. He had forgotten how new Kirstie

was to passion's ways and how uncertain she was about
him and the rightness of their being together like this.
Clasping her small chin in his hand, he turned her face
toward his and brushed a kiss over her lips.

"Ye fret yourself o'er naught, my dark angel," he
said, stroking her blush-warmed cheek.

"Naught?" she muttered, wishing she could so easily
accept her own wanton behavior, her brazen compli-
ance with what was, by every rule and law she knew of,
a sin. "I have no shame," she whispered. "I should
disgust you."

"Ye delight me." He moved slightly inside of her,
letting her feel the truth of his words.

"Weel, of course, for ye get what ye want when I cast
aside all rules and modesty."

"True." He briefly grinned when she gave him a
disgusted look, then quickly grew serious. "Ye are a
beautifully passionate woman, Kirstie. Trust me to ken
what I speak of when I say 'tis a gift, something ye
should be proud and pleased with. Dinnae kill what is
so beautiful with fears of sin and a foolish modesty. Ye
chose to come to me. Can ye nay just accept your own
choice?"

Kirstie wanted to, desperately. She did not like how
her worries and fears robbed some of the beauty from
what she and Payton shared. While it was true that he
had done his utmost to seduce her into his bed, the
final decision had been hers. Somehow she was going
to have to fully accept that and, more important, be
comfortable with it. Her time with Payton could well be
short-lived and she would be the worst of fools to taint
it with fears of sin and her own passionate nature. No
one in this house had condemned her for becoming
Payton's lover and, for now, she would let their attitudes
guide her and ignore the carping voices in her head
which tried so hard to spoil it all.

As she wrapped her arms around him, she became
aware of the fact that Payton's manhood now filled her,

and that he was moving ever so slightly, as if he could not help himself. "Ye want to do it again?"

He chuckled against her neck. "Aye. Ye intoxicate me."

Payton had thought that he could go slowly, savor each thrust, each sigh and shiver, but Kirstie's passion grew wild and demanding again. He swiftly found his control torn to shreds by her response. It was all too soon that he found himself again collapsed on top of her, both of them trembling from the force of their releases. He smiled faintly with a blend of chagrin and delight even as he succumbed to a need to rest.

As dawn's light seeped into his bedchamber, Payton woke and reached for Kirstie. Yet again he tried to go slowly, to make the pleasure last, and yet again he failed. He had just gained enough strength to move out of her arms when a knock sounded at the door.

"Roderick and his hounds are coming down our street," Ian announced.

CHAPTER ELEVEN

Kirstie tucked the blanket a little more securely around a sleeping Robbie. She wished she could find such peace, but doubted she would do so for quite a while. After Ian's warning had shattered the morning, Payton had gotten them both dressed; then they had helped take the sleepy children down into the cellar. Now she huddled in the small, dark room with six children and prayed that Roderick would not get past Payton. It was not a pleasant way to start the day.

She glanced around the hiding place Payton had readied for them. It was lit by one candle, which she had been given strict orders to extinguish the moment she heard anyone enter this part of the cellars. The place was surprisingly dry and fresh of smell. There were blankets, pallets, a chamber pot, drink, and food. The children revealed that they had learned too young the ways of hiding, of remaining utterly silent. It was good that they could do so, but very sad as well.

"What is that smell?" asked Callum in a very soft whisper as he leaned against her side.

Even as Kirstie was about to ask what smell he meant,

the odor reached her nose. Following the example of the grimacing children, Kirstie placed a hand over her nose. The smell was already easing ever so slightly before she recognized it. It was a particularly strong mix of what was used to clean the floors, especially if one wanted to kill off any fleas or other tiny vermin. Kirstie would not be too surprised to discover Alice had added very little to dilute what she had been curing in a small shed behind the house. Since that had consisted of the men's urine, Kirstie knew that, if the dogs were brought down here, all they would smell would be Ian and Payton, if they could be made to put their keen noses to work at all.

"It smells like p—" began Moira, her voice surprisingly soft for such a young child.

"Aye," Kirstie quickly interrupted in an equally soft voice. " 'Twill distract the dogs. They willnae be able to smell us."

"They willnae be able to smell anything for a fortnight if they put their noses to that," said Callum.

"Is Mama going to make the whole house stink?" David asked.

Surprised at how quickly David had taken to calling Wee Alice his mother, it took Kirstie a moment to reply. "I certainly hope not. Yet, we must nay complain and we will help her if she needs to clear it all away, for 'tis done to help us." She almost smiled at the look of dismay that crossed all their faces.

"So the monster willnae find us?" asked Moira, edging closer to Kirstie and placing one tiny hand on the blanket covering Robbie.

"Aye, so the monster cannae find us," replied Kirstie. "Now, we must be verra quiet. The dogs have ears as keen as their noses. We shall sit here being verra quiet and still until Sir Payton comes to let us out."

"It willnae be too long, will it?"

"Nay, I dinnae think it will be too long."

Kirstie prayed she was right, then turned her prayers

toward giving Payton and Ian all the guile and strength needed to turn Roderick away at the door. Roderick would not only have to be turned away, but would have to leave without gaining the smallest suspicion that he had been fooled or lied to, she realized, and began to pray even harder.

Payton almost laughed at the way Roderick, his men, and the four hounds with them recoiled when they entered his home. With what Wee Alice was vigorously scrubbing the floor with, if one flea leapt off a dog, it would be dead before it hit the floor. Ian liked to jest that the reason Wee Alice loved him was because she had bad eyesight and a poor sense of smell. Payton was beginning to think the latter just might be true. Unless she had some trick up her sleeve, it was going to take days for his house to stop reeking.

" 'Tis early," Payton said, fixing a cold look upon Roderick, "and I believe the game is more plentiful outside the town walls."

"I dinnae hunt rabbit for the stew pot," said Roderick, making no effort to hide his dislike. "I am hunting my wife."

"I had heard that she had drowned." Payton frowned and rubbed his chin. "If I recall, the one who told me made mention of the tragedy simply because she puzzled o'er your lack of grief."

"A mon keeps his grief to himself. He doesnae display it to please some foolish wench."

"Of course not. Ye will be pleased to ken that ye were behaving with great monly fortitude." Payton decided it might be wise to temper his sarcasm, for Roderick's eyes were narrowing with a look of growing suspicion. The man might just have enough wit to wonder what was causing Payton's heavy disdain. "So, she didnae drown, aye?"

"It would seem that she didnae," replied Roderick.

My men Wattie and Gib saw her last eve.'' He sighed.
''I fear I tempered the truth a wee bit when I spoke
of what happened that day. It wasnae a pleasant day
shattered by a tragedy. Nay, I fear my wife and I were
quarreling. She is a tempestuous lass.''

Fearing what he might say in response to Roderick's
portrayal of a saddened, concerned husband, Payton
just nodded, silently encouraging the man to finish his
fable.

''With a show of great drama, she plunged into the
river. Thinking she sought to take her own life, I struggled to pull her from the water, but the currents swept
her away. 'Twas fear for her immortal soul that made
me hide the truth of what happened that day. Now it
appears that my torment was for naught. If my men are
right, my wife not only survived, but hides from me.''
He shook his head. ''She is obviously still angry with
me.''

''Ah, another woman, was it?''

''A mon has his needs and is often too weak to resist
the many temptations of the flesh.''

''The lasses can easily beguile a poor mon. Indeed
they can. But, why do ye bring the dogs to my home?''

''The trail they followed led here.''

Payton felt confident that his look of shock and surprise was convincing. ''How could that be? I have ne'er
e'en met your wife. S'truth, didnae e'en ken ye were
married until rumors of your wife's death were spread
about.''

''The dogs sniffed out the trail and it led right to
your door.''

''They appear to have lost the trail now.'' Payton gave
the seated, panting dogs a telling glance. ''Your wife may
have paused by my door, but she didnae walk through it.
I allow few women into my home. Especially another
mon's wife.''

The big, dark man holding the dogs' leads snorted.

"Ye have had near half the lasses in Scotland. Tup them in the road, do ye?"

"Gib, silence," Roderick said and then he looked at Payton. "I am sure Sir Payton wouldnae lie."

"Of course not. I suspect I *have* had half the lasses in Scotland." Payton ignored Ian's snort of laughter. "I did not, er, tup any of them here, however. The women of my clan often stay here. And, I believe my feelings about soiling my own nest are no secret. But, please, feel free to search."

Roderick hesitated only a moment before signaling his men to look around. "I mean no insult, Sir Payton," he said as his men moved forward, urging their dogs on. "I dinnae accuse ye of lying to me, but my wife has an unusual skill, ye see. She could easily have made your house a refuge and ye wouldnae e'en ken she was here."

"She can make herself invisible, can she?"

"Nearly. The woman can skillfully flit in and out of the shadows. She can be as still and as silent as one, as weel. 'Tis a most unladylike trick, but I place the blame upon her brothers. Too often they treated her as just another lad. I brought home a wife who lacked all training. It was a long time ere I felt she could be presented to anyone outside of Thanescarr."

Payton wondered almost idly if he had ever wanted to hit someone as badly as he wanted to hit Roderick MacIye—repeatedly. It was a good thing Kirstie could not hear this. He had no doubt that she would be enraged, more for the insult to her brothers than to herself.

The return of Roderick's men, with a scolding Alice close behind them, diverted Payton from his thoughts. Alice could sound positively shrewish, he mused with a flicker of amusement. That faded quickly when he saw how Ian moved to stand between his wife and Roderick's men. Gib and Wattie had suddenly turned to face Alice, their fists clenched.

"I would strongly suggest that your men leave my serving woman alone," Payton said.

"Gib, Wattie," Sir Roderick called. "Leave the woman be. We have interrupted her cleaning."

"Cleaning?" Gib muttered as, after giving Alice one final glare, he started out the door. "The place smells like a cursed garderobe. I wouldnae be surprised if the dogs are near ruined for a sennight."

"We have recently suffered a plague of fleas," Payton said and shrugged. "The woman claims this is the way to end it. One must wonder, however, if the cure could prove far worse than the illness. Then, too, I wasnae expecting any visitors so didnae think this would be inflicted upon anyone." Payton was mildly satisfied when a slight flush colored Roderick's cheeks, revealing that the man had understood the subtle rebuke.

"I thank ye for your patience, Sir Payton," Roderick said, and, after a somewhat curt bow, he and his men left.

"Bastard," Ian muttered, then frowned at his wife. "And what game were ye playing? Trying to see how hard ye could push those fools ere one of them knocked ye on your arse?"

Alice crossed her arms over her fulsome breasts and glared at the door Roderick had just gone through. "They were making a mess of my clean floors."

"Ah, aye, the floors." Payton grimaced. "Ye do have a way to get rid of the smell, I pray."

"Och, aye. Scrubbing with something less foul, a few rinses, and a few fresh rushes. Although the smell may linger a wee while in the cellars. I was a wee bit heavy-handed down there. I was anxious, ye ken, and wanted to be verra sure those beasties couldnae smell Lady Kirstie or the bairns." She looked at Payton. "Can we let them out now?"

"Nay just yet. I want to be sure that fool has given up the hunt for the day. We must also hope that he decides 'tis a waste of time to use the dogs."

"I will follow them," Ian announced, even as he headed out the door.

Alice sighed. "I hope my lads are nay too afeared in that wee, dark room."

"They will be fine," Payton assured her. "They have Kirstie with them."

"Aye, true enough. I will start scrubbing away this stink, then."

"Ye dinnae think we ought to leave that for a wee while in case the bastard comes back?"

"Nay. What I put down should have taken away any trail those beasties might follow. Until Lady Kirstie and the bairns start walking about again, and laying down a fresh trail, leastwise. 'Tis fortunate they didnae go inside the bedchambers, for I wasnae certain I had the time to hide all sign of the bairns or Lady Kirstie. By the time those fools stomped up there, however, they had ceased trying to get the dogs to sniff out their prize and only looked into each bedchamber."

"That was a fine touch of good fortune. I hope it stays with us for a while."

"Do ye think he believed ye, Payton? 'Twould be best if he looked elsewhere and ne'er returned here."

"It would be best, but we must remain prepared. We can only pray that he doesnae think too long on how the dogs led him to my door, or how convenient it was that we chose this verra day to make my house smell like a privy. If he does, he could come up with some answers that will turn his search back on me."

"Curse it, the dogs took us right to that pretty bastard's door," grumbled Gib as he sat down at the table and poured himself a tankard of ale. "They didnae do that at any other house."

"Nay, they didnae," murmured Roderick.

Slouched in his chair, Roderick sipped his wine and stared somewhat blindly at one of the tapestries gracing

the walls of his great hall. Gib was not known for his
keen wits, but this time he was right. They had covered
the whole town and, although the dogs had picked up
Kirstie's scent, as well as Callum's, numerous times, not
once had they gone straight to another door. At Sir
Payton's house the dogs had acted just as they had when
they had sniffed out that wretched hole in the ground
Kirstie had plainly used as a hiding place. Unfortunately,
it was obvious she had not used it for some time except
to hide from Gib and Wattie, if the reactions of those
two fools were anything to go by. The idiots had tried
a little too hard to hide the fact that they recognized
the place. Roderick suspected that was where they had
lost Kirstie last evening.

Several things about the confrontation with Sir Payton
Murray troubled Roderick as well. Why had the man
been awake and dressed so early in the morning? It
could be that he had had work to do or had just arrived
home after entertaining some woman, but Roderick
did not think so. Sir Payton had acted appropriately
surprised and somewhat outraged, but Roderick simply
could not shake the feeling that it was, indeed, all an
act. There had been a cold look in the man's eyes, the
occasional glimpse of a fury greater than was warranted
by the intrusion into his home. Then there was that
reeking concoction that woman had been spreading
throughout the house. He knew some of the remedies
used to rid a house of fleas could be foul, but *that* foul?
And it just happened to have been spread all over Sir
Payton's house at the exact time Roderick's hounds
were clinging fast to Kirstie's trail? Such a coincidence
was difficult to accept.

Roderick drummed his fingers on the arm of his
ornately carved oak chair. The more he thought about
all that had happened at Sir Payton's house, the more
suspicious he became. Sir Payton was one of those foolish men who wasted his manly beauty on women. The
idiotic wenches tumbled over themselves in their

attempts to catch him between their thighs. Roderick was not sure when his wife might have made Sir Payton's acquaintance, but he could all-too-easily see her going to the handsome, highly lauded knight to plea for aid.

And if she had done so, he thought with a sigh, then Sir Payton now knew too much. He, too, would have to die. For a brief moment, Roderick felt a pang of regret. Sir Payton was the only man who had made Roderick consider the possibility of expanding his sensual experiences to include men. The man's beauty could stir lustful thoughts in a stone. Sir Payton, however, only lusted after women, so there had been no chance to test his ability to gain his pleasure in some new way.

So, Sir Payton had to die, decided Roderick, all regret vanquished by his own deeply rooted sense of self-preservation. And probably those two rather unpleasant-looking servants, too, Roderick mused. He grimaced as he realized the death toll was beginning to rise. A lot of very careful planning would be needed. The fault for that could be laid directly at Kirstie's feet. If his cursed wife had just drowned as any proper lady would have, he would not have to be dealing with all these complications.

"I think the bastard is hiding her," grumbled Wattie before shoving a hunk of cheese into his mouth.

When Roderick looked at the man, he wished he had not. Wattie had the manners of a pig, and Roderick suspected he might well be maligning the pig. Struggling to ignore the way Wattie chewed with his mouth open so wide it was a miracle the food did not simply fall out, Roderick decided it was time to start on Sir Payton Murray's downfall.

Roderick nodded. "I believe he kens where she is, too. The mon was certainly trying to hide something and I feel increasingly certain it was my errant wife."

"So, we go back and cut us a few throats?"

"A pleasant thought, but much too ugly. The mon is too weel known, too much admired despite seducing so many wives. His death would be carefully scrutinized. And, if my wife is found dead alongside him, I would become verra suspect indeed. Nay, we must proceed carefully, play a verra subtle game."

"And what game would that be?"

"Since I believe he is the source of the rumors causing me such difficulty, I believe I will begin to give him a taste of his own medicine."

"What good will that do?" asked Gib.

"It will leave him without any allies. By the time I am done, Sir Payton Murray will be fortunate if e'en one of his own kinsmen bothers to attend his funeral."

"He is gone?" Kirstie asked the moment Payton let them all out of their hiding place.

"Gone from town and I am fair certain he willnae be using the dogs again," Payton replied as Alice shooed the children away, herding them to her kitchen. "It wasnae easy to face the mon, to listen to his lies without acknowledging them as such." He put his arm around her slim shoulders and led her out of the dark cellars.

"Ye dinnae sound verra certain of your victory o'er the mon. Nay as certain as I would wish ye to be."

Payton sighed. He wanted to reassure her, wanted to make her feel safe. That would be a mistake and he knew it. Kirstie needed to know what he suspected and be fully aware of the dangers that still existed. If nothing else, such knowledge might make her more amenable, more ready to obey any commands he gave her.

Roderick had given no sign that he was suspicious, but Payton could not shake the feeling that the man was, or soon would be. The man could not have successfully hidden his evil for so many years without having some wits. Sir Roderick had erred in not seeing the threat Kirstie was and then by not making very sure she was dead. He would not make that mistake again. Nor would he wish any of her allies to live very long, either.

"Are we nay to dine with the others?" Kirstie asked, hesitating just inside Payton's bedchamber door when she saw the food laid out on a small table before the fireplace.

After nudging her further inside his room, Payton shut the door and led her to a seat at the table. "Nay, not this night. Ye and I need to thrash out a few facts and rules concerning the trouble ye are in. If we had to weigh every word because we didnae wish to afright the children, we would accomplish verra little."

"Oh." She abruptly sat down. " 'Tis bad, is it?"

He sat down and poured them each some wine. "It might be. I dinnae think he believed me."

"Roderick called ye a liar?" Kirstie felt outraged over that insult to Payton, even though he had, indeed, been lying to the man.

"Nay, in truth, he was most apologetic. The problem is that the dogs led him straight to my door."

Kirstie helped herself to several slices of roast lamb and an assortment of lightly seasoned vegetables. She was a little surprised that worry over Roderick did not seem to dim her appetite at all. It was probably because she had spent too much time over the last five years being hungry to allow worry or fear to stop her from filling her belly when food was at hand. She idly noted that being the bearer of grim news did not dim Payton's appetite, either.

"Ye mean I spent the whole day locked up in that wee, dark room and he still kens I am here?" she asked.

"Aye and nay. As he stood there, I would say he believed me, believed ye may weel have drawn near to my door, but ye didnae come in and I didnae see ye. I am just nay sure how long he will believe it. If he has any wit at all and thinks too long on the matter, I fear he will decide I was lying."

"He is clever when he wishes to be." She finished off a thick piece of bread. "And his dogs are verra good hunters."

"Who wouldnae follow the wrong trail." Payton sighed and savored a mouthful of turnips. "So, if those dogs didnae lead him directly to anyone else's door, he has to wonder why they came to mine."

"I suspect he will. So, the children and I should leave ere he comes back and brings more men with him."

"Nay, ye and the children arenae leaving." He held up his hand when she started to argue. "He must tread warily with me for all the same reasons I must do so with him. Aye, and a few more. After all, if he believes I am aiding ye in any way, then he will believe ye have told me everything." He frowned slightly when she paled.

"Then he will most certainly want ye dead," she whispered and then shook her head. "Nay, I cannae allow that. I foolishly thought that, because ye and Roderick were so evenly matched, that ye would be safe. I forgot, or chose to forget, how virulently he fights to keep his secrets. And, now that he believes we have met, he will be eager to silence ye."

"Kirstie," he snapped, grasping her by the wrist and yanking her back down into her seat when she started to rise, "ye chose me to aid ye in this battle. I chose to accept the challenge. I didnae accept it with any qualifications such as, if it grows dangerous, I will be done with it. Ye must cease thinking of leaving each time Roderick draws near to me."

"But, I dinnae want ye hurt or killed or hunted."

"Just ye and the bairns? Aye, he may have forgotten about the wee ones, but nay Callum."

"Callum could stay with ye." She knew her arguments were foolish, but fear for his safety forced her to offer them.

"He willnae and ye ken it. The moment ye cast me aside as your champion, Callum will step up to take my place. He will consider it his duty to help ye and keep ye safe. And, if ye are caught, he will try to rescue you. Ye ken it weel, lass, for all ye are struggling to deny the truth. The other truth ye keep trying to deny is that the moment Roderick learns that ye ken who I am, that ye might have confided in me, he will wish me dead. Ye cannae take the battle away from my door any longer, lass. If 'tis any comfort, love, Roderick would have cast a suspicious eye my way soon anyway, for he will track down the source of the rumors that begin to cause him so much trouble.''

She took a deep drink of wine as she thought over all he had just said. Kirstie admitted that she had boldly chosen him as her champion, but wavered over that choice at every hint of danger. She could not seem to make up her mind as to whether he was an ally or someone else she needed to protect. One chose a champion to fight a battle, not to stand at one's side only to shoo him away once things grew dangerous. That was foolish. And so, she thought as she frowned at him, was that last thing he had just said.

"Ye wouldnae have started those rumors had I not told ye what Roderick was.'' This time she held up a hand to stop his arguments. "I panicked. 'Tis as simple as that. The moment I approached ye, I put ye in danger. I must accept that and cease trying to halt what I started. I cannae. All I would do is separate the targets Roderick will take aim at and, in the end, that will probably aid him, nay us.''

"Now ye show some sense.'' He briefly raised his goblet in a toast before taking a drink.

"Aye, occasionally I do so,'' she drawled, "and ye would certainly think so this time as it means I agree with ye.'' She ignored his grin. "Nay, we are in this together 'til the end and I shall try to cease trying to put all back as it was when I was the only one Roderick wanted dead. In truth, it was ne'er only me, but Callum and, perhaps, e'en the younger children as weel. And, 'tisnae about us, either, but the bairns.''

"Aye, 'tis for the bairns.''

Kirstie sighed. "So, if Roderick decides ye were lying,

that ye *are* helping me, what do ye think he will do next?''

"I have no idea.''

"None?''

"Weel, I am certain it willnae be a direct attack. Nay, 'twill probably be subtle.''

"I see. And as ye wait for this subtle attack, what am I supposed to do?''

"Hide.''

CHAPTER TWELVE

Something was wrong. Payton moved amongst the courtiers and richly dressed women and sensed a change in the air. His presence seemed to stir an uneasiness amongst some, a coldness amongst others. Only one or two women cast him a flirtatious glance. No man cornered him to garner a piece of the favor they all thought the regents had blessed him with. Since Payton doubted anyone had started to believe his denial that he had any special blessing or favor from those worthies, it had to be something else. It was increasingly clear that no one wanted anything to do with him.

Even as Payton considered cornering one of the people who had sought his favor only recently, he spotted Sir Bryan MacMillan about to leave the great hall. Although it felt strange to hurry through the crowd with no hindrance, almost as if people stepped aside for fear of accidentally touching him, Payton did not hesitate in chasing Sir Bryan down. The man was no gossip himself, but he heard a great deal of what was being said. Payton caught up with the man just outside the great hall. He noticed that Sir Bryan was not surprised to be accosted by him.

"Ah, good. I have been watching for ye for two days." Sir Bryan caught Payton by the arm and led him down the narrow, torch-lit hallway. "We shall go to my room and talk."

The fact that Sir Bryan had been watching for him made Payton tense with a growing concern. He felt the walk to Bryan's room was painfully long, and the silence they maintained a little too ominous. By the time they reached the man's room, Payton was eager to demand that Bryan tell him everything he knew. He held his tongue, however, as the man poured them each some wine, then directed Payton to one of two small benches set before the fire.

"It was, perhaps, nay such a good time for ye to be away from court," Bryan said.

"I had business to attend to." He had had safety measures to be plotted and enacted, as well as devising escape routes and seeking out secure hiding places, but he was not ready to tell Bryan that. "Being the eyes and ears of the Murrays at court doesnae put bread upon my table. I was only gone for three days. It takes that long for the Regents to decide and agree upon what color tunic the wee king ought to wear."

Sir Bryan grinned and nodded, then quickly grew serious again. "Unfortunately, it takes but a day for gossip and rumor to spread and blacken a mon's good name. Did ye nay notice a change in the air when ye arrived?"

"Och, aye. A bite of frost. So, someone seeks to tarnish my name?" Payton inwardly cursed, certain who it was, yet a little surprised that anyone would still accept the man's word about anything.

"Aye. It seems Sir Roderick's young wife isnae dead." Sir Bryan's green eyes widened slightly at the harsh curse Payton muttered, but did not comment on it. "He is most aggrieved that, after he endangered his own soul trying to hide what he believed was her suicide, he now discovers she but tricked him. His men espied her in town. She was followed to your house, yet ye denied ye had e'er met her. As he says, what is a mon to think, but that ye have stolen away his wife, that the two of ye planned it all so that ye might be together.''

"And none questioned this tale? None wondered if, mayhap, a mon I have warned so many about just might lie about me?''

"Sir Roderick strongly suggests that your foul campaign against him is born of the fact that ye have always coveted his wife. And, let us be brutally honest, Payton, ye arenae innocent of the sin of cuckolding a mon.''

"True, but I have ne'er had to steal another mon's wife and hide her away.''

"Nay, they come to ye most easily and readily. A fact that irritates many a mon, especially those who have a wife they believe has entertained ye in her bed or one who would like to. The tale caters to the envy and jealousies of far too many for them to discard it.''

"Despite the fact that the accusation falls from the lips of a mon who buggers little boys? Beats them? Has e'en killed some? They see that foul stain upon God's earth as some font of truth, do they?'' Payton quickly took a deep drink to still his tongue, but could tell by the look upon Sir Bryan's face that he had already said too much to have it ignored.

" 'Tis what ye implied before and Uven's feelings about the mon caused me to heed the warning, subtle as it was, but are ye certain, Payton? Are ye verra certain? If 'tis only his wife who claims such things,'' Bryan began cautiously.

"Nay, not just his wife.''

Payton realized he was going to have to tell the man everything. Roderick's attack was a clever one, although Payton was surprised it had worked so well. In truth, he was a little surprised the man had done this, for Sir Roderick was a proud, arrogant man. Yet he was telling all who would listen that he had been cuckolded, that his wife had left him. It was, perhaps, a sign of the man's desperation, but Payton was not in the mood to fully appreciate that possibility.

"Does it put in doubt all the warnings I gave about the mon?" he asked.

"It weakens them, but nay with the laddies themselves," replied Bryan, and he sighed. "I think many of them kenned what the mon was, but didnae dare act so until we who should protect them started to acknowledge it. I think some were e'en asked directly about the truth of the rumors. So, nay, all your warnings havenae been ignored. Those who now feel the warnings were, as Sir Roderick claims, naught but ugly slander, probably didnae believe them to begin with or didnae want to. Yet, Payton, it doesnae matter much to his claim that ye stole his wife."

"I didnae steal her. She came to me, along with five children she had rescued from her husband, plus one other she found later. A poor lad of but seven years who was beaten nigh unto death." Taking a deep breath, Payton proceeded to tell Sir Bryan everything from the moment Kirstie had found him lurking beneath Lady Fraser's window.

"Jesu," Sir Bryan muttered when Payton finished his tale. "The mon wants gutting." He frowned. "Yet, ye hold his wife from him. Nay matter what the reasons, that could cause ye a great deal of trouble if 'tis proven or that fool is believed. Unless ye can prove Sir Roderick has done all ye say, then ye become the one who has erred. Because of your reputation with the lasses, Sir Roderick doesnae have the same need to actually prove what he claims. Some of his kinsmen are here and they are already making some verra dire threats."

"I cannae understand how it is his kinsmen havenae seen what he is," Payton muttered.

" 'Tis a difficult thing for people to accept. Yet, stealing a mon's wife—"

"She isnae his wife!" Payton snapped, then sighed and nodded his acceptance when Bryan moved to refill their goblets.

"They were married by a priest," Sir Bryan said.

"I dinnae care if the pope himself said the words— she isnae his wife. He ne'er bedded her. Not once in five years. The marriage was ne'er consummated."

"But, that could be the answer to this trouble. If ye bring her forward and she allows herself to be examined, once she is proven a virgin, it will weaken Sir Roderick's claims against ye, and strengthen yours against him."

"I wish I had thought of that."

"Ye wish? Oh, dear."

"Aye, she isnae a virgin now."

"Ye seduced a virgin who had sought your protection?"

"Aye." Payton shook his head. "I suppose that isnae much better than stealing a mon's wife. But, ye havenae seen the lass. And, she was in my home for three weeks, tormenting me."

"Tormenting ye?" Bryan asked, unable to keep his amusement out of his voice.

"Fine, I ken there is no excuse, though I had thought those might serve." He smiled briefly when Bryan laughed. "She was in my home for a week ere I finally admitted to myself that I had to have her. Then she told me nay for a fortnight. And suddenly, she walks into my bedchamber and says aye. Weel, I am only a mon, ye ken."

"Weel, we cannae use my excellent plan, that is certain. We shall have to come up with another. Mayhap ye should tell your family all about this. I am rather surprised ye havenae done so already."

"I was afraid that, if I couldnae find some hard proof of Roderick's crimes, all I would do is turn the wrath of his rather powerful family upon my kinsmen. By telling ye, I may have already risked that."

"Their wrath is swiftly turning your way now. Roderick

isnae openly asking for their aid, but they see his shame
as theirs. I think the only reason they havenae showed
up at your door to cut ye into wee, bloody pieces is
because they are hesitant to start what could be a long,
bloody feud with your kinsmen. I sensed that from the
cautious way they questioned me about ye just yest-
ereve."

"I hope ye were appropriately outraged over this slur
against me," Payton drawled.

"Aye. I bristled most impressively at the heavily
implied insult and strongly reminded them that the
last thing ye needed to do was steal a woman for your
pleasure," Bryan replied with a faint smile, then grew
serious again. "They are hesitant to act simply upon
Roderick's word. I got the feeling he isnae weel thought
of by his kinsmen."

"But that willnae stop them from avenging this
insult."

"Nay. I would guess ye have a sennight or less ere
they bestir themselves to act." Bryan stood up and patted Payton on the shoulder. "Go home, keep yourself
out of sight for a wee while, and think of a plan. I wish
I had more cunning, but I am a verra poor plotter. I
will, however, keep an ear to the ground and alert ye
to any approaching threat. And, if any of your other
kinsmen come round, I will send them to you."

"If they hear these rumors, ye willnae have to." Payton finished off his wine and started to leave. "Ye watch
your back. If Roderick e'en thinks I have told ye the
whole story, he will want ye dead."

"I will be careful. If naught else, the nightmares your
tale will undoubtedly give me will remind me of the
danger. And, 'tis my opinion, 'tis past time ye had some
allies, some who ken the full truth. Go, and come up
with a clever plan. I will try to grasp at one myself, but
I shouldnae hold out much hope."

"Ah, dinnae belittle yourself, cousin. Ye are clever.

Ye are just nay verra devious, which isnae such a bad thing."

And devious was what he now had to be, thought Payton, as he headed home. He had slipped away from the castle like a thief in the night, which had galled him, but he knew it was the wisest way. If Roderick's kinsmen came face-to-face with him, they might not wait to be shown some proof of Roderick's claims. It might soothe his pride to stand fast and prove Roderick lied through some manly trial by fire, but he could also get himself wounded, even killed. Kirstie and the children needed him hale and ready to protect them. So, he would sneak around and try to think of some way to come at Roderick from behind.

By the time he entered his home, he was angry. Where were the people he had thought his friends? Payton could not believe how quickly everyone had turned against him, had distanced themselves. It seemed only Bryan, a kinsman only through marriage, was ready to defend him and stand by him. Striding into his ledger room, he poured himself a large tankard of wine and wondered if he had fallen too completely into the shallow ways of court life, into the ways of empty flattery and fleeting, false intimacy.

A pounding on his front door startled him out of his increasingly morbid thoughts. When Kirstie burst into his ledger room, he tensed. She looked afraid.

"Who is it?" he asked, setting down his tankard and walking toward her.

"I dinnae ken," she replied. "I was caught out in the hall as the door opened and this was the closest room. I hope ye have a place for me to hide in here. Nay matter who it is, they cannae find me here."

That was truer than she knew, but he would have to tell her all about the newest twists in their campaign later. Payton grabbed her by the arm, led her over to a heavy tapestry hung upon the wall, and pulled it aside.

Behind the long tapestry was an alcove, just the right size for an armed man to hide.

"Ye have some verra odd little niches and rooms in your house, Payton," she murmured.

"Stranger than ye ken." He pointed to a piece of stone which stuck out just a little. "Push that in and a door will open behind ye. Hide in there if ye e'en think ye may be discovered here. Now, get in there."

The moment she stepped up into the alcove and turned to face him, Payton moved to kiss her. She was just leaning toward him when she heard Ian arguing with some woman, the voices rapidly drawing nearer. Kirstie placed a hand upon Payton's chest and scowled at him when, a heartbeat later, she recognized the woman's voice. The startled look upon Payton's face indicated he had not expected this visitor, but that only eased Kirstie's annoyance a little. She could all too easily recall that, when she had first approached Payton, he had been about to crawl in this woman's window and spend a long, lusty night in her arms.

"Am I to be stuck here whilst ye tryst with Lady Fraser?" she hissed.

"Dinnae be an idiot," he admonished, then gave her a quick kiss before dropping the tapestry back down in front of her. "Do what ye do so weel—be verra still and verra quiet."

Kirstie hastily swallowed a sharp curse. The sensible part of her knew Payton had arranged no tryst, especially not here where he was hiding so much. When it came to the fulsome, fair Lady Fraser, however, Kirstie knew she could not be completely sensible. The woman had all Kirstie felt she lacked, such as a highly praised beauty and full curves. She could not fully banish the fear that Payton would look at his little dove Lady Fraser and wonder why he was bedding a scrawny crow.

"So, here is where ye are hiding," said Lady Fraser as she flung open the door to the room and glared at Payton, ignoring the scowling Ian close at her back.

"M'lady?" Payton noticed Ian nervously looking around the room and reassured him with a quick glance at the tapestry before signaling him to leave. "I wasnae expecting ye. Have I been a callous swine and forgotten some assignation we arranged?"

"Ye are a callous swine," she said as she marched up to him, "but, nay, no assignation was planned. Now I ken why. I tried to catch ye at court, but ye slipped away. Where is she?"

"She?" Payton began to think he had made a lucky escape when he had been drawn away from the woman's window, for she was acting both jealous and possessive. He had obviously missed seeing this aspect of her character when he had considered having a liaison with her.

"Lady Kirstie MacIye, that wee shadow of a wife Sir Roderick must claim. She is why ye have been ignoring me. I cannae believe ye would choose that too-thin child o'er what I was so willing to give ye."

"It pains me, m'lady, that ye are so quick to judge me in the wrong, so ready to believe the whispered lies of a mon like Sir Roderick MacIye." Payton wanted to tell her that he did, indeed, prefer what Kirstie could give him, but stung vanity had brought Lady Fraser to his door, and he knew it would be very unwise to add to her sense of injury, even if he could admit to Kirstie's presence.

"Sir Roderick isnae whispering. He is fair to shouting his claims of insult. Why would he shame himself with talk of being cuckolded by ye, of ye stealing his wife away, if it wasnae all true? That makes no sense at all."

"Nay? The mon's wife has deserted him. 'Tis something all would soon learn of e'en if he didnae admit it. Mayhap he but chooses to accuse me o'er any others. I do have something of a reputation. He may think to dim his shame with the sympathy of others. And mayhap he seeks to turn all eyes away from him, away from his own sins."

She crossed her arms beneath her chest and frowned

for a moment. "Oh, ye mean all that talk about him favoring the wee lads. Someone did mention that most of the talk about that was coming from you. Although, why ye should worry so o'er the matter, especially when the mon seeks out those ragged, unwanted wretches cluttering every alley, I dinnae ken. And, what does that have to do with ye stealing his wife?"

Payton was appalled by the way the woman showed no concern at all for the abused children. Suddenly, he knew that, even if he found himself alone again, he would not seek out her bed. He would feel soiled. It was unsettling enough to think that he had once lusted after this woman. He saw it all as even more proof that he had been at court too long, had become too thoroughly ensnared in the emptiness of it all.

"I didnae steal his wife," he said, fighting to hide his sudden distaste for this woman.

"Oh." She suddenly smiled and wrapped her arms around his neck. "Weel, then, since we are alone—"

"Ah, such temptation." He touched a kiss to her mouth before gently tugging her arms away. "Yet, I must find the strength to turn away from it." Seeing the anger darkening her face, he hurried to add, "Sir Roderick may be tossing lies about, but his kinsmen are listening. I must warn my own kinsmen of the trouble that may soon kick in my door, a trouble that could all too easily darken their thresholds as weel. I must work fast, hard, and untiringly if I am to turn aside this trouble before it becomes some senseless, bloody feud."

It took several more moments of explanations, flatteries, and false, vague promises, plus a few kisses, before he got her to leave. About the only good he could think of which might come from Lady Fraser's visit was that the woman would tell everyone who would listen that Lady MacIye was not with Sir Payton. The moment he returned from escorting Lady Fraser to the door and pulled aside the tapestry, Payton decided he was right to think that. Kirstie was looking at him as if he was some foul muck staining her slippers. It struck him as odd that he should find Kirstie's apparent jealousy a pure delight, yet be irritated by Lady Fraser's.

"She is gone now," he said as he helped her out of the alcove and kept a firm grip upon her hand to keep her from leaving.

"Aye, trotting home to her bed to think on all the delights ye promised her," she snapped, then inwardly cursed herself for sounding like a jealous shrew.

"Nay. If ye think o'er what was said, I ne'er said I would do all that, just that I would like to."

Kirstie stared at him in furious amazement. "And that is supposed to make me feel better?" She scowled at him when, after a moment of what looked to be surprise, he suddenly grinned. "Ye find this amusing?"

"Nay, not ye. Myself, I fear. After pouring honey all o'er Lady Fraser, I find it rather amusing that, when I open my mouth to speak to ye, I promptly stick both feet in it." He pulled her into his arms, ignoring her stiffness. "Ah, lass, she means naught, though she obviously thinks she ought to. In truth, as she stood there acting as if she had rights I ne'er gave her, I thought how fortunate I was that ye pulled me away from her window that night."

She started to relax against him. "I am sure it is still open for ye."

"It can stay open 'til the winter's snow blows in. I willnae be crawling through it. Nay, when she shrugged aside the plight of the children as if 'twas naught, I kenned that, nay matter what happens atween us, I willnae be sharing her bed. 'Twould leave me feeling soiled."

The woman's callous dismissal of the abuse of children had both saddened and infuriated Kirstie, but she was a little surprised that Payton would find it so distasteful. If, as Ian said, Payton simply took what was offered, why should he care what a woman thought or felt? It was probably one of those manly attitudes she would never understand. She had come across such puzzles with her brothers from time to time.

"Oh!" She leaned back to look at him as she recalled some of the other things she had overheard. "Ye now ken Roderick's plans."

"Aye. He means to do to me as I did to him." Payton moved to a chair and sat down, pulling Kirstie down onto his lap. " 'Twas something of a shock to discover that I could become a pariah in but a day or so. He is telling all who will listen that ye and I planned your supposed drowning so that we could be together and that, e'en when ye were seen coming to my house, I denied e'en kenning who ye were. I am the vile stealer of wives and he is the poor cuckolded victim."

"And people are actually listening to such nonsense?" she asked.

"I fear so." He began to idly rub his hand up and down her leg, subtly inching up her skirts so that, soon, he could easily slip his hand beneath them. "As Sir Bryan says, some of that readiness to heed the mon's tale is my own fault. I have cuckolded a few men." He ignored her snort of disbelief over his claim of only a few. "Yet, I had thought I had friends there, ones who wouldnae believe such a tale, might e'en come to my defense."

"Obviously Sir Bryan is a true friend." She stroked his cheek and nestled her face against his neck in a silent show of sympathy over his obvious disappointment.

"He is a cousin by marriage."

"We both ken such a thin relation doesnae stand by ye nay matter what. He does it because he is a friend."

"Aye, I suppose he is, and far truer than most. 'Tis clear the others only tried to ingratiate themselves with one they felt held the favor of the regents as he once held the favor of the king. Now that I may risk losing that favor, they dinnae want to be within a mile of me. I decided I must have been too long at court, for I wasnae aware of the falsity of so much that is said and done. 'Tis probably time to let another Murray come to court to keep an ear to the ground. I have become too deeply sunk into the game of empty flatteries and fake smiles."

She nodded. "My father said it was probably a good thing we are such a small clan no one notices, for otherwise we might have to go to court. He said it was a midden heap of lies, betrayals, and hunger for power. Said the people there were like one of those dogs ye think is all friendly, sweet-natured, and obedient, until, one day, when ye are nay looking, it bites ye right in the arse." She smiled when he laughed, pleased she could raise his spirits, if only briefly. "Lady Fraser seemed willing to believe in ye," she murmured.

"For a wee while. It soothes her vanity."

"Weel, I suspicion she has some right to be a wee bit vain. She is verra beautiful." Kirstie could not fully repress a sigh. "Verra fulsome, too."

Kirstie gave a small squeak of surprise when Payton suddenly stood up with her in his arms. She quickly wrapped her arms around his neck to steady herself. It was not until he was opening the door that she recovered from her shock enough to say anything. Even as she opened her mouth to speak, he opened the door, and there stood Ian. Kirstie groaned and hid her blush-warmed face against Payton's neck.

"I came to tell ye that we will dine in an hour," Ian said, grinning widely.

"Ah, good," said Payton as he started up the stairs to his bedchamber. "That should be enough time."

Hearing Ian laugh, Kirstie groaned again. Then curiosity banished her embarrassment. She lifted her head to look at Payton as he entered his bedchamber and kicked the door shut behind him.

"Enough time for what?" she asked.

"To show ye that bigger isnae always better," he replied.

Kirstie opened her mouth to tell him to stop his non-sense. Then she realized what he planned to do and quickly shut it again. In all honesty, she could not think of a more pleasant way to spend an hour than letting Payton Murray try to convince her she was more desir-able than the very well endowed Lady Fraser.

CHAPTER THIRTEEN

It was not easy, but Kirstie hid her feelings of horror over the bloody and bruised little boy Callum brought to her. She had come into Payton's ledger room to try to compose a letter to her family, one that would tell them enough to assure them she was safe, yet not enough to alarm or enrage them. That problem seemed very small compared to the one that confronted her at the moment.

She heartily wished Wee Alice was home as she sat the boy down and, with Callum fetching the things she needed, did her meager best to tend to his injuries. Poor Simon seemed unable to stop shivering, even after she served him some watered wine and honey cakes. The way he devoured the honey cakes, revealing all too clearly that he was starved for food, both saddened and infuriated her. By the looks of the couple who were supposed to care for children like Simon, the Darrochs fed their own healthy appetites regularly. She pretended not to notice how Simon shoved two of the cakes into the pocket of his ragged coat.

"Better now, Simon?" she asked, although the boy still acted terrified.

"Aye," he answered and quickly took another gulp of wine. "I *had* to come here."

"Of course ye did," she murmured in a soothing voice, although she thought it a rather odd thing to say.

Kirstie wished someone else was at home, that it was not just herself and Callum. It felt odd to be so alone. Since Roderick had come to his door a week ago, there had been an uncomfortably close guard kept on her and the children. Today, however, being warm and sunny, had prompted Wee Alice to convince Ian that the children needed to get out. With the judicious use of coats and caps, she felt they should be able to safely take the five youngest out into the wood to collect herbs and berries. Callum had been invited to go along, but had declared himself Kirstie's guard for the day. Ian had taken one of the three guards Payton had posted outside with him and Payton was back at court trying to dim the poisonous effects of Roderick's campaign against him. That left two guards outside and, although she scolded herself for being a nervous coward, Kirstie suddenly did not think it was enough.

And why had those guards not brought Simon to her, she asked herself as she slowly stood up. It was possible Simon had gotten to the back entrance unseen, but not very likely. Kirstie did not like to be suspicious of a child, yet what better way to keep her too occupied to notice anything was wrong than to send her a battered child in need of care? Had she not stayed in one place, never questioning, never looking?

"Callum, did ye see Donald when ye opened the door to Simon?" she asked.

"Nay." Callum scowled. "He should have been in the back, aye?"

"Aye." She saw how pale Simon was and began to think it was not all due to the pain he must be feeling. "And Malkie?"

Callum started to glare at Simon. "Nay. Him neither."

Kirstie looked at Simon, who started to cry. "Oh, Simon, my poor laddie, what have ye done?"

"He has assisted me in taking back what is mine."

A chill so sharp it made her shiver went through Kirstie as she turned to look at the man standing in the doorway. Roderick looked much the same, fair in coloring and solid in build. Although her eyes had been somewhat spoiled by Payton's beauty, she had to admit that her husband was handsome in his way, except for the look in his pale blue eyes. At the moment, those cold eyes shimmered with malevolent triumph.

Wattie and Gib lurked right behind him as they always did. A widely grinning Gib stepped forward and Kirstie tensed, subtly pulling her dagger from the sheath hidden beneath a thin opening in her skirts. The man held a tiny, silently weeping girl, and Kirstie knew exactly what had forced Simon to help these men. Beating the boy had obviously not been enough. She eased herself between the men and the children after Gib shoved the little girl toward her and she ran straight to Simon.

"Run, Callum," she ordered, keeping her voice low in the hope that a gloating Roderick would not hear her.

"Nay, I must protect ye," Callum said in an equally soft voice as he stood beside her, a dagger in his hand.

Glancing at the boy, Kirstie noticed the big knife he favored was still sheathed at his side. She idly wondered just how many weapons the boy now carried. Keeping her gaze fixed upon Roderick, who seemed to be content to stand there and savor his victory for a while, she knew she would have to give her valiant protector a very good reason to leave.

"Simon, take your sister and start edging toward that big tapestry on the wall," she ordered, still keeping her voice low and trying to move her lips as little as possible.

"Why are ye helping that traitor?" muttered Callum.

" 'Tis clear how ye got that poor boy to help ye," she

said to Roderick in a normal voice, but intending the explanation for Callum. As she had hoped, all three men fixed their gazes upon her. "Beating the child wasnae enough?" In a whispered aside, she ordered Callum, "Go. Someone needs to tell Payton what has happened and as soon as possible."

"But, he will kill ye," Callum whispered back.

"Nay too quickly. He likes to gloat. Go. Now." A faint whisper of sound told her he was obeying her with as much stealth as possible.

"The boy was surprisingly reluctant to assist me," drawled Roderick. "I told him my dogs had trailed ye and Callum right to the well at the children's home, but the boy dared to lie to me and claim he had ne'er seen or heard of either of ye. Our attempts to persuade him to be more truthful failed, so we decided he might care more about his sister's life than his own. Or yours. Ye do collect a rather sad clutch of allies, m'dear."

"Such brave, stout men ye are, threatening and pounding on bairns," she sneered.

"Ye should be more temperate in your speech, m'dear. Ye are now back in your husband's loving grasp."

"I am nay leaving here."

"Oh, aye, ye are." He started to walk toward her, Gib and Wattie slinking along behind him.

She held her dagger out, smiling coldly when all three men stopped. "Aye, I see ye hesitate. But then I am nay a child and I am armed. Ye ne'er were any good at confronting an enemy to his face. Or hers. And, there isnae any river near at hand for ye to toss me into."

"I wouldnae try that again. At some time during our five years of marriage ye might have told me ye could swim."

Kirstie wondered just how insane her husband was. He sounded irritated, even grieved, that she had kept a secret from him, a secret that had ruined his plan to murder her. Roderick was acting as if she had failed

him as a wife, even committed some grave sin with her
reluctance to confide everything in him, her husband.

"We didnae talk much, Roderick," she replied with
a hard-won calm.

"Those little bastards are escaping," yelled Gib.

Roderick cursed even as Gib and Wattie bolted forward. Kirstie managed to trip Wattie, but Gib reached
the tapestry the children were just disappearing behind.
He suddenly bellowed and staggered back, a dagger
buried deep in his upper arm. Kirstie breathed a sigh
of relief when she heard the scrape of stone on stone
and knew the children had shut the hidden door behind
them. As Gib and Wattie wasted several moments taking
turns trying to open the door into the passageway the
children were fleeing down, Kirstie faced her husband
again.

"Ye are a troublesome lass," Roderick said in a tight,
cold voice that told Kirstie he was having difficulty
restraining his temper. "Where did they go?"

"Why should I ken what little hidey-holes and escape
routes Callum has found?" she asked, moving slightly
when Gib and Wattie moved to flank Roderick, for she
wanted to keep all three men in sight.

"E'en if ye havenae searched this whole house for
places to hide and ways out, that little bastard Callum
would have told ye of all he found. Despite all my efforts
to educate him, he retains a softness for the lasses."

"Educate him? Is that what ye call the foul perversions
ye force on the children? Education?"

He shook his head and sighed. " 'Tis evident the
lecherous Sir Payton hasnae added much to your understanding of the pleasures and needs of the flesh. I do
the children no harm. In truth, I give many of them a
far better life than they had, for I give them warm clothing, food, and clean beds. I but ask a small service in
return for my largesse. What harm is there in that?"

She wondered if he truly believed what he said. Kirstie

had the chilling feeling that he did. "And the ones ye kill?"

Roderick shrugged. "They would have died anyway, if left where they were."

"Ye are long overdue for killing, Roderick," she said, her voice icy, her tone fierce, as she wondered if she could do it herself.

"Nay, my curse, ye are." He made a languid movement with his hand. "And ye have played this game quite long enough. I dinnae intend to be here when those thick-witted guards wake or one of your champions returns."

Kirstie inwardly cursed. That had only been a tentative hope, but he had just effectively killed it. She tensed and adjusted her grip on her dagger as she prepared for the attempt to capture her. They would undoubtedly succeed, for she was no match against three men, but she hoped she could inflict some memorable pain before they succeeded.

"Get her, lads," Roderick ordered his men. "Do watch out for that dagger. She may ken how to use it."

For a few moments, Kirstie was able to hold Gib and Wattie at bay. She even gave each man a painful, if minor, wound. Unfortunately, that only increased their determination to get her. The men were not particularly smart, but they did know how to fight. They also proved very skillful at keeping her away from the door and window. Kirstie doubted she would have been able to get through either, but she would have liked the chance to try.

When Wattie managed to get behind her, Kirstie knew it was over. She managed to give Gib another good scratch with her dagger, however, before Wattie wrapped his thick arms around her. A soft cry of pain escaped her when Gib viciously twisted her wrist as he took the dagger out of her hand. Despite knowing she had little chance of breaking free, Kirstie wriggled and kicked in Wattie's hold as he turned to face Roderick.

The gloating, malicious smile on her husband's square face so infuriated Kirstie that she went very still for a moment. She knew his glee was born of the knowledge that he could now murder her at his whim. It was past bearing. Kirstie gave him what she suspected was an equally malicious smile, then kicked him in the groin as hard as she could.

Kirstie was able to savor her success for one brief moment. Roderick went white, clutched himself, then sank to his knees. Both Gib and Wattie cursed as Roderick nearly sobbed with pain, then retched. She detected a note of admiration in Gib and Wattie's voices. It had been a vicious strike from someone who should have been cowed, and Kirstie suspected the two brutes respected that even though they would never tolerate it.

As Roderick staggered back to his feet, Kirstie braced for the retribution she knew would come. Since it would be far too troublesome for them to carry her away while she was still concious, she knew she would have been knocked out anyway. At least she had struck a telling blow herself first, and there was some satisfaction in that. The fury sparkling in Roderick's eyes told her she would suffer a far more punishing blow than she might have before, however.

Even expecting the strike, and knowing it would be a forceful one, when it came it was still a shock. Her head snapped back and, despite the blinding pain in her jaw, she was fleetingly aware of a sharp one in the back of her head, as well. As blackness rolled over her, Kirstie heard Wattie cursing and knew that the second pain had come from the back of her head smashing into Wattie's jaw. She smiled.

"Jesu, Roderick," Wattie muttered, holding Kirstie's limp body with one arm as he tested his jaw for breaks with his other hand. "Ye could have warned me."

"Ye kenned we would have to silence the bitch,"

Roderick said as he rubbed his knuckles. "Is her jaw broken?"

After checking Kirstie's jaw, Wattie shook his head. "Nay," he replied as he flung her body over his shoulder. "We best get out of here." He did not wait for any response, but immediately headed for the door.

"What about those three brats?" asked Gib as he and Roderick followed Wattie out of the house.

"We will get them," said Roderick as they walked past one of the unconcious, tightly bound guards.

"Sure we shouldnae kill those guards?"

"At the moment, what I am doing is perfectly legal. I am simply retrieving my chattel. Cluttering my path with dead men gains me naught, could e'en cause me trouble. 'Tis probably best Callum slipped away. I would have been sorely tempted to use the ungrateful little bastard's body to send Sir Payton a clear and bloody message. That may have been satisfying, but it would also have been a mistake."

"Then ye probably cannae kill this bitch too soon," said Wattie when they reached their horses.

Roderick mounted carefully, cursing softly over the lingering pain in his groin, and waved Wattie away when he tried to hand him Kirstie. "Ye carry the bitch." He watched as Gib helped Wattie mount, then settle the unconcious Kirstie in the man's arms. "And, aye, I shall be forced to keep her alive for a while. However, I plan to make her deeply rue each added moment of life." He kicked his mount into a gallop, knowing his men would follow him closely all the way back to Thanescarr.

Callum slipped out from behind a tree and watched the three men carry Kirstie away. He had suspected the man would take her back to Thanescarr, but had needed to be certain. His fingers wrapped tightly around the hilt of his knife, he strode back to where Simon and his sister Brenda stood by the unconcious guards. As he walked past the well, he filled a bucket with water and tossed it over the guards' faces. While they sputtered awake, he cut their bonds.

"What happened?" Malkie asked in an unsteady voice as he cautiously sat up.

"Sir Roderick took Lady Kirstie," replied Callum. "She made me leave to take this traitor to safety."

Malkie looked at Simon, his eyes widened, and then he looked back at Callum. "Did ye do that?"

"Nay, though I would have liked to." Callum sighed. "For a wee while, 'til Lady Kirstie made me see that he couldnae help being a sneaky, cowardly traitor. If ye look close, ye can probably see a wee bit of a lass sticking out around Simon. 'Tis his sister Brenda cowering behind the fool. Roderick and his swine got hold of her and made Simon help them."

"I am so sorry," whispered Simon, wiping at the steady flow of tears on his bruised face with a ragged sleeve. "They told me they would kill her like they killed my fither."

"They told ye they had killed your fither?" asked Callum.

"Aye." Simon took several deep breaths and began to grow steadier.

"Then ye had best stay with us. Ye and wee Brenda."

"Nay. I ken 'tis my fault Lady Kirstie got took away. Me and Brenda will go back to the Darrochs."

"And be dead faster than I can spit. They told ye they murdered your fither. Think they want ye telling anyone about that? Nay. Stay here." Callum sighed somewhat dramatically. "I suspicion I can forgive ye." He looked at Malkie and Donald, who were watching him with a mixture of amusement and astonishment. "They rode out toward Thanescarr. Thought they would, but followed a ways just to be sure. Lady Kirstie was all limp, but I dinnae think she is dead."

"Payton is going to skin us alive," muttered Malkie as he stood up and helped a groggy Donald to his feet.

"Should I go fetch him?" asked Callum.

"Nay, lad. Ye would barely get to the castle ere he would be headed home and he would still have to come here first. That is, if he is e'en at the castle. Nay, stay here, rest, and eat, and start thinking about ways we might get into Thanescarr to get her ladyship out of there."

"I dinnae need to rest or eat, and I already ken how to get into Thanescarr."

"Weel, ye cannae run off and save her all by yourself."

"I ken it. I will go fetch Strong Ian. I ken where he went and Sir Payton will be wanting him here, ready and waiting, aye?" When both Malkie and Donald nodded, Callum carefully checked his weapons, then cursed. "I am missing a dagger. Stuck one in that pig Gib. Hope he didnae steal it."

"Just how many knives do ye have on ye, lad?" asked Malkie, staring at Callum in wonder.

"Had six. Still, I suspicion I dinnae need that many to go and fetch Strong Ian home. The ones I need to keep watch for are all riding fast for Thanescarr, arenae they?" he muttered and kicked at a stone. "I wasnae a verra good protector."

Malkie patted the boy on the shoulder. "Neither were we, lad, and we dinnae have the excuse of being only eleven."

"I shouldnae have heeded her when she told me to take Simon and Brenda to safety. I should have stayed by her side."

"Nay. Ye did just as ye ought. Ye helped the children, ye obeyed your lady's command as ye should, and now ye are here to help us rescue her. She probably kenned ye have information that could help us and wanted to be sure ye lived."

"Weel, mayhap." He took a deep breath to steady himself. "I will go fetch Ian home."

Watching the boy trot away, Donald looked at Malkie. "Are ye sure that lad is only eleven?"

Malkie laughed. "Aye. Eleven going on thirty. Come, Simon and Brenda. Best we get inside. Callum may not need rest and food, but I do. I will need all the strength I can garner to face Sir Payton with the news that we lost his lady."

Callum hurried along the path Ian had told him they would take to the woods. He felt afraid, tears stinging his eyes, and he hated the feeling. Although it had been a long time since he had seen Roderick, one look at the man had brought all the old, ugly feelings back, and he still felt sick. He hated that feeling, too.

Strong Ian was teaching him how to be strong, but now, Callum knew he was not strong enough yet. He was still a scared little boy inside. He wanted to sit down and cry, wail like a wee bairn. Callum swore he would not let Sir Roderick make him weak again, would not let that man make him cry.

Starting to run, he told himself that Kirstie loved him. He had to save her. She was the only one who had ever cared about him and he could not let that beast have her. Losing Kirstie would also make Sir Payton, Strong Ian, and Wee Alice unhappy, and he could not let that happen, either. They were all kind to him, treated him like a normal little boy, even as a soon-to-be man, even though they all knew about what Sir Roderick had done to him. He had a place with them, one where he did not have to be afraid or ashamed, and he would not let the beast take it away.

He felt a sob choke him and swallowed it. Despite all his prayers, the beast was back. He was making everything dark and frightening and horrible again. Callum started to mutter every curse he knew. He would not let the beast win. He would not let the beast hurt his lady and his friends. Then he felt someone grab his arm and panic ruled.

"Here, now, laddie, what ails ye?" Ian's eyes widened

when Callum pulled a dagger from inside his sleeve.
"Now, 'tis Ian, lad. Aye? Ye ken I willnae hurt ye. Ye
can put the knife away."

Callum stared at the dagger in his hand, then at Ian.
He had almost stabbed his friend, the man who was
helping him get strong. It was all the beast's fault, he
thought as he sheathed his knife. When a worried Alice
handed him a wineskin, Callum drank greedily from it
and felt the cool cider start to calm him.

"The beast has taken Lady Kirstie," he said, and
frowned when Alice started to wipe his face with a clean
scrap of linen. Then he realized his face was wet with
tears. "I was running so fast the wind stung my eyes
bad."

"Aye, laddie, it can do that sometimes," she said and
began to pat the shoulders of the five children now
huddled all around her skirts. "Do ye mean Sir Roderick
when ye speak of the beast?"

"Aye." Callum gave them a quick explanation of what
had happened. "I couldnae protect my lady," he confessed in a soft, unsteady voice, and fixed his gaze upon
Ian. "I wanted to, but she told me to go, to take Simon
and Brenda away."

"Which is exactly what ye should have done," said
Ian. "Get the bairns in the cart, Alice. We need to hurry
home."

"This is all my fault," Alice said, fighting tears. "Ye
would have been there to help her if I hadnae forced
ye out here."

"Ye didnae force me, and 'tisnae your fault, either.
Get in the cart, lad," he told Callum. "Ye need to rest
and get your strength back as I am thinking we will
need your help to get Lady Kirstie back."

For a while Callum did as he was told, but he was
quick to get his strength back. Soon after his breathing
had grown steady and the trembling in his body had
faded, the cart he shared with the other children grew
too confining for him. He needed to do something, but

he knew he could not help Lady Kirstie, not yet. They had to get Sir Payton and make a plan. Finally, too agitated to sit still, he hopped out of the cart and moved to walk beside Strong Ian, who walked at the front of the cart Wee Alice drove, while the guard Angus walked behind.

"I thought I told ye to rest," Ian said to Callum, but his voice was calm, carrying no hint of a scold.

"I ken it," Callum replied, "but I was getting agitated e'en though I ken we cannae do anything yet."

"Agitated, is it?"

"Lady Kirstie taught me the word. It has a nice sound, I am thinking."

"Aye, it does. Makes ye sound clever, too."

"Good. But, I will try to be calm. We need to make a plan to get my lady back."

"Aye, we do," agreed Ian. " 'Tis hard to go slow at times, but 'tis for the best, and I suspicion we will have to make Payton recall that. Ye go charging in blind and all afire and the only thing ye will have on your side is luck. Weel, luck is a verra fickle thing. Nay, 'tis best to pause and use wit and cunning, especially when your enemy expects ye to come to him."

Callum lightly bit his lip, then asked quietly, "Sir Payton will want to rescue Lady Kirstie, aye?"

"Of course he will, lad. I will have to keep a tight grip on the reins to stop him from charging off blind to rescue his lady."

"Is she?"

Ian frowned down at the boy. "Is she what, lad?"

"Is she his lady? I thought she might be, but then I sometimes get to thinking she might just be someone he likes to tup."

"Ah." Ian glanced back at his wife, saw that she was busy talking to the other children so would not be listening to him, and then he looked back at Callum. "Ye really shouldnae speak of your lady that way, but I ken what ye mean. So, I will speak plain to ye. Aye, Payton is a bonnie rogue and has tupped more than his share of lasses. He doesnae see your lady as just one of those. I have been with him near all my life and I am certain he doesnae see her as just a bonnie lass to warm his bed for a wee while. For one thing, if one lass said *nay*, he would just go and find one who would say *aye*, and he didnae wait a fortnight to do it. He would have waited e'en longer for your lady."

"So, do ye think he will marry with her, make her truly his lady?"

"Now there is where I grow a wee bit uncertain. I think he would be a pure idiot not to." He exchanged a brief smile with Callum, who nodded his agreement. "I think they are a perfect match, but 'tis they who have to see it and they do seem intent upon making it all so verra complicated." Ian was thrilled when the boy chuckled, but forced himself to act as if it was no grand thing, as if the boy had not so recently been weeping and terrified.

Callum slipped his hand into Ian's and felt the man's steady calm wash over him. "I am so sorry I pulled a knife on ye. I was afeared of the beast again, for a wee while," he confided softly. "He took Lady Kirstie and I thought he would soon be turning everything sad and horrible again. But, we willnae let him, will we?"

"Nay, laddie, we willnae." He briefly, lightly, squeezed the boy's hand. "We will get wee Lady Kirstie back and put things right again. And, there may be some good to come of this."

"Oh, aye? What?"

"Weel, I am thinking having a wee taste of losing the lass might be enough to shake some sense into Payton."

CHAPTER FOURTEEN

"He doesnae seem to be verra sensible yet," Callum whispered to Ian as he watched Payton storm around the great hall.

Ian bit back a smile. "Nay, but I think he needs to rant a wee while."

"Oh. I hope he finishes soon as we need to do some planning and go get my lady."

"If he doesnae, I will go and give him a wee knock offside the head." He could not fully suppress a smile this time when Callum solemnly nodded as if that was a perfectly reasonable solution.

Payton saw Ian's fleeting smile and had to fight the urge to grab the man by the front of his doublet, shake him vigorously, and demand what he could possibly find so cursed amusing. He grasped the mantel of the huge fireplace, stared into the cold hearth, and fought for calm. He did not have to look behind him to know what waited there. Ian, Malkie, Donald, and Angus all waited for orders. Callum waited to tell him all he knew about the ways in and out of Thanescarr and to hear how they would rescue Kirstie. He was not sure why the poor, battered Simon was there, but suspected guilt made the boy want to do something to help.

He had arrived home in a foul mood, eager to find some calm and comfort in Kirstie's slender arms. The news that Roderick had taken Kirstie had been a hard blow. The man's talk of cuckoldry and wife theft had gotten Payton banished from the court. Now the man had Kirstie. Roderick was winning. It was intolerable.

His fear for Kirstie had soared swiftly and was like a live thing inside of him. There was a small scrap of comfort to be found in the knowledge that Roderick could not murder her now. Too much attention had been drawn to him and his wife. In truth, Roderick's talk of being a poor, cuckolded husband would now work in Kirstie's favor. If she turned up dead too soon after her husband had taken her back, everyone would assume Roderick had killed her for her unfaithfulness.

What troubled Payton were the thoughts of all the other things that could happen to Kirstie while in her husband's grasp. He could clearly recall all Callum had told him the day Roderick had discovered Kirstie was alive, all the man's two lackeys had said. Roderick could be handing her to Gib and Wattie even now. Those two brutes could hurt her badly, could easily kill all the sweet passion inside of her, with their abuse.

"Payton?" Ian called, his voice holding both sympathy and a call to action.

"Aye, my tantrum is done." He walked to the table where they all sat, poured himself some wine, and sat down to face them all. "Have ye thought of all the ways we might get into Thanescarr, Callum?"

"I have," Callum replied. "I think I ken them all. As I told my lady, I like to ken where the hiding places and the boltholes are. Didnae work so verra weel at Thanescarr, for Roderick kept a close watch on me. But, then, Kirstie and I found a few more. 'Tis how I escaped, how we got the bairns out."

"Do ye think Kirstie will try to get out through one of these ways?"

"She willnae be able to get to them. He will lock her in her bedchamber. I am nay sure why, but there is a way in to there, but nay a way out unless someone is in the passageway and opens the door for ye. There is no one at Thanescarr now who will do it for her."

"But, there are ways into Thanescarr that Roderick doesnae ken about?"

"Aye. And, I can get ye from one of them to the passage outside her bedchamber."

"Good. 'Tis enough. Odd that the mon doesnae ken such things," Payton murmured, suffering a flicker of doubt.

" 'Twas nay his home until he turned one and twenty," Callum said. " 'Twas some cousin's. Few of the people his cousin had still work inside Thanescarr and them what do willnae tell Roderick anything, if they e'en ken about the bolt-holes."

"Good, then our plan is simple. But, first," he looked at young Simon, "did ye hear the men say anything about what they planned to do with Lady Kirstie?"

"Gib asked if the laird was going to put her in the cage, but the laird said he couldnae." Simon frowned. "Said there were too many eyes turned his way right now."

"He didnae say exactly where he might put her, though?"

"I dinnae ken. He said he would put her where she belonged. Wattie said he didnae ken how that was any good, as she had slipped out of there before. The laird said she wouldnae do so this time as, by the time he gets her back to Thanescarr, the cursed doors will have a bolt on the outside."

"Then he has put her in her bedchamber," Callum said. "He used to lock her in there, but caught her slipping back in one night and realized she could pick the lock. That was one reason he decided he had to kill her. He kenned she had seen too much, had been wandering about free for too long not to have seen a lot.''

Payton nodded, the formation of a sound plan helping him gain some calm. ''Then Callum will lead me and Ian inside. Malkie, ye, Donald, and Angus are to make sure no one discovers our bolt-hole.'' He smiled gently at Simon, who was struggling to stay awake. ''And ye, Simon, are to go to bed.''

''I am so sorry, sir,'' Simon said as he slowly stood up. '' 'Tis all my fault.''

''Nay. Ye held firm when 'twas only yourself being threatened and hurt. 'Tis enough. Ye were wise enough to ken the mon was speaking true when he threatened your wee sister. 'Twas right that ye protected her. Now, get some rest.'' The moment Simon left, Payton looked at Callum and cocked one eyebrow. ''I hope ye heeded what I just said.''

''Aye,'' Callum said, struggling to look innocent. ''We have a plan now. I heard it all.''

''I meant what I just said to Simon and weel ye ken it. Ye are to cease calling him a coward and a traitor. They threatened his sister and he had to think of her. I am sure the fact that they told him they had murdered his father counted a great deal in his decision to believe their threats.''

Callum nodded. ''I will stop. Since they followed my trail right to him, 'tis my fault, in a way, that he e'en had to make that decision. So, are we going to go after Lady Kirstie now?''

''Verra shortly. I want the shelter of nightfall. Roderick is expecting us, but I would rather he didnae ken we came until it is too late for him to stop us.''

''In and out like a wee breeze.''

''Aye, lad, exactly like that. Roderick thinks he is winning at the moment, but he will soon realize he has but begun to lose.''

* * *

Kirstie slowly opened her eyes. For a moment, it did not seem strange to be lying on her old bed in Thanes-carr; then her wits began to clear. Panic surged through her and she fought it back down. She knew she had every right to be afraid, but refused to let herself be ruled by that fear. It would gain her nothing, but would certainly please Roderick.

The pain in her jaw was enough to bring tears to her eyes, as was the throbbing from the knock on the back of her head. Very carefully, she tested her jaw, relieved to find it was not broken. One of her teeth was a little loose, but she knew from past experience that that would heal itself if she was careful and Roderick did not hit her there again for a while. As slowly as possible, she rose until she was sitting on the edge of the bed. She clutched the thick, carved bedpost to steady herself as she fought back waves of dizziness and nausea.

It was several agonizing minutes before she felt she could move again, and, cautiously, she got to her feet. Kirstie inched her way over to the window. From the angle of the sun and the sparse activity in the bailey below, she judged it to be nearly nightfall. Roderick had obviously hit her very hard indeed for she had been unconcious for nearly four hours, perhaps more. That did mean, however, that if she could get out, she would have the shadows of nightfall to aid her in her escape.

Then she heard a chilling noise. It was the sound of a bolt being drawn back—on the outside of the door. Roderick had turned her bedchamber into a very effective prison. The window was too high to escape through. There were no secret ways out of her room, only in, and that one required someone to open it from the other side. Now it appeared that Roderick had made sure she could not pick the lock on her door, or on the one leading into his bedchamber. Escape would require a great deal more work than she was capable of at the moment. Kirstie refused to think that escape might now be impossible, for such thoughts destroyed hope and she desperately needed hope to cling to.

Roderick stepped into the room and she felt a chill go through her. With an outward show of calm, she sat down in a chair before the fire, a little surprised that there had been one built for her. Roderick walked over to stand in front of the fire, blocking a lot of the heat. Kirstie found herself hoping a stray spark would catch his rich clothing afire. She had not realized, until seeing Payton's elegant yet subdued attire, that Roderick was a coxcomb.

"I suppose ye have already tried picking the locks," Roderick said.

He was so pleased with himself, she mused. "I havenae had the time yet. I have only just awakened from your little love tap." She touched her jaw, not surprised to feel a swelling there, and suspected the bruising would soon be very colorful.

"Weel, ye may as weel nay waste your time."

"Aye. I gathered that when I heard the bolt being drawn on the outside of the door ere ye came in. Ye obviously planned weel for my visit. There was nay need to trouble yourself. I dinnae intend to visit for verra long."

"Ah, Kirstie, ye just dinnae understand, do ye?" Roderick shook his head. "Ye will ne'er leave Thanescarr, nay alive. Ye have betrayed me once too often, from our wedding night to your feeble attempts to blacken my name with slanderous lies. And, of course, ye have cuckolded me with Sir Payton Murray."

That was a subject she would prefer him not to linger on for too long. Roderick had not wanted her as a true wife, wanted no woman at all. It was not something she could prove any longer even if she ever got the chance to do so. If Roderick wanted to brand her an adulteress, she could find herself in some serious trouble if she managed to survive the trouble she was in now. Since she had just spent a month in the near-legendary Sir Payton Murray's house, even if she could manage to lie and deny any affair, no one would ever believe her. Kirstie did not know why Roderick cared what she may or may not have done with Payton, unless he intended to use it as an excuse for her death. That made little sense for, even if the wife was guilty of adultery, people frowned on the husband killing her for that sin. So, she thought, what game did he play now?

"Slanderous lies?" she drawled. " 'Tis but the truth finally being told." She watched him repeatedly clench and unclench his hands and braced for a possible attack. "Ye hurt children, Roderick. Deny it all ye will, pretty it up with lies about giving poor lads food and clothing all ye wish to, but that is the plain truth. And, one of these days," she added in a hard, cold voice, "I will prove that there is innocent blood on your hands, that ye killed some of those children."

"Ye try to blacken my name to hide your own sins."

"Oh, nay. Whate'er sins I may have committed pale in comparison to the ones which stain your soul."

"Your sins grow daily, wife. Ye keep adding to the blood upon your hands, despite all of my efforts to stop ye."

"What madness do ye speak? I am nay the one with blood on my hands."

"Nay? Ye keep dragging others into this, keep telling others those lies about me until I am forced to act to silence them. Ye ken weel my need for privacy, how virulently I protect it, yet ye keep endangering others with your tales of imagined woes and crimes."

"Ye tried to kill me!" She could not believe how completely Roderick lied to himself, how he spoke of his cruelties and murders as if they were of no consequence.

"Ye wouldnae shut up!" Roderick took a deep breath and said more calmly, "Weel, ye have now given me three more to deal with."

"What do ye mean?" she demanded, a chill slipping down her spine.

"What do ye think, ye foolish wench? Ye have drawn Sir Payton and those two rather ugly servants of his into our troubles. Dinnae try to deny it. Once I had time to consider the matter, I realized 'twas Sir Payton who was blackening my name. The lies he was telling could only have come from you. Now I must silence him and it willnae be easy. I shall have to spend many long hours plotting how to be rid of him and his servants without bringing any suspicion upon myself. Fortunately, I dinnae need to be so careful concerning that little traitor Callum."

Kirstie found it all very difficult to comprehend. The man spoke of the murder of four people, one only a child, yet he sounded merely irritated over the time and effort it would take to do it without risking the gallows. He also tried to blame her for it all. Worse, she could not completely dispel the guilt he was stirring inside of her.

"Ye speak of murdering four people as if 'tis naught but an inconvenience," she murmured, unsure of what to say, for she knew there was little chance she could talk him out of it, yet she felt compelled to try.

" 'Tis an inconvenience, one ye keep inflicting upon me. And for what? Troublesome, wee brats others toss aside?"

"Weel, ye willnae find it so easy to kill Payton or Strong Ian and his wife. And, if ye think ye can do so and remain unscathed, ye are a fool. Payton's family will start hunting for his killer before his blood has e'en dried."

"Oh, nay, I dinnae think so. I have been verra successful in blackening his name, far more successful than he has been in trying to blacken mine. The mon has cuckolded too many men and roused the envy of many another. 'Twas verra easy to bring him down. I doubt his kinsmen will e'en want to ken what plot of mud he will be rotting in.''

"Ye try to judge others by the inconstancy of the court's fools and flatterers. The Murrays willnae be so quick to believe what ye say or to condemn one of their own. Nay, they will seek answers and will demand blood for blood. Ye may weel succeed in silencing Payton, Wee Alice, Strong Ian, and e'en Callum, but the Murrays and their allies will soon root out all your dark secrets. Then it will be ye who will rot in the mud, banished by kith and kin, your grave pissed on by every child ye have abused.''

It puzzled her that he did not hit her. Kirstie could see that he dearly wished to. Roderick had rarely practiced such restraint in the past so she had to wonder why he did so now. He wanted her dead so he should not fear that he might accidentally kill her if he released his rage.

"Why have ye come here? To gloat o'er imagined slights? To try to pass your own sins onto me?'' she asked. "Ye waste your time. We really have naught to say to each other.''

"Nay? Mayhap I have decided to forgive ye and accept ye back as my wife.''

"I was ne'er your wife.'' For the first time, Kirstie truly believed that.

Roderick ignored her. "Aye, 'tis time for us to become a true family. 'Tis time ye had a child.''

Kirstie crossed her arms over her chest to hide the trembling that suddenly seized her. Roderick did not know she had overheard Gib and Wattie speak of his plans to get her with child, using them as studs. She did not want to believe he would do such a thing, then told herself not to be such an idiot. A man who could do what he did to children was capable of anything. Considering what fate he probably intended for the child itself, she should not really be so deeply shocked over how he wanted to obtain that child.

"Ah, so ye have decided to try to be a mon again,"
she said, and watched him actually start to swing his fist
at her only to stop it, shaking slightly from the effort.
"Tsk, such a temper ye have."

"One does wonder why ye seem so intent upon stirring it up."

"Does one?" She did, and did not really have an
answer for that. "I dinnae believe I am quite ready to
have a child."

"Bearing children is one, mayhap the only, useful
thing a woman does. 'Tis also your duty as my wife."

"Just as it is your duty to give me one, but ye seem
unable to do so, so where does that leave us?"

Roderick crossed his arms over his chest. "I could
wait to see if that great lover Sir Payton has bred ye,
but, nay, I think not. 'Tis possible the bairn would look
just like him and that could cause some difficulty. Nay,
I shall have my lads see to it. Come, why look so appalled?
Ye were willing to spread your legs for Sir Payton. Ye
can do it for the men I choose." A knock at the door
drew his attention and he moved to open it, keeping a
wary eye on Kirstie as he did. "Curse it, Wattie," he
hissed at the big man standing there. "I told ye I would
tell ye when."

"Your kinsmen are here," Wattie said. "They want
to talk with ye. Now."

"Jesu, what could they possibly want to talk about
now?"

"Weel, ye be telling the world and its mother that Sir
Payton Murray stole your wife, that ye are a cuckold. I
suspicion they feel ye ought to do something about that
insult, aye? Going to tell them ye got the bitch back?"

"Nay, not yet," Roderick replied. "I suppose I must
talk with them." He looked at Kirstie. "I suggest ye get
some rest, my dear. Ye will be needing your strength
later."

Once alone, Kirstie slowly folded over until her head
rested upon her knees. She felt cold, chilled to the bone

with fear for herself and all those she cared about. The insanity festering within Roderick also left her afraid. He meant all he had said, was not merely trying to frighten her. Yet, because of that, he had frightened her far more that he ever could have with threats and his fists. There was no reasoning with such a man and no way to guess what he might do. He would do things and act in ways no sane man could ever hope to anticipate. That made him a very dangerous man indeed.

And there was no way she could warn Payton, she realized, and fought the urge to weep. Payton had to know that Roderick would want him dead. He already knew that Roderick wanted Callum dead. But, would he know that Ian and Alice were also in danger? And what about the other children sheltering in his home, now numbering seven? Roderick might not know that they were there, but if he went after the others, he would soon discover them. He had not mentioned Simon and Brenda, but if reminded of them, he would undoubtedly want them silenced as well. Then there were Payton's three guards to consider.

She slowly straightened up, tightly gripped the arms of the chair, and stared blindly into the fire. Six adults and eight children. No sane person would ever think he could execute so many and get away with it. But, then, Roderick was not sane. She doubted he even thought of them all as people, merely obstacles to his ability to continue his perversions in peace.

The door was unbolted again and Kirstie tensed, fearing Roderick had sent Gib and Wattie to her already. Gib was there, leering at her and looking as if he had not been wounded at all, but he simply guarded the doorway as the kitchen maid Daisy brought Kirstie a tray of food and drink. Gib was not very bright, but he might have as strong a sense of self-preservation as Roderick did. Kirstie wondered if she could stir up a little dissension in the ranks.

"Ye do ken what Roderick plans now, dinnae ye?" she asked.

"Aye. He plans to let me and Wattie breed a bairn on ye," Gib answered.

"Nay, ye fool, I speak of all the people he is planning to kill. In truth, he is probably planning to have ye and Wattie do the killing so 'twill be your filthy necks the hemp will soon be kissing."

Gib shrugged. "Been past worrying o'er a hanging for a long while. 'Tis just a matter of when and for what. They can only hang me once, ye ken. And, I think I will enjoy killing that pretty bastard ye have been tupping for a month. Sir Payton's tupped near half the women in Scotland and the other half wish he would tup them. The man sore needs killing."

"And, of course, his three guards and his two servants will simply stand back and let ye have at him?"

"I suspicion old Roderick has a wee plan or two for them as weel or they will fall in the fighting. I dinnae much care. Old Roderick's kept us from hanging for this long. Suspicion he will continue to do so. Clever is old Roderick."

"Old Roderick is insane," she snapped, "and I begin to think it is contagious."

Gib frowned for a moment, then nodded. "Aye, the mon is probably mad as a March hare. After all, he would have to be to prefer wee lads to a woman." He wrapped his arm around Daisy's thick waist, yanked her close to his side, and nuzzled her dirty neck.

The way Daisy paled a little, and the look of frightened disgust on the woman's face, had Kirstie fighting the urge to attack Gib and try to free the maid. Common sense told her to stay in her seat. All she would accomplish was the chance to nurse a few new bruises and, quite possibly, some rough retribution for Daisy. Then she realized that Daisy was staring at her, that most of her wriggling and sounds of distress were to keep Gib occupied. Once Kirstie met her gaze, Daisy cast a pointed glance at the tray, then winked. It took every ounce of willpower Kirstie had not to look at the tray to discover what Daisy might have hidden there.

"Let go of me, ye fool," snapped Daisy as she wriggled free of Gib's hold. "The laird is demanding food and drink for his guests and I need to get back to the kitchens."

"Go on with ye, then," Gib said, somewhat roughly shoving her out the door. Once out in the hall himself, Gib paused in shutting the door to leer at Kirstie. "I will be seeing ye later. Me and Wattie. Best ye rest some. Ye will need your strength to handle big men like me and Wattie."

Kirstie stared at the door as he shut it and bolted it. She wondered idly if, in the ten years he had lived here, Roderick's insanity had seeped into the very walls of Thanescarr, only to ooze out now and then to infect others. Gib might not be insane, but he was most certainly not quite right in the head. Somehow he, and undoubtedly Wattie as well, had grown to manhood without one single scrap of conscience. She supposed she should not be surprised. Such men were the only ones who could serve Roderick so faithfully.

She turned her attention to the tray Daisy had set down on the table next to her chair. When she touched the square of linen on the tray, she knew whatever Daisy wanted her to have was hidden inside it. Within the folds of the linen was a plain but very sharp dagger. As Kirstie tested the feel of it in her hand, she wondered what Daisy thought she could do with it. The ones working in Roderick's kitchens had always been sympathetic to her, although their help had always been severely restricted by their fear of Roderick. Kirstie would have preferred some help getting out of Thanescarr, but knew they had taken great risks to slip her a weapon and she was grateful. It did make her feel a little less helpless.

Forcing herself to eat something, Kirstie chewed on

a piece of bread, and studied the dagger. If she was very lucky, she might be able to kill Roderick if he came to visit her alone again. She might even be able to kill one of the men who would try to bed her later, but she knew she could never kill or incapacitate both Gib and Wattie. Once she struck one down, the other would kill her without thought or hesitation. Despite all she might suffer in the next few hours, she really did not want to die. Of course, the knife might have been sent so that she could kill herself, but she doubted it.

Kirstie had the feeling that the ones in the kitchens expected her to perform some miraculous escape. She dearly wished she was not about to disappoint them all. About the only way out she could see at the moment was through the window and that would be suicide. The best that would accomplish would be to give Roderick the difficult chore of trying to explain why his missing wife was crushed and bleeding all over his bailey. When Kirstie realized she was actually seeing that as a good thing, she decided it was time to start praying for a miracle.

CHAPTER FIFTEEN

"Are ye sure Ian will fit?" asked Payton as he stared into the dark hole Callum had uncovered.

From where they stood, Payton could see the men upon the walls of Thanescarr. The trees and brush had been allowed to grow so thick and wild, however, that he felt confident none of those men could see him or the others with him. It seemed odd that a man so protective of his secrets as Sir Roderick would be so careless about the ones his own keep held.

" 'Twill probably be a wee bit tight for a few yards," replied Callum, "but, aye, he will fit. 'Twas made to let a fully armed mon pass through."

"I will follow ye in for a ways," said Malkie. "Ye may need help if ye are caught fleeing and, ye ne'er can tell, someone might have finally discovered this, amble along the passage, see it is open, and send up an alarum."

"Oh, I didnae think of that," said Callum.

"Nay? Truly?" Malkie's wide grin removed any sting from his sarcasm. "Go on. Let us be done with this."

Payton heartily agreed with that sentiment as he followed Callum into the dark, dank passage. Ian and Mal-

kie quickly slipped in behind him, leaving Donald and
Angus to guard their route of escape. It only took a
few yards for Payton to decide he hated small, dark
passageways. What Callum had claimed was only yards
soon felt like miles to Payton.

When they reached the wider part of the passage,
Payton had to stop. He took a few deep breaths to calm
himself as he watched Malkie light a candle. Malkie
dripped some wax on a piece of stone jutting out from
the wall and set the candle down in it. Payton found that
even that faint light was enough to calm his lingering
unease.

" 'Tis like a cursed coffin," muttered Ian as he lit the
shuttered lantern they had brought with them.

"Sometimes the dark can be a verra safe place," murmured Callum as he studied the floor for a moment.
"It doesnae look as if anyone has come this way, nay
since Lady Kirstie and I last used it."

"But, we will still have to pass through some that are
weel used?" asked Payton.

"One or two, but none of those as weel used. We will
have to pass by a few places where we had best be verra
quiet. Want me to hold up my hand to tell ye when we
get near them?"

"Good enough. Lead on, lad."

Payton was astounded at how quietly the boy moved.
Callum also appeared very confident about the direction
he took, yet it looked to be a confusing maze to Payton.
It was not until they took a second turning that he
caught sight of the odd painted scratchings upon the
wall. He signaled Ian to bring the lamp closer.

"What are these?" he asked Callum when the boy
joined them.

"Lady Kirstie and I made them," the boy replied.
"The arrow means ye go straight down here. The three
doors there are the openings ye pass ere ye see another
useful passage. See the letter 'R' on that second door?
It means ye have to be verra quiet going by that place.

It opens behind Roderick's chair at the head table in the great hall. The sun on the first door means ye can get outside through it, but only into the bailey. 'Tis why the sun is frowning. The goblet on the third door means ye can get from there into the place where they store barrels of wine and ale.''

"Clever," said Ian.

"Aye," agreed Payton. "Can we see into the great hall?''

"We can." Callum pointed to the little circles on either side of the door and Payton realized they were eyes. "Do ye want to look in, then?''

"It might be wise. Might tell us just where Roderick is.''

Callum nodded and started on his way again.

"She turned his own keep against him," Ian whispered to Payton. "I would wager she made a close study of the whole underbelly of his keep. She could come and go as she wished, and spy on him whene'er she wished to, as weel.''

"It would certainly seem so," agreed Payton. "And, she did so for about three years. Something tells me the mon still doesnae ken how she found out so much or how she got the children away from Thanescarr. She is, after all, just a lass, one of a breed he has naught but contempt for.''

A moment later, Callum held up his hand. Silently, Payton approached the hole the boy pointed to. Putting his eye to it, Payton was able to see the length of the great hall. He also saw that Roderick was there, deep into an argument with several other men. There was a similarity of appearance that told him these were probably some of his kinsmen. Payton was especially pleased to see that Gib and Wattie were also there.

He listened to the argument for a while before signaling Callum to lead on. Roderick's kinsmen wanted him to do something to avenge what they saw as a stain upon their honor. For reasons even Payton could not understand, Roderick was trying to counsel patience, but that only seemed to be making his kinsmen angrier and suspicious.

Something was going to have to be done about the MacIyes, Payton decided. If that argument was any indication, Roderick's kinsmen were considering acting on their own. Roderick was beginning to be seen as a man without a care to the honor of the clan or, worse, a coward. A confrontation with the MacIyes was drawing dangerously near and Payton would prefer it happened on his own terms.

A noise up ahead of them pulled Payton from his thoughts and caused them all to stop. Ian quickly shuttered the lantern. Payton drew his sword even as Callum pulled the large knife he kept sheathed at his side. They could clearly see the flickering of light ahead of them, but it was impossible to see who held it.

"I ken there is someone there," called a shaky female voice. " 'Tis Daisy, the kitchen maid."

Callum cautiously moved closer and, although Payton could not see what the boy did, he saw Callum visibly relax. "What are ye doing here, Daisy?" asked Callum.

A well-rounded woman stepped away from the wall. "Callum! We thought ye might be dead." She peered in Ian and Payton's direction. "Who ye got with ye, lad? Someone to help the lady?"

"Aye. Is she in her bedchamber?" Callum asked as he sheathed his knife.

Daisy nodded. "Locked in tight, she is. I remembered ye saying ye could get into her room, but nay out, save through the doors. Thought I might be able to find that secret way and let her out, but I been standing here for a long time, nay sure which way to go, and too scared to just set off looking. Coward that I am, I keep fearing I will get lost and, a few years from now, some poor fool will stumble o'er my poor old bones." She sighed and shook her head.

"Ye did your best. We will get my lady out now."

"Best ye do so and quick. The bastard means to set Gib and Wattie on her. Would have done it by now, but his kinsmen arrived, demanding to see him. Took some bread in to them a wee while ago and decided those kinsmen willnae be staying too much longer. They looked ready to spit on the laird and walk out. Soon as they go, I think Gib and Wattie will be going to Lady Kirstie's bedchamber. I gave her a dagger, but it willnae help her much against those two brutes, 'less she sticks it into her own sweet heart, poor lass."

"My lady wouldnae do that. She would kill one of those pigs instead. That is what she would do," Callum said.

"No need to get so heated, lad. I thought she might use it on one of those ugly fools, that I did. 'Course, she kills one of them and the other will just up and snap that lovely neck of hers. But, at least she would go down fighting, aye?" Daisy gasped, then sighed when Payton stepped up to her, bowed, and kissed her hand. "Oh my, oh my. Ye must be Sir Payton. Ye are a bonnie one, arenae ye? Why, ye are as bonnie as I suspicion our fine lad Callum will be."

"I thank ye, Daisy," Payton said. "And I heartily thank ye for getting a dagger to Kirstie."

"Och, weel, if 'tis gratitude ye wish to show, there be a fine niche just back here—"

"He belongs to Lady Kirstie, Daisy," Callum said.

"Do ye?" she asked Payton.

Payton smiled faintly. "I rather think I might."

"Ah, weel, she be a good lass with a heart near as big as the sea. Oh, and who be this fine figure of a mon?" she asked as Ian moved to stand beside Payton.

"He is marrit," said Callum.

"Weel, what the wee wife doesnae ken," began Daisy as she stroked Ian's arm.

"Marrit to a verra fierce, verra mean woman."

Daisy sighed. "Weel, off with ye, then. I will keep

watch here. Any fool comes round and I will keep him so busy ye could move a whole army right on past him."

After a few more yards, Callum paused at the foot of some narrow stone steps, leaned closer to Payton, and whispered, "We must be verra quiet now. We will be going past rooms that often have someone in them, and Lady Kirstie and I didnae have the time to test them all to see if ye could hear someone moving back here or see the light they carry."

Payton nodded and carefully followed the boy. The constant need to maintain silence, as well as the brief confrontation with Daisy, was costing them precious time. Although he ached to come to swordpoint with Roderick and his faithful hounds, Payton knew that now would be a very poor time for such a meeting. Getting Kirstie out of Thanescarr unseen and safely back to his home before anyone even realized she was gone was the most important thing. The longer they took to reach her, however, the greater the chance was that they would not find her alone.

Callum suddenly stopped again and Payton tensed. It was soon obvious that the boy was making use of another peephole. Callum then put his mouth near the hole and made the sound of the mourning dove. After a long, tense moment, the sound of a blackbird came back, faint but clear. The sounds were repeated twice more with slight variations before Callum grinned at him.

"She is alone," he announced, and started to open the door.

Payton quickly moved to help him with the heavy door. Callum was the first to step into the room and was immediately swept up into Kirstie's arms. Even as Payton had to smile over the way Callum protested the intimacy all the while he returned the hug, he realized he was actually feeling a little jealous of an eleven-year-old boy. A heartbeat later, Kirstie was in his arms, and he swiftly wrapped them around her, holding her close.

It occurred to Payton that Kirstie meant a great deal to him. Although it was a poor time to have such a revelation, he could not ignore it. The strength of his fear when he had thought her lost to him, the depth of his concern over what might be happening to her, and the joy he felt over having her safely back in his arms had only one explanation. There was a great deal more here than passion, even more than liking and respect. He thought he might even be approaching that elusive emotion called love, but whether he felt that or not did not matter at the moment. Payton was very sure of one thing—he was going to keep Kirstie. Now all he had to do was make her understand that.

He was abruptly yanked from his thoughts when he became aware of how badly she was shaking. "Kirstie?"

Kirstie gave him a quick, hard kiss to distract him from asking any questions. The miracle she had been praying for had arrived. She did not want to waste any time talking. Despite her various pains and the cold fear she could not shake, she wanted to leave. Now.

"We must go," she said, grasping his hand and pulling him back through the door he had just entered through. "There isnae any time to talk. Later. I will tell ye all that was said and done. Later."

Payton decided not to argue. He followed her out, pausing only to help Callum shut the door behind them. They moved swiftly and silently until they reached the place where Daisy still waited.

"Oh, thank ye God," Daisy muttered, and gave Kirstie a brief hug. "Ye go, lass. Go and find a safe place."

"I will." Kirstie handed the woman the dagger that had brought her such comfort. "Here, take this back."

"Ye can keep it."

"Nay. Ye dinnae want anyone to notice it is missing." She glanced at the well-armed trio waiting for her. "I am weel protected."

"Aye, that ye are." Daisy hugged her again and whispered, "Make him come with a yell once for me, lass."

Although she could feel herself blushing, Kirstie winked at the woman and whispered back, "I will. Watch your back."

"Always." Daisy watched them disappear into the dark, sighed, and headed back to her kitchens to await the uproar.

Roderick stared at the empty bedchamber in open-mouthed disbelief. He was only faintly aware of how Gib and Wattie cursed as they fruitlessly searched the room. Somehow she had escaped him again. Frowning slightly, he moved to look out the open window, but was not surprised when he did not see her body sprawled on the ground below. In truth, he was disappointed. It would have solved so many of his problems and been relatively easy to explain.

"She didnae go out that way, did she?" asked Wattie as he moved to stand by Roderick and look out the window.

"Oh, nay, nay! She didnae! Please say she didnae!"

The woman who had cried out those words suddenly pushed her way between Roderick and Wattie. She stared out the window, then sighed, and wiped the tears from her round face with the corner of her somewhat dirty apron. It took Roderick a long second look to recognize the kitchen maid Daisy. He hastily stepped back, away from the smell of turnips and sweat.

"Ye gave me such a fright," said Daisy.

"What are ye doing here?" demanded Roderick.

"I came to collect the tray I left when I brought her some food earlier," Daisy replied as she moved toward the table.

"Food? I ordered no food brought to my wife." He marched over to study the remnants of Kirstie's meal. " 'Twas a cursed feast! I ne'er ordered this!"

"Weel, someone did for I was given this tray and told

to bring it up here." Daisy shrugged. " 'Tisnae my place to ask questions."

"I am cursed! Surrounded by fools and traitors!" Roderick cleared the table with one sweep of his arm.

Daisy knelt down and began to clean up the mess he had just made. She went slowly about the chore, listening to Roderick rant. Gib and Wattie tried to offer plans for getting Lady Kirstie back, but the laird was beyond listening. From what Daisy could understand, the man was only interested in killing Lady Kirstie and anyone else she had ever spoken to. Although she had always suspected the laird was not right in the head, Daisy began to think the trouble Kirstie and her allies were causing the man was pushing Sir Roderick deep into insanity. She winced when he finally left the room, for the curses and threats he was bellowing out were almost painful to listen to.

As she got to her feet, she realized Wattie and Gib were still there, staring at her with a look she easily recognized. "What do ye two fools want?"

"Weel, now, Daisy," replied Gib as he wrapped an arm around her waist and pulled her close, "me and Wattie came up here all hard and ready for a good tupping and the bitch is gone. But, we are still hard and ready."

"Ah, I see, and ye think I ought to take care of that," said Daisy, struggling to look alarmed.

"We will give ye a shilling each," said Gib even as he tugged her toward the bed.

"What? Why should we be paying her?" demanded Wattie even as he started to take off his clothes.

" 'Twill make her work harder, isnae that right, Daisy?" asked Gib as he, too, started to take his clothes off.

"Aye, if ye give me the shillings now and if one of ye fools shuts the door."

Daisy quickly grabbed the shillings from Gib and slipped them into the pocket of her apron. If she was lucky, she would get away with the coins before one of the men thought to steal them back. As she undressed, she watched a now-naked Wattie walk to the door and shut it. He was a pig with very little skill, but he was hung like a bull. It was the same with Gib, although he could reveal a trick or two when he was feeling kindly. She also knew they would take her whether she said aye or nay. By agreeing to it, she would save herself a few bruises.

Even as Wattie shoved her down onto the bed and climbed on top of her, Daisy told herself she was helping Lady Kirstie in a small way. If both men wore themselves out using her, they could not be working to calm Sir Roderick down or trying to get Lady Kirstie back for him. The lady would have time to get away, to prepare for Sir Roderick's next attack. Daisy winced as Wattie slammed into her, but then Gib started to feast on her breasts. Between the two of them, she mused, she might actually gain a little enjoyment out of it all. She thought of the man Lady Kirstie would be bedding down with and sighed with a mixture of envy and happiness for the little lady. Closing her eyes, Daisy pictured the two men she had seen in the passageway and soon decided that imagination was a very fine thing indeed.

Kirstie sat on Payton's bed and watched him wash up. She had thanked everyone, told a little of her story to assure them all she had not been hurt, and then allowed Alice to take care of her. The woman had bathed her, fed her, and given her a very mild potion to ease her pain and calm her. Kirstie felt a great deal better, almost as if she was a little drunk, but she knew her fear had not gone away.

When Payton tugged her robe off her and nudged her under the covers, she was more than ready to curl up with him. She moved into his arms the moment he got into bed beside her. As she ran her hand up and down his side, she realized her fear was mostly for him, for the danger she had placed him in. Yet, when he held her so close, she felt safe. It made little sense, but she decided some things did not have to. She wondered if, deep in her heart, she simply could not believe that God would allow the ugliness that was Roderick to destroy the beauty that was Payton, inside and out.

"Are ye sure this is the only hurt he inflicted?" Payton asked, gently kissing her badly bruised jaw.

"Aye, and I hurt him first," she said as she kissed his throat. "I was certain he didnae plan to carry me out kicking and screaming. So, I got in one verra painful kick ere he knocked me out."

Payton rolled onto his back and Kirstie rapidly accepted his silent invitation. She greedily savored the taste and feel of him. The way he stretched slightly as she kissed his chest and stroked his arms reminded Kirstie very much of a contented cat. Payton reveled in being touched and kissed. Kirstie decided it was past time she gave him a full dose of what he so thoroughly enjoyed. She suspected Alice's potion had eased her modesty and reticence right along with her pain and fear, for the things she was thinking of doing to Payton should have shocked her right down to her toes. Instead, they excited her and made her eager to begin.

She slowly kissed her way down to his taut stomach and stroked his strong thighs. His manhood hardened and twitched against her breasts, so she almost idly rubbed herself against him, delighting in his soft groan of pleasure and approval. When she moved her kisses to his long legs, she slowly dragged her hair over his groin, and heard his breathing quicken. All the way down his well-shaped leg she kissed him, gave him small, gentle bites, then soothed away any possible sting with strokes of her tongue. It was what he had done to her and she quickly discovered that Payton found it as arousing as she did.

Kirstie next discovered that Payton had very sensitive

feet. She saw that he was almost as intrigued and surprised by that as she was, which told her she had actually found something about him, something intimate, that no other woman had. A little unsure of exactly how to take advantage of that, Kirstie did her best. It proved to be more than sufficient. In fact, Payton looked ready to stop her play because she was pulling him too close to the edge, and Kirstie did not want that. She still had plans, daring plans that she felt sure she would be too cowardly to try later, after Alice's potion had worn off, so she quickly moved to make her way up his other leg.

It was as she kissed the smooth skin of his hip that she grew hesitant. Kirstie could sense a tension in Payton, but was not sure what it meant. He had loved her with his mouth, but she knew that did not mean he wanted her to do the same to him. Or, worse, he wanted it, but would think she was little better than a whore for giving it to him.

"Ye dinnae have to," Payton said quietly. "I would ne'er have ye do something ye didnae really want to."

The obvious disappointment behind his words was all the encouragement Kirstie needed. She turned her head and slowly ran her tongue up the impressive length of him. Soon, she was lost in the pleasure of giving him such pleasure.

Payton gripped the sheet in his hands and clung desperately to every scrap of control he could muster. She was definitely going to kill him. Since many women did not offer him such a pleasure, he had had little experience with it, but he quickly decided Kirstie had a natural skill men would be willing to die for. She seemed to know exactly when to ease back to allow him to regain some control and thus make the pleasure last. When she took him into her mouth, however, he knew even her innate skill could not help him to last much longer. Allowing her free rein over his body had left him too hungry for her.

A soft cry of surprise and disappointment escaped

Kirstie when Payton suddenly grabbed her under the arms, dragged her up the length of his body, and joined their bodies with a little more force than finesse. She swiftly discovered that there was delight to be found in this as well. It was not until his cry of release thundered in her ears that Kirstie gave herself over completely to her own needs. As she collapsed in his arms, she had to smile. She had certainly lived up to her promise to Daisy.

This time Kirstie roused from her sated stupor before Payton did from his. She rose and donned her robe, tying it loosely. After she washed herself, she brought a damp cloth back to the bed to cleanse Payton. The way his manhood twitched with renewed interest as she bathed it made her smile, especially when she saw how boyishly proud of himself Payton was. Seeing the remainder of the potion Alice had made still sitting in a tankard on the table by the bed, Kirstie sat down on the edge of the bed and began to sip at it. Earlier, she had only accepted half of the medicine, but the ache in her jaw and the back of her head were nudging at her. So, too, was her fear. This added amount of potion might make her fall asleep, but now she did not care. When Payton curled up behind her, tugged the edge of her robe out of the way, and kissed her hip, she wondered if she might be acting too hastily. There were many more pleasant ways to dispel fear.

"Roderick is utterly insane," she said and calmly met Payton's startled gaze. "He claims 'tis all my fault he has blood on his hands."

Payton sat up, outraged, but struggling to hold his tongue. He did not want to distract her from what she was about to say. Although he had suspected she had not told him everything, he had tried to be patient, willing to give her time to recover from her ordeal.

"He feels I dinnae understand what he does with the children, thinks himself some wondrous benefactor who asks but a small service for all he so kindly gives them.

I have betrayed him from the start, he says, right from
our wedding night when I had the effrontery to become
a woman. If I would cease telling such lies about him,
he wouldnae have to kill anyone. Oh, and any poor
children he has killed are of no real concern. They
would have died anyway, aye? He now feels he must
kill all of ye. Ye, Alice, Ian, your guards, Callum most
certainly, and the other bairns. And me, of course, but,
mayhap, only after he has had Gib and Wattie work to
breed a child on me."

"Jesu."

"Exactly. There were many other words, other twisted
accusations, but that is the heart of what he said, what
he believes. I had thought him, weel, nay quite right in
the head because of his lust for children, but 'tis so
much more. And, as his madness became clear to me,
I grew verra afraid, Payton. How does one fight that?"

He moved to kneel on the wolfskin carpet at her feet,
slipping his hands beneath her robe to stroke her thighs.
"The same as ye would fight a sane mon. Aye," he said
when she looked doubtful. "Mayhap it will be a little
more difficult to guess which way he will jump, but it
can be done. We ken what he wants, what he will try to
accomplish. 'Tis but a question of when and how. And,
nay matter how frightening his insanity, how different
he seems from other men, one thing about him will
always remain quite completely normal."

"Oh? And just what about Roderick could possibly
be normal?"

"If ye cut him, he bleeds. If ye run a sword through
his heart, he dies."

"All ye say is true, and yet, I am still afraid. If ye could
have heard him, Payton. If ye could have seen the look
in his eyes." She quickly finished off Alice's potion and
set the tankard down, noticing almost absently that her
hand shook a little.

"I would probably have found it all as chilling as ye
did, but I would still ken that I could defeat him, hurt

him, kill him.'' He opened her robe, ignoring her soft protest. "I shall have to do my duty as your champion and banish your fears." He kissed the inside of her thighs until he felt her start to soften and open to him. "I shall make ye forget all about your mad husband."

"Actually, there was one other thing I discovered whilst being held by Roderick.'' Kirstie found that watching Payton caress her could be a very heady thing.

"And what was that?'' he asked as he kissed her taut stomach and savored a moment of anticipation for what he would delight in doing next.

"It pains me to say this, but ye were right. Roderick has nay right at all to be called my husband. So, I have decided that I have none." She was not sure what that fierce look of delight on his face might promise for their future, but it stirred something deep and hot inside of her. "I am nay longer a wicked wife, simply a wanton maid."

"Interesting." Payton pressed a kiss to the dark curls between her soft, white thighs. "I wonder if a wanton maid tastes different from a wicked wife."

By the time he had thrice stroked her with his clever tongue, Kirstie was not terribly interested in his opinion so long as whatever decision he came to did not include stopping to tell her about it.

CHAPTER SIXTEEN

"Hah! He looks fine to me."

Even as Payton's sleep-drugged mind realized that someone was in the room, he recognized that somewhat loud voice. He muttered a protest when the soft breast he had been nuzzling was abruptly replaced by the crumpled linen sheet beneath him. Resisting the urge to look around for Kirstie, who had slipped out of his arms with a dizzying speed, Payton turned his head and glared at the big, fair-haired man standing about a yard from his bed. Although he loved his cousin Gillyanne dearly, he was not so sure he was pleased to see her, either. Certainly not now, when he had been about to indulge himself in a little morning delight.

"Gilly, Connor, what are ye doing here?" he asked and started to sit up, only to feel a whisper of movement at his back which told him Kirstie was still in the bed.

"I *had* to come see ye, Payton," Gillyanne said, moving closer and trying to look over Payton as he cautiously turned onto his side, facing her. "Something kept telling me ye were in danger, that ye needed help."

"Did ye bring the twins?"

"Nay, of course not. My feeling said ye were in danger. I couldnae bring my bairns here. So, I hope we can solve your problem rather quickly. I already miss my bairns." She edged even closer to the bed and scowled at the well-rumpled covers behind him. "Curse it, Payton, I am sure I saw a woman in that bed. Connor?" Gillyanne frowned when her husband did not move to her side. "Why are ye still standing so far away?"

"Weel, aside from the fact that I have no great wish to see your cousin naked, I think I had best stand still as long as someone has a knife pointed at my backside," replied Connor.

Gillyanne peered around behind Connor. "Oh, 'tis a lad. Ye can put your knife away, laddie. Connor willnae hurt ye."

"I wouldnae be too sure of that," Connor drawled.

"Ye best tell me what ye are doing here quick-like," said Callum, "or I will be sticking this knife up your arse."

Connor quirked one brow at a grinning Payton, but spoke to Callum. "Ye ought to be careful who ye threaten, lad. If ye annoy me, I could hurt ye."

"Ha! And I could bugger ye with this blade. Now, where is my lady?" Callum peered around Connor and scowled at the bed. "I dinnae see her and she ought to be there."

"Payton," snapped Gillyanne, "cease that cackling and tell the lad who we are."

A quick pinch on his backside urged Payton to reassure Callum. "Kirstie is fine, Callum. She is just hiding. These people are no threat to us." He nodded at Gillyanne. "This is my cousin, Lady Gillyanne Murray, now MacEnroy, and her husband, Sir Connor MacEnroy. I believe we have us a few more allies, lad."

"Here now, lad," said Ian as he appeared in the doorway, "why are ye pointing your knife at Sir Connor's arse?"

Callum frowned at Ian, even as he sheathed his knife.

"I saw him come in here and, not kenning who the big bullock was, I was worrit that he would hurt my lady. Oh, and mayhap Sir Payton, too. He doesnae seem too quick or alert when he is naked, ye ken. So, I pulled my knife on this Sir Connor MacEnroy here."

"Weel, that certainly was quick thinking," Ian said, "but ye picked a poor place to point your blade at, lad. Stick a mon in the arse and ye willnae bring him down. Ye will just make him angry. Nay, ye want to point it here," Ian instructed, indicating a particularly vulnerable spot on Connor's lower back.

Payton opened his mouth to tell Ian to take his lessons somewhere else, then groaned when he saw what lurked behind his man. A glance at Gillyanne revealed his cousin staring wide-eyed at Wee Alice and the seven children with her. Gilly looked at Callum, then looked at Payton, and opened her mouth.

"Dinnae start," he said, halting the questions he knew she would pummel him with. "Go to the great hall," he began.

"Where is Lady Kirstie?" demanded Moira as she hurried over to the bed, looked around, then glared at Payton.

"She is hiding," replied Payton, and he glared briefly at Gillyanne, "because there are so many people in the room."

"I dinnae see her." Moira's bottom lip began to tremble. "Did the monster get her again?"

Before Payton could reply, he felt movement behind him. One pale, slim arm curled around him from behind and the small, elegant hand briefly stroked Moira's cheek. A brief glance over his shoulder revealed only a mass of tossled black hair and smoky grey eyes. What little he could see of Kirstie's face was brilliant with blushes.

"See, my dear one," Kirstie said, "I am fine. I just need a wee bit of privacy ere I join ye in the great hall."

Moira nodded, turned to face everyone, and bellowed, "Get out! My lady is naked!"

"Oh, it wanted only that," Kirstie muttered and hid behind Payton's back.

Payton fought hard against the urge to laugh as little Moira marched over to the group and pointed her finger at the door, impressively regal in her silent command. Alice, her face contorted slightly as she obviously fought the urge to laugh, quickly pushed everyone out of the room. The huge grins on the faces of Connor, Ian, and Gillyanne only added to Payton's strain.

Just as the door closed, Payton heard Callum ask Moira, "How did ye ken she was naked? Did ye see her paps?" and his control broke. He roared with laughter. Even the sight of a vividly blushing and beautifully naked Kirstie leaping from the bed did not calm or distract him.

"Oh, aye, ye can laugh," Kirstie muttered as she started to dress. "I am so glad my embarrassment entertains ye so. And, I suspicion ye thought Callum was hilarious. He said *paps,* Payton. He wanted to ken if Moira saw my paps!" Her words were muffled as she struggled into her gown. "Ye have to talk to that boy. In truth, if he is wondering about such things, 'tis past time someone talked with him. And his language!"

All the while she talked, going from complaining about Callum's language to complaining about Payton's callous indifference to her mortification and back again, she continued to dress. She grabbed up her brush, realized she was standing by the bed, and slowly sat down. For a moment, she just stared blindly at her brush.

"Oh, Payton, how can I face those people?" she asked.

Recovered now, Payton sat up, took the brush from her hand, and began to gently untangle her hair. "Ye worry too much, Kirstie. They willnae condemn ye. In truth, once the whole tale is told, I may weel face a sharp scold from my cousin. A family secret, love—Gilly is probably one of a rare breed of Murray women. She actually married Connor before she bedded down with him. And, she once told me she chose him out of the three lairds trying to marry her so that they could claim her dower lands, because she thought he could show her what passion was." He nodded when she stared at him in wide-eyed shock. " 'Tis the truth."

"Ye mean they dinnae care for each other?"

"Oh, they do now. Gilly kens Connor loves her as she loves him, though she admits she probably willnae hear it said too often. A hard, private mon is our Connor. Kenning how much it would mean to her, he gave her some verra pretty words at the christening of their twins, and he looked near to emptying his belly as he did so." He looked at her quizzically when she smiled.

"My brother Steven is the same. His wife Anne says she kens he loves her, but they have been wed for four years and she has only heard him say it thrice. Once just before they wed, for she wasnae going to marry him unless he did, once when she had their first child, and once when he thought he was dying. Fool thought he had a growth in his belly."

Payton got up and started to get dressed. "He didnae though, aye?"

"Aye. He was just bound up inside. A purging was all he needed." She smiled when he laughed, then grew serious again as she tied her hair back with a ribbon. "I really dinnae have much choice, do I? I have to go and face them."

"Aye, ye do." He took her by the hand, tugged her to her feet, and gave her a quick, hard kiss. "Trust me, Kirstie, they willnae condemn ye for sharing my bed. Dinnae believe they will e'en think about the matter verra much. And, once we tell them about the battle we are fighting, they will think ye are a near saint."

Kirstie rather doubted that, but allowed Payton to lead her down to the great hall. Payton skillfully curtailed his cousin's many questions, promising a full telling in his ledger room after they broke their fast. By the time she,

Payton, Ian, the MacEnroys, and Callum gathered in Payton's ledger room, Kirstie was feeling more at ease. Gillyanne was open and friendly and, once, when she met Sir Connor's gaze, he gave her a brief wink. She did wonder how so many people could be so accepting of something she had always been told was a sin. Inwardly shrugging, she sat down next to Payton and braced herself for what would undoubtedly be a disturbing retelling of all that had happened and of the danger they still faced.

Payton opened his mouth to start relating the tale of their battle with Sir Roderick, then frowned at Callum, who sat next to Ian. Ian had confided to Payton about the state the boy had been in when he had arrived in the wood to fetch Ian back to the house yesterday. For the first time, the man had clearly seen the scars Roderick had left upon the boy, the deep fear of the man Callum still held. It had only been a day since Ian had seen that crying, terrified little boy Callum tried so hard to hide and Payton had to wonder if it was far too soon for Callum to hear all this again, to relive so much through what would have to be told now.

"Callum, mayhap ye—" he began and raised his brows a little when Callum vigorously shook his head.

"Nay, I will stay. I am an ally, too, aye?" Callum said with a hint of anxiety. "Aye, I am. I am fighting, too. I helped save my lady."

"That ye did, Callum," Kirstie said and smiled at him. "Ye are my champion, too."

"And a promising fighter, too, lad," said Ian, patting the boy on the shoulder.

"E'en more promising as soon as he learns not to stick a knife in a mon's arse," drawled Connor and he winced dramatically when Gillyanne pinched his arm, then winked at Callum, who grinned.

"Fine then, Callum," Payton said, "ye can stay and add anything ye think is important." He saw the uneasy look on the boy's face, the hint of shame despite his air of determined bravery, and added softly, " 'Twill be just fine. Trust me. They will ken who holds all blame in this." He smiled when the boy hesitantly nodded, but knew, sadly, it was going to take a very long time before Callum ceased to feel that pinch of shame, that sense that somehow he was the one to blame.

Payton looked at his cousin, who was doing a poor job of hiding her impatience to know everything. "Did ye really have a feeling that I was in danger?"

"Aye," Gillyanne replied, scowling at him, "and ye are courting e'en more danger if ye keep hesitating to tell me just exactly what is going on."

After grinning at her, Payton quickly grew serious. He began to tell them everything that had happened since he had met Kirstie, everything he knew about Sir Roderick. Callum, and Kirstie added very little. Gillyanne looked increasingly upset while Connor looked increasingly grim. To Payton's relief, neither of them looked at Callum unless he spoke, for Payton was sure the boy would misunderstand such glances.

"I will go and kill him for ye," Connor said after a brief but weighted silence. "I could get close. He doesnae ken who I am. I suspicion ye would want him to die slow and hard. I have a few ways to ensure that."

Kirstie blinked, trying not to show her shock as she studied the man who spoke so calmly of going to kill a man, and do it in a way that would leave him to die slow and hard. She certainly felt that was what Roderick deserved, but it was a little chilling to hear such a handsome man speak so blithely of doing it. When she looked at Payton, she relaxed a little. He was grinning at the man.

"Ye would do it, too, wouldnae ye?" said Payton.

"Aye," replied Connor. " 'Tis a mon's duty to protect the wee ones. Predators like Sir Roderick MacIye should be killed. And slow is best. Men like him are scared of dying. Deep in their black hearts they ken there is nay salvation for them. So, ye leave them dying, leave them with a long time to want to die so the pain will end, but terrified of doing so. A long time to think on all their sins and just how they will be made to pay for them." He shrugged. "Sad to say, it doesnae usually happen that way. The bastards usually die quick."

Everyone, even Gillyanne, looked as if that all made perfect sense to them. Kirstie knew that, in her heart, it all made sense to her, too. She agreed with the man. She was just not sure she ought to.

"Ah, your lass looks uneasy," murmured Connor. "A soft heart is a good thing in a lass, but mayhap not now, not with this mon."

"I ken it," Kirstie replied, then grimaced. "I just wasnae sure it was right to be so heartily in accord with it all."

Payton draped his arm around her shoulders and kissed her cheek, ignoring her blushes as he turned back to Connor. "At the moment, my biggest concern is his family. They see Roderick's claims of cuckoldry and wife theft as a deep insult to their honor, to their clan's honor. They grow angry and restless with his reluctance to do anything about it except talk and complain. It may be best if Kirstie and I find somewhere to hide until I can talk to some of them. If I can get them to heed the truth about Roderick, I think they will nay longer be a threat and, quite possibly, nay longer help Roderick in any way."

Connor nodded. "Their feelings are just. They need to ken that they are based on lies."

"I dinnae think ye should hide away, Payton," Gillyanne said. " 'Twould be as if ye are admitting your guilt. It would give the weight of truth to Sir Roderick's lies. The MacIyes would see it thus and feel free to hunt ye down. If ye are running and hiding, it then becomes verra difficult for anyone to guard your back. All of that simply helps Sir Roderick in his plan to be rid of both of ye."

"True, yet," Payton shrugged, "what else am I to do?

Invite the MacIyes here for some wine and conversation?''

"Aye, exactly that. A bold approach, one that will intrigue them and make them wonder if ye just might be innocent.''

"Or give them a fine chance to cut me into wee, bloody pieces.''

"Gilly makes a fine little potion," Connor said, and exchanged a brief grin with his wife. "From what ye have told us, the MacIyes sound a fair-minded lot, but they think the honor of their name has been stained. Feelings could run high and that makes for a dangerous situation. And, once ye start telling them what a foul beast Sir Roderick is, there is nay judging how they will react to that. If ye tried to tell me the like about one of my close kin, my first thought would be to cut your lying tongue out. They might feel the same.''

"Exactly," agreed Gillyanne, "so we get the men here and serve them some mildly dosed wine. When they fall asleep, we tie them to their seats. They will listen to ye then and with no cutting out of tongues." She sighed. "I wish I had a potion that would make them believe ye. That will be the most difficult thing to accomplish.''

"Then I will help make them believe it," said Callum.

"Oh, nay, Callum," Kirstie protested. "We couldnae ask that of ye.''

"Ye didnae. I offered.''

"As will I.''

Kirstie stared at the two people standing in the doorway, as did everyone else. "Michael? Eudard? What are the two of ye doing here?'' She saw how her brother limped as he walked toward her, Michael close behind him. "Your leg—''

"Is mostly healed, although a stiffness might linger,'' Eudard replied. "I would have come sooner except that Aunt Grizel threatened to tie me to the bed.''

"But I sent Michael to tell ye what was happening and I wrote to ye—''

"Aye. Dear Eudard, dinnae worry, I didnae drown. Kirstie. Verra soothing, that."

"I was writing a better one. Started it yesterday, but something interfered."

"Of course it did. Why dinnae ye introduce me and Michael to your friends, and then we can discuss that, er, interference."

As Kirstie quickly did so, Payton studied her twin brother. They were certainly much alike in looks, making Eudard a very handsome young man, but he was a great deal larger than Kirstie, being at least six feet tall, broad-shouldered, and muscular. Michael Campbell looked to be about fourteen or fifteen, and lanky, as most youths were. With his black hair, deep blue eyes, excellent skin, and elegant features, it was easy to see why Roderick had fixed his perverse attentions on the youth. Although he was now too old for Roderick, the man had obviously felt it was too dangerous to kill the boy—or Michael, unlike Callum, had been adequately cowed.

"I heard what ye have planned," said Eudard as he sat down in the chair Ian had fetched for him, "and Michael has told me a great deal ye neglected to, Kirstie. Howbeit, if ye would be so kind, I would like to ken just how much trouble ye have gotten yourself into since that day ye didnae drown."

Kirstie briefly told him of each incident, fighting to ignore the way he kept looking from Payton to her and back again. "So, ye see, it has been somewhat difficult, but everything is fine now."

"Oh, aye, I can see that," he drawled and rolled his eyes, before fixing his gaze upon Payton. "So, is this the lecherous, too-bonnie-for-his-own-health lad ye are cuckolding your bastard of a husband with?"

The question was asked so mildly, it took a moment for Kirstie to realize the import of it. "Where did ye hear that?" she demanded, hoping a swift offense would divert him. "Oh, Jesu, that news hasnae reached home, has it?"

"Nay. I heard it in an alehouse. Some MacIyes were talking about ye and what to do with him. 'Tis how I kenned where to find ye, something else ye neglected to tell me. So, is he?"

"I really dinnae think this is the proper place or time for us to discuss this," she hissed.

Eudard shrugged. "I will be here for a while. We can discuss it later." He looked at Connor. "Several MacIyes are staying at the Hawk and Dove. Several more are at a wee house on the upper High Street, one marked with their clan name."

"They are nay staying with Sir Roderick?" asked Gillyanne.

"Nay," replied Eudard. "Odd, dinnae ye think? Ye may not need to work so verra hard to convince them that he is naught but filth they had best quickly scrape from their boots. 'Tis clear there is little affection between him and the others. The ones I o'erheard at the inn dinnae like him at all. If he wasnae one of the laird's sons, I dinnae think ye would be hearing from them at all."

"Now *that* sounds verra promising," said Connor. "Some of them might already suspect what he is."

Before Payton knew it, Connor and Gillyanne were gone, hurrying away to deliver invitations to the MacIyes to come to Payton on the morrow and to make certain that Gillyanne had all she needed to make her potion. Ian took Callum off to show him the best places to aim his knife and Michael, deciding that sounded interesting, went with them. Kirstie was headed out the door, babbling excuses about needing to check on the children and seeing if there was enough food for everyone, before Payton had even seen her stand up. He glanced around, then looked at Eudard, and realized he had been left alone with his lover's twin brother. The way Eudard slowly smiled was not particularly comforting.

"That was an impressive escape your sister just made," Payton said.

"Aye, she is verra good at that," said Eudard. "Learned the trick of it when she was but a wee lass. With eight brothers, retreat is oftimes the best way. So, ye are the mon who has stolen Roderick's wife, tempting her into committing adultery."

"She isnae his wife," Payton snapped, then groaned when he realized how telling his reaction had been. "He ne'er bedded her, ye ken. Ne'er consummated the union."

"Ah, I thought not. Of course, ye have undoubtedly rectified that."

"I have nay wish to fight with Kirstie's brother, especially her twin brother."

"I have nay great wish to fight with ye, either. Nay anymore. When I first heard this tale, I was rather hot for your blood. Ranting on about all the ways I would kill ye. Geld ye first, of course."

"Of course. Only to be expected."

"Then Michael verra quietly said, 'She is alive.' I, being a calm mon, a reasonable mon, naturally tried to clout him offside the head with my walking stick and demanded he tell me exactly what he meant by that."

Eudard had a very odd sense of humor, Payton decided, and studied the thick, carved stick the man held. "I hope ye missed the poor lad."

"Aye, he is admirably quick on his feet. He then said he didnae have a sister, so couldnae guess how a mon would feel if he discovered his sister had been debauched by a bonnie rogue." He nodded faintly when Payton winced. "But he does think, in Kirstie's case, wasnae it more important that she was alive, that she was safe and protected, and that someone was helping her fight her perverted bastard of a husband? Being as I am so fond of hearing a hard truth, I tried to hit him again. He skipped away, still yapping at me, and we played that game for a wee while. Then I decided he might be right, and I was tired, and it was probably a good thing I have a limp or I might have hurt the lad.

Of course, he is impudent. A sound rap with a stick wouldnae have been completely amiss.''

"Quite right. I occasionally think that about Callum and he is but eleven. 'Tis probably for the best that I resist the urge.''

"True. He has suffered enough. So has Michael.''

"Oh, I wasnae thinking on that, though ye are right.''

"Nay? Then what were ye thinking of?''

"Callum has knives. Seven at last count.'' Payton smiled faintly when Eudard laughed. "Right now he needs to fair bristle with weapons, I am thinking.''

"Aye, and my sister had need of you. Mayhap not in that particular way," he drawled, "but in many another. It pinches that she didnae come to us, but I can understand why. Ye live in Roderick's world and, kin for kin, coin for coin, ye can match him. Ye have kept her alive, ye have kept her safe, and, I think, ye have made her happier than she has been in five verra long years. So, nay, no fighting and no interfering. Nay now. Later, if she survives this, but ye break her heart?'' He shrugged again. "We shall see.''

Payton frowned slightly. "I cannae say I wouldnae break her heart, though 'tisnae my intention. My intentions are all that is honorable. I just thought I would wait until she isnae wed to Roderick any longer ere I speak to her. When she is a widow, I will make her my wife.''

"Fair enough. More than fair. So, I may now rest easy and ignore the frolics going on beneath my verra nose.''

"I but pray ye can convince her of that. Mayhap, the next time she skips by, ye could try to trip her with that stick.''

Eudard grinned and then held his hand out when Payton stood up. "Heave us out of this chair.'' Once on his feet, Eudard walked to the door at Payton's side. "That fellow Ian is teaching the young lad how to fight?''

"Aye. Down in the cellars, if ye are of a mind to see it.''

"I believe I am. Lead on."

Just as they neared the door to the cellars, Kirstie walked out of the kitchen. Before she could escape, Payton caught her round the waist and held her to his side. She blushed furiously, then started to frown in confusion when she realized Eudard was grinning. Since Payton had no intention of speaking to her of marriage yet, he suspected her brother's easy acceptance of their sharing a bed was going to puzzle her.

"What are ye doing now, Eudard?" Kirstie asked her brother.

"Going down to watch Ian train the lads," Eudard replied. "And what are ye planning to do?"

"Weel, I was going to—" She screeched in surprise when Payton picked her up and tossed her over his shoulder.

"We are going afrolicking," Payton drawled.

"Ah, missed your morning one, did ye?" Eudard grinned.

"Exactly."

"Weel, have a wee frolic for me. And, I will now pretend that I am blind as weel as lame."

Payton heard Kirstie gasp and felt sure she had received her brother's less-than-subtle message. He suspected he would still have to indulge in some soothing of her renewed concerns, but, as he started up the stairs, he decided he was more than up to the task.

CHAPTER SEVENTEEN

"I cannae believe it worked!"

Neither could Payton, but he just smiled at Kirstie as she, Gillyanne, and Callum slipped into his great hall. He had covered his back well enough, but it had still been a risk. It pleased him to have been proven right about the MacIye sense of honor and fair play. The fact that they had been willing to talk instead of simply cutting his throat on the spot for the perceived insult to their family, meant that they would be willing to listen. Unless they were too enraged by the trick he had just played on them, he thought as he looked over the six unconcious men and grimaced.

"Six of them?" Gillyanne asked as she quickly checked each man to be sure they were all simply unconscious and had suffered no ill effects from her brew or from falling on the floor.

"Eight," announced Connor as he walked in dragging an unconcious MacIye, Strong Ian following with another.

"Did ye hurt them badly?" Gillyanne frowned at the two men Connor and Ian tossed onto the floor.

"Nay much."

"They thought they had me cornered after they slipped round Malkie, Donald, and Angus," Strong Ian explained, "but Connor came up behind them and slammed their heads together."

"Simple is always best," Payton murmured and grinned when Gillyanne muttered a few well-chosen curses as she checked the men's heads. "Eudard and Michael?"

"Here," said Eudard as he, Malkie, and Michael entered the room only to pause and gape at the MacIyes. "Eight of them?"

"I would have brought more," said Connor.

"I am flattered," said Payton.

Connor shrugged. "Ye are little, but ye are slippery."

"Was that a compliment?" Kirstie asked softly as she came to sit beside Payton's chair.

"I think so." He looked at Michael and Callum as they came to sit near him. "Are ye sure about this?"

Callum turned from watching the men tie the MacIyes to their chairs. "Aye. Ye and Kirstie are fighting for me and the other bairns. Ye have risked your lives and your good names. Now your kinsmen have begun to step into the fight. If telling what happened to me and all I ken and saw will help, I must do it."

"And no one here will be telling anyone what they hear," added Michael. "It has to stop. It *has* to."

Payton briefly clasped the youth on the shoulder. "It will."

By the time Wee Alice had brought in food and some untainted drink, and left to watch over the children, the first of the MacIyes was rousing. Gillyanne and Kirstie set some wine, bread, and cheese before the men while Connor and Eudard stood behind four of the MacIyes, and Strong Ian and Malkie stood guard behind the other four. The MacIyes were disarmed, but, if released from their bonds they could still prove dangerous. Gillyanne and Kirstie were just slipping back into their seats flanking him, when the last of the MacIyes opened his eyes. Almost as one, they all glared at him.

"We were willing to talk," growled the eldest of them, Sir Keith.

"Oh, aye, and then ye meant to chop him into wee bits," muttered Kirstie.

"And ye, our kinsmon's wife, dare to cavort with another right before our eyes!"

"We are nay cavorting! We are just trying to stay alive, Uncle."

"Uncle?" Payton asked.

"Aye," replied Kirstie, still meeting Sir Keith's hard glare with a fierce one of her own. "They obviously felt ye were a formidable opponent. Ye have Sir Keith, Roderick's uncle, and next to him is his firstborn son Tomas. Then there is another uncle, Sir Thomas, and his firstborn son William. On t'other side of the table are four of Roderick's brothers—Sir Andrew, Sir Brian, Sir Adam, and Sir Ross. 'Tis clear my husband's clan holds the honor of the MacIyes more dear than Roderick e'er has."

"Certainly more dear than his whore of a wife does. Ow!" Sir Keith glared back at Connor, who had sharply rappped him on the head with his knuckles. "The lass is here carrying on with the pretty fool. All of the king's court can speak of naught else. Do ye expect us to do naught but smile and wish her a fine time?"

"Lady Kirstie did not seek me out because of my pretty face or rumored skills in the bedchamber," Payton said. "She sought someone to help her after her husband tried to drown her." He was a little surprised by the sudden, tense silence of the MacIyes.

"I wonder if their silence o'er that charge is because they ken Roderick would do such a thing or because they arenae verra surprised that I might drive a mon to try it," drawled Kirstie, then smiled when Gillyanne laughed.

"Ye be quiet," Payton ordered her gently before turning a hard look on the MacIyes. "Now, if ye gentlemen swear ye will behave and hear us out, we will untie you. 'Tis time ye heard the truth."

After exchanging looks with his kinsmen, Sir Keith nodded. "We will nay be fighting ye today."

The moment they were untied, the MacIyes began to help themselves to the food and drink set before them, confident that this time it would be safe. "What do ye want us to believe the truth is?" asked Sir Keith.

"Roderick tried to murder his wife," Payton replied. "He chased her down and threw her in the river. The mon forgot she could swim."

Sir Andrew snorted, then muttered, "That sounds like something that fool would do."

"So, he tried to kill her," said Sir Keith after exchanging another round of glances with his kinsmen. "He failed. Most lasses would flee to their kinsmen for shelter or enter a convent. But, she didnae. She ran to ye. Why?"

"I was closer," Payton drawled and winced when Gillyanne kicked him in the shins, painfully reminding him that these were not men he should antagonize. "Lady Kirstie had already begun to search for a champion ere her husband tossed her in a river. When she pulled herself out of the water, she sought out the mon she had finally chosen—me. I fear she heeded the many flattering, but somewhat exaggerated, tales of how I rush to help the helpless, rally to righteous causes, and so forth. She needed a champion, ye understand, for she kenned exactly why her husband had tried to drown her. Lady Kirstie had discovered why, after five long years of marriage, her husband had yet to bed her."

After another heavy silence, Sir Andrew said, "Curse it, I had always wondered. He likes the men, eh?"

"Lady Kirstie wouldnae care about that."

"I would have found some way to compromise or to end the marriage verra quietly," Kirstie said.

"But, I fear her husband's secret is verra dark

indeed," said Payton. " 'Tis nay men he lusts after, but children." He waited patiently as his allies quelled the furious protests his guests made. "Come, gentlemen, we all ken that such evil exists. 'Tis nay banished from this world simply by denying or ignoring it."

" 'Tis a foul, black deed ye accuse our kinsman of," said Sir Keith. "Why should we heed what ye say?"

After closely studying the faces of the men, Payton replied, "Because I speak the ugly truth and I think some of ye are nay so surprised."

"Nay," said Sir Andrew. "I willnae believe it."

The vehemence of the man's denial told Payton that Sir Andrew was probably trying to convince himself of his own words. For a brief moment, he had hoped there was a way to save Michael and Callum from having to tell their tales. It did not really surprise him, however, that the MacIyes needed much more to accept that their clan, their closest blood, had bred such evil.

"I will speak first," said Callum, slowly standing up.

"And who are ye?" demanded Sir Keith.

"No one important. Just one of the wretched wee ones who creep about the streets and alleys of a town trying to find enough to survive another day. One of those ye fine gentlemen dinnae heed, save to kick the wretch aside if he stumbles into your path. 'Tis where Sir Roderick found me. 'Tis where he finds many of his prey. I doubted his tale of giving me a better life, but he dragged me away with him. I was soon shown that I was right to doubt his promises." Taking a deep breath, Callum told his tale in a flat, hard voice, and with the occasional coarse bluntness of a child of the streets.

Kirstie reached out and took Callum's hand in hers. It tore her heart out to hear all that had happened to Callum, to the other children Callum had seen come and go, even though she had known or guessed most of it. She saw tears on Gillyanne's face and did not look at the woman again, afraid she would give in to the grief choking her. The MacIyes just stared at Callum. Each one had lost all color and several looked as near to weeping as she felt.

"Brave lad," Payton murmured, briefly clasping Callum's shoulder as the boy sat down again.

"I just kept telling myself it isnae my shame," Callum replied. "All of ye keep saying so, and I think I begin to believe it."

"And so ye should, for 'tis the truth," Payton said.

"Ye are no street waif," said Sir Keith in a hoarse voice when Michael slowly stood up.

"Nay, sir," replied Michael. "I am the fourth son of Sir Ronald Campbell, laird of Dunspeen, a small, poor holding."

"Jesu," whispered Sir Keith, "the sons of lairds as weel?"

"Nay so verra many," Michael said, "and fewer still of any family of great standing. The bastard's greatest shield is our own fear and shame, isnae it? I am near to emptying my belly at the thought of speaking about what I suffered, though I have been too old for him for a while now, and of all I saw and heard. Yet, when I met the wee ones Lady Kirstie saved, I kenned that it will ne'er stop unless someone speaks out. Silence might save my pride and heart, but it allows that bastard to keep visiting his evil upon the innocent."

"Sit down, lad. Ye need say no more. The lad Callum told us more than we need. Jesu, more than any mon wishes to hear."

Michael sat down. "Do ye believe it, then? Did ye guess what he was?"

"A wee bit, but 'tis one of those things one fights to blind oneself to. We couldnae ignore it enough to give him our own bairns to watch o'er, though, could we? If he did manage to get to any in the family or others upon our lands, no one spoke out about it. Or, they died," he added softly.

Payton could tell by the tormented look upon the older man's face that he was thinking of far too many possibilities, of children whose deaths may not have been the tragic, but all too sadly common, natural loss of a child. "And now?"

"He is dead to us," Sir Keith said, and the other MacIyes muttered their agreement, even Roderick's brothers.

"Will ye make that known?"

"Aye, but nay the reason why, if we can avoid it." He rubbed a hand over his face. "The whispers have begun, fed by ye, I suspect. When 'tis known we have cast Roderick from the clan, most will feel those whispers are all true." He looked straight at Payton. "Ye will kill him."

There was only the barest hint of a question in the man's voice. "Aye. I will."

"Weel, that was unpleasant," said Eudard when the MacIyes finally left.

"Aye," agreed Payton. "Most families can count a rotted branch or two upon the family tree, but 'tis nay usually one as evil as this, thank God. Now they will fear there is bad blood within their lineage. 'Tis to be hoped they willnae hold fast to such foolishness for too long." He looked at Callum. "Ye did weel this day, lad. As did ye, Michael," he added, and lightly slapped the older boy on the back.

Callum shrugged. "It helped that I was verra certain no one here would e'er repeat what I said, just as Michael claimed."

"I had thought they might ask for the right to deal with Roderick themselves," said Kirstie.

"They obviously dinnae want to spill the blood of such a close kinsmon," said Payton. "I am glad of it. That right should be ours."

Kirstie filled her goblet with wine and took a long drink. She felt relieved that they would not have to fear the MacIye clan anymore, but also felt sad for Sir Keith and the others. They were good men, had always been kind to her. That their proud name should be so stained by Roderick had to be a hard blow.

Now the only one they needed to watch out for was Roderick and whatever men he could hold at his side. She had no doubt that, when the MacIyes made it known that Roderick was dead to them, they would also avow the innocence of Payton Murray. Guilt would prompt them to ensure all the hounds were removed from the hunt, leaving Payton free to fight Roderick. She knew it would not be easy, but suspected Payton did as well.

"Your name will soon be cleared," she said to Payton.

"Do ye think so?" he asked.

"Oh, aye. The MacIyes may not be able to draw Roderick's blood, but they want him dead. Dead, buried, and forgotten. They will make it clear that ye are no wife thief, for they will wish ye to be able to fix all of your attention and skill upon bringing Roderick to justice."

"And so your name will also be cleared."

"Ah, true, although I dinnae believe I have loomed so verra large in all of this. If naught else, few people ken who I am. Roderick didnae allow me to mingle with verra many people. Afraid of what I might say, I suppose."

"What do ye plan to do now?" asked Connor.

"Take my ease," replied Payton. "I am nay sure for how long, but I mean to wait until Roderick is thoroughly cast off, and all ken it. I also want it kenned that I have a rightful vengeance to enact so that I may hunt the beast down without fear of any consequences. Nay for myself as much as for Kirstie."

"And ye believe the MacIyes will openly give ye the right to hunt their kinsmon?"

"Aye. As Kirstie says, they want the shame of him dead and buried. There have been whispers about the mon and not all of them begun by me or Kirstie. Once his kinsmen cast him out, those whispers will, indeed, be seen as the truth. Although no one will speak openly of his crimes, they will shun him for them. And, they will silently condone whate'er justice I mete out.''

"Gilly and I will take ourselves to the king's court, be your eyes and ears.''

Payton had to bite back a smile, for Connor's tone of voice revealed what a painful sacrifice he felt he was making. "Ye dinnae have to.''

"Aye, we do. Ye and the lass cannae go, nor can Eudard, for he is her kinsmon. But, ye need to ken when the path is cleared for ye to act openly and forcefully against that bastard. Since word went out that ye stole that bastard's wife, ye havenae been able to do much at all save hide behind guards and closed doors, occasionally getting word from Sir Bryan. Rest. The furor will die down soon and Gilly and I will tell ye exactly when ye can show your pretty face again. Ye will need all your strength and wits about ye then." He lifted his goblet of wine. "To victory.''

"Aye," agreed Payton as he and the others all joined in the toast. "To victory, and may it be soon.''

Kirstie sat in the middle of Payton's huge bed, dressed only in her shift, and brushed at her damp hair. The confrontation with the MacIyes had been trying, somewhat exhausting, but their success eased a lot of that. If only she could so easily rid herself of all the twinges of shame and embarrassment she felt over so openly sharing Payton's bed. Just as she had thought she had accepted it all, the number of others who knew had greatly increased. His family did not seem to mind, the children acted as if it was all perfectly acceptable, Strong Ian and Wee Alice seemed almost pleased, even hopeful, and her own brother offered no condemnation. It seemed she was the only one concerned about it all. Perhaps it was time she just asked one of the others exactly why they accepted the arrangement so easily, especially her brother. All of Payton's reasons why she should feel no shame made perfect sense, but she could not completely ignore the fact that he gained something he wanted when she agreed with him. And, he was certainly no stranger to the sin of adultery or lust.

"Ye are thinking on sin and penances again, arenae ye?" drawled Payton as he tossed aside the last of his clothes, sat down behind her, and took over the pleasant chore of brushing her thick hair.

"Someone ought to," she mumbled, wondering how the man could be so unconcerned about his own nudity. "No one else seems to be."

"Nay so long ago ye didnae, either. At least, nay for a few hours."

"I ken it. I am nay so sure why I keep fretting myself o'er it now. 'Tis just that, weel, now a whole new lot of people ken it. And, weel, adultery, *mmpfh.*" She briefly considered nipping the palm of the hand he had clasped over her mouth, but thought he might actually like it unless she did it hard enough to truly hurt.

"Is a sin, and, I will confess, though I am nay above using the women willing to commit it, I have little respect for most of them. Ye, however, are no adulteress."

"I am a wedded woman," she said as soon as he removed his hand.

"Ye may have said the vows, but the marriage was ne'er consummated, therefore 'tis invalid. I had thought that ye had decided that was so."

"So, then I am just a wanton?"

Payton set the brush down, wrapped his arms around her, and pulled her back against him. "Ye are my lover." He traced the delicate shape of her ear with his tongue. "Ye are my comrade in arms. Ye are nay Sir Roderick's wife, nor have ye e'er been. Ye are mine," he said, his voice soft and husky as he kissed her neck.

"At this time, aye, I am." She forced away the hurt caused by the knowledge that her time with Payton would end either because Roderick beat them or because Payton tired of her once they had won their battle.

As he shifted their positions on the bed so that she was sprawled beneath him, Payton decided that now was probably not a good time to tell her he had no intention of letting her go. She was still Sir Roderick's wife, sometimes in her own mind, and definitely in the minds of too many others. Payton knew that no matter how many pretty and heartfelt words he gave her, how many promises of fidelity and forever he uttered, Kirstie would not completely believe him. He had to wait until he could make her his wife.

Kirstie shivered with a sudden rush of desire as Payton began to kiss her legs. The flare of embarrassment she had suffered when he sprawled between her legs quickly faded. She was a little astonished that she could be so enflamed by a kiss on the soft skin at the back of her knee. It was not until he kissed each hip that she realized he had pushed her shift up to her waist. Shock at how exposed she was to his gaze made her try to close her legs, but his broad shoulders prevented that attempt at modesty.

"Payton," she cried softly in protest when he knelt, his gaze fixed upon that place she wished to shield as he stroked her thighs.

When his gaze met hers, she gasped. The desire she could read there was almost hot enough to burn away the last shreds of her modesty. To see that she could stir this man to such passion could easily make her vain.

"Ye must ne'er try to hide such beauty from me," he said, leaning forward to kiss her hard and fast.

She was thinking of protesting such a meager kiss when he tugged her shift off and tossed it aside. He kissed, caressed, and even licked his way from her throat to her breasts. When he drew the taut, aching tip of one breast into his mouth, Kirstie stroked his back and shoulders, holding him close.

Kirstie murmured her disappointment when he

began to move his kisses to other parts of her heated body. She was just thinking that it was easy to cast aside all modesty when he caressed her, when he touched his lips to the soft curls shielding her woman's flesh. Even she could hear that her trembling protests were weak, her voice thick with desire. She liked this, yet was shocked that she did. Her thoughts on her own inexplicable confusion were completely scattered when he stroked her with his tongue. She could be shocked and embarrassed later, she decided, as she twined her fingers in his hair to hold him close while she offered herself up for his stunningly intimate kiss.

As she felt herself draw ever nearer to that sweet abyss passion always sent her tumbling into, Kirstie struggled to get Payton to join with her, but he ignored her demands and then her pleas. He drove her to the heights with his mouth. Her body was still shaking and tingling from the strength of her release when Payton propped her legs up against his shoulders and joined their bodies with such force she knew she would have been thrown up against the headboard if he had not had a firm grip on her.

For one brief moment, she saw him clearly. The look of intense, nearly feral passion upon his beautiful face should have alarmed her, but instead, it caused her desire to start climbing again, to start scrambling back up those blinding heights she had only just hurled herself down. His gaze was fixed intently upon the place where their bodies were joined as he thrust in and out with a fury and growing speed that could well leave her feeling a little bruised in the morning. One glance was almost more than she could bear, and, closing her eyes, she allowed her body to rule her. He placed one hand down on the mattress as his body shuddered, the warmth of his seed spilling inside of her only intensifying her own bliss. When he collapsed against her, she forced her weak, trembling arms around him, holding him close as they both struggled to recover their wits and

strength. She liked the way he remained joined with
her as they both tried to grasp some calm and rationality,
so she wrapped her arms and legs around him more
securely, holding him as close as possible.

" 'Tis nay wonder women flock to your bed," she said
when she finally regained enough sense to speak.

Kirstie forcefully pushed aside the thought of how
many women there were out there who had shared this
bliss with him. The moment she had entered his room
that first night, she had known she was about to join
the ranks of far too many women. It was foolish to
torment herself with thoughts of all the other women
who had held him close like this. He made a noise
that was an even blend of curse and laughter, and she
welcomed the interruption of her own painful thoughts.

"Ah, lass, I have ne'er done that before," he said,
shifting a little to resettle himself more securely inside
of her as he felt himself begin to harden again.

"Truly?" She was somewhat astonished when his
almost idle caress of her breast caused a renewed quick-
ening low in her belly.

"I suppose I should be flattered ye thought me experienced in that sort of loving. Nay, I sometimes gave a
rare, fleeting kiss to speed the wench toward my goal,
toward satisfying my wants and needs, but nay more
than that. They were women I but borrowed, used for
a wee while, and nay more. Ah, but ye are mine, have
only e'er been mine. No other mon has kenned the
sweetness of ye and I have a need to ken the fullness
of it." He propped himself up on his forearms and gave
her a deep, stirring kiss. "And, ye are verra sweet indeed,
my dark beauty. Like the richest, rarest honey. Sweet
and warm and definitely tasting like more." He began to
move, measured, penetrating thrusts intended to gently
restir that fierce passion she gave so freely.

She could feel the sting of a fierce blush upon her
cheeks, but his words stirred her. As she felt her desire
revived by his gentle caresses and almost idle cadence,

she stroked the back of his strong legs with her feet and decided to cast aside all worry about sin. She had done it before and it should not matter that his cousin or her brother now knew about them. According to all the rules of the church and society, she became a sinner the moment she went to his bed, the moment she even thought about doing so. Fretting over the matter would not change that, would only sour all they could share, as would worrying over who might know about it. She acted out of love and there was no changing that, either. There was also the ever-present shadow of Roderick looming over them. Soon he would find himself disowned, dispossessed, and scorned. That would enrage him, make him rabid in his need for revenge, and he would blame her for it all. From the moment he had thrown her in the river, her life had been in danger. It was past time to cease fretting over how she spent what few peaceful hours she had. There was always the chance that she might not have many left.

CHAPTER EIGHTEEN

As she peered out the window of the room the children slept in, Callum on one side of her and Michael on the other, Kirstie wondered just how big Payton's family was. It had been a week since the MacIyes had arrived and three days after that the first of a horde of Murray kinsmen had begun to arrive. Payton was very particular about introducing her to each and every one, but she was not sure why. Most seemed very surprised to find her in his home and she began to think the rumor that he let no women in this house was actually true. Most stayed only long enough to find out what Roderick looked like, what men were with him, and where they should look for the man.

Roderick was in hiding. The MacIyes had not only disowned him, they had taken back his lands, his source of wealth, and most of his small army of men. He was now a "broken man." His clan had also cast him out swiftly, openly, and completely. As suspected, the moment they had done so, all the dark rumors about Roderick were seen as true and he was utterly shunned. Several men who either suspected or now knew he had

defiled their sons were also hunting him, eager to make
him pay for an insult they had no real wish to discuss,
but which everyone now suspected.

It was somewhat amusing, and she and Gillyanne had
certainly giggled over it often enough, but Payton was
now seen as a wondrous hero, a near saint of a man
who had risked his good and honorable name for the
sake of children. There was certainly some truth to it
all, yet it was spoken of in such ridiculously flowery
terms it invited ridicule. It was obvious she and Gillyanne
were not the only ones who thought so as there had
been several tussles amongst Payton and the seemingly
never-ending flow of cousins and brothers. Connor also
made the occasional subtle jest, as did Ian.

"Payton has a verra big family," said Callum, sounding a little envious.

"They arenae all blood kin," said Michael. " 'Tis
rather fine that that doesnae seem to make any difference, though." Michael looked at Kirstie. " 'Tis why ye
chose him, isnae it? Ye kenned his family would all be
quick to help him."

Kirstie nodded. "One of the reasons. I had heard
that the family was large and that a strong bond existed
e'en amongst the most distant. I will confess, though,
that I hadnae realized it would be like this. Nay wonder
the MacIyes were hesitant to act upon Roderick's claims.
They kenned the trouble that would descend upon
them."

"As it is now descending upon Roderick. The bastard
willnae be able to find a hole dark enough or deep
enough to hide in."

"Nay. It willnae be long now e'er it is over. I but pray
nothing bad happens to us or any of the ones aiding
us."

"Ah, there ye are," said Gillyanne as she peered into
the room, then hurried over to them. "Payton wants ye
to join him in his ledger room, Kirstie."

"Weel, at least I can be fair sure I am nay about

to be lectured again,'' Kirstie said and smiled when Gillyanne laughed.

"And he wants to see ye as weel, Callum,'' Gilly said.

Callum frowned. "He wants me to meet some of his kinsmen? Me alone, I mean?''

"Aye. Some of the MacMillans.'' Gillyanne cast a quick, telling look at Kirstie, then hugged Callum. "Ah, that is good, my braw laddie. Fight those dark, ugly feelings. Dinnae let that bastard steal away the joy of a friend's touch or a truly loving embrace. If ye turn from such things, ye will ne'er feel aught but the cold.'' She straightened up, smiled at everyone, and headed out the door. "Dinnae be too long. Why dinnae ye come with me, Michael.''

As soon as she and Michael were gone, Callum looked at Kirstie. "She is always doing that.''

"Doing what?'' asked Kirstie as she nudged him toward the door.

"Hugging me and saying those odd things. 'Tis as if she can see right into a person's heart. I ken there are bad feelings inside me, but I keep them there. I hide them, ye ken, because I dinnae like them.''

"But, Lady Gillyanne can see them?''

"Aye, and she kens I want them gone. Do ye think she is a witch?''

"Och, nay,'' she said as they made their way down the narrow stone stairs. "She just, weel, kens things, kens a person's feelings. Nay all of them and nay all the time. Does it trouble ye? Do ye wish me to speak to her?''

"Nay. Weel, it does trouble me a wee bit, but I think that may be good for me. I dinnae like these feelings, but I am nay getting rid of them, am I? Just hiding them. When she says those things, I think on them for a wee while, and I think some of the bad feelings are getting weaker.'' He shrugged. "Mayhap 'tis just because she sees them and talks about them.''

"Sometimes looking straight at such feelings and having someone who understands, someone ye can speak to, can help. And, mayhap she does it so that, when she has to go home, ye will be able to work on making those bad feelings go away all by yourself.'' She gently stroked his soft, bright hair as they paused before the heavy door to Payton's ledger room. ''Ye havenae been free and safe for verra long, Callum. Wounds take time to heal, and a heart's wounds can take the longest. And, the sad thing is that ye will mostly have to heal yourself. People who care about ye can help if ye let them, and I think ye ken that ye now have a lot of people who care about ye. Aye?'' She smiled when he nodded. ''Good. When those dark feelings try to take hold, ye remember that. Always remember that.''

''I will.''

''Trust me, kenning that, believing that truth, is the best medicine. Now, best we see what his grand lairdship wants.'' She smiled again when he laughed and they walked into Payton's ledger room.

A gasp caught her attention even as she shut the door behind them. A tall, handsome, auburn-haired man was very pale. He clutched the back of a chair as if he needed the support to remain standing. She glanced at the other two guests with Payton and Ian, quickly recognized the boy as the one she had mistaken for Callum, and recalled Payton saying he was his cousin Uven. They truly did look almost exactly alike. The other man in the room was also handsome, slightly older than the other two, and his hair was a much darker red. He wavered between concern for the man who looked so pale and a delight which appeared whenever he looked at Callum.

Kirstie felt a slight twitch at her skirts and looked at Callum. He was pale and he was staring at the boy Uven as if he had seen a ghost, a look Uven was returning in kind. She realized he was clasping her skirts in one hand so she reached down to take that hand in hers. Callum clutched her hand, holding on tightly even as Payton walked over to them and led them to a seat.

"Gentlemen, this is Lady Kirstie MacIye and this handsome boy is Callum," said Payton as he poured the pale man a large tankard of wine. "Kirstie, Callum, allow me to introduce Sir Bryan MacMillan, Uven Mac-Millan, and Sir Euan MacMillan." Each one bowed slightly as his name was said; then Payton crouched by Callum, who sat hard up against Kirstie. "Do ye see it, lad?"

"Uven looks like me," Callum said. "He isnae my brother, is he?"

"Nay, but I strongly suspect he is your cousin." As he rose to his feet, Payton looked at Sir Euan. "Is he?"

Sir Euan nodded, took a long drink of wine, and sank down into the seat he had been clinging to. "Aye, he is." He looked at Payton. "When I was told about the boy, all the facts I sought were right. The right mother, the right town, the right time, the right name. Bryan added to it all by discovering I had been lied to, that the woman and child hadnae died upon a childbed. Yet, it was difficult to believe." He looked at Callum. "But, Jesu, he is Innes to the bone."

"Who was Innes?" asked Callum, curiosity easing his fear enough for him to speak calmly and clearly.

"Your father," replied Sir Euan. "Your mother was—"

"Joan, the swineherd's youngest daughter." Callum shrugged when Kirstie and Payton both stared at him in surprise. "I always kenned who my mither was, but she died when I was three, near four, years old."

"I was told she died bearing a child, taking that child to the grave with her."

"Nay. She got a fever and went to her father's house. Thinking she was dying, she wanted him to care for me, but he spit on us. Told us he wouldnae waste the slop he fed his pigs on such a whore and her bastard. He tossed us off his wee scrap of land and my mither was near dead by the time we reached her sister's home. She didnae want us, either. I remember my mither saying she might shame her sister into caring for me if she died right on her hearthstone. She did. It didnae. When the cart took my mither's body away, I followed it, and I marked where she was buried so I could find her place again."

"And then what did ye do?"

"Lived about the town for a wee while. Then, when I was about seven, I was taken to Thanescarr."

"So, ye ken what your birthday is?"

"Aye. The fifteenth day of May, 1455. Mither told me it was exactly a week before old Father James died. I was the last bairn he christened. It helped me remember because I just had to ask someone how long ago it was that Father James died."

"That, too, fits. The swineherd told me ye and your mother were dead. I didnae like the look of the mon, but I couldnae think of any reason why he should lie to me. 'Twas Bryan who tracked down the sister and finally got the truth. They just left ye in the streets?"

Callum nodded. "They didnae want a bastard. So, ye ken who my father was?"

"Aye. Sir Innes MacMillan. He came home at summer's end twelve years ago, intending to tell his father about a lass he meant to have to wife. Sadly, he was attacked by thieves and left for dead. He dragged himself home, but 'twas clear to all that he was dying. Fevered though he was, he struggled to tell us about your mother. I swore I would find her and be certain she was cared for. That gave him peace, but it proved a promise I couldnae keep. Winter set in hard and 'twas nearly a year ere I could set out to find Innes's Joan. It was a hard blow to hear that she had died, e'en harder to ken that Innes's child had died with her. Innes was the only surviving child of Sir Gavin MacMillan of Whyte mont and the mon was heartbroken when I had to bring him the news. But, now, I can tell him Innes's child lives, that Innes left a son.''

"A bastard.''

"Ah, nay. 'Twas a handfast marriage, true, but ye were born within the year. I have papers, ye ken. A witnessed handfast agreement, and now proof of when ye were born and christened. Nay, it may nay be as good as a priest-blessed marriage to some, but ye arenae a bastard. And, it wouldnae matter if ye were. Sir Gavin certainly wouldnae care.''

"Are ye saying ye wish him to go to Whytemont, to Sir Gavin?'' asked Payton.

"Weel, aye. He is Sir Gavin's heir,'' replied Sir Euan.

Payton looked at Callum and saw the fear, the uncertainty, in the boy's eyes. "What do ye say, Callum?''

"I,'' he began, and looked from Payton to Kirstie and back again, "but, there are bad things about me, there are—''

"Nay, lad,'' said Sir Euan. "There are bad things about Sir Roderick, nay about ye. Ye were a child, a child with no one to stand for him, may God forgive us. And, though ye may take insult o'er this, the truth is that ye are still a child. Dinnae let what happened hold ye back from reaching out for what is rightfully yours. I ken the tale, as does Sir Bryan, and so will Sir Gavin, but we will tell no one else if that is how ye wish it. The word about Sir Roderick has spread far and wide already, however, so I cannae promise it will all remain some great secret. Few things do.''

Callum nodded. "I ken it. It doesnae matter so verra much, nay if it puts an end to that mon.''

"And we dinnae need to go now. I wish to see the end of this, as weel. So, ye have time to think on it. If ye are still uneasy later, then Sir Gavin would be more than willing to come here. Ye can take it as slowly as ye wish.''

Kirstie felt Callum immediately relax. She was so happy for the boy, she felt like crying. He was unsure now, undoubtedly afraid of being taken from the odd family that had developed in Payton's home, but he would soon accept his good fortune. He just needed time and she was pleased that the MacMillans understood that. When she caught him studying Uven as hard as that boy was studying him, she felt even more hopeful.

"So, ye are my cousin?" he asked Uven.

"Aye. My grandmither and yours were sisters," Uven replied. "I think that is why we look so much alike." Uven moved closer. "Where did ye get that big knife?"

"I got this one when I first came here." Callum pulled a knife from his right sleeve. "Ian gave me this one." He pulled a knife from his right boot. "Payton gave me this one. This one in my left boot is from Wee Alice, Ian's wife. Malkie gave me the one in my left sleeve. And, see this one strapped inside my shirt? Donald gave me that one. And look at this one on this side with the sheath inside the waist of my breeches. Angus gave me that one."

"Can ye use them?" asked Uven, the challenge clear in his voice.

"Aye. I can show ye, if ye like." Callum stood up, then frowned and looked at the men. "Oh."

"Go on, lads." Ian stood up and started to herd the two boys toward the door. "I will come along to keep an eye on things, aye?"

Callum stopped just as Ian opened the door and looked back at Sir Euan. "I would have to live with him, aye?"

"Aye," replied Sir Euan. "That doesnae mean ye cannae go where ye wish when ye wish, however."

"I will think on that, too, then." Callum looked at Uven. "Come on, then. Mayhap we can find that big-nosed boy, too."

The moment the door shut behind Ian and the two boys, Kirstie looked at Payton. "Ye gave him a knife?"

Payton shrugged. "I didnae ken he had so many."

"It seems I am the only one who hasnae given him

a knife. And, big-nosed boy? He is still calling Simon names, isnae he?''

"Ah, weel, he isnae calling him a traitor or a coward anymore." He almost smiled when she groaned. "Leave it be for now, love. Simon and Callum are evenly matched in size and strength, but Simon is a year or more older than Callum. I think they are, weel, testing each other to see who will be the head of the pack."

Kirstie rolled her eyes, then grew serious again as she looked at Sir Euan. "I ken ye were hoping Callum would just come along with ye," she began.

"Aye, I was," he said, smiling faintly, "but I am nay surprised by his hesitation. It may not look a proper family to others, but to Callum, this is his family, here with ye and the other children. The moment Bryan told me what the boy had endured, and e'en he didnae ken it all, I understood that there may be a problem or two."

"There are two things that are important to Callum. He needs to feel safe and he needs to ken that he is accepted, that what happened to him hasnae left him unacceptable, e'en unclean."

"He will soon come to understand that none who matter amongst the family would e'er fault him for what happened to him, just as most reasonable men would-nae fault or turn from a woman who was sorely abused against her will. In truth, 'tis nay what others might think or believe which matters, but what Callum comes to believe about himself."

Payton nodded. "Exactly. We have been working on that. He needs to gain pride in what he can do, pride in who he is. I think, as he comes to ken the MacMillans, starts to accept and believe he truly is one, that will help. 'Tis nay just what that bastard did to the boy, but what his mother's family did, what this whole town did, that has left the boy with the feeling of being unwanted, undeserving. Ye can hear it occasionally in certain things he says. I believe his mother loved him dearly, for he seems to be able to accept the validity of a motherly sort of affection.''

Sir Bryan nodded, then sighed. '' 'Tis astonishing that he can accept any affection at all. I always thought a very young child had the blessing of forgetfulness, yet, sadly, Callum recalls verra clearly what happened when his mother was dying, though he was verra young. And, hearing how he was forced to live upon the streets at such a tender age.'' He shook his head. ''The most difficult part of that was the realization that I rarely heed the plight of the wee ones who appear so ragged and uncared for. I live here, yet not once can I recall seeing that boy. For all I ken, he was one I tossed a coin to at some time.''

''Weel, since ye are feeling so guilty, and, as ye say, ye live here, there is this place which calls itself a home for foundlings and orphans—''

As Payton began to stir his cousin's outrage over the plight of the children in the Darrochs' care, Kirstie quietly excused herself. She was just stepping into the hall when Sir Euan joined her and quietly shut the door behind them. The man looked so serious, Kirstie began to feel a little nervous. In her experience, such a solemn look upon a man's face often meant he was about to give her bad news or say something he knew she would not like.

''I wished a private word with ye about Callum,'' he said.

''He is a good lad,'' she said.

''A verra good lad. Far better than I had hoped for. Innes would be proud.''

''And exactly what is your part in all of this? Ye are verra involved in it all. Are ye close kin to him?''

''Just a cousin, but Innes and I were as close as brothers. He was the truest of friends and I still miss him. Despite his wounds, his hard life, and all else that is so verra different from Innes and his life, I can see a great deal of my friend in the boy.'' He smiled faintly. '' 'Twill be an honor to help Sir Gavin in the raising of him. The mon will love the boy, m'lady. Ye need ne'er worry on that. And nay as some ghost of his lost son, but as the boy he is. Of course, he is also the continuation of that small branch of the MacMillan clan."

Kirstie smiled and nodded. "A heritage can only help Callum gain that pride that ne'er should have been stolen from him."

"Aye. And I do realize all that has happened to the lad cannae be ignored or forgotten for it has shaped him, and will probably continue to do so. What I wished was a few moments of your time so that ye could tell me about the boy. I think it would help if I learned as much as possible, for it would be too easy to step wrongly, to cause an unintentional hurt, or misjudge something he says or does."

"A verra good idea." She linked her arm with his. "Come to the gardens with me. There is a pleasant spot there. 'Tis private, and, e'en better, 'tis near impossible for anyone to creep up and listen unseen."

Payton frowned as he approached the couple sitting so close together on the stone bench. He had heard their laughter as he had approached, could now see their ease with each other. They looked very good together. So good that Payton felt an overwhelming urge to pound Sir Euan MacMillan into the mud until he was not quite so cursed handsome any longer.

Jealousy, he thought, and was so startled he stopped too abruptly and nearly stumbled. He was jealous, blindingly so. He did not like seeing Kirstie so close to or so at ease with another man. She was his. Payton did not think there had ever been a time in his life when he had felt such a primal, fierce possessiveness over a woman. He had rarely practiced fidelity except out of convenience, and had never expected it of the women he had bedded. Yet, the mere thought of another man touching Kirstie had him clenching his hand on the hilt of his sword.

He took several slow, deep breaths to subdue this new and fascinating emotion. Neither Kirstie nor Euan was doing anything to warrant it and he did not wish to insult either of them. Payton slowly started toward them again. He would, however, make it as clear as possible to Sir Euan that this lass was taken.

Kirstie smiled at Payton as he stepped up to her. She blushed a little when he idly stroked her braid, but was beginning to become accustomed to the way he seemed inclined to touch her all the time, even when they were not private. The brief look of knowing amusement that crossed Sir Euan's face troubled her a little. It was evident that Payton's actions told the man they were lovers. She quickly shrugged off that embarrassment when the man smiled at her with the same easy and open friendliness he had before. Kirstie did wonder why it felt as if Payton had just clenched his hand tightly over her braid, but the feeling passed so quickly, she decided to ignore it.

"I thank ye for telling me so much about Callum," said Sir Euan as he lifted her hand to his mouth and lightly kissed the back of it. "I will be sure to tell Sir Gavin all ye have told me ere he meets the boy."

"We decided it would probably be best if Sir Gavin came here to meet Callum," Kirstie said, frowning a little when Payton took her hand in his and idly rubbed his thumb over the place Sir Euan had kissed. That that action seemed to cause Sir Euan a great deal of silent amusement stirred her curiosity, but she forced it aside, for Callum's needs were far more important. "I was hoping that would be acceptable to ye, Payton."

"Aye," replied Payton, "for I can see how it would help the lad. He will be more at ease here. Better that than to take him to a strange place to meet a mon who, sadly, is nay more than a stranger to him." Payton fixed his gaze upon Euan, only mildly annoyed by the man's amusement, for it revealed that he had read and understood Payton's silent message, that silent but forceful declaration of ownership well known amongst men. "I suppose ye will come with the man."

"Oh, aye," replied Sir Euan as he stood up. "I assume Bryan is prepared to leave."

"He is, although Uven was reluctant."

Euan smiled. "Good. Then Callum has already accepted one MacMillan as kin, and been accepted. 'Tis a start." He bowed to Kirstie, "M'lady," then winked at Payton. "And may I say that, for a mon I suspect has ne'er done so nor felt inclined to, ye did that verra weel. I had nay trouble understanding. A shame ye would choose to do it in this particular instance, but that, too, I fully understand. Good day."

"What was that all about?" asked Kirstie as she allowed herself to be pulled to her feet and into Payton's arms.

"He was complimenting me on my sense of responsibility," Payton answered and kissed her. "Wine?"

Brief though the kiss was, Kirstie was feeling somewhat heated. "Aye. Alice sent some out to us, kenning that we might have a lot to talk about. And, 'tis warm." Kirstie suspected she had had a little more than she should have because she was thinking some very scandalous things as she nuzzled Payton's throat. "Did ye just come to fetch Sir Euan?"

He slid his hands down over her backside and pressed her close. "Aye and nay. I was thinking about honey. Warm, sweet honey," he added in a soft voice as he kissed her ear.

Kirstie was now certain that she had had too much wine, for the flush upon her cheeks had little to do with shyness or embarrassment. Payton's words stirred a fire within her, a sudden aching need that demanded attention. That need seemed to free her as much as it startled her. She wanted to blame the wine for that, too, but finally confessed to herself that it was more, so much more. For some reason, her love for him was flowing strong in her veins at the moment, filling her heart and feeding the need his heated words had stirred within her. Suddenly, she decided to let her heart lead her. Their time together was swiftly coming to an end and, perhaps, she was more willing now to throw all caution to the wind.

She wriggled out of his arms and smiled at him. "Honey? Ah, then, ye must follow me."

Payton watched her skip away, the smile she sent him one of the most sweetly lecherous come-hither smiles he had ever had the privilege of seeing. There was an air of delight about her, the air of a carefree maid. For some reason, Kirstie was feeling unrestrained, untroubled by thoughts of sin and propriety, of the needs of the children or the threat of Roderick.

"So, why are ye standing here puzzling o'er this mood of hers and nay hurrying after her to enjoy it until it fades, ye great idiot?" he murmured, then hurried after her.

CHAPTER NINETEEN

Payton stopped abruptly to look around him. Kirstie had led him to a magical corner of his own gardens. It embarrassed him a little that he had not known about it. His only excuses were that his gardens were large and he was a busy man. He often sat on the bench where she and Sir Euan had been talking, enjoying the solitary peace, the scent of the flowers, and the sound of the birds. It was a good place to find some calm, to think, and he simply had not bothered to go any further.

As he studied the small enclave of trees and honeysuckle, a part of him was sorry he had lacked the interest to study his own gardens more extensively. Another part of him was pleased that the first time he saw it, it was with Kirstie. Now there would always be a special touch of magic to the place. Especially, he mused as he leaned against the thick trunk of one of the trees in the circle, if Kirstie was still in her playful mood. He smiled as she walked over to him, the look in her stormy grey eyes stirring the heat in his blood in a way no other woman ever had.

" 'Tis lovely, aye?" She looked up at the canopy of

leaves and branches over her head. " 'Tis as if some fairy or wood nymph made herself a home here. I found it shortly after I came to your home. Ye must love it here.''

"Aye, but I am ashamed to admit that this is the first time I have seen it," he said.

"Truly? Dinnae ye like gardens? This one is so large, I rather assumed ye had had some hand in the making of it.''

"I hired the lads who tend it. Nay, I found the bench amongst the roses and went no further. Ere the Murrays gained this house, this garden was planted, and many a Murray woman has made her mark here. I now own the property, including the land ye can see running out behind the house. I see that that is used weel. In truth, I had ne'er realized just how much land was taken up by this pleasure garden. 'Tis beautiful.''

"Oh, aye. I have come here often to sit beneath the roof of leaves or in the swing.'' She pointed to the small, carved seat suspended from the branches overhead by two thick ropes.

" 'Tis good to have a place to think." His eyes widened slightly when she blushed. "And just what do ye come out here to think on, love?" he asked as he took her by the hand and pulled her close.

Bravery was a fleeting thing, she mused, as she faltered in her plans, but then the magic of the place seeped into her blood. It was a wild place in a way, a secret place where she could be free of constraint. Kirstie suspected it had always affected her so and that was why she had often had such sensuous daydreams whenever she was here. Now the object of all of them was in reach and the spirit of the place seemed to demand that she fulfill a few of those sensuous dreams.

"Ye with your chest bare," she said quietly, encouraged by the way his eyes gleamed with a growing desire.

"As ye command, m'lady." Payton swiftly shed his doublet and shirt.

"So chivalrous ye are to grant a lady her wish." She gave him a slow, deep kiss, fighting her own rising passion even as she worked to rouse his. "Ye have such beautiful skin," she murmured as she moved her kisses down to his broad chest. "So warm, so taut, and the taste of ye is so verra fine upon my tongue."

Payton wanted her to decide that something else tasted very fine on her tongue, but he suppressed the urge to suggest it. He combed his fingers through her hair as her kisses warmed his skin and heated his blood. As he looked up at the thick canopy of trees, he decided it was a perfect place for some unrestrained loving. Kirstie seemed to be in the mood for such sensual indulgence and he was curious as to just how unrestrained she might get.

"Was this all ye thought on?" he asked.

"Och, nay." She knelt down and tugged off his boots. "Ye were always quite naked. I thought ye would look perfect naked here in the sun-dappled shade." She slipped off his hose and braies, then ran her hands up and down his legs. "Of course, for the first few weeks I thought on it, I didnae quite picture this proud fellow being as impressive as he is," she murmured, curling her fingers around his manhood. "Or," she added in a soft, husky voice, "that I would find him such a delight . . ."

He groaned out his appreciation as she stroked him with her tongue. She took a leisurely pleasure in him, enhancing the delight she was giving him with her warm kisses and the gentle touches of her hands. She caressed his hips, his thighs, his buttocks, and even the heated area at the base of his erection. As if she sensed the growing intensity of his need, she slowly took him into her mouth. Despite her intuitive skill and his own desire to make the pleasure last as long as possible, in what he considered was far too short a period of time, he knew he was close to losing all control.

"Ah, love, ye must cease," he said, although he could not make himself pull her away.

"Ye grow bored?" she asked, gently nipping the inside of his thighs.

"Jesu, nay, but I will soon be beyond control." He gasped when she did something exquisitely clever with her tongue. "I willnae be able to pull back and 'tis said that women dinnae like that."

"Ah, I suppose 'tis that grand, all-kenning *they* who say that, aye? Weel, how often are they right, I ask ye?"

When she took him back into the damp heat of her mouth, he lost all ability to protest, to even think clearly. His gaze fixed upon her, he relinquished all control. It was not until he sat slumped against the tree that he realized how completely he had done so. A little uncertainly, he looked at Kirstie, who was curled up at his side, idly stroking his stomach. If the faint smile on her lips was any indication, they were indeed wrong. He decided it would be wise to say nothing, for the very last thing he wanted was to embarrass her or make her uncomfortable, so much so that she hesitated to do it again. That would be a great tragedy, he thought, and bit back a grin.

This interlude was proving something he had suspected from the beginning. Kirstie was a passionate woman, sensual and giving. Doubts curtailed her enjoyment for now. She was a woman brought up to believe some rules should not be broken, yet she had done so to be with him. Once they were married, once their passion was sanctified, he had hopes that the restraint she so often practiced or felt would be greatly eased.

He noticed a slight flush upon her cheeks. Pleasuring him had obviously stirred her desire, which remained unsatisfied. Gently grasping her by the chin, he turned her face up to his and kissed her. Keeping her drugged with kisses, he slid his hand beneath her skirts. He found her more than ready for a quick pleasuring, and it stirred him deeply to know she had reached such a state through loving him as she had. It took but a few strokes of his fingers to bring her her release and, when she slumped against him, he tugged her over until she straddled him.

"I thought ye brought me here for some honey," he murmured as he undid her bodice and caressed her breasts.

Those husky words quickly brought Kirstie out of her pleasant lethargy. She blushed a little when she realized she sat astride him, her breasts bared. There was no mistaking what he was asking for, but she was not sure she felt quite as bold as she had when she had brought him to this place. Then he began to kiss and suckle her breasts with a slow, seductive gentleness that made her think one more bold, reckless act could not hurt anything.

Payton leaned back against the tree. He watched her closely as he grasped her by the hips and tugged her up onto her knees. His body was hardening at the thought of what might happen next.

"Lift your skirts, Kirstie," he said.

"Oh, Payton, I cannae," she began to protest even as she felt her blood heat at the thought of doing such a brazen thing.

"Ah, lass, show me your beauty. Offer me your sweetness." He lightly stroked her legs when she grasped the hem of her skirts, then hesitated. "Aye, show me heaven, love. Surrender to me as I did to ye."

His soft, deep voice wove a spell around her and Kirstie slowly lifted her skirts. When he looked at what she revealed, she faltered a little, far too aware of how exposed she was. "Oh, Payton, I cannae—"

"Hush, my dark beauty." He caressed her with his fingers and heard her breath catch. "Hush and let me pleasure ye. Tuck your skirts up, love."

She obeyed him without hesitation, blindly seduced by his rich voice. When he kissed the inside of her thighs, his soft hair brushing against her so intimately, she shivered with delight. It was not until he nudged her legs farther apart that she regained a scrap of awareness over exactly what she was allowing.

"Payton, I dinnae think—"

"Good. Dinnae think. Feel. Revel. Succumb to it all as I did." He kissed the silken-soft line of skin where her slender thigh joined her body. "Sigh. Moan. Cry out my name. Cry out for mercy."

Even as she smiled faintly over those last words, Kirstie realized he was kissing her everywhere but where her body now ached for the touch of his mouth. "Payton?" She looked down at him, meeting his gaze even as he kissed her low on her belly.

"Ask me, my heart. Ask me to love you."

"Ask ye? How brazen. How shameless. How wanton."

"How intoxicating. How enflaming. How verra much I want to hear ye say it."

And just how was she supposed to resist that, she thought as she threaded her fingers into his hair. "Love me, Payton."

"Ah, my bonnie blackbird, how can I do aught else? Except, mayhap, make ye cry for mercy. Twice."

She was just puzzling over the odd question when the import of his final words struck her. Kirstie opened her mouth to question that plan when she both saw and felt him stroke her with his tongue. All clarity of thought fled her mind. She succumbed. She reveled. She surrendered all—her doubts, her fears, her body, her heart. Kirstie let passion become her master and, if that master came in the perfect form of one Sir Payton Murray, she saw nothing wrong with that.

When had she gotten naked, Kirstie wondered as she slowly roused herself from a sated oblivion. She blushed as she recalled exactly when she had been relieved of all of her clothes. She glanced up and, if she judged the fading light correctly, more than two hours had passed since Payton had threatened to make her cry for mercy—twice. Kirstie was increasingly certain that she had done so more than twice. It was then that she became aware of the fact that the weight upon her back was Payton. When her rapidly waking mind recalled her to how he had gotten there and why, she blushed even more.

She certainly had reveled, she decided, and wondered if she was simply too tired to worry about it all. After what they had just indulged in for several hours in their private leafy bower, Kirstie thought she ought to feel riddled with shame. There was the small sting of embarrassment, and a twinge of concern about whether or not people were actually supposed to do such things, but nothing else.

It could be the soft magic of their trysting place, she thought as Payton moved off her and she slowly sat up, but she had the feeling she had finally reached a turning point. Kirstie realized she was not really even trying to find reasons for why she had behaved as she had done for the last few hours. At least none beyond the facts that she loved Payton and she loved the way he could make her feel. There had always been a part of her that had felt that was enough, and it had apparently finally won out. When she watched Payton stand up and stretch, looking gloriously tempting in his nakedness, she decided that part of her which felt that only the loving mattered was probably right. Sensing a flicker of interest in her body, she quickly reached for her clothes.

"Ah, time to come out of the wood, is it?" Payton asked as he stepped up behind her.

" 'Tis late," Kirstie said as she shook out her clothes. "I am surprised no one has come looking for us."

Payton decided it would be very unwise to say what he was thinking, that if anyone had approached their bower in the last few hours, the noises she had made would have warned them to stay away. He idly brushed the grass and leaves from his body as he admired her fine lines. When he noticed that she had some of the same debris on her front, he started to brush her off as well. He was not only surprised by the way her nipples hardened in invitation as he lightly brushed his hand over her breast, but at how his body began immediately, if a little slowly, to respond to that invitation. He could tell by the look upon Kirstie's face that she felt the same way.

"Jesu," she muttered as she slapped his hand away, "we need a bucket of cold water thrown o'er us."

Laughing softly, he began to help her dress. "I shall let ye leave here first," he said as he finger-combed her hair and then began to lightly braid it. "I will follow ye in a wee bit."

"Do ye really think that will fool anyone?" she asked and almost smiled as she looked herself over. "I believe I might look as if I have been, er, trysting." Glancing at his scattered clothes, she added, "I suspect ye will, too."

"Quite possibly. And, considering that we have both been gone for a long while and were last seen in the garden together, we could probably stroll in, looking as neat and prim as if we had just been to Mass, and they still would think we had been out trysting. Howbeit, nay need to tempt them into actually saying anything. I cannae promise that all of my brothers and cousins will keep their big mouths shut and I am too worn out to pound them into the mud. Which, of course, I would have to if they spoke out."

"E'en if all they said was 'Good eve, m'lady?' "

"That would depend upon the look in their eyes as they said it."

Kirstie laughed, recognizing the nonsense, the dark threats that would never be carried out. Her brothers did the same. She suspected Payton probably had pounded a few of his vast multitude of male relations into the mud, just as her brothers had thrashed each other on occasion, but it was now probably remembered quite fondly. Men, she thought, were sometimes very confusing.

Payton pulled her into his arms and kissed her passionately. As he ended the kiss, he decided it may have been ill-advised. Kirstie looked adorably dazed, but he was naked and hard, while she was dressed and preparing to leave.

Feeling the proof of Payton's desire pressed against her, Kirstie quickly stepped out of his hold. "Enough. I need to go and help Alice as the number of people she must cook for has grown rather alarmingly. I believe your brothers Brett and Harcourt will join us this evening," she added as she hurried away and laughed softly when she heard him curse.

The sound of Kirstie's laughter made Payton smile and he watched her until she disappeared around a turning in the path. He realized her mood was still light and carefree. This time when the passion had faded there had been no doubts or fears to be seen, no regrets, no fleeting looks of shame. Kirstie had gotten up, gotten dressed, and simply talked, even teased him. There had been a slight blush upon her cheeks until she had donned her shift, but nothing else.

As Payton began to dress he looked around the quiet bower, the place where he had finally held a Kirstie who truly let her passion rule. It had been hot, exciting, and exhausting. He did not think he had ever spent a more sensuous, more passionate, or more fulfilling time. In truth, after the way they had just glutted themselves, he was surprised either of them could walk, let alone talk coherently, get dressed, and rejoin the others.

Something had changed, he thought as he tugged on his boots, then leaned against the trunk of the tree closest to the wall of his garden. Payton did not want to believe it was some sensuous magic within the bower or the wine Kirstie had drunk while talking to Sir Euan. He was certain it went deeper than that. If not, this new, freer Kirstie would fade away and that was unacceptable.

The Kirstie who had just frolicked with him here had broken free of the bonds of guilt, shame, and fear. Payton did not want those bonds to return, yet unless he knew what had changed, what had finally freed her, he was not sure he could stop her from returning to what she had been before.

It was past time he married her, but she had to be made a widow first. Payton decided it was a good thing there were so many acceptable reasons to kill Sir Roderick, for he could all too easily see himself wanting the man dead just so he could claim Kirstie. He wanted to openly mark her as his. He chafed at even the small acts of discretion they did practice. He wanted their union sanctified so that Kirstie need never fret over the right or wrong of their lovemaking again, so that she never again choked some of the life out of her passion with such concerns.

Payton was not fool enough to think they would always indulge themselves as they had done here. They would never survive it. Yet, when he went into her arms at night, he wanted to find that same, sweet wanton who had so beautifully exhausted him in the cool shade of this bower. Marriage would ensure that—Payton was certain of it.

A rustling in the leaves above his head caught his attention, pulling him out of his deep thought. Even as he started to look up, a noose slipped over his neck. Payton grabbed at the thick rope, but it quickly tightened so he could not throw it off. He was pulled hard against the wall and realized that was where his assailant was, not in the tree. As he was dragged up and over the wall, he struggled to get some of his fingers beneath the rope to try and ease its killing grip. Blackness crowded his mind as he fought to breathe—and failed. At the top of the wall, his dimming gaze became fixed upon the tree and the last thought he had was to wonder why he should think he could see Callum.

When Payton came to his senses, he found himself

draped across the saddle of a fast-moving horse. The moment he realized why it was that he could not breathe without pain, he grew enraged. He flung himself upward and grabbed the rider. It was easy to toss the man out of the saddle, but not so easy to right himself and take the man's place. After he had lost conciousness during his near-hanging, his captors had obviously treated him roughly, for he ached in nearly every part of his body. He could almost hear Ian scolding him for acting without thinking first.

For one brief moment, he savored the sweet taste of victory as he sat upright and held the reins of the slowing horse. Then something slammed into his back, high up on his right shoulder. A heartbeat later the pain came. The next thing Payton knew, he was hitting the ground, hard. He had only enough time to consider how lucky he was not to have broken his neck before he was yanked to his feet. The pain that followed as the knife was pulled from his back almost sent him to his knees.

"Curse it, Wattie, ye could have killed him," complained Gib as he joined his friend and looked at Payton hanging limply in Wattie's grasp. "I think ye have."

"Nay." Wattie tossed Payton back onto the ground and sheathed his knife. "But, what if I did? He is for dying anyway."

"That he is, but we may have use for him as a live hostage," Sir Roderick drawled as he stood over Payton, then nudged him roughly over onto his back. "Still, this may have served some purpose. Ye seem to have taken the fight out of the mon."

"He killed Ranald," said Gib. "Broke his neck when he threw him off his horse. Only have five men now."

"Five will be enough."

"A hundred thousand wouldnae be enough to keep ye safe, ye perverted swine," Payton said, his voice little more than a raspy whisper. "My kinsmen hunt ye now."

"Aye, I have seen all the pretty Murrays skipping through the wood. They havenae found me yet, have they? They willnae, either. As soon as I have the ransom for your bonnie hide, I will kill ye and my traitorous wife and then I am off for France."

"I have kinsmen there, too."

"And some rather vicious enemies as weel, I hear. Mayhap I should join forces with them."

That was a chilling thought, nearly as chilling as the knowledge that he was going to be used to draw Kirstie into a trap. His only comfort was that there would probably be enough people around to keep her from making some foolish sacrifice on his behalf. Payton knew he was in too poor a condition to do much more than stay alive as he waited for the ransom he knew would come, and then get out of the way of the fighting. It was not much, certainly neither glorious nor heroic, but he would do it to the best of his ability.

His pride rebelled at the thought of just lying there in ignominious defeat, silently accepting of it all, and he struggled to sit up. Sweating and shaking slightly, he managed it, his hands braced against the ground to hold him upright. Payton looked at Roderick and wished that, after first learning about the man's crimes, he had simply killed him.

"If ye had been a clever lad," said Payton, "ye would have fled to France by now. Ye might have gained a few more months of life."

"And leave ye and my whore of a wife to rut yourselves blind? Nay, I think not. Although, if I had realized how skilled she was with that mouth, I may have found the occasional use for her. Mayhap I will test her skill ere I kill her. And, I must say, after watching ye exercising your much-heralded skills, I cannae see how ye can think I am perverted. Such a waste of a beautiful mon," he said and shuddered.

"She sure was enjoying herself," drawled Gib.

"Aye," agreed Wattie, grinning widely. "Opening them pretty legs wide and letting him bury his face in her quim."

"Your wife was riding his tongue like it was the finest bit of meat she had e'er taken inside her."

"And he sure seemed to like it. Couldnae get enough. She must taste real sweet."

" 'Cause she be clean. No dirt or nits or sweat, just pure bonnie quim. Wouldnae mind having me a lick or two of that."

Their crude talk enraged Payton, but his weak body refused to act upon that anger. They were defiling the beauty of the time he had spent with Kirstie in the bower. He prayed she would never find out they had been observed. Then his anger eased as he realized Gib and Wattie were not even looking at him, that their words were not intended to taunt him. Both men were looking at Roderick and smirking faintly.

Payton looked at Roderick as well and his eyes widened slightly in surprise. The man was pale and shaking slightly, but not with rage. Roderick looked ill, utterly disgusted, and even horrified. There was a strange, glazed look in his eyes, and Payton got the feeling that Roderick was looking at something in his past. Roderick, at least, had probably not watched him and Kirstie very much. It was apparent that the man had a strong distaste for such intimacies.

"Hell, we dinnae e'en have to wait for a turn," continued Gib. "While ye are seeing how good your wee wife can play your pipe, me and Wattie can play with t'other end."

"Aye," agreed Wattie, "I think I would like having them bonnie white thighs hugging my ears. I could e'en tell ye later if she tasted as good as your mither."

The speed with which Roderick drew his sword and had the point pressed against Wattie's throat startled even Payton. He had suspected there was a dark secret there, one both Gib and Wattie knew, and one that could explain Roderick's revulsion concerning sex with a woman. Payton rather wished he had not learned what that dark secret was, however. There were many ways

Wattie's remark could be interpreted and none of them was good. Some were appalling and Payton suspected it was probably one of the latter. It certainly explained why Roderick had never been able to hide his perversions behind a normal relationship with a woman. It also explained why the man kept two such crude, unattractive men close at hand despite his love of beauty. Wattie and Gib were an intricate part of what had obviously been a very dark and perverted past.

"Nay, Roderick," Gib said in a soft, soothing voice that was surprising in such a big, rough man, "ye cannae kill Wattie."

"And why not?" asked Roderick.

"Because, even though he is an idiot who doesnae ken when to keep his mouth shut, ye dinnae have the men to spare. We need every sword we can muster to get to France, aye? Now, let us forget this, and get out of here. We have a ransoming to deal with, aye?" Gib breathed a sigh of relief when Roderick backed away and turned his attention back to Payton. "Shall we tie him up this time?"

"Aye," replied Roderick as he sheathed his sword. "Get the ropes. I will just make sure that he cannae cause ye any trouble as ye bind him."

Payton saw the booted foot headed his way, but could not avoid it. The force of the kick sent him sprawling onto his stomach. As his dimming gaze became fixed upon a clump of trees, he wondered why the blow had not broken his jaw. He wondered, too, why he was always so slow to lose consciousness. But mostly, he wondered why he thought he saw Callum again.

CHAPTER TWENTY

"Does anyone ken where Payton is?" Kirstie asked as she looked around the great hall, but did not see him.

She looked from Brett to Harcourt, who had moved to flank her, then inwardly sighed. They were both near an age with her, Brett newly turned one and twenty and Harcourt but eighteen. They were both stunningly handsome young men with thick black hair, but Harcourt had amber eyes, and Brett had lovely green eyes. They were also both looking as if they wanted to say something she would probably want to hit them for.

"We rather assumed he was with you," Harcourt said.

The smile the young man gave her undoubtedly set many a lass's heart aflutter. Kirstie gave him a narrow-eyed look to let him know she was not impressed. "Does it look as if he is with me?"

"He isnae here. Roderick has him," gasped out Callum as he staggered up to Kirstie.

Even though she helped Callum sit down at the head table, calmly told Brett to get the boy some water, and dampened a small linen square in the finger bowl so that she could bathe Callum's face, Kirstie felt as though she was frozen inside. She wanted to think Callum no more than a terrified little boy who saw monsters under the bed, but she could not. Waiting for him to calm enough to speak clearly had her screaming inside. Not even the sight of eight strong men crowding around her and Callum eased her fear by very much. She was only faintly aware of Alice and the children being sent out of the room.

"I went to the garden to talk to Sir Payton," Callum began, then glanced at Kirstie and blushed, "but he was busy, so I walked about for a while." He leaned closer to Kirstie and said, "Didnae see naught but the clothes and that Payton was naked. Peeked once more to see if ye were, too. Sorry."

She supposed he thought he was whispering, but Kirstie knew that every man there heard him, and she found that she did not care. " 'Tis nay matter, my dear one. So, ye came back later?"

"Aye, and ye were leaving so I climbed up one of the trees to wait. Knew Payton wouldnae be leaving for a wee while, for he was still naked. Got looking at something else and, when I looked back, Payton was standing near the garden wall, alone. I was just starting to climb down when a rope was put round his neck." He grabbed Kirstie's hand and awkwardly patted it when she paled. "Nay, he is alive. Last I saw him, he was alive."

"I will remember that," she said and kept hold of his hand. "Go on."

"So, scrambling back up the tree, I looked about for who threw that rope. I saw Gib and Wattie climbing down off the wall, pulling Payton up and over the wall by the rope. Roderick was there, too. So was his mon Ranald. Oh, and Colin, too. Didnae recognize the other men, but there were four of them."

"Good lad," said Ian. "What did they do to Payton?"

"Took him. Ranald tossed him over his saddle and they all rode off. I was afeared they had killed him."

"But, they didnae," Kirstie said.

"Nay, they didnae," agreed Callum. "I followed. They werenae galloping, but they were going a wee bit fast, but I followed their trail as ye taught me, Ian. Then I had to hide because they had stopped. Ranald was lying on the ground and Gib said Payton had killed him. Payton was bleeding high up on his shoulder, but he was sitting up, alive," he stressed, glancing at Kirstie again. "They argued, then Roderick pulled his sword on Wattie, but Gib calmed everyone down. Then Roderick kicked Payton in the face, which laid Payton out flat. They tied him up, tossed him onto Wattie's saddle, and rode off."

"Ye did weel, lad," Ian said, patting him on the shoulder.

"Nay, I couldnae follow them anymore. I tried, but then I thought I best get back here to tell ye what had happened. I kenned I wouldnae have been able to if I had gone any further, but mayhap I should have."

Ian shook his head. "Nay, ye needed to do just what ye did. Their trail is clear, aye?"

"Aye. They arenae doing anything to hide it."

"And ye ken how to get back to where ye had to leave that trail." He smoothed his hand over Callum's hair when the boy nodded. " 'Tis good, lad. Verra good. I think they will be asking for a ransom." Ian looked at Kirstie. "And we both ken what part of the ransom might be. We had best start making plans so we waste nay time once the demand is made."

"Is there time?" asked Kirstie, finally regaining some calm as she accepted the fact that Payton was still alive and it appeared Roderick intended to keep him that way for a while.

"Och, aye, lass," replied Ian. "I may have misjudged the mon by nay thinking he would come so near to us, but I am certain of this. The fool obviously cannae leave, cannae run for his miserable life. He wants ye and Payton to suffer."

"He blames us for what has happened."

Ian nodded. "A mon like that ne'er blames himself. What we have to do is make him think he is getting what he wants, then take it away without any of our own getting hurt." He signaled the men to join him at the far end of the table.

Kirstie poured herself a large tankard of wine and took a deep drink. It had been such a beautiful day. She had thought her troubles near an end. Roderick was being hunted down, the children were safe, and she had finally allowed herself to be free with Payton, to revel in her love for him and the passion they shared. She did not dare even think of how she would feel if it proved to be their last time together.

"This is all my fault," Kirstie murmured.

"Och, nay, it isnae," said Brett as he sat down beside her.

" 'Tis, and I thought plans were being made. Shouldnae ye be with them? Oh, and I should probably be there with them, too. Although, they didnae ask me."

"Nay, for ye will go where they tell ye to and do as they tell you. As will I. And your part cannae be fully decided upon until we ken what that bastard wants. And, 'tis nay your fault."

" 'Tis. I brought all this trouble to his door. I set him right in the path of a madmon who murders people simply because they irritate him. I also led him out into that place in the garden where they took him from."

"Wheesht, and him kicking and protesting every step of the way. Ye are stronger than ye look."

"And ye are far more annoying than I would have guessed."

"I do my best." He winked at Callum when the boy laughed, but then grew serious again. "No one, and most especially not Payton, thinks that this is your fault. Ye needed help, for yourself and the bairns. The moment ye presented this trouble to Payton, he could do naught else but join the fight. Nay, not if he wished to retain any honor or continue to call himself a mon."

He glanced toward the door. "Ah, Connor and Gillyanne. Now there is a mon one wants fighting at one's side," he said as he hurried over to Connor and they both joined the men.

Gillyanne sat down next to Kirstie and briefly hugged her. " 'Twill be fine. Payton may come home a wee bit battered and bruised, but he *will* come home. And ye will, as weel."

"Have ye had another, ah, *feeling?*" she asked Gillyanne.

"I dinnae ken. All I do ken is that when I heard the news, I wasnae afraid."

"Wish I could say the same."

"Have faith. Payton is no fool and no one could have better men on one's side," she added with a nod toward her husband and the others.

Kirstie reminded herself of Gillyanne's words as she slowly rode toward the meeting place Roderick had named in his ransom note. She was not alone and neither was Payton. Although she was not quite sure what the men were doing, she knew she and Payton would be watched over and then rescued. All she had to hope for was that they were all right about Roderick, that he would not simply cut her throat, that he would want to talk, perhaps even gloat. It had certainly been his way in the past, but he was desperate now.

The moment she entered the little copse where Roderick waited, Wattie yanked the reins of her horse out of her hands. Gib pulled her out of the saddle and dragged her over to Roderick. A moment later, Wattie appeared with the bag she had had secured to her saddle. As he opened it and he, Gib, and Roderick all peered inside, she prayed they would not look too closely at the contents. There was money aplenty to glitter in the light, but beneath a thick layer of coin lurked rocks from Payton's garden.

"Weel, it looks as if your liaison with this fool has actually brought me something more than humiliation," drawled Roderick as he quickly closed the bag before Wattie could do what he so plainly wanted to—touch the money. "He isnae so verra pretty now, is he?" he added, with a nod toward Payton.

It was difficult not to run straight to Payton's side. Blood stained the front of his shirt and there were raw marks all around his throat. From what she could see, he was covered in bruises as well. For a brief moment she met Payton's gaze and read a fleeting look of hope there, but she also saw a strong hint of despair. She glared at Roderick, blaming him completely for Payton's pain and his apparent low spirits.

"Ye have your money," she said. "Ye can let him go now."

"Oh, can I? How kind of you." Roderick shook his head. "Ye cannae really expect to leave this place alive, can ye?"

"Nay, I suppose it was foolish to think ye would e'er honor your word like a true gentlemon."

She had guessed that he might strike her for that, but was still surprised when his fist struck her cheek. Kirstie fell to her knees, but quickly rose to her feet again. Payton was struggling against his bonds, obviously eager to get to Roderick and make him pay for that brutality. She could almost be glad that Payton was tied to the tree, as Roderick thought he had what he wanted, and might no longer hesitate to kill Payton.

"Gallant as always," she muttered.

"And why should I behave gallantly toward such a little whore?" Roderick asked with a pleasantness that sent chills down her spine. "From virgin to slut in less than a month, but ye were always a quick learner, werenae ye? Yet, ye being such a wee, grey whisper of a lass, I was astonished at how brazen and greedy ye can become once your clothes are off. And ye certainly have acquired a taste for a mon, havenae ye? I had considered

letting ye show me some of the fine skill ye displayed.
For someone with such an irritatingly sharp tongue, yon
gentlemon obviously found it sweet enough when it was
put to such good use.''

Kirstie was horrified. He had watched her with Payton
in the garden earlier. If she judged the leers on the
faces of Gib and Wattie correctly, so had they. Then she
got angry, very angry. They had had no right to do that.
What had occurred between her and Payton in that
garden had been beautiful and private. These pigs were
ruining that memory with their crude talk.

''Actually, the more I think on it, the more intrigued
I become,'' said Roderick. ''I ne'er thought to teach a
woman a trick or two. Aye, in fact I think I will give ye
a try. If ye are as good as Sir Payton seemed to think ye
were, I might allow ye to live for a little while.''

''Ah, weel, there is a problem with that. Ye see, I sip
upon only the finest of wines.'' She cursed when he
struck her again, but this time she held herself upright.
''And if I am going to be sticking something in my
mouth, I want it at least to be big enough so I ken it is
there,'' she added in a furious voice.

Payton groaned. Why was she trying so hard to enrage
the man? He had been pleased when she had recovered
so quickly from her horror over realizing their lovemaking had been observed. The rage she had then displayed
had astonished him. Now he was terrified she was going
to get herself killed.

Perhaps there was no rescue coming, he suddenly
thought, and felt the chill of fear snake down his spine.
Payton shook his head, ignoring the throbbing pain
that resulted. There would be a rescue made. With only
Gib and Wattie close at hand, that left all five of Roderick's remaining men out in the surrounding wood, easy
targets for the ones who would be coming for him and
Kirstie. This argument she was pushing the man into
could prove dangerous. Once she may have known her

husband's limits well, but he had changed in the last few weeks, become more insane and angry.

Before he could think of something to say, something that would warn her to be careful yet not warn Roderick or his men that a rescue may be imminent, Kirstie punched her husband. It was a good punch, skillfully executed and forceful. It knocked Roderick flat on his backside, but to Payton's dismay, the man came up swinging. Kirstie went down beneath Roderick in a flurry of skirts and petticoats and it was hard to see who was doing what to whom. Roderick finally got her pinned onto her back and Payton bellowed out a cry of outrage and denial when he saw the glint of a knife in the man's hand. He could feel the warmth of his own blood upon his wrists as he struggled to break free of his bonds.

A loud yell caused Kirstie to look and see what Roderick held. The knife was already plunging down before she moved, so she was unable to avoid it altogether. Kirstie screamed from fury as much as pain when the knife plunged into her side, for she realized he had intended to give her a vicious gut wound. Then, suddenly, Roderick was climbing off her, backing away. As she sprawled there on her back, struggling to regain the strength to move, she watched in horrified fascination as she was encircled by the children.

"Jesu, 'tis the bairns," muttered Ian. "Alice isnae going to like this."

"How did they get here?" asked Brett as he crawled up beside Ian and stared into the clearing.

"Followed us and met up with Callum where we left him. What about the men Roderick had set about in these woods?"

"Two preferred to die. Three decided to take their chances with the justice. They are fools if they think they willnae hang, but 'tis their gamble to take. What do we do about this?"

"Get up as close as we can." He turned to Eudard, who had just appeared at his side. "Tell everyone to carefully encircle the camp. I dinnae want any of the children hurt. They can judge if it is time to do something or wait until I give a signal." The moment Eudard left, Ian went back to scowling into the camp.

"I suspect they just came to watch, but when Kirstie was hurt, they couldnae sit still," Brett said.

"They willnae be able to sit at all for a few days after this," muttered Ian. "Come on, best we get a little closer."

Payton really hoped he was having a vision brought on by pain and loss of blood. He did not want what he was seeing to be real. The children were not really out there standing around Kirstie like a tiny guard. Unfortunately, there was no denying the very real glint of the sun off the blade of Callum's knife.

Then he tensed but forced himself not to look around. If the children knew where they were, then so did the adults. The fact that the children had run right into Roderick's camp with no warning and no pursuit seemed to indicate that Roderick's perimeter guard had been eliminated, or soon would be. He hoped something happened soon, before any of the children got hurt and before Kirstie lost any more blood.

"What are ye doing here, Callum?" demanded Kirstie, dismayed by the lack of force in her voice.

"Protecting ye," Callum answered.

Callum gave her one brief, sharp glance that told her he was not telling her everything he wanted to because everyone was listening. A look at Simon gained her the same silent message. The others were out there, but for some reason, the children had eluded their grasp and run to her. It was possible they had simply reacted to the sight of Roderick raising his knife. It was also possible that they had drawn closer than the adults and they had seen no one to help her when she had needed it. Either way, they were now in danger.

"What are these brats doing here?" snapped Roderick.

"Stopping ye from killing our lady," Callum replied in a hard voice. "And Sir Payton," he quickly added.

"Robbie," Kirstie called and smiled weakly when the boy hurried to her side. "Help me sit up. Slowly," she hissed out when the movement caused her wounded side to punish her with a shaft of excruciating pain. "Do ye have a knife?" she whispered, and the boy nodded. "Then I want ye to sneak o'er to Sir Payton and help him to get free of those bonds. He is wounded, too, ye ken, so he may need ye to stay beside him in case he needs your help to get out of here."

"I can do that," Robbie said, "but ye are badly wounded, too."

"And have more help right here than I need whilst Sir Payton has none."

The boy nodded and slipped away. Kirstie noticed that Wattie and Gib had their gazes fixed upon her and relaxed a little. So long as she and the other children held Roderick's attention, Robbie ought to be able to do as she asked without any danger to himself. She turned her thoughts to a way to keep Roderick's attention on her and Callum, for if he remained interested, so would Gib and Wattie.

"I dinnae like this," said Gib.

"Nay, the brats are a nuisance," agreed Wattie.

"They are more than a nuisance."

"Do ye think Callum can use that knife, then?"

"Think, Wattie," Gib ground out between tightly gritted teeth. "Where did the children come from? Why werenae they stopped by Colin or one of the other men? How did they e'en ken where we were?" He nodded when Wattie's eyes widened and he looked around nervously. "Exactly. The bitch's allies are out there. Or Payton's. Not much difference to us. Or Roderick."

"We should warn Roderick, then."

"He willnae listen anymore, Wattie, e'en if we could do it quiet-like. And whoe'er is creeping up on us will notice if all three of us just leave. Nay, old Roderick willnae leave. He thinks he can kill them and go to France and live like a laird there. Time to tend to ourselves, lad."

"Shame about the money."

"Something tells me there isnae as much in there as we think."

Wattie nodded. "A trick. Makes sense. Where can we go?"

"Weel," Gib started inching back, toward the wood and their horses, "I was thinking the borderlands. They are said to be a rough, lawless people there. Go to one of the border clans, like the Armstrongs. 'Tis said they are a hard lot of thieves and murderers. Aye, we will see how they do things." He looked toward Roderick, who was engaged in a glaring match with Callum. "See ye in hell, Roderick, m'lad."

Brenda stepped out of the shadows by the big tree her brother Simon had picked for her to hide near. She watched the two men who had hurt Simon disappear into the wood, then spat on the place where they had just been standing. She looked toward her brother, saw him notch his bow, and knowing they would soon go home, she started to amble back to the camp.

Roderick drew his sword and held the tip to Callum's chest. "It would appear that your dagger is a wee bit short, eh, laddie? The question is, do I kill ye first or my traitorous wife?"

"Roderick, dinnae be a fool," Kirstie said as she tried to edge herself between her husband and Callum. She could hear Payton cursing and prayed he would not try anything foolish once Robbie got him free. "Ye cannae win this."

"Nay, probably not, but I can make it cost some people verra dearly." He turned the sword point on her, smiling faintly at the soft gasp of the children. "I believe I shall take ye to hell with me, m'dear. I wouldnae want to be alone."

Kirstie could almost feel the tense silence as Roderick started to swing his sword. Then there was the sound of men hurrying through brush and onto open ground. She could hear Payton cry out with a strange mix of fury and denial and some other strong emotion. All that settled in her mind, but made little impression. Her gaze fixed upon Roderick's sword, she used what little strength she had to shove Callum down onto the ground and held herself as the perfect target above his squirming, cursing little body.

There was a threatening whisper of a sound Kirstie knew she ought to recognize. It passed right by her. Callum suddenly went very still. The swing of the sword halted abruptly and the point of the blade was slowly lowered to the ground. Kirstie looked at Roderick to see what had changed his mind about her execution, and frowned. There appeared to be an arrow sticking out of Roderick's eye, but Kirstie's weary, pain-drugged mind was having trouble accepting what her eyes told her. Roderick's face was frozen in a look of surprise and then he slowly crumbled to the ground. Callum nudging her off him brought her to her senses.

"Simon," Callum snapped as he stood up and glared at the other boy. "Ye killed him!"

"Aye, I did," Simon said calmly as he retrieved his arrow and cleaned it off.

"But, *I* wanted to do it. I had a right to do it."

"He killed my fither. Nay with his own hands, the murdering coward, but he had it done, and all because my fither warned me about what that bastard did to boys."

Callum frowned a moment, then nodded. "Fair enough. But, when did ye learn to use a bow like that and what if ye had missed and hit me or our lady?"

Payton, helped over to sit down next to Kirstie by his

brothers, was about to say the same thing, and far less kindly, when Simon quietly replied, "I never miss."

"Never?"

"Never have, nay with anything I throw either. My fither said I had the finest eye he had e'er kenned. I look at it, stare at it a wee bit, and I can hit it square." He frowned when Brenda strolled up to his side after nudging her way through the crowd of men. "I told ye to stay hidden 'til it was over."

"Saw ye aim your arrow and kenned it would be done soon," Brenda said, smiling faintly when everyone stared at her, for it was the first time she had spoken since coming to live with them. "I saw the men who hurt ye and I spat on the ground where they stood and cursed them with warts and boils."

"Ye saw them, lass?" asked Payton, slipping his good arm around Kirstie, calmer now that he could see her wounds were painful, but would heal. "They slipped away, aye?"

"Aye," replied Brenda. "They guessed your men were out there. They decided to go to another place."

"Did ye hear where that place was?"

Brenda nodded. "The borderlands. They want to go thieving. Said they would go and join up with the Armstrongs."

"Are ye sure they said the Armstrongs, lass?" Payton asked in a choked voice, fighting not to join in the growing round of laughter amongst the other men, if only because he suspected it would hurt.

"Aye, the Armstrongs. A hard lot of thieves and murderers, Gib said. They willnae be back, will they?"

"Och, nay, lass, they willnae be back." He laughed, then winced when it hurt his shoulder.

It took Kirstie a moment to figure out why the men were all finding that so amusing, then sighed. "Another cousin, right?" she said and shook her head when he laughed, wincing even as he did so.

CHAPTER
TWENTY-ONE

His Uncle Eric was right, thought Payton. Waking up
to a sword at your throat was not a pleasant experience.
Sir Eric loved to jest that there was nothing that could
cool a man's morning ardor faster than finding four
armed men encircling the bed. Next time he saw his
uncle, Payton was going to have to tell him that seeing
eight armed, glowering men was not just chilling—it
could probably make a man impotent for a week. Which
was a true shame for, after almost a fortnight of lying
beside Kirstie, unable to do anything more than hold
her close while they both healed from their wounds, he
had woken up feeling very ardent indeed and more
than able to tend to the matter. He did not think these
men would be content to wait an hour or so while
he indulged himself. They looked a little too eager to
immediately cut him into very small pieces.

After studying the men surrounding his bed, he began
to understand why they looked so murderous. Payton
had the feeling he was looking at Kirstie's family. These
men had the same black hair, the same handsome features as Eudard, and at least two of them had eyes just

like hers. Since one of those was the oldest one amongst the group, Payton suspected that man was her father.

Payton felt Kirstie move against his side and quickly warned her, "We have company, love."

"Oh, dear."

Kirstie clutched the bedcovers as tightly as she could to cover herself as she looked at her family. Since Roderick's death, the guard around Payton's house had been greatly eased. She deeply regretted that at the moment. She found it a little amusing that they had arranged themselves around the bed in a tidy order from the oldest to the youngest. Then she decided she could not be fully awake yet, for there was nothing amusing about this tense, somewhat dangerous confrontation.

"Good morning, Fither," she said calmly, then looked around at her brothers. "Ye brought them all."

"Aye." Elrick Kinloch looked down at his daughter, his stormy grey eyes narrowed. "We got word that ye had been wounded. Then your wee message appeared saying your husband was dead, ye had been a wee bit wounded but were fine, and that Eudard was here so I shouldnae worry."

"And, ye shouldnae have worried, Fither. I was weel taken care of." She grimaced at that poor choice of words when two of her brothers laughed, only to be glared into silence by her father. "Allow me to introduce—"

"Sir Payton Murray. Aye, I have heard of the rutting fool."

"Ye really shouldnae insult a mon in his own home."

"I will if he is lying naked in a bed with my only daughter."

"He was wounded, too," Kirstie said, pointing to the still-red scar on Payton's shoulder and the fading marks upon his throat. "It was a verra trying time."

Elrick sheathed his sword, but his stance remained an aggressive one. "And ye had to comfort each other, did ye?"

"Weel, it was easier for everyone to care for us this way." It was not working, she mused, studying the angry look upon her father's face. "Now, I ken ye said ye have heard of Sir Payton Murray, but he doesnae ken who ye are. A mon ought to ken the names of those who invade his home waving swords about, dinnae ye think so? So, Payton, this is my father, Sir Elrick Kinloch, and my brothers Pedair, Steven, Colm, Malcolm, Blair, Aiden, and Aiken," she said, pointing to each one lined up around the bed.

"I pray ye will pardon me for nay getting up to greet ye more properly," drawled Payton.

"Payton," she whispered when she heard the hint of belligerence in his tone, "didnae ye notice that I was trying to calm my family down?"

"To be honest, love, I couldnae really puzzle out exactly what it was ye were doing."

She decided to ignore him as he was obviously going to act all manly and aggressive and she already had eight of that breed to deal with. "So, Fither, now that ye all ken each other, perhaps ye could leave us alone for a wee while and—"

"I wouldnae leave ye alone with this fool. Ye have been alone with him too much and look where it has gotten ye. And, I couldnae leave now if I wanted to."

"Why not?"

"Because someone has a knife stuck in my arse."

Kirstie sighed. "Callum, these are my father and my brothers. They willnae hurt me."

Callum peered around the tall, broad-shouldered Elrick. "It wasnae really ye I was worried about. When I saw these men creeping about up here, I moved fast to keep a watch on them. Soon recognized that they were your kinsmen, but kenned they might be a wee bit angry with Sir Payton."

"Oh, nay," muttered Eudard as he stepped into the room, his tossled hair and mussed clothing indicating that he had hurried out of his bed.

"Ah, the valiant guardian of his sister's virtue," drawled Sir Elrick, glaring at his son.

"I really need to get some sort of secure latch for the door," murmured Payton, wincing faintly when Kirstie pinched his hip.

"Fither, why dinnae ye come to the great hall with me," said Eudard. "Alice is setting out food to break your fast."

"And leave these two alone?"

"They need to, weel, they need some privacy, dinnae they? Ye cannae have a reasonable talk here."

"Mayhap I dinnae want a reasonable talk. Mayhap I just want to give out a few commands and toss in a few bloodcurdling threats to make sure I am obeyed."

"Weel, mayhap I want to have a reasonable talk to ye first," Eudard said through gritted teeth. "I truly need to talk to ye first. Now. Please."

Sir Elrick sighed. "Fine. First tell the wee lad to get his knife out of my arse."

"Callum!" Kirstie and Eudard yelled at the same time.

Callum rolled his eyes and sheathed his knife. "Thank ye, Callum, for worrying o'er me and trying to protect my arse from them what would sneak in and try to cut off bits I might sorely miss," he muttered.

Payton grinned at the boy. "Thank ye, Callum. I most certainly would miss those bits."

"Ye may still lose them, so ye can swallow that big smile of yours," growled Elrick. Then he looked at Callum. "Hungry, laddie?"

"Aye," replied Callum. "Always."

"Ye do ken that if ye stick a knife in a mon's arse, ye willnae bring him down, dinnae ye?"

"Aye, Ian told me. Said it would just make him angry. He showed me the best places to stick a knife, but I didnae think I ought to try to cut the liver out of one of my lady's kinsmen."

"Verra thoughtful of ye, lad," drawled Elrick as the

last of his sons left the room and he followed them, Callum at his side.

Kirstie blinked as the door shut behind everyone, leaving her alone with Payton. She had always thought it would be nice if Payton and Callum met her family, but she had never imagined this sort of a meeting. What really troubled her was what was yet to come. She knew her father would be demanding marriage. Instinct told her Payton would feel honor demanded that he comply. Kirstie was not sure she could hold firm against both men and her own foolish desires.

"Payton," she said, but he was already getting out of bed and disappearing into the small adjoining room where they kept the bath, the chamber pot, and most of their clothes. "Payton!" she called.

"No time to talk now, love," he called back. "I dinnae think your father will be leaving us alone for too long."

"I can talk and dress at the same time," she grumbled as she got out of bed and tugged on her shift.

She turned to go into the little room only to find the door shut. Although Payton was not heavily burdened with a sense of modesty, she knew there were some things even he would wish privacy for. Kirstie sighed and sat down on the bed to wait for him. A few minutes later, he came out, still lacing up his doublet, kissed her on the cheek, and left. She stared at the door, her mind telling her that he had just made a hasty escape, but that made little sense. Then she realized the men would quickly start to discuss her future whether she was there or not, and she hurried to get dressed.

Payton breathed a sigh of relief when Kirstie did not come after him. He then cursed as he made his way to his great hall. All his clever little plans had just been utterly ruined. He had been waiting for them both to heal so that he could propose marriage to Kirstie in a romantic setting, one where, if she hesitated to accept him, he could seduce her into saying aye. Being caught in bed with her by her large, well-armed family would certainly ensure that she married him, but there would be no chance to woo her to the idea, to soothe any doubts or fears she might have.

At the doors to his great hall, Payton hesitated, took several deep breaths to prepare himself for the confrontation he knew awaited him, and stepped into the room. Nine tall, dark Kinlochs turned to stare at him; he beat down a brief urge to turn around and leave, preferably at a very swift pace. He straightened himself and walked to the head of the table, indicating with a wave of his hand that everyone should sit down. For a little while silence reigned as everyone helped themselves to food and drink. Payton used the respite to prepare himself.

"Eudard tells me ye have already told him that ye intend to marry my lass," Sir Elrick said as he slathered honey on a thick piece of bread. "Said ye told him that when he first arrived and that is why he didnae geld ye."

"I did say that," Payton admitted. "I had hoped to present my suit to your daughter within the next few days."

"Couldnae find the time whilst ye were bedding her for the last month or more?"

"She was still married," Payton reminded him. "Now that she is a widow, I need nay hesitate."

"I do thank ye for killing that bastard."

"I am nay the one to thank. At the time I was tied to a tree, bruised and bleeding. The boy Simon did the deed."

"Ye prepared him for the slaughter and kept my lass alive whilst ye did so. It might have been better if ye had kept your breeches tightly laced as weel, but that doesnae change the fact that she is alive because ye helped her. 'Tis why I didnae pin ye to that bed with my sword."

"I commend ye for your show of restraint," Payton murmured and wondered if that really was laughter he had just briefly glimpsed in the man's eyes.

"Callum, m'boy, do ye think ye can take my lad Aiken here and find us a priest?"

"Nay, Fither!" cried Kirstie as she entered in time to hear her father's question. "Ye cannae do this." She hurried to the table to take a seat on Payton's right.

"Oh, aye, I can." Sir Elrick looked at Callum and Aiken. "Go on with ye. She willnae be changing my mind." He nodded when the pair hurried away, then fixed a stern look upon his daughter. "But ye will try, will ye not?"

"Of course," Kirstie replied. " 'Tis nay as if I was some maid, Fither. I was a wife and am now a widow."

"And your point is?"

"Weel, 'tisnae uncommon for such women to, weel, frolic a wee bit and no one pays any heed."

"I do. And we all ken ye were no wife to that piece of filth."

Kirstie looked at Payton. "Dinnae ye have anything to say?"

Payton shook his head as he spooned some stewed apples over his porridge. "They found us naked in a bed together. I am nay sure there is much one can say."

He was not going to make even the smallest protest, Kirstie realized. She looked at Ian, who had slipped into the room behind her and taken a seat at the far end of the table. He just smiled. Next she studied the faces of her family, only to find that even Eudard looked stern and unbending. She had no allies. About the only way she could see to put a stop to this was to flee and she knew her father would have planned for that. The moment she had entered the room she had become trapped. It truly would be a waste of time to argue, but she decided to try anyway.

"Fither, ye dinnae need to hold a sword on him," Kirstie snapped as she knelt beside Payton before a

plump, balding priest. "He hasnae made e'en one protest."

"E'en the best of horses can balk at the last gate,"
Sir Elrick said.

"Ah, me, why am I nay surprised by the scene?"
drawled a deep voice from the doorway to the great
hall.

Payton cursed and looked toward the couple walking
over to him. "Hello, Father. Mother." He introduced
everyone, despite still kneeling before the priest, Sir
Elrick's sword at his back. "I suppose Gillyanne wrote
to ye."

"Aye." Sir Nigel Murray looked at the priest. "Carry
on."

Kirstie stared at Payton's handsome father and stunningly beautiful mother and felt wretched. They both
smiled at her and she managed a weak smile in return.
She wondered why they were not trying to stop this, or
even asking a few hard questions. Was she the only one
who saw the problems in such a marriage? Everyone
else seemed either pleased or determined. She could
understand the children being happy about it all, for
they were too young to know all that was wrong with
being forced to marry someone. It was everyone else's
attitude that confused her, including Payton's. He did
not seem even mildly annoyed over this indignity.

A nudge from Payton turned her attention to the
priest. Despite her confusion and doubt, she heard herself dutifully repeat her vows. It startled her when Payton
produced the rings required, finely wrought gold bands,
one of which fit her perfectly. Why, she thought a little
dazedly, would a carefree, licentious rogue have such
rings on hand? Did he keep a small chest full of such
tokens to give his lovers?

Then it was over. She was married. A widow for barely
a fortnight and now a wife again. She thought it very
sad that her first husband had married her because she
looked like a child and her second husband had married

her because he preferred her to a precise and painful gutting by her angry father.

Once on her feet, Payton kissed her. It was no delicate, chaste kiss and she was soon clinging to him. There was no anger in his embrace, just a fierce, possessive ardor. Then Kirstie found herself freed, Payton's curse still tingling against her lips. When she saw how he rubbed the back of his head and glared at her father, she realized that odd noise she had heard had been her father rapping on Payton's head with the hilt of his sword.

In the confusion of the hearty congratulations, which she found somewhat misplaced, Kirstie found herself separated from Payton. She finally saw him talking seriously with both her father and his. Certain that the three men were planning her life, she started toward them, only to be brought up short by the grip of a small, delicate but surprisingly strong hand on her arm. She looked into the beautiful green eyes of Lady Gisele and wondered why Payton's mother was not berating her for forcing her son into marriage.

"You did not wish to marry my son?" Gisele asked.

"If Payton and I were to be married, I would rather it had been done without nine swords prodding him to the altar," Kirstie replied and was a little surprised to see the amusement upon Lady Gisele's face.

"A very manly performance, *oui*? And, I would leave them to talk now. Another manly thing 'tis best to let them do. You can correct their mistakes later, *non*?"

"This whole business was a mistake."

"Was it? You do not love my son? Gillyanne was most certain that you did." She smiled and touched the blush that quickly heated Kirstie's cheeks. "I have waited a long time for someone to love my son."

"A lot of women have loved your son. He is probably the most loved mon in Scotland." Kirstie realized just the thought of all the women Payton had known had her scowling at his back and she quickly turned her attention back to his mother, who was smiling a little too knowingly for Kirstie's comfort.

"A lot of women have wanted Payton," Lady Gisele said. "Like they want a pretty ring, or the finest house in the town, or the richest gown. They have not loved him. They want to hold the beauty of him and have everyone know that they do, but they see no more, look no deeper. He knows this so he does not linger, but flits from flower to flower. I think he flitted a little too much," Lady Gisele smiled when Kirstie briefly laughed, "but that is a man's way."

"How do ye ken I am nay the same as those other women?"

"Such a woman would ne'er risk all, e'en her life, for street waifs." Lady Gisele winked. "And, of course, I have Gillyanne's assurance that you love him."

"What I feel doesnae matter all that much. Payton was forced to marry me and that can ne'er be a good thing."

"Child, do you truly believe my pretty but very pig-headed son could be forced to do anything he did not wish to do?" She slipped her arm through Kirstie's and started to walk toward where the children were gathered. "I know you will not heed me in this, but my son is exactly where he wishes to be. Now, I wish to meet these children."

"Ye need nay scowl at me, laddie," said Sir Elrick. "Ye had weeks to take care of this matter and dinnae give me that nonsense about her being married. She wasnae really and ye kenned she would soon be a widow. I would ne'er have thought ye the shy, reticent type."

Payton scowled at his father when the man laughed. "Ye did notice this mon was holding a sword on me, didnae ye?"

"Aye," Nigel replied. "If I had found my lass abed with a mon, I believe I would have done the same. Ye

ken weel how I reacted when I first learned about your
sister Avery and her Cameron. Circumstances made this
sort of thing impossible and the fools got married ere
I could figure out a way to make them.''

"I wanted to woo her.''

"Thought that was what ye were doing," said Sir
Elrick. "Of course, most of us do our wooing with our
clothes on." He studied Payton for a moment, a glim-
mer of amusement in his storm-grey eyes. "After all the
practice ye have had, I would have thought ye would
be able to get it right by now.''

Ignoring his father's laughter, Payton said, "I didnae
woo any of those other women. Didnae have to. Didnae
want to.''

"Cocksure little bugger, isnae he?" Elrick exchanged
a grin with Nigel, then fixed a stern gaze on Payton.
"And, ye willnae be wooing any other lasses from now
on, laddie. I willnae be pleased if ye hurt my lass. Aye,
I ken 'tis my fault she was wed to that piece of filth, but
he was good at hiding what he was and she didnae tell
me anything, did she? Kept all this misery secret, then
turned to ye.''

"First—I believe in holding to vows made. 'Tis why
I was always careful to make none and why I was, admit-
tedly, a little slow to decide to make some to Kirstie.
Second—Kirstie didnae tell ye about Roderick because
she was sure ye would all come riding to her rescue and
probably kill the mon.''

"No *probably* about it.''

"Exactly. And that would have turned the wrath of
the MacIyes upon ye and yours. Kirstie kenned that the
powerful and much larger MacIyes would decimate her
family and clan. She came to me because she felt I
was of an equally powerful and large clan. E'en more
important, I had the ability and knowledge to expose
the bastard so that no one would care if he was killed.''
He shook his head. "My only regret is that I didnae get
to do the killing.''

"I see. Galls me to admit it, but she may have been right. And the boy Simon who did the killing? Is he all right? Twelve is young to have felled your first mon."

"He is fine," replied Payton. "A little unsteady at first, but there were so many reasons to kill the mon, the justice of it soothes his unease. At the moment he struck, Roderick was about to separate Kirstie's head from her shoulders." Payton briefly glanced at the marks still visible upon his wrists where he had savaged them in a frantic and futile attempt to break free of his bonds. "I could do naught to help her or Callum, who was with her and would have been next." Payton looked at Elrick and knew he had revealed some of the torment he had felt at that time, one that still haunted him.

"Ah, lad, ye love my wee lass, dinnae ye?"

"Aye, but it will be difficult to make her believe it after this."

"Just tell her, Payton," said Nigel, and shrugged when his son looked at him. "I fear your winning way with the lasses only hurts your cause now. Pretty words and soft flatteries willnae do it. She kens that ye are skilled at those and gave them out freely to others. Nay, plain words, lad. And, ye may have to repeat them. Speak from the heart, son, and dinnae worry if it isnae elegant. It just has to sound like the truth to her."

"Wise words," Payton murmured. "I will try to heed them, but 'tis nay easy to bare one's heart when ye dinnae ken what the one ye offer it to is feeling."

"For a lad who has been said to have bedded half the lasses in Scotland, ye arenae too wise about women," said Elrick. "Or, mayhap ye have ne'er had too much to do with the right lasses. Kirstie is sharp of tongue and stubborn, but she obeys all the hard rules, the ones that say a wife keeps to her vows and a maid keeps her chastity. She broke them all to be with ye."

Payton stared at his new father-in-law for a moment, then slowly smiled. "Aye, she did, didnae she?"

"I would appreciate it if ye didnae look quite so lecherous when ye say that.'' Elrick spoke sternly, but his eyes brimmed with laughter.

After grinning at Elrick, Payton looked around for Kirstie. ''Might as weel start a wee bit of wooing now as 'tis a wee bit early to start my wedding night.'' He suddenly noticed the three men standing in the doorway of the great hall. ''Curse it. The MacMillans are here.'' He briefly explained about Callum. ''I believe that is Sir Gavin with Bryan and Euan. I also believe this could take a lot of my time.''

''I suspicion my lass will understand. Tend to it. We will keep her busy. If naught else, she has some explaining to do.''

''And your mother and Alice will be more than willing to stand as her kinswomen and do whate'er it is that women think they need to do for a wedding night,'' said Nigel.

As soon as Payton was gone, Elrick looked at Nigel. ''Ye have no objections to all this, do ye?''

''Nary a one,'' said Nigel. ''I have always believed ye should marry when ye find a women who fits ye, but I was beginning to think Payton would ne'er find one. Worse, I began to think he was becoming too much the courtier, too accustomed to fleeting liaisons and empty, false friendships. He fell into it all at a verra young age.''

''Och, aye, a bonnie lad like that would.''

''He was becoming blind to it all. This business reopened his eyes to the rot that can lie beneath the rich clothes, the power, and the heady sex. All my wife cared about was that the lass truly loved Payton. Our niece Gillyanne, who has a way to sense such things, assured her that Kirstie did love Payton for what he is, nay just what she sees, and that Payton loves Kirstie.''

''Do ye think the fools will sort that out?''

''It may take a wee bit of time.''

''Aye. Weel, it will do the laddie good to actually have to work for what he wants from a woman.''

Nigel nodded. ''A struggle can only build character.''

"Exactly. How long do ye think we should give them?"

"A month or two. Even an idiot ought to be able to sort it out by then."

"True, true. And if they prove to be complete idiots?"

"Then we take them aside and knock some sense into them."

"Sounds like a good plan to me."

CHAPTER
TWENTY-TWO

"Ah, lass, ye do look bonnie," Alice said as she stood back to admire Kirstie.

" 'Tis certainly a lovely night shift," Kirstie murmured, then blushed as she looked herself over. "And, er, delicate. Verra delicate."

Gisele nodded. "A perfect temptation, teasing the mon with wee glimpses of what he wants."

"Mother," Kirstie was a little startled by how quickly she had grown at ease with the title Lady Gisele insisted upon, "I dinnae think I will shock ye by saying your son has already glimpsed all I have, little as it is."

"Which makes it even more tempting when you hide it." Gisele smiled at Kirstie's confusion. "Believe me."

"Aye," said Alice, "and ye may as weel enjoy playing the temptress now as ye probably willnae feel comfortable doing it later."

"I dinnae feel comfortable doing it now." Kirstie frowned at Wee Alice. "Why should later matter to how I feel?"

"Weel, some women dinnae feel comfortable showing

much of themselves once the bairn starts to round them."

"The bairn?"

"Wheesht, didnae Lady Gillyanne tell ye?"

"Tell me what?"

"That ye are carrying, lass." Alice shook her head when she saw how shocked Kirstie was. "When did ye last bleed?"

"Why, just before—" Kirstie realized how long ago it was that she had first bedded down with Payton and hastily sat down on the bed when she felt her knees grow weak. "I think it has been a while. Oh, dear."

"Payton will be thrilled," said Gisele as she patted Kirstie's shoulder and made no attempt to hide her own delight.

"Come, lass," said Alice, "with the fertile ground both ye and the lad sprung from, can ye really be so surprised?"

"Nay, I suppose not," replied Kirstie, torn between delight over the child and fear that Payton would see it as just another shackle binding him to a wife he had not chosen. "Payton will feel e'en more obligated to me now."

Gisele shook her head. "Foolish child. You have sunk yourself into a morass of self-pity, *oui*? I understand why and sympathize, but shake it off, lass. Do you know that Payton has bred no bastards at all? His caution and control are near legendary amongst the lads in the family. 'Tis obvious he exercised neither with you and you should look hard at the why of that."

"Weel, the passion is rather, er, strong," she began, blushing furiously.

"I truly do not wish to remind you of what a rogue my son was, but there is no hiding from that truth. Payton has been no stranger to passion for far longer than I care to think on. He has ne'er left his seed in a woman, and do not tell him I know that as I think it might embarrass him. Foolish lads believe they can hide such things from their mothers and I kindly allow them to think so.''

'' 'Tis a puzzle, and I will think on what it means.'' Kirstie sighed. "Yet, he is such a beautiful mon. When he walks into a crowded room half the women there want him and the other half have probably had him and want him again. I am a little dark lass, Mother. I have seen what he is accustomed to and I dinnae compare weel at all.''

"You have your own beauty, child. Do you think my boy would want you if you did not, eh? He has no need to struggle so hard to get a woman into his bed, and, I must say, we were all delighted by how long and hard ye made him struggle for you.''

Kirstie blushed. ''Gillyanne told ye everything, didnae she?''

"It was a very long letter, *oui*." Gisele gently took Kirstie's face between her hands. "Tell him, child. Tell him what you feel. Tell him what you want. Tell him what you need. Set it before him and see what happens, see what he says. This night begins the whole rest of your life. Start that life with the truth. And, when you are satisfied with what he offers, and I know you will be, tell him of the child. But, only then, or you will always wonder if the child was part of why he accepted being married to you.''

Kirstie was still considering Gisele's advice when she suddenly found herself alone. She sighed, reached for the tankard of mead Alice had poured for her, and had a drink. One thing Lady Gisele had said had truly struck home. She had been feeling very sorry for herself and she did need to stop. The marriage may not have come about as she would have liked, but it was done. It was time to cease pouting over what she did not have and look at what she did have. Even more important, it was time to look at what she could have if she tried hard enough.

There was no question that Payton was a husband

many women would envy her for. Although she had
seen little of him since they had said their vows, he had
revealed no anger or regret. There had certainly been
neither of those emotions in the kiss he had given her
after they had finished their vows. Payton would keep
the children and few other men would do so. Simon,
Brenda, Moira, and Robbie would have a home with
them. So would Callum, although, after today, she
believed it would not be a permanent home, that Callum
would accept his grandfather. There was passion, hot
and fierce, and she had no doubt that he shared it
with her. She also felt fairly confident that Payton liked,
trusted, and respected her. Although she ached to be
loved, she recognized the value of those gifts.

Tell him what you feel, Payton's mother had advised,
and it was good advice. Kirstie was just not sure she was
brave enough to bare her soul like that when there was
no guarantee of an equal return. Yet when would be a
good time, she wondered. And who deserved the truth
more than Payton, who had risked his very life for her?
She had another drink of mead, but the truth could
not be washed away with the heady brew. Lady Gisele
was right. It was best to start their married life with the
truth. At least he would know he was getting everything
she had to offer a man, even if he could only return
some of that. She would also finally know where she
stood in his affections. It would let her know how much
she had to work for or if there was any point in even
trying for more.

She was just starting her second goblet of mead when
Payton entered the room. He wore only a loosely tied
robe and his beautiful hair was still damp from his bath.
Her newly made resolutions faltered badly. How could
she possibly hold onto a man like him? Little dark lasses
did not have bonnie knights like Sir Payton Murray lay
his heart at their tiny feet. Yet, she told herself firmly,
her decision had been a good one. She just needed to
get her courage back, and the way he looked at her as

he poured himself some mead would certainly help. Such a heated, hungry look from such a man should be enough to give any lass courage.

"How did the meeting between Callum and his grand-father go?" she asked, hoping to calm her nerves with idle conversation.

Payton could see that Kirstie was nervous and decided to let her set the pace for a while. "Surprisingly weel. We shall have Sir Gavin as a guest for a wee while, but then I do believe Callum will be ready to go and see what will be his new home."

"Oh." She truly was happy for the boy, yet it hurt to know he would soon leave her. "Sir Gavin had no trouble accepting Callum despite what had happened to him?"

"Nay. He asked the lad if the mon was truly dead and Callum told him how Roderick had died. Then he asked if Callum kenned where the mon is buried and Callum told him where. Then the old mon asked if Callum had gone to piss on his grave yet."

Kirstie was shocked, yet could not completely hold back a laugh. "He truly asked that?"

"Aye, and Callum smiled. Told the mon he had done it—twice—and had been careful to drink a lot ere he went there."

She shook her head. "Such strange creatures men are." She sighed and stared into the dregs of her mead. "I am sorry for today, for how my family arrived and forced ye to the altar."

"Love, no one can force me to do anything I dinnae want to. It made your father feel better to wave his sword about so I let him, but nay more than that."

"I see," she murmured, although she really did not. How could any one man resist the persuasive power of nine swords?

Payton set his goblet down and gently took her face between his hands. "I wanted to marry ye, lass."

"Ye ne'er said so, ne'er hinted at it."

"Eudard kenned it. I told him so the day he arrived."

"Weel, that certainly explains his attitude." She found that confession was enough to renew her courage. "Payton, I need to say—"

"Aye," he kissed her to halt her words, "and I have things I need to say as weel, but first, we get naked."

Still dazed from the heat of his kiss, Kirstie meekly allowed him to strip her of her clothes. "Ye need to be naked to talk to me?"

"Twill help."

When he shed his robe, she looked at him and sighed. "I am nay sure I will be able to talk much with ye naked." She reached out to curl her fingers around his erection. "The sight tends to muddle my thoughts." She moved closer and kissed his chest as she lightly stroked him, enjoying the soft sounds of pleasure he made. "I just think about touching ye." Kirstie licked him. "And tasting ye."

It was surprisingly easy to maneuver the much stronger Payton around until he was sprawled on the bed. At first, Kirstie had thought it odd that he would wish to be naked in order to talk seriously, but now she saw some distinct advantages to it. Making love to him would fire her own passions and she was sure it would be easy to confess all then. As she crouched over him, she kissed him with all the love and need within her.

"Now, are ye verra sure ye wished to marry me ere ye woke up with my father's sword at your throat?" she asked as she encircled his still-lightly-bruised neck with soft kisses.

"Oh, aye. Ye ken that something must have made Eudard so calm about ye sharing my bed."

She did. It was the only thing that made any sense. "Weel, that is good. I wouldnae wish to be doing this to just any fool." Kirstie trailed kisses down his broad chest. "I do so want ye, Payton. All the time. I think ye are a pestilence, but I dinnae really wish to be cured."

"I must be suffering the same disease." He shuddered

when she ran her tongue slowly up and down the length of his manhood. "We willnae get much talking done if ye do that."

"Nay? How about if I do this?" She took him into her mouth.

For as long as he could, Payton enjoyed the pleasure she so freely gave him. They were not going to get much talking done now, but he decided they could easily talk later. It might even be better, for they would both be too exhausted to move, no matter what was said. Then, knowing how close he was to the edge, Payton dragged her up his body, and eased her down on him.

"Ah, lass, this is all I need. This is what is right, perfect."

"Truly?" She leaned down and brushed her lips over his, moving ever so slowly. "Do ye ken what I need? I need ye, Payton Murray. I need ye here. I need to see ye when I wake in the morning and when I go to sleep at night. I need to ken that, whene'er I have some news to share, or burden I need eased, that ye will be there. I need to ken that, e'en when I am the veriest shrew, ye will still be there. I need to ken that, when what little beauty I have fades into wrinkles, ye will still be there."

Payton stared at her, his mind fixed entirely upon her words, even as she taunted his body with her tiny movements. "And I need the same," was all he could think to say.

" 'Tis good, then."

"Verra good."

"And I want things, Payton. I want ye to think about me now and then. I want ye to hold fast to your vows, for it would tear the heart right out of me if ye didnae."

He smiled faintly as he stroked her hips, then gasped as he felt her tighten around him. "I have wanted no other since setting eyes on ye, lass, and I will ne'er want another."

"And, Payton Murray?" she said very softly as she pressed her lips against his.

"Aye, my dark beauty?" he said, speaking against her mouth.

"I want ye to love me as I love ye."

Kirstie suddenly found herself on her back, a taut, intense-looking Payton above her. His body trembled as she wrapped her limbs around him. It was a little bit more of a reaction than she had anticipated. However, it revealed that he was willing and eager to accept her love, seemed deeply moved by her words. That had to be a good sign.

"Say it again," he ordered in a hoarse, slightly tremulous voice. "Say the last three words again."

"I love ye," she whispered.

"Ah, Jesu, lass."

Kirstie found herself being made love to with a ferocity that was both intensely exciting and somewhat astonishing. She caught his fever very quickly and gave herself up to it. He was muttering sweet, hot words against her skin, words she suspected she ought to heed more closely, but her rising passion deafened her to all but the seductive tone of them. Kirstie was also aware of the fact that Payton had lost control, and that knowledge only heightened her desire, for she knew instinctively that no other woman had seen him this way. She, little dark lass that she was, had the legendary Sir Payton Murray, the great lover renowned for his control, his finesse, and his seductive artistry, slamming into her so fast and furiously they were rapidly edging up the bed. Her last clear thought was that she was glad she had piled the pillows against that hard, ornately carved headboard.

When Kirstie felt the touch of wet linen, she opened her eyes and saw nothing. It took her dazed mind a minute to realize the pillows had toppled onto her face. Still a little embarrassed at being so personally attended to by Payton, she did not immediately remove the pillow.

A moment later, Payton returned to lie at her side, lifted it off, and kissed her.

"Say it again," he whispered against her cheek.

Although she blushed, too painfully aware that while he kept demanding the words, he offered none in return, she whispered back, "I love ye." She squeaked a little when he pulled her into an almost too-tight hug.

"Mine," he said.

"Weel, aye. We are wed now." It was a little sad, she mused, that she could find satisfaction in that display of manly possessiveness.

"Nay, I mean mine in every way. In body, in law, and in heart."

"I think I have been yours since the beginning," she said, finding hope in the fact that he was so obviously pleased by her admission and decided to be completely truthful. "Nay in law, true, but in all other ways."

"And I was an idiot not to see it. I have been an idiot in many ways." He brushed a kiss over her lips and held her gaze with his as he idly stroked her lithe body and braced himself to speak from his heart. "The passion we shared was clear to me and I was greedy for it. I respected your stand, your determination to hold to vows given and a few hard rules, but resented it as weel. Yet, when ye finally came to my bed, I did not see, or didnae want to, the importance of that. To ye."

" 'Tis difficult to see what is nay revealed and nay spoken of."

"Ye revealed it, lass, in every sigh, in every embrace. I but chose to keep calling it passion." He touched a kiss to her forehead. "I decided quite a while ago that I must lack the capability of being in love, for I have ne'er been, that I am nay a loving mon."

"Oh, nay, Payton." She rubbed her hands up and down his arms when he moved to settle himself on top of her. "Ye are a verra loving mon. 'Tis there to see in how ye are with your family, to hear in how ye speak of them. 'Twas there to see in how ye not only championed the cause of the children, but in how ye treated them."

"Then I refused to recognize it as such. I looked too closely, too hard, at every feeling, perhaps." He shook his head. "It matters naught how I became misguided, just that I was, that I had convinced myself I wasnae destined to love a woman, or was incapable of it, so I put a different name to all I felt. I did that time and time again until I could nay longer delude myself."

Kirstie felt herself tense, terrified she was misinterpreting his words, yet certain she was not. "What are ye saying, Payton?"

"I am saying that when the passion we shared proved to be the best, the fiercest, the most satisfying I have e'er kenned, I decided we were a perfect match in desire. Then, when Roderick took ye and I was near maddened with fear for ye, I decided I cared for ye. That was when I decided ye were mine and, as soon as ye were free, I would marry ye."

"Ye ne'er said a word."

"Nay, for ye were still a married woman, by law and in your own mind." He combed his fingers through her tangled hair. "Then, when ye came to ransom me, I finally saw it all clearly." Payton raised his hand and idly studied the marks there, marks which would fade, but would undoubtedly leave behind a few scars. "When he struck ye, when he raised that knife, I kenned the truth. I was cold with fear for ye and gripped by a blinding rage that he would dare to hurt ye, to take ye from me. When I saw him start to swing that sword toward this pretty neck," he kissed her throat, "I would have gladly maimed myself just to get free and stop it, or take the blow in your stead. I was watching ye die and it was killing me."

Kirstie took his hand in hers and kissed the marks around his wrists, anxious to ease the torment that memory so clearly brought him. "Ye could do naught. Ye were wounded and tightly bound. And, my head still sits upon my shoulders. But I am so sorry that ye had to hurt your beautiful hands.''

Payton took her face between his hands. ''Every time I see the scars, I will remember what ye mean to me. I will remember how desolate I felt at the thought that ye would be taken from me. I will remember that I nearly lost all chance to tell ye that I love ye.''

Despite suspecting what he would say, Kirstie's doubts had remained strong enough to leave her stunned when he finally said the words she so longed to hear. She stared at him, unable to think of anything to say. When he kissed her, she clung tightly to him, fighting back tears of joy.

''Say it again,'' she whispered, and felt him smile against her shoulder.

''I love ye, my dark beauty, my heart, my wife.'' He smiled and kissed the corners of her eyes. ''Thank ye for nay crying.''

She laughed softly. ''Ye ken women too weel.''

''Nay, I kenned whores, adulteresses, women to whom it was all a game or a salve for their vanity. Aye, the women in my family are like ye, and I did learn from them—yet, I believe I forgot too much as I dallied amongst the courtesans and courtiers. Ye have reminded me of all I truly value in a woman, all that I truly hungered for.''

''Oh, my, ye give me a grand standard to live up to.''

He laughed. ''Ye have already done so. And, as I vowed before that priest, there will be no others. I need no others and I will want none. I havenae since I first saw ye. Ye didnae believe me the first time I told ye that, but I pray ye will believe me now.''

''Aye. I think those fears began to fade when ye made your vows before that overfed priest. Ye are a mon who would hold to a vow, e'en one made whilst a sword was held to your back.'' She exchanged a brief grin with him, the memory of their wedding now one full of amusement for her. "What do ye want from marriage, Payton?"

Payton frowned a little. "Weel, companionship." He grimaced. "Nay verra romantic. I want someone I ken will be there with me, for me. Someone I dinnae have to play the courtier's game for, whom I can be myself with, warts and all. I ken the passion will ease, will change in some ways o'er the years, so dinnae fear I think only on that. I want to ken that nay matter how much this shell of mine—this covering that so many think is so beautiful—nay matter how it softens, or wrinkles, or becomes scarred, it willnae matter to ye because ye dinnae love it, ye love me."

"Oh, aye. E'en in the bonniest, much of that gift is one bestowed by youth. Age can change it, battle can steal it, disease can fade it. I ken all of this. I am nay such a fool as to love a shell, nay matter how bonnie it is, or how looking at ye can make my breath catch in my throat. After all, Roderick was a handsome mon, aye?"

"Aye, but too few others understand the need to look beyond that gloss. I ken ye see me as more than a bonnie mon who happens to please your eye. So did my heart."

"So, ye want companionship." She stroked his legs and felt him shift against her. "And passion."

"And bairns. I would ne'er ask ye to bear more than ye want," he hurried to add, "but, ah, lass, I do want bairns. Bonnie little lasses with storm-grey eyes and night-dark hair."

"There is a verra strong chance that I will bear a lot of laddies," she said.

"Aye, I ken it, but one wee lass would be nice, if God wills it."

"Weel, we can judge his benevolence in, oh, about seven months, mayhap a wee bit more."

Kirstie waited for the moment the import of her words finally settled in his mind. The sudden delight that bloomed upon his face was all she could have hoped for. Now that she knew he loved her, she felt only joy over his reaction to the news. Payton wanted and needed her. That made the child she carried a much-valued gift and not just another obligation.

Payton placed an unsteady hand upon her still-taut belly. "Are ye certain?"

"To be honest, I am still trying to believe it. I was told by Wee Alice only a short while ago when she helped attire me in that fine linen shift ye so quickly cast aside." She blushed and looked away as she said, "I havenae bled since shortly after we first met and I should have. Twice, I believe." Then she smiled at him. "And, Gillyanne says 'tis true."

He held her tight, then kissed her. "Thank ye, lass. And, ye will be fine."

She could sense the hint of fear beneath his somewhat foolish command. "Oh, aye, I will." She stroked his cheek. "With such a champion by my side, how could I be anything else but verra fine indeed?"

"So, e'en though I am now your husband, your love, ye still see me as your champion?"

"Oh, aye. My love, my husband, and my champion. The champion of my heart. Always."

Please turn the page for an exciting sneak peek of
Hannah Howell's HIGHLAND GROOM!

Scotland, Spring 1471

Isla groaned as eight of her fourteen brothers crowded into her small cottage. They looked around, each wearing an identical scowl of disapproval. None of them liked or tolerated her decision to move out of the keep. Unfortunately, not one of them understood that their often overbearing protectiveness had been smothering her, either. Even though one or more of them stopped by several times a day, she was enjoying her new found freedom. That, she feared, was about to end.

"It has been nearly a year," announced Sigimor, her eldest brother, as he and his twin Somerled crouched by the cradles of their nephews. "In a fortnight the year and the day come to an end."

"I ken it."

Isla put two heavy jugs of ale on the huge table that occupied almost half of her main room. She had realized that she would never be able to stop her brothers from coming round as the mood struck them so had arranged her living area accordingly. A huge table, sturdy benches, and extra seats hanging upon the wall until needed, had all been made specifically for her brothers. She had arranged a small sitting area more to her liking on the other end of the great hall which made up most of her bottom floor. A low, somewhat rough addition to the back of her home held the kitchen, a tiny pantry, a bathing room, and a small bedchamber for her companion. The high loft, which served as the upper part of her home, was where she had done things to please herself alone. She had the sinking feeling her brothers were going to force her to leave her little cottage just as she had gotten herself comfortably settled.

"The lads need their father," Sigimor said as he let his nephew Finlay clasp his finger.

"Fourteen uncles arenae enough?" she drawled, setting eight tankards on the table.

"Nay. Their father is a laird, has land and coin. They deserve a part of that."

"It would appear that their father isnae of a like mind." It hurt to say those words, but Isla fought to hide her pain. "Ye want me to go crawling to a mon who has deserted me?"

Sigimor sighed and moved to join his brothers at the table as Isla set out bread, cheese, and oatcakes. "Nay, I want ye to confront him, to demand what is rightfully due your sons, his sons."

Isla also sighed as she sat down next to her twin brother Tait. She had hoped her brothers would not use her sons' rights or welfare to sway her, but suspected she had been foolish to do so. They might be rough, loud, overbearing, and far too protective, but they were not stupid. Her weak point was her sons and only an idiot would not realize it.

"Mayhap another week," she began and groaned when her brothers all shook their heads.

"That would be cutting it too close to the bone. We will leave on the morrow."

"But . . ."

"Nay. I will admit that I am fair disappointed in the lad . . ."

"He is of an age with ye," muttered Isla.

Sigimor ignored her. "For I believed all his talk of needing to clear away some threat and prepare his keep for a wife. 'Tis why I settled for a handfast marriage. I felt a wee bit uncomfortable insisting upon witnessed documents, but now I am glad that I did. He cannae deny ye or the lads. We can make him honor the vows he made." He studied Isla closely for a moment. "I thought ye cared for the mon. Ye wanted him bad enough."

"And I thought he cared for me," she snapped. "That was obviously utter foolishness. For just a moment I forgot that I am too poor, too thin, and too red. The mon was just willing to play a more devious game than usual to tumble a maid."

"That makes no sense, Isla," argued Tait. "He let us ken where he lives."

"Are ye sure of that?" She nodded when her brothers looked briefly stunned. "We just have his word on that and I think we can assume that his word isnae worth verra much."

"We will still go," said Sigimor. "If we discover it was all a lie, a trick, then we will ken that we have us a mon to hunt down." He nodded when his brothers all muttered an agreement. "So, Somerled will stay here, as will Alexander whose wife is soon to bear him his first child. They can watch the young ones. I, Gilbert, Ranulph, Elyas, Tait, Tamhas, Brice, and Bronan will ride with ye. A few of our men and a couple of our cousins, too, I am thinking."

"Tis nearly an army," protested Isla.

"Enough to put weight behind our words, but nay enough to be too threatening."

Isla tried to talk them out of their plans, but failed. The moment her brothers left, Isla buried her face in her hands and fought the urge to weep. She had done enough of that. A soft touch upon her shoulder drew her out of her despondency and she looked at Gay, her companion and the wet nurse who helped her sate the greed of her sons. Brutally raped, cast off by her family, and then suffering the loss of her child had left young Gay terrified of men, a near silent ghost of a girl who still feared far too many things and grieved for all her losses. Gay always hid away when Isla's brothers stomped in for a visit.

"Ye must go," Gay said in her whispery voice.

"I ken it," Isla replied. "Yet, when he didnae return for me, didnae e'en send a letter or gift, I realized I had been played for a fool and did my grieving then. I buried all of that verra deep inside of me. I dinnae want it all dug up again."

Gay picked up a fretting Finlay, handed him to Isla, then collected Cearnach. For a few moments, Isla savored the gentle peace as she and Gay fed the babies. Looking at her sons, however, at their big, beautiful eyes, she was sharply reminded of the man whose seed had created them. The pain was still there, deep, and, she suspected, incurable.

For a few brief, heady weeks she had felt loved, desired, even beautiful. At twenty years of age, an age when most considered her a spinster, she had finally caught the eye of a man. And such a handsome one, she mused, and sighed. That should have warned her. Handsome men did not pursue women like her. In truth, no man had ever pursued her. She had let loneliness, passion, and a craving for love steal away all of her wits. Going to the man as her brothers wished her to would only remind her too sharply of her own idiocy. Not that she ever completely forgot it, she muttered to herself.

"It must be done for the laddies," Gay said as she rested Cearnach against her thin shoulder and rubbed his back.

"I ken that, too," Isla said as she did the same to Finlay. " 'Tis their brirthright and I cannae allow it to be stolen from them. Weel, if there even is a birthright and we dinnae discover that the mon told us naught but lies. Ye will have to come with us."

Gay nodded. "I will be fine. I hide from your brothers because they are so big, nay because I fear them. They fill the room and I find that hard to bear. I will find other places to slip away to when we get where we are going." She frowned. "I just cannae abide being inside a place when so many men are about. I ken your brothers willnae hurt me, but that knowledge isnae yet enough to banish all my blind fears."

"Quite understandable."

"Do ye still love this mon?"

"I think I might which would be a great folly. But, 'tis time to stop hiding for fear I will be hurt. I must needs seek out this bastard for the sake of the laddies, but I begin to think I need to do it for myself, too. I need to look the devil in the eye, find out just how big a fool I was, and deal with it all. Of course, if he is there, was just hoping I would fade away into the mists, 'tis best to confront him with his responsibilities. And then I can do my best to make him utterly miserable."

When Gay laughed briefly and softly, Isla felt her spirits rise. Gay was healing. It was slow and there would always be scars, but soon Gay would recover from the hurts done to her. It made Isla a little ashamed of her own cowardice. If, after all she had suffered, little Gay could heal, then so could she. And, if she did meet her lover again, she would be a lot wiser and a lot stronger. She would not fall victim to any more foolish dreams.

"My children need a mother."

"Och, he is back to talking to himself again."

Sir Diarmot MacEnroy smiled at his brother Angus who sat on his right. On his left was his brother Anthony, or Nanty as he was often called. They had come to attend his wedding and he was heartily glad of their company. The brother he really wished to talk to was his eldest brother Connor, however, but that man had only just arrived with his pregnant wife Gillyanne. Ignoring Gilly's protests, Connor had immediately insisted that she rest for a while and had dragged her up to the bedchamber they would share. It would be a long while before he saw either of them again. Diarmot just hoped there would be some time before his wedding in which he could speak privately with the man.

"Just uneasy about the wedding," Diarmot said.

"Thought ye wanted to marry this lass."

"I do. I just need to remind myself of why now and again."

"She is a pretty wee lass," said Nanty. "Quiet."

"Verra quiet," agreed Diarmot. "Sweet. Biddable. Chaste."

"Completely different from your first wife," murmured Angus.

"Just as I wanted her to be. Anabelle was a blight. Margaret will be a blessing." A boring one, he mused, and probably cold as well, then hastily shook aside those thoughts. "Good dowry and a fine piece of land."

"Does she ken about the children?" Angus asked.

"Aye," replied Diarmot. "I introduced her. She seems at ease with the matter. Her father wasnae too happy at first, nay until he realized the only legitimate one was wee Alice. Once assured that any son his daughter bears me will be my heir, he calmed down."

"There willnae be what Connor and Gilly have, will there?" Nanty asked, his tone of voice indicating that he already knew the answer to the question.

"Nay," Diarmot replied quietly. "I thought I had found that with Anabelle, but 'twas naught but a curse. Nay every mon can be blessed with what Connor has, but then no mon deserves it more." Both brothers grunted in agreement. "I now seek peace, contentment."

He ignored the looks his brothers exchanged which carried a strong hint of pity. Since he was occasionally prone to feeling the pinch of it for himself, he did not really need theirs. It was time, however, to set his life back on course. He had drifted for too long after the debacle of his marriage to Anabelle, descending into debauchery and drunkenness which had left him with a houseful of children, only one of whom was legitimate by law even if he was not certain that little Alice was truly his child. Then, as he had finally begun to come to his senses, he had been attacked and left for dead. The months needed to heal had given him far too much time to think. That had led to the coming marriage to sweet, shy, biddable Margaret Campbell. It was the right step to take, he told himself firmly.

It was late before he got a chance to talk privately with Connor. Diarmot had almost avoided the meeting he had craved earlier for the looks Connor and Gilly had exchanged while dining with Margaret and her family had not been encouraging. It was possible Connor might try to talk him out of the marriage and Diarmot feared he was too uncertain of himself to resist such persuasion. As they settled in chairs set before the fireplace in his bedchamber, Diarmot eyed his elder brother warily as they sipped their wine.

"Are ye certain about this, Diarmot?" Connor finally asked. "There doesnae seem to be much to the lass."

"Nay, there isnae," Diarmot agreed, "but that is what I want now."

"Are ye being prompted by your injuries, by that loss of memory?"

"My injuries are mostly healed. And, aye, my memories are still sadly rattled with a few unsettling blank spots remaining from just before and just after the attack upon me. But, those things have naught to do with this." He sighed and sipped his wine. "Not every mon has the luck ye have had in finding Gillyanne. I tried and I failed, dramatically and miserably. Now I seek peace, a woman to care for my home, my bairns, and to share my bed when I am in the mood. Nay more."

"Then why did ye wish to speak to me?"

"Weel, I havenae seen ye for months," Diarmot began, then grimaced when Connor just stared at him with wry amusement. "I think, like some foolish boy, I wanted ye to say this is right, to give your approval."

Connor nodded. "But, ye arenae a small boy any longer. Ye are the only one who can say if this is right or not."

"Ye arenae going to give me your opinion, are ye."

"I am nay sure ye want to hear it," Connor drawled. "Also nay sure what ye want my opinion on. By all the rules, ye have arranged yourself a good marriage, gaining land, coin, and a sweet, virginal bride. By all the rules, ye should be congratulated by most everyone."

"But not by ye or Gilly."

"I cannae see into your heart, Diarmot. I cannae be sure what ye want, what ye seek. To be blunt, I look at that sweet, shy, biddable bride ye have chosen and wonder how long it will take ere ye have to be reminded that ye e'en have a wife."

Diarmot laughed and groaned. "About a month. I can see the same ye do, but 'tis what I think I need. Yet, something keeps nagging at me, weakening my resolve. One of those lost memories trying to break through the mists in my mind. The closer the time to say my vows draws near, the sharper the nagging. I have more and more dreams, strange dreams, but I cannae grasp the meaning of them."

"What is in these dreams?"

"Nonsense." Diarmot sighed. "Last night I dreamed of a scarlet elf poking at me, cursing me, and telling me to clear the cursed mist from my puny brain ere I do something stupid. Then there were some angry fiery demons, near a dozen of them, bellowing that I had best step right or they will be cutting me off at the knees. Then, for a brief moment, all seems weel, until the first blow is struck. 'Tis the beating, I think, for I wake up all asweat, the fear of death putting a sharp taste in my mouth."

"The last I can understand," Connor said. "Ye were helpless. No mon wants to die, but to be set upon in the dark by men ye cannae recognize, who beat ye near to death for reasons ye dinnae ken, would stir a fear in any mon."

Diarmot nodded. "I can understand that part. I just wish that, upon waking with that fear, I would also hold the memory of the who and the why."

" 'Twill come. Now, elves and fiery demons? Nay, I dinnae understand that. Gilly might. Could just be some trickery of your mind which is struggling to remember." He shrugged. "That would explain all the talk of clearing the mists and the like. Mayhap ye should postpone the wedding."

"And what reason could I give? Dreams of scarlet elves?"

"Weel, that could do it," drawled Connor, but his obvious amusement quickly fled. "The return of your memory. Just tell Sir Campbell ye sense a danger behind what happened to ye and, since the memories are struggling to return, it might be best to wait and see if ye finally recall what that danger is."

For several moments Diarmot sat sipping his wine, staring into the fire, and considering Connor's advice. It was good advice. The increasingly strange dreams he was having could indeed mean he was beginning to remember the attack upon him. Then he shook his head. It did not really matter when his memory returned, whether it was before or after his marriage. He might not recall what the danger was, but he was absolutely sure it was his danger alone. If it started to reach to others, it would reach for his betrothed as swiftly as it did for his wife.

"Nay, it would just cause more trouble than it would solve," Diarmot finally said. "All my instincts tell me this danger I face is mine and mine alone."

"But, if ye are wrong?" Connor asked quietly.

"Then I have already drawn Margaret into my danger by betrothing myself to her."

"True. At least, as your wife, you would have better control o'er the protection of her. Weel, I dinnae think I have helped ye much. I sense ye are still uneasy." Connor stood up. "Years ago I would have looked at your bride's bloodline, her land, and her dowry and said good lad. Once I wed Gilly, I lost that blindness."

"And if Gilly had turned your life into a near hell upon earth as Anabelle did mine? Would ye wish to risk giving any lass that sort of trust, e'en power, ever again?"

"Nay," Connor replied immediately. "Ye made your point. I just wish it wasnae so."

"So do I, but, far better a wife so unexceptional I forget she is about, than one who rips my heart and soul to shreds."

Connor walked to the door, but paused on his way out to look back at Diarmot. "There is a third choice and ye have until the morning to decide."

"What third choice?"

"No wife at all."

Diarmot was still considering Connor's parting words as he watched the dawn brighten the sky. He had slept very little, troubled by that strange dream again as well as his own uneasiness. Although there were any number of times in his life that he knew he should have thought twice, this constant worrying over something was unlike him.

It was possible that his memory was beginning to return, although he wished it would not do so in strange dreams. He could not understand how that should make him question his decision to get married, yet that seemed to be what it was doing. Until the strange dreams had begun, he had been content with his choice of bride and his plans for the future. In fact, he could not figure out what scarlet elves and fiery demons had to do with anything.

Suddenly realizing he had missed the dawn because he had become so lost in his own thoughts, Diarmot cursed and rang for his bath. Enough was enough. Illness and a strange reluctance to bed any of the willing lasses around Clachthrom had kept him celibate for a year. That was what was disordering his thoughts and dreams. In a few hours he would be a married man again and he could do something about the problem.

Constant company and the final preparations for the wedding feast kept him busy and he was glad. Diarmot wanted no more time with only his own tangled thoughts for company. It was as he walked to the church with Connor at his side that Diarmot realized he was not going to be able to go blindly to the altar, marry his bride, and get it over with. Connor was tense with the need to say something.

"Weel, what is it?" Diarmot grumbled.

"I was rather hoping ye would take the third choice," Connor murmured. "So was Gilly."

"Why?"

"Weel, Gilly says Margaret is indeed sweet, shy, and biddable. She also says she is, er, empty."

"Empty? What does that mean?"

Connor shrugged. "Not much emotion in the lass."

"Good," Diarmot snapped, although Gilly's impression troubled him. "I have had my fill of emotion. Anabelle drowned me in emotions, good and bad. Calm would be a nice change."

"It could also be teeth-grindingly dull."

"I dinnae care." He looked away from Connor's expression of wry disbelief. "I may not find any fire in my wife's bed, but at least when I choose to go to her, she will be there. She may nay welcome me verra heartily, but she willnae be welcoming anyone else, either—mon nor woman."

Connor whistled softly. "Ye caught Annabelle with a woman?"

"Aye, although the woman fled ere I got a good look

at her. Anabelle thought it all verra funny. Said she and
the lass had been lovers for years. Tried to tell me I
couldnae call that adultery. I could keep ye entertained
for days on all the tales I have of Anabelle, her lovers,
her rages, her wailing spells, and her wanderings. It was
like trying to live in the heart of a fierce Highland storm.
After that, dull sounds verra sweet to me.''

Diarmot was relieved when Connor said no more. He
did not like pulling forth the painful memories of his
time with Anabelle. Such memories, however, did serve
to remind him of why he had chosen Margaret. He
craved peace, he thought, and walked toward the church
with a surer step.

It was as he knelt beside his bride that his doubts
trickled back. A voice in his head kept saying this was
wrong, although it offered no explanation. Margaret's
hand in his was cool and dry, her expression one of
sweet calm. What could possibly be wrong?

Just as the priest asked if anyone knew why Diarmot
and Margaret could not marry there was a disturbance
at the doors of the church and a clear, angry woman's
voice said, ''I think I might have a reason or two.''

Shocked, Diarmot looked behind him and his eyes
widened. Marching toward him was a tiny woman with
brilliant copper hair. Behind her strode eight, large,
scowling red-haired men. She held a bundle in her arms
and a small, dark-haired girl walked beside her holding
another.

''Weel, now, Diarmot,'' drawled Connor, smiling
faintly, ''it seems your dreams have become prophetic.''

''What?'' Diarmot glanced at Connor who was slowly
standing up.

''Did ye nay dream about the scarlet elf and a troop
of fiery demons?''

Diarmot decided that, as soon as he found out what
was happening, he would pound his grinning brother
into the mud.

ABOUT THE AUTHOR

HANNAH HOWELL is an award-winning author who lives with her family in Massachusetts. She is the author of thirty-three Zebra historical romances and is currently working on a new historical romance, IF HE'S WILD, coming in June 2010! Hannah loves hearing from readers and you may visit her Web site: www.hannahhowell.com.